THE EVIL THAT MEN DO

'Holds the reader like a hostage in a web of high-voltage intrigue and violence . . . Frightening authenticity'

Publishers Weekly

'One of the best bar-room fight scenes ever put on paper'

Scotsman

'Fast and gripping skullduggery' *Birmingham Post*

'Excellent reading' *Current Crime*

'A gripping look at the state use of fear to maintain law and order'

Glasgow Herald

'Razor-slice storytelling' *Kirkus Reviews*

The Evil That Men Do

R. Lance Hill

CORONET BOOKS
Hodder and Stoughton

First published in Great Britain 1978
by Hodder and Stoughton Limited

Coronet Edition 1981
Second impression 1984

British Library C.I.P.

Hill, R Lance,.
the evil that men do.
I. Title
823'.9'1F

ISBN 0-340-26466-7

The characters and situations in this book are entirely imaginary and bear no relation to any real person or actual happening

Printed and bound in Great Britain for Hodder and Stoughton Paperbacks, a division of Hodder and Stoughton Ltd., Mill Road, Dunton Green, Sevenoaks, Kent (Editorial Office: 47 Bedford Square, London, WC1 3DP) by Cox & Wyman Ltd, Reading

To Helen, at the time
of the Philippines

Quick rising the sun, summer hurries on.
Splendid the song of birds; fine, smooth weather.
I am of golden growth, fearless in battle.
I am a line, my attack a flash against a host.
I watched through the night to keep a border.
Murmuring ford water in heavy weather,
The open grassland green, the water clear,
Loud the nightingale's familiar song;
Gulls play on the bed of the sea,
Their feathers glistening, their ranks turbulent. . . .

from Gwalchmai's *Boast*,
translated from the Welsh.

DJAKARTA, INDONESIA. 3:53 A.M./17 June/1974.

The naked lightbulb cast a flat ugly pall in the night.

Forlorn, it hung like a treefruit from the side of a house that had once been blessed with charm and dignity, but was now lame and flagging, blemished like a grand dame diseased of poverty. In back was a sunken garden gone to jungle. Beyond that, the *Kali,* a moving toilet masquerading poorly as the city's central canal.

Other houses on the lane exhibited the manicured outerwear of thoroughbred families, serving only to emphasize the sluttishness of the one fallen from grace. Some of the smug were thankful for the shrubs and willows that rampantly smothered much of the unsightliness. Some decried that as well. However, thoroughbred families know when it is ill-advised to voice complaint. Such opportunities for discretion are provided when black automobiles and drab military vehicles come and go from a house at all hours of the day and night. In Djakarta one learns not to see such things. Ever. Not even when the lights flicker for hours on end. Or when the plumbing backs up and the flush comes red.

There were two military vehicles and one black car parked beside the house.

The ensemble made a tidy row under the light, the black car in the middle, the other two as close as lusting escorts. All three appeared empty, and were, except for the panel truck nearest the house. Behind the wheel was a soldier in the uniform of the Indonesian army. His hands were clasped on his belly, his head back on the seat, his mouth an open hole.

He had been sleeping for two hours.

Outside, the temperature was 29 degrees Celsius, the equivalent of 84 degrees Fahrenheit. In the day it had reached 114 degrees Fahrenheit. Birds had plummeted from the trees. Humidity made snapping noises with radio waves. People waded in the *Kali.*

The house appeared cool despite excesses of climate. All windows were shuttered.

Heat oozing from the pavement beneath the black car made the confined space a boiling cauldron. If the man lying pressed between the asphalt and floorboards made the slightest slip in his labors, the space would become his crematorium. If he made a noise sufficient to wake the soldier, or if the others came out of the house before he finished, he would be delivered into the hands of a man who could kill him without his dying. His sweat ran profusely.

Assael Ganot was carefully and quietly affixing C-4 plastic explosive to the entrails of the automobile. For Assael Ganot to be doing what he was doing required he be exceptionally courageous . . . or committed . . . or cavalier. Most members of the elite Mossad possessed varying parts of the prescription, though certainly the accent was on commitment. The Mossad was the deadly efficient Israeli intelligence organization, and Assael the demolitions expert in a commando squad of six members. His commander and one of the surveillance team were watching from a house across the street, the balance waiting in a freighter on the bay.

Assael lowered his arms to rest, letting the blood flow back from where it had thinned. He was young, only twenty-two, but cramps are hurried by heat. Even with the back of his head on the pavement there was little room to turn it. The sheet metal planed his face as he did so, prompting him to silently curse the nose he considered at other times his prized feature.

He normalized his breathing, rhythmically, each intake spreading his ribs against the underbelly of the car. Bathed in perspiration, the juice mingled with road grease and became rivulets speeding into his eyes and ears. His hands were wet and slippery. Pressing them against his shirt did not help; it was wet enough to be wrung.

The glow from the lightbulb skipped across the pavement, flickering ominously again. He knew what that signified. The knowledge chilled him, his sweat rearing up cold and clammy. Assael shivered in the heat.

The flickering meant that electrical current was being drawn from the house circuits to be passed through the bodies of human beings within. Each dimming of illumination meant a fresh charge administered. Sometimes the light quaked, nearly vanished, for long seconds. Dutch electrical standards had not been of a high order when the house was erected in their colonial era. Had they been, the lights would not dim.

Assael shut his eyes from the spastic sight. A harsh fetid odor from the canal hung heavy near the ground. To Assael, who had never smelled anything to rival it—not even Syrian cadavers baking in the deserts of the October War—the stench seemed caustic enough to rot the tires around him.

But, he knew he must finish, and soon. Four plugs of C-4 had been taped already, two on the transmission tailshaft housing forward of the front seat, and two more to the driveshaft just forward of the rear seat's proximity. A plug was fixed independently at both 45 and 315 degree angles on the housing and shaft. The charges were designed to kill one man, regardless of the location he assumed in the car. Such perfection was largely immaterial. There was enough explosive on the drivetrain to powder a small building, much less dismantle a common American sedan.

Assael moved painfully forward, crabbing on his shoulder blades, buttocks, and heels. A sharp slagging of metal caught his chest and tore it. He sloughed on, adding his blood to the sweat and oil, concerned more with the sound of tearing fabric than with his skin.

The car was a Chevelle, an intermediate model manufactured by General Motors. That put the starting motor at the lower right rear corner of the V8 engine, providing easy access from below. The Israeli squirmed until the round cylinder and its piggy-back solenoid was directly overhead, then strained to see into the gloom around it. He was unable to make out the all important terminals on the solenoid. A bad omen. He would be forced to use a light.

The young commando's preparations had been thorough and meticulous. Once the surveillance team informed him of the type of automobile used to chauffeur the subject, the commander had rented an identical unit from Hertz. Assael spent hours under it, tracing wiring harnesses, measuring distances by hand-spreads, plotting points of placement, cutting wires to precise lengths, committing all to memory. He was a stone cold professional selected for a squad comprising the best the Mossad could cull from ranks. He knew explosives as he knew the roof of his mouth. The mission was one of the heart, and he in turn was the heart of the mission. His plugs of plastic would rend the subject into jelly. Assael would be a lion in the Mossad.

He slid his hand below his beltless trousers and into the dampness near his genitals. The shunning of a belt was just another precaution; belts snag and scrape at inopportune times. When he extracted his hand it held two coils of double wire. Each coil had a brass alligator clamp on one end, a small round blasting cap resembling a firecracker on the other.

The crucial part of the operation was now. Electrical blasting caps dictate respect bordering on fear. Caps are the fuse that fires first, thereby setting off whatever larger charge they are mated to; without them the plastic explosive being just so much inert putty. Caps must never fail and are assembled with a machined neurosis that makes a fuse *want* to fire regardless of appropriate inducement. In rash hands they often rebelled fatally.

Assael unravelled the wires, gingerly holding the closed cap ends between two fingers and slipping them inside his shirt so they would not be jostled while he worked. From between his teeth he took an object no larger than a fountain pen. This was a fiber-optics light, having a frosted plastic tube the size of a pencil projecting from one end, thus directing illumination down the tube to project in a concentration equal to the tube's diameter. Besides the intense convergence of light provided, the preeminent feature of the device was that it was undetectable until quite close.

The pencil-beam played on the automobile's starter solenoid a few inches from Assael's face. There they were, the three terminals jutting out. The larger one in the middle posed the threat; it directly connected to the car's battery and therefore was a constant source of current. If he were to so much as brush that terminal with one of the clamps, the caps would detonate. It would be all over. No, it was the smaller outrigger terminal he would have to fasten his clamps to, scarcely a thumbnail distrance from the live terminal. His touch would have to be steady and sure.

Once the clamps were fastened he could ease himself back to the plastic plugs where he would tuck the caps gently into the craters formed in the C-4. That would complete the exercise. He could then crawl back through the bushes to the canal.

After, it would be simply a matter of waiting. Waiting for them to come from the house . . . for the subject to get into the car . . . for his driver to turn the ignition key. Other members of the squad would conceivably hear the explosion all the way to the freighter. They would smile and cuff each other in the macho ritual of triumph.

Hinges squeaked on parched metal. Assael closed the light, his breath seized. He lowered his head and turned his eyes. A pair of army issue boots were a few feet to his right. The soldier was coming around to the car, near enough to reach out and touch.

Across the street the commander of the squad grew tense as he watched the drama from a second floor window, his eye to an infrared spotting scope that afforded a view as clear as though it were high noon.

"Aei," he whispered anxiously.

"What? What is it?" the man next to him wanted to know, moving to see what he could.

"The soldier woke up," the commander said tightly. "Next to the car."

"I see him," the surveillance man confirmed. Though he did not have benefit of an infrared instrument, he was trained to see in the night and could make out the form of the soldier between the truck and the car. The trick was in knowing that the center of the eye is a dead zone at night, its nerves the ones used primarily to detect colors. By focusing ten degrees or so from the desired object and rotating the vision around this field, the more sensitive nerves were brought into play and a suitable image transmitted.

"Is Assael out of there yet?" he asked the leader.

"No." The man looked at his watch. "Six minutes more are required. Minimum." The commander dealt in absolutes, even in speech.

"What is the scrotum doing? I can't see enough."

"Pishing. Against the truck."

"Move, you pig," the surveillance man hissed, as if to will it by word. "Go back to your truck and sleep the long sleep."

The commander elbowed him away from where he was encroaching on the window. The man slumped against the wall.

They waited, only two in a room belonging to a teenage girl in an empty house. The occupants were on vacation in Japan.

The surveillance man fidgeted with his hands incessantly. For the past while he had been fingering a pair of girl's panties. The rite annoyed his senior.

"His bladder doesn't stop," the commander marvelled.

"He's filling his boots so his feet will be cool," the other said derisively, stretching the silk bridge of the panties tightly over his fist. "Go back to your wet dreams in your wet boots, you scrote."

The commando leader was annoyed by the man's solitary bantering, considering it unbefitting a professional.

Then, as though heeding instruction, the soldier walked back to settle as he had been behind the wheel.

The commander lowered the scope in relief.

"He went back?" his companion queried.

The commander snatched the panties and sent them flying into the darkness of the room. He had little patience for the inspirations resorted to in times of waiting. Surveillance men were a peculiar breed by any measure. His personal suspicion was that they would be peeping in bedroom windows of their own volition anyway. This way they at least had a worthy purpose. Still, the man deserved his respect. When assigning this mission the heads of the Institute had extended him full discretion in choosing his squad of four men and two women. Each of them had performed faultlessly thus far, all aware that promotions were for the taking on this one, knowing that entire careers had taken seed in less vital operations. The likelihood was that he himself would advance to the inner circle of the Institute.

In a house across the way was a man the Institute very much wanted dead. The briefing in Tel Aviv had been conducted in a mood of enmity more pronounced than that reserved for Black September, the virulence on display then causing him wonder. It still did. He did not know enough. Only that the man, thought to be named Clement Moloch, was known to most only as The Doctor. And that he apparently moved from country to country instructing various nefarious organizations in methods of interrogation.

Assael said he had heard rumors. Of unspeakable tortures, perpetrated by this Doctor. Of monstrous methods devised and imparted to others. Of service to the most barbaric of regimes. According to Assael's reasoning, it must have to do with the Israeli prisoners tortured by the Syrians in the aftermath of the October conflict.

Beyond the conjecture, the commander had only his orders to go on. The major-general had given him a passport photograph that had been altered by a skilled hand at some time, a date and some anticipated zones of interception in Djakarta, and a directive to remove the man from the face of the earth at all cost.

Costs thus far had been substantial. Members of the squad were registered as seaman in the employ of the Biscayne Traders Shipping Corporation, a Mossad front incorporated in Liberia's curtain of anonymity. A tramp freighter, part of the Biscayne apparatus, was chartered solely so that they would have legitimate endorsement to be in Djakarta. Ostensibly, the freighter was in port for repairs to her pumps, but the instant the mission concluded she would be blessed by a wondrous recovery and make straight for the congested shipping lanes.

In the eight days spent observing the house, any doubts of its function were quickly laid to rest. Too many trucks brought too many prisoners. Too many men and women were sent cowed and stumbling through the gauntlet of soldiers between the trucks and the house. Too many of them had been carried out prone and shrouded. The house was an interrogation center for political prisoners, a chamber of horrors.

The Grey Eminence known as The Doctor had been inside up to thirteen hours a day. His exit was usually made in the early hours of evening, in time to have dinner with his wife and children at the Commissioner's compound where they were quartered. This day was different. This day he had not left as darkness fell, and the commander had been quick to put into motion the only plan he deemed left him.

He raised the scope and scanned the scene again. The sweep of filtered beam detected no movement. In the truck the soldier's head lay back, his mouth open again.

Assael would have allowed four or five minutes for the soldier to reclaim his sleep. That meant the explosives would be set and primed inside of four minutes. In seven minutes the young commando should be clear of the car. The success of the mission was at hand. They were close.

Under the car, Assael closed the last clamp as gently as a caress, drew his hand away, and allowed his lungs to function once more. Wires from the clamps hung down, curling on his face and neck, leading to the blasting caps in the folds of his shirt. Artless wires. Umbilicals of death. Caution would have to be taken they did not nudge the clamps against the live terminal.

The soldier's urine had wormed under the car and formed a pool where his right leg rested. Moving rearward to place the caps in the plastic would necessitate a slide through the puddle. The prospect was a trifling incidental now that the clamps were set.

He reached into his shirt to extract the caps, holding them by the closed ends with enormous care.

From somewhere across the still air he heard the oriental timbre of a gamelan—the Indonesian xylophone. Late for music, he thought. Or early, depending on your reason of reference and level of discomfort.

He squirmed slowly toward the rear of the car, shifting a bit to center, full into the urine, playing out the wires as he went.

The pencil-light, now off, caught on the emergency brake cable and was pulled from his mouth, falling to the pavement with a clatter. Assael came rigid as a man on a blade. His ears took the attention of a blind man's. His eyes closed, the better to hear. At least the noise had been partially dispersed by the waiting urine pool. Small mercies. He waited.

Sounds were those of the night. Crickets. A dog barking. The engine of a light plane far off. A screen closing somewhere along the lane.

If the soldier had stirred, Assael had not heard him. No squawk came from the door hinges. Boots had not appeared from the truck. The soldier could be listening too, and waiting, unsure whether his drowsiness had betrayed his ears. Assael deliberated, the pragmatic commando temper reckoning quickly. The eager blasting caps decided for him; counting risk was now a luxury to be jettisoned.

Both caps in one hand, he groped with the other for the pencil-light, his fingers making tracks in the wetness there. Where was the damn thing? There. There it was. He placed it, wet, back between his teeth.

The last few inches were taken on his back, bringing the deposits of C-4 into view above. His shoulder blades were raw and hurting, stung by the acidity on the ground. But the wires leading forward were lax and unhindered for placing the caps. The moment of truth. Once the caps were joined with the C-4 there was no turning back.

His hand crept furtively for a place he could not see, like feeling for a woman—the delicate touch taught in Demolitions. Fingers found the crevice in the plastic plug. The first cap went home.

That was the moment the gamelan player chose to halt his serenade.

The commander felt regret when the music ceased. The sound had been pleasantly foreign, appropriate for the heavy heat of nights like this. It reminded him of where he was, a soil far from his own.

In looking away from the window he noted the surveillance man had his head against the paper of the wall. Oil from his hair would leave a smear. He jerked a finger and the man moved his head away, knowing without asking.

When the family returned the house would have to appear untouched. Those cursed panties had to be replaced in their drawer.

"What is this?" he said suddenly, as headlights showed in the street.

The spotting scope rose urgently.

Outside, a grey Mercedes had swung into the drive by the house across the way, its headlights shining full in the face of the waking soldier. The beams flicked to high and back, spurring the soldier to start the truck.

"What are they doing?" the surveillance man wondered aloud, having taken up a position back of the window. "Is Assael clear yet?"

"Under the car," was the terse reply.

The truck was backing up, the Mercedes taking its place next to the house. When the truck stopped it too activated its headlights.

The commander stood, his attention fastened to the window, his chair knocked over by the reflex motion. The man behind caught it before it struck the carpet.

"What is that Mercedes doing there?" he demanded of the subordinate, more accusation than question.

"I don't know. Maybe—"

"Maybe a switch," the commander finished for him.

"It cannot be . . ." the man said in his imploring way.

"It is," the senior confirmed stiffly, watching their fears pantomimed for them.

The Mercedes halted so that its passenger doors were adjacent to the side of the house, scarcely a stride away. A man stepped from the house and opened both doors of the German car, glancing in at the driver. This man was recognized by the commander as having been at the house daily. He was a high ranking officer of the Indonesian security agency, named Epatj. Upon confirming the driver's identity, Epatj presented his back to the street and stood like a shield at the door.

Three men, all in batik shirts out at the waist, emerged and stepped into the rear of the Mercedes. An older man followed, thick in stature, white hair caught passing in the light, face lowered. The Doctor. The center seat in front was his. Epatj got in beside him, slamming the door in accustomed military manner.

With that the Mercedes backed into the street and in a single fluid sweep leapt away. Less than a minute passed from its initial appearance. The commander watched his quarry disappear untouched; taillights receding.

"How did this happen?" the commander snapped.

"They used the American car . . . always. . . ." the other defended haltingly, shaken by the realization their chance had slipped away and his surveillance team would be held largely responsible. Someone on the other side had been exceptionally clever. "He must have suspected," he said, grasping.

"Impossible. They did this purely as a precaution. You should have known."

"What if The Doctor wasn't with them? Are you certain you saw—?"

"Confirmed," his superior interrupted. He repeated, "How did this happen?"

"I don't know how it happened." Then he remembered Assael. "We've got to get Assael clear . . . before someone uses that car."

"The house still has a dozen soldiers, and the one outside," the commander said. "We can't help him. You could pray . . . and do it better than you did your reconnaissance."

His voice carried more optimism than conviction. The scope showed him the soldier, and the truck still with its lights on. Anticipating. Waiting on something.

A uniformed officer came from the house, walked briskly to the black car, nodded to the soldier in passing.

"Gott in Himmel!" the commander rasped, turning on his heel from the window and dropping the scope in flight. His companion sped after him.

Assael felt a frieze of hypnotic tranquility embrace him as he watched the wing-tipped shoes of the officer approach . . . as the door opened and the automobile grunted under the settling weight . . . at the sound of keys so close and sweet.

Assael Ganot never heard the snap of the starter solenoid. Instead he became, at 4:06 A.M., a swirling red dust shot from a hurricane.

C-4 plastic is not a selective explosive, as are some. Of high velocity characteristic, its fury radiates indiscriminately in every direction. Where the black car had been—and Assael Ganot—the dense clay was pulverized to a crater of nearly two meters in depth. Most of the side of the house was laid open. The officer was reduced to a clump of pounded rags. Components of the automobile splashed down in the canal for a considerable distance. Even the soldier in the truck was killed, shredded by the imploding shards of glass.

The commander and his underling flew down the rear steps of their lair and into the night on silent crepe soles, the rooftops washed in fire flashes behind them.

To the freighter, where the celebration awaiting them was aborted as soon as the others saw their faces. Permission was granted to put to sea almost immediately.

Within forty-eight hours the Institute in Tel Aviv received a coded message that was not altogether unexpected. In it the United States Central Intelligence Agency curtly suggested the Mossad suspend all interest in The Doctor.

As has become the custom of most quasi-bureaucratic entities, merit is not necessarily a condition for advancement in the Mossad. Therefore the tainted commander went on to a somewhat more enhancing mission in the early days of July, 1976, at an obscure airfield in Africa called Entebbe.

The foiled operation in Djakarta signalled the last attempt made on The Doctor's life by any group or individual for the following four years. The prevailing consensus arrived at was dogmatically clear: The Doctor had too many patrons in too many towers, who had made him one of their own, and, like themselves, had pronounced him an untouchable. To try was not only futile, but presciently suicidal.

The word had come down. Everyone heard.

•I•

A PLACE TURNED PRIMITIVE . . .

• 1 •

Morning came gently in The Caymans, skimming across a still sea to reach for the coral and then the beach, flashing on sand as white as a winter moon in halo. Above, a mackerel sky was blown into chalk tailings by the high trades.

There had been a light shower in the night. Still, as the dawn spread, the break between water and sky was difficult to distinguish for the unpracticed eye, even in a mounting sun. Look for the fishing skiffs. They had been on the break for hours.

Little Cayman is a flat plate of beaches and reefs seventy-four miles east-northeast of the Grand isle, the least populated of the three Islands with only a few dozen rooted inhabitants living well clear of the tourist flyways. On the north shore there are colorful Caribbean names like Grape Tree Bay, Mary's Bay, Snipe Point, Crawl Bay, and Bloody Bay Point. But few people, and fewer places for them to live. Fishermen, mostly.

Midway between Grape Tree and Crawl, the man sat on the open veranda of a beach house and watched the cloud streamers overhead. He often spent time absorbed with the formations and shadings of sky. The vastness was what unfailingly fascinated him. He found that the longer he watched the more infinite seemed the power there. The power was of perspective, and therefore awesome, particularly when contemplated from a mere bud of ground in the tracts of the Caribbean. His sky gazing was a private balm, there for him regardless of where he went or when he needed it. The reserves could always be drawn upon. Day or night.

Once or twice he had contemplated learning to fly an airplane. The ticklish part was that heights disturbed him. Gravity's pull was frightening and he doubted he could overcome the helplessness. He was a solitary man and he knew himself, knew his limits. Besides, rattling about the heavens in a noisy metal contraption was like a cow swimming. There was no grace to it, no freedom. Only illusion and struggle. The man remembered how Jones had put it: "He had no call for it at all."

In his left hand he held a valve spring from a truck engine, a tight winding of thick wire. He squeezed the spring between his fingers and palm with monotonous replay, crushing it until the coils touched and formed a solid cylinder, then releasing the spring, crushing, releasing, over and over.

The cycle would go on for fifty closings, then to the other hand for fifty, then back. He did the repetitions absently and with a seeming indifference to the effort.

Though partly shaded by the palms in the heat of the day, the small house was bleached by the sun. It looked old, and was, with a mantle of history. The man had a history, too.

This corner of the Caribbean was the romantic and bloody Spanish Main of the seventeenth and eighteenth centuries, and the Australian pine ringing the cove had made it a favored blind for the buccaneers. Among them had been Henry Morgan and Edward Teach, the latter more accustomed to the name Blackbeard.

Here they had portioned and hid their booty, chained their slaves to iron stakes—the remains of both can still be found with the cactus back of the pines—healed their wounded and patched their ships, ravished their wenches against the palms, and eaten sweet turtle steaks and drunk grog beneath the sunset reds of evening.

Weeks of land-locked carousing made the nautical desperados touchy and eager for the sail. Turtles would begin to shun the cove and the pirates would have to stroll further to pick mangos. They hacked at each other with swords. They beat their women. They dug up their shipmates' coin.

But men who lived by their wits were too innately resourceful to let idle hours pass without sport and bounty. On nights of small moons they would trudge to a windward shore and walk a donkey up and down the water's edge with a lantern hung round his neck. From offshore the swaying lantern looked every bit like the light of a ship in safe waters. Many a dumbstruck vessel was lured onto the shoals in this manner and raucously plundered by the inventive donkey-walkers.

The first house, built of thatching, was burned by the British when they trapped a gang of desperate pirates there, and, having them vastly outnumbered, slaughtered them on the spot. Thinking there was treasure buried beneath the floor, the Brits had torched the place and dug it up. The talk was that they had then spaded more than twenty bodies into the hole, some still swearing. This is likely true, for the people of the island have little use for fancy. There is no need. Doubloons still swell out of the beach once in a while.

The second house, the one standing on the gravesite, was constructed of ship's timbers and hull spikes. A century of storm lashings had left it unimpressed. The house was born in the year 1863, the man in 1946; both in summer.

In the night the man had swum to the coral reef about two-hundred meters from shore. It was just after the shower passed and the moonlight caught the gliding schools of gobies a fathom or two below. Like swimming on a carpet of neon, he had once thought.

His night swimming was always bare. Which has no particular significance, at least on the surface of things.

The friendly grouper the man had christened Quasimodo was waiting at their usual rendezvous station, three stones from the shore drop-off. The man dove and held his fist out. The grouper bumped it with his snout and followed the man the rest of the way to the reef. The fish would wait for him to swim back to shore, biding his time by poking about in the shallows and trailing the shadow the man cast on the bottom. Sometimes he would have to wait for hours while the man walked the sandspit alongside the coral.

Quasimodo, a creature of habit, missed the man when he was away, which was about a third of the time. The fish became depressed then, but a jewfish is patient if nothing else. The man always returned to the house, and always swam to the reef at night. He was always alone.

Four hours of sleep was enough, simply all that his metabolism required. He slept from eleven till three in the morning. The house was without a bed, deliberately. He slept on the centennial planking, and in fact had not slept a full night in a bed for something over seventeen years.

Despite the strength required to close the spring the man was neither large nor imposing in stature. Instead his form suggested sinew over modest bone, in place of blunt biceps on concrete pins. A fathom was sufficient to cover him to his hair.

He blended agility and quickness of motion, a tempo of anticipation, and an outsized capacity for stress. Even his casual movements were balanced, by a large measure kept in check, and best seen when crossing the jagged coral in unshod feet. He was a mongrel whose mind came silky and sure the more immediate the urgency. Risk made it hum.

Body scars implied past experience with threats to his life; wandering white lines on his chest and shoulders and back, and small craters from old impacts—like photographs of the plains of the moon. And not the coarse scars of the fishermen, caused by running rope and flailing fish, instead these told tales of skewering weapons and unwholesome projectiles—the leavings of violence.

The features of his face were a good measure short of perfection, but on the whole were orderly and not altogether unpleasant. Barring close scrutiny, the overall impression could even be considered pedestrian.

By birth his skin was American fair. Now it was tobacco-leaf browned by the tropical sun, for he had lived here since Vietnam. Except for his times away.

Living in seclusion on a sparsely peopled island in the Gulf Stream would be too lonely an existence for most to contemplate. The man had not found it so. His cove, his house, his sand, and his sea were his place of peace between certain wars. A lonely day had never encroached on his life. He was content and wholly attuned with his own company. And there was always the matrix of living things about. The plane brought books and magazines and day-old papers from the mainland.

The Island knew him, but did not know of him. The people were cordial and he stopped to speak with them when they used the same path. Poor fishermen, with enormous pride hard earned, prized their privacy and extended the same without reservation. They left the man alone and had long since tired of wondering about him. He was one of them. His house was like theirs, untethered of electricity, using oil-burning lamps at night. He washed his own clothing, and waved to passing families in boats. He did not seem disposed to waste. He ate fish, and shared the Islander's disdain for those who fished for sport.

At midday the man had a lunch of yellow-tailed snapper and melon cropped that morning.

He needed fresh bread. Maybe he would fetch some from Santiago's wife that evening. Santiago had promised him a bag of 10/15 shrimps, and would probably want a game of darts, too. He would leave in time to walk back at dusk and watch the terns dip for flying fish.

When he got back he'd have a pit fire on the beach and butterfry some of the shrimps and drink what was left of the Israeli wine. It would be late, but he could wait. Besides, Santiago's wife would put a bowl of turtle rice in his hands as soon as he came in the door. She always did. The next time he was away he would have to get her some lengths of material. He made a mental note of it.

When his meal was finished and his dishes cleaned he lit his pipe and stretched in the hammock. Books 1 and 2 of *The Geek* by Craig Nova took him to three o'clock. The battery-powered cassette played Paul Whiteman while he read.

The sun swung enough to take the shade from the hammock. The book's drawings had stirred him. If he allowed himself to dream of women he would wake with a headache. There was a woman on Cayman Brac who liked him and had sex with him whenever he went there. She was from Alabama and worked as a guide for the cave tours. The last time he'd been there, six weeks back, they'd gotten drunk on rum and made love in one of the caves. She talked of going back to college in Alabama, and she might have for all he knew.

He left the hammock and went off down the beach on his bicycle for an aimless excursion.

The bicycle, like most in the Islands, had a sloping crossbar in the manner of a girl's bike. In that way it could be used by most anyone in a family, of any age, because the bicycle was truly the predominant utility of transport.

Back in the South Bronx, from where he came, a man of the street would not be seen on a bicycle past the age of eight or nine years. But before that he would never allow himself to be seen on a girl's bike under any circumstances.

The man guided the fat tires around the point of the cove and beyond, moving the pedals languidly, crunching over dried Sargasso weed drifted in from far out, and steering into a few inches of water for short stretches to let the wheel spokes fan moisture on his bare feet and legs.

A man on a bicycle was coming toward him on the beach.

The interloper was still a good distance away, too far to discern who it was. The man watched as the distance narrowed.

It may have been because his attention was on the approaching bike instead of his own trajectory, but he struck a conch shell in the water and it turned the wheel at right angles, his momentum pitching him over the handlebars, mincing his feet in the ocean as he tried to keep them forward of his weight. He could have righted himself with a few more steps, but chose not to and dumped himself in the shallows. It was the same Caribbean people flew thousands of miles to swim in, so why not? There were only his shorts to get wet.

Santiago stopped his bicycle with one wheel in the water and laughed at him, his teeth worn sharp as a dog's and whiter.

"Hey, you fell on your ass, darlin," he observed in the curious Islands dialect of Scotch brogue and King's English. The lilt at the end was like singing.

"Astute, amigo, astute," the man said, rolling his head under the water.

Santiago laughed again, lifting his Panama hat and wiping the band with the tail of his shirt.

Santiago had been born on the island and had his name before Hemingway wrote so brilliantly of his Santiago. Since then most families had named one boy-child in honor of the old man who had killed the great marlin.

This Santiago was old, a fisherman for food, descending from a sailor shipwrecked generations past. The sun and salt seas had twisted his skin until it resembled the creased vinyl used on the seats of speedboats. As for the color, it was like the hot brier round the bowl of a pipe.

Santiago could find fish as effortlessly as he found sleep, and had taught the man something of it. That had not been an easy task, because the man had been alien to the sea when he came here.

Santiago knew the currents as a man knew his wife, and went straight for them whenever he took the man fishing; that way they had little rowing to do and even less need of the sail. One time the man had gone out alone and had not returned for another night and part of a day. He had failed to find the current. Yet he was not angry with himself in failure. And that had astonished Santiago, so much so that he had told his wife of it. Such a tolerance of oneself was a trait of the old, not the young. But then, there was much of the man that did not fit his years. They could spend hours in the skiff without speaking, looking at the horizon or down into the black hole where the line disappeared, then the man would pass food, or the water jar, silently, or would say something funny for them to grin at. Santiago's wife said she thought the war had forced the man old. Because he had said, only once, that he had been in Vietnam.

So Santiago had taken him out to learn the currents, without the fishing lines, and after that the man had never failed to catch the current again.

Beyond that, Santiago had little in common with Hemingway's Cuban. When Santiago was newly married he had left the Islands and taken his wife to Detroit, where he had worked twenty-seven years in the Fisher body plant filing fenders and doors for Cadillacs. They had lived in a cheap flat off Trumbull Avenue and saved their money, returning to Little Cayman before they were sixty and with enough savings that the island's economy left them virtually retired.

They still mourned all of those years spent away from the Caribbean, and lived no better or worse than the poorest fisherman, though they could afford to. They had enough.

"You are well, my friend?" the man asked him.

"I am ancient and dry of de spit, and dass de truth,"

he replied, handing the man an envelope. "Here, mon, a stone-tablet I wrestled all de way from de town for you."

The man stayed seated in the ocean and opened the envelope with his small finger. Santiago laid his own bicycle over, then wheeled the man's dripping bike onto the sand.

"Two telegrams in two days," Santiago said, snapping his fingers. "Juss like dat, a celebrity."

"Overnight sensation," the man agreed, adding wryly, "and if pigs had wings they'd be eagles."

Santiago laughed heartily and slapped at the water. "Dass a beauty, mon. I like dat one. Dass American south?"

"Yes, and west."

"Pigs with wings. Can't you juss picture dat?" He filled his cheeks, folded his arms and flapped around the man in the water, "Hhh-oink. Hhh-oink."

The spectacle caused the man to laugh. "Think of the *guano* you could make."

"Wooo, mon." the old man exclaimed, his eyes big against his dark face, "and drop from great heights."

"It wouldn't be safe to go out of doors."

"A new industry for de island. We all be filthy rich . . . filthy, anyway. Every fishermon gon have a flock."

"Or herd."

They laughed until the humor was spent, then Santiago offered a hand and pulled the man to his feet.

"De telegram. Does it mean we won't fish in de mornin?" Santiago asked.

"Did you get the shrimps?"

"Three pound. Didn't bring dem cause . . . you know, de telegram."

The man shook his head, his hair flicking water away. "Yes. My friend from Mexico is coming on the evening plane."

"Ah. Mister George, de journalist," Santiago nodded. "Dat is good though. Him I like. Only met him de three times he come here, but I think he is—what's de word—a gentlemon of substance and learnin?"

"The Hidalgo family is one of the oldest and most revered in Mexico," the man said, inspecting a scrape on the top of one foot. The salt in the water made it tingle, but would also heal it. "They were instrumental in the Revolution of 1810, fighting the Spanish armies with Indians and bandits and peons. You know, amigo, he once told me how his forebears ran up to the Spanish cannons and placed their straw sombreros over the muzzles, thinking that would stop the shot. They had never seen cannon before."

"Lord above," Santiago marvelled. "Dass an innocence."

"They were times of innocence for some, I suppose." The man looked out on the water. "They never last long."

"You want I should meet his plane, bring him in de boat?" Santiago offered. "I'll put on de motor."

"If you are willing," the man said, although it was the same procedure used the three previous times George Hidalgo had come to visit him; the only person, in fact, who had ever stayed. This visit would not be social in nature. The man knew his friend was finally coming on business, and he suspected what that business was.

"Sure, mon," Santiago said. "Glad to do dat."

"Come to the house, I'll make you some tea."

The man removed his wet shorts and hung them on the handlebars. They mounted their bicycles and headed towards the cove. The young man, who now rode naked, was known as Holland.

•2•

While the naked man and the elder were pedaling their bicycles on the rim of the outland cove, George Hidalgo was walking a carpet five miles above the level of the sea, the jet airliner headed due east out of Mexico City, having just cleared the jungle-crusted limestone of the Yucatan on its course to Grand Cayman Island.

Restless, impatient, George had left his seat to stroll the aisle. The plane was occupied to only one-third of capacity, and most of the passengers napped, read, or sipped drinks. They paid him no mind.

For him the flight was the culmination of years of frustration and anguish so acute and consuming as to have forever altered his life's course. Or at least he hoped it was the culmination.

He had prayed that morning, rising in darkness, to approach the Shrine of the Basilica on his knees. The Basilica, and The Virgin, so wise, so rich, so luxuriously cool in the hours of daybreak, had not comforted him this morning. The reason was elementary. His prayer was that a man named Holland would consent to kill a man known as The Doctor.

Had they known, tens of thousands of others in a multitude of countries would have joined him in the solemn bidding.

Upon leaving the Basilica he had walked home through the streets of the gathering markets. There, Alvaro had brought him fresh *limón* and avocado in the garden while he threw grain to the tapaculos and caught his breath from the long walk.

Mariana had telephoned while he was out, to confirm lunch at her villa.

They had been married once, when they were very young. And they were not much older now. It had been two years since she had last mentioned Nietzsche, Kafka, or Rimbaud, and that alone was promising for them. If she had truly put her Nietzsche period and all of its fashionable trappings behind her, then he thought much was possible. If he could put The Doctor and all of the bad baggage his being had visited on his life behind him, then everything was possible.

George had wanted to marry Mariana at first sight of her and after her first utterance. They had met at a reception where she was introduced to him formally as *Señora* Mariana Ordonez. He had asked her how she liked to be called. She had said, with mischievous allure, "often."

Now they met frequently to talk and make love. Mariana believed they loved each other more now than they did then. George didn't know, though there were times when he needed her desperately—times like this.

He wished she were with him in the plane. He wouldn't need to walk the aisle.

At midmorning he had gone to the study, and sat at his desk under the portico, intending to work on his book. In truth there wasn't a manuscript, just a drawer of tape recordings and a cabinet swollen with notes and cuttings. Combined, they represented eight years and one marriage of work; Mariana would call it obsession.

The commitment of the book was to document the existence of one of the most hideously depraved men in all the darkest ranks of history; a man who had stood in blood to the ankles and had the love of pain in his soul; a man whose mark George had first seen eight full years before.

George Hidalgo was a journalist. Words came easily, if that's not too immodest a claim for him, but not words for this synonym for evil so outsized as to defy the very essence of the word. He feared that words would be worthless anyway. Writers don't end lives that cry for it; Diogenes held a lamp, nothing more.

By eleven A.M. the manuscript remained virgin paper, the tapes and cabinet undisturbed, lurking under lock and key.

At that point Alvaro had appeared with the mail and a bundle of newspapers.

A summary of his credentials had been requested by the Catholic Institute for International Relations.

The *Rhodesia Herald*, ever mindful of government censure, had dutifully related the day's count of "Soviet backed terrorist atrocities." Rhodesian security forces commit no atrocities on the pages of the *Herald*. Nothing had changed.

In the same bundle, *The New York Times* had found Rhodesian tobacco slinking off to Russia, the militant champion of black Africa, and to Canada, the servile bastion of the righteous embargo. Nothing had changed.

Beneath the trappings of war, commerce continued. And the hand-tooled Bibles were selling nicely, thank you, as Holland was wont to say.

George had put the unopened balance of mail and newspapers in a box with other unopened chronicles of madness. Mariana made a habit of going to the house when he was away and helping Alvaro drag the boxes into his brother's room. The room had been empty since Patrick Hidalgo was murdered, except for the boxes. Mariana wanted to burn them. They would, when they had an occasion to rejoice. Holland, if he chose, could provide that occasion.

Luncheon with Mariana had been by the pool, on tiles laid out in a pattern of lotus petals. The fragrance of the *copa de oro* plants and scented water was soothing, but not as soothing as the scent raised on his former wife by the hot sun.

After lunch they had moved closer to the pool to sit with their feet in the water. He sipped *mezcal* moodily, watching the worm at the bottom of the bottle drift lazily about in its tomb of spirits.

Mariana went into the house and came back to lie naked in the sun.

He applied oil, rubbing his palms in circles on her legs and stomach and sides, ascending with the narrative: "Look, this is how your body is made. It has marvelous form, hasn't it?"

Her laugh had disrupted his oil painting.

Mariana was particularly sensitive on the underside of the wrist and opened like a flower when he nibbled there. She then moved her wrists on him with a touch so delicate that she stroked the fine hairs rather than the skin.

He licked her temples when a drop of perspiration appeared.

They harmonized their breathing, entering each into the other in the matinee of afternoon sun, then lazed in the water, and made love again.

Somehow even that hadn't lightened his crabbed thoughts. She knew, and he felt wretched.

Whenever a plane was to take him away, he would see Mariana. He was often on a plane. In the past his work had taken him to Vietnam, the Golan Heights, Angola, Beirut, Belfast, and more. He used her that way, yet with her consent, for they spoke almost daily and she could sense when demons were present. In fact, Mariana knew to the day, eight years before, when the demons had first alighted. She didn't know the apparition was The Doctor, didn't know George had never set eyes on him, didn't know he lacked the courage to confront The Doctor even on paper.

She did know the marriage had started to come apart then, on Bouboulinas Street in Athens.

The thought of that first fateful encounter caused him to stop his pacing, and lean against the bulkhead, feeling the thundering vibration of the jet engines worming through the aluminum skin to his back, stainless turbine blades humming euphoria through set teeth; oscillations of the womb.

Athens seemed a long time ago and far away.

That day George Hidalgo had gone to the headquarters of the civilian security police to meet with a high ranking gendarmerie officer in anticipation of the usual interview of denial. The Greek military junta had little time for questions of censure from meddling foreign journalists, but he had a story to file with a leading British daily and had pestered the officer unmercifully during the past week.

An awkwardly hesitant policeman showed him into the lieutenant-general's office only after he had refused to leave the building. The same policeman had seen him there the day before and knew he had the appointment. George didn't understand. Not at that moment, anyway.

While he waited he readied the recorder and scanned his notes.

It was then he heard the scream.

The sound was so unlike anything he had ever heard that he found himself standing. The pad fell to the floor. But he clung to the recorder, the reels turning.

The shriek had erupted with an energy he could only imagine, a harrowing pitch of surreal intensity that mounted and peaked and held for so long he began to doubt it human, instead the echo of some tormented machine. But no, it was human. In agony we know our tribe. What the scream said of the ageless complexities of pain was that moment etched permanently into the farthest recesses of his mind, only to hurtle back across the graveyards whenever he tried to sleep.

The cry was sustained for more than a minute, then fell to a clamorous barking that rose and fell, finally becoming a lapping guttural haunting that ebbed through cracks in the door like a black blood. The whole of his skin moved.

From another direction he heard, "The Lord is my shepherd; I shall not want . . ." Then silence.

In a place turned primitive, he wanted out—to flee.

By the time the door was wrenched open he was sitting with as much calm as he could muster, the recorder and note pad safely in the clasped briefcase.

The lieutenant-general and two policemen picked him

up by the arms, carried him into the street, then threw him onto the stones like a cur that had trespassed. His furious-faced bouncers had said nothing and George wasn't about to compound the situation by confirming he'd heard the offending scream.

At the hotel Mariana was disturbed nearly as much by his agitated condition as she was when she heard the recording. He took her to the solitude of a park. The tape had to be played at recorded scale and to do so at the hotel would have invited disaster.

The first playing unnerved her. He played it twice more, their eyes locked together as they listened. Mariana put her hands in her hair and said the sound was "apocalyptic," in keeping with her manner of speech when she read Russian history in airport lounges.

That evening the lieutenant-general came to the hotel with soldiers and took them in custody to the airport. On the way George recited Article 5 of The Universal Declaration of Human Rights, astonishing everyone, but most particularly himself. Despite having read The Declaration before he would not have thought he'd retained anything beyond the intent.

The officer's reaction was to spit on his shirt.

Later he was to learn that The Doctor had been in the building on Bouboulinas Street that day.

The hand of the stewardess on his arm caused him to open his eyes, embarrassed to realize he had been standing with them closed.

"Are you feeling well, sir?" she inquired.

"Oh, yes. Thank you. I was lost in thought for a moment." His hands were damp.

"Pleasant thoughts, I hope," she said, smiling. She too was Mexican.

He nodded a lie.

"I'll have to ask you to take your seat now, sir," she said. "We'll be starting our descent soon."

The steamed paper towel he wiped his hands with was scalding in the center. He bent to peer through a window, could see only an unbroken blue. "How is the weather? Do you know, by chance?"

"It's clear, as usual," she said. "The Islands are as close to a paradise as anywhere I know."

He returned her smile and walked to his seat. He gazed at the curved ceiling.

Upon sending the first telegram he had not even been certain that Holland was still alive. Such rudimentary consideration was what it meant to know the man, and such safe assumptions were not within the scope of their relationship. He considered himself Holland's friend. With the exception of Santiago he was likely the only one Holland allowed that distinction. And Santiago did not know what Holland's profession was, while George did. Indeed, in simply knowing his profession, it would probably have been as safe to suspect Holland was dead as to suspect he was alive.

But he was alive, and would be expecting him.

He detected the familiar slackening in pitch of the engines. He tucked the case firmly between his legs and fastened his seat belt.

George Hidalgo took a deep breath and became aware that most of his anxiety had left him. He knew the reason too. He was closer now to the man with the singular name.

Not even The Virgin in the Basilica had been able to provide such calm, such peace of purpose.

•3•

In the hours following, George Hidalgo was often reminded of what the stewardess on the plane had said of paradise.

On the short hop from Grand Cayman to Little Cayman the pilot of the Cessna slowed his craft and pointed out a group of dolphin racing the plane's shadow, the mammals rocketing in and out of the water with no discernible splash—and a like betrayal of whatever propelled them at their prodigious speed.

Santiago waited at the south tip of the island, standing in freshly pressed whites, his hat in his hand. George extended the walking stick he had brought him, and an Indian dyed scarf for his wife. The old man was genuinely moved. There were times, more frequent now, when his back was eased by walking with a stick, and this was a proper one with an Irish stamping, and, as George pointed out, had whole sections meant to be carved by the owner—a pastime Santiago utilized to while away the hours of fishing.

George sat in the prow of the boat, the spray raining over him, forming beads on his arms. He gazed at the royal palms and the beach and marveled at the technicolors of the coral outcroppings below the surface.

Santiago serenely brayed what sounded an Islands chanty. Minutes passed before George realized the song was not a chanty at all, but Santiago's version of *Crazy,* originally composed by one Willy Nelson.

At the cove, Holland waded to his knees to take George's bag and shoes, his visitor rolling his pants up and slipping over the side. Santiago handed Holland the shrimps and fresh bread, then pointed his boat away. Moments later the motor's noise was lost beyond the break of land. The cove was as still as it once had been between pirate callings.

George hung his spare clothing in the house while Holland strung him a hammock on the veranda. They talked of the things people talk of when they have not been together for some time. The trip George had made to South Africa the month before interested Holland.

A severe drought was common throughout the Caribbean, extending as far south as Tobago. Poor people were starving to death in Haiti. "They scarcely needed the drought for that," George pronounced. "President For Life Jean Claude 'Baby Doc' Duvalier will see to it."

For seven weeks Holland had been back on his island. George did not ask where he had been prior to that. Enlightenment was not volunteered. No matter. Better not to know.

Holland asked after Mariana, seemed pleased to hear of renewed romance. He liked Mariana. She did not like him, exactly, but neither did she dislike him. It was just that she had not been able to get a fix on him the one time they met for a few days of vacation at Las Hadas, on the Pacific. They spent an afternoon alone sailing the bay while George played a round of golf. Afterwards she had returned to the room, fuming. Holland had spoken only a dozen words to her during the afternoon. She was convinced he had been deliberately rude. George explained that it was as natural for Holland to be unspoken as it was natural for her to speak of art and literature and music. In the days that followed she came to know that when he did speak it was with warmth and a remarkable knowledge of much that interested her. He introduced her to the recordings of the American Big Bands and she became nearly as ardent an aficionado as he. One day Holland spoke French to a woman on the beach who became his companion for the duration of his stay. George was certain he had done it only so that Mariana would have someone to talk with. Still, Holland's quiet was a source of mystery to her, as were the sulfurous scars evident when he wore bathing trunks.

By the time George was finished his swim Holland had banked a fire in front of the house and was heating butter in a cast-iron skillet. In a hole dug in the sand were two bottles of wine resting in sea water.

George helped him rinse fresh fruit in the ocean. The sun, half gone, had brushed everything in clarets of red. The water looked bloody and even the sand had the glow of a blast furnace as they squatted by the fire.

George looked around. "Like this, the sun reminds me of a line I read somewhere: 'Forged in the smithy of the mind.' "

"Uh-huh," said Holland.

"Would you live here if you felt differently about your country?" George said, the words chosen carefully.

Holland put the first few shrimps in the skillet, the butter singed to a mahogany where it ringed the metal. "Henry James said 'It's a complex fate being an American.' The man could lift his shit, I'd say."

George did not pursue it. He knew the reason why Holland, an American citizen by birth, felt he could no longer live there. His self-imposed exile was a condition of conscience and conviction; a protest so private and deep that George was the only one who knew.

He also knew that if one were to unjustly discredit the United States of America in the presence of Holland, that person had best move quickly.

"You didn't come for the sunset, George," Holland said quietly. "What brings you?"

George prepared his thoughts, squirming his folded legs deeper into the sand, seeking stability. To broach the subject so early was unexpected.

"Do you recall my mentioning The Doctor?"

"A time or two." Holland did not look up. "I thought it might be that."

"It's what I've wanted for five years. I'm not sure of the proper term. We—I'm not alone in this—wish to have The Doctor disposed of."

"Hold this, will you?" Holland said, extending the handle of the skillet. "Don't let it rest on the coals just yet." He reached into the hole and filled two tumblers with wine.

"Is that how you put it?"

"You want him killed, George."

"Yes. That is what we want."

"You want me to kill him."

"Yes."

Holland took the skillet from his hands, handed him a set of tongs. "The shrimps are ready."

He looked into the pan. "I'm not sure I should be eating shrimps and drinking wine and discussing having a man killed. It's not an altogether agreeable sensation."

"You're a journalist by choice," Holland observed, reaching with his own tongs, "not necessity. You've met deadlines by writing beside your plate about body counts and mortar casualties. We're just talking."

This last struck a note of discord. Coupled with Holland's earlier statement that he was contemplating six months or more on the island, it made George wonder if Holland had anticipated his purpose and already reached a decision.

Holland raised his glass. *"Es irrt der Mensch, so lang er strebt."* The toast, 'Man errs so long as he strives,' was familiar to George.

"Of course," he nodded. The first shrimps dripped butter on his chin as he bit into them. "These are incredible."

"Closer to 10's than 15's," Holland calculated. "You said you're not alone."

"You've heard me talk about them as well," he responded quickly, eager now that Holland seemed at least willing to hear more. "My Godparents, Hector and Isabelle

Lomolin; as dear to me as my own father and mother. Our families are very close."

"They fled Chile after the coup and set up a refugee center or something in Mexico City?" Holland recalled from memory of past conversations.

"Not exactly. They didn't flee. And it's a clinic they have, not a refugee center. The clinic was originally conceived just for those expelled or escaped from Chile, but now they're accepting patients from other countries as well."

"What other countries?" Holland wanted to know.

George threw his hands up for emphasis. "Wherever the governments have institutionalized political torture to stay in power. There are more than seventy such countries now, and those are only the ones that are known. Were you aware of that?"

"I should think there are a good deal more than that," he said.

He put more shrimps in the butter. He cut a thin wedge of lime, squeezed it between his teeth. A heavy fish leaped in the shallows. His attention dwelled on the erasing ripples.

"Look," he said at length, "I know you've been taken up with this Doctor and what he does for years now. But you've come here wanting me to do something for others besides yourself. You'd better tell me about them. From the beginning."

George got to his feet and began shuffling a small arc on his side of the fire, the dry sand sifting through his toes. A spider marched toward the fire. Holland scooped it up and set it down a yard past.

He would have to relate that which he knew would be important to Holland: the nuances of the Lomolins, their position in Chile, their home there, the visits. Even Patrick, not because his brother had any bearing on the subject at hand, but because Patrick had been so much a part of the time—and Holland knew there had been an only brother killed.

George's mind tumbled back to initial visions. To the most pleasant of the memories.

From the time of his first recollection the Hidalgo family would make the annual trip to Santiago to stay with the Lomolins. Their home was made a wonderful place for a child, despite not having children of their own.

There were so many rows of books the house seemed constructed of them. Where there were no volumes there were lighted maps, some with mountain ranges thrusting from their surfaces and great rifts and waterways etched in vivid relief. Paintings of disturbing dimension and humbling grace hung in every room, and there was music, from the earliest of morning to the last of evening, which first brought George to regard it too as a form of light.

He had images of after dinner debates that were a tradition, coursing from room to room and even into the garden, nourishing all things with knowledge and wisdom, judgment and tolerance. He followed the discourses as best he could, a transfixed but respectfully silent observer too young to participate. When he was of school age they used him as a stringer, dispatching him to the bookshelves for a particular work of reference. This soon led to his debut, occuring amidst a discussion of the French Revolutionary Calendar.

That memory was like yesterday. Somewhere he had read the year of the calendar's inception as 1793, therefore disputing his father's claim of 1788. Postings of opinion were taken; Mother and Hector on his side, Father and Isabelle in opposition. A record of the Revolution was consulted and the date of 1793 affirmed.

The exhilaration he felt! . . . a child's first triumph in the realm of adults . . . and in such formidable company. His parents were pleased, even proud.

He ran to the garden to tell Patrick, but his brother had never shown much interest in the debates and George was certain did not grasp the significance of his excitement. Besides, Patrick was then involved in an adventure of his own.

The garden was the favored gathering place of the children from the privileged neighborhood, and Patrick, though younger than George, had discovered girls that summer—a full two years before his brother's own lust came galloping along. George was not sure who discovered who, or what, but the young ladies, many of whom were older than Patrick, displayed equal enamor and came every morning to play.

This time he was feeding them spoonfuls of raw ground

coffee, believing it to be a frothing aphrodisiac that would ultimately have the maidens throwing off their crinolines to reveal the source of all virgin mysteries. What it did was get them all sick as dogs, and put them in the proverbial house where canines reside.

Alas, no mysteries were solved, and George promptly forgot all he knew of the French Revolutionary Calendar. The mysteries had long since gone the way of all virgin thoughts and misconceptions, although the mysteries of ladies are, of course, eternal.

And Patrick? Patrick was like a proud-cut horse from that summer on. Until he was murdered, and that may always remain something of a mystery.

On the eleventh day of September of 1973 the country of Chile was taken in a military coup d'etat.

From that hour on Hector and Isabelle Lomolin were without a homeland. They were attending a medical conference in Edinburgh, and the wanton slaughter and gluttonous ammanity descending on Chile that day was to forever prevent them returning. Hector tried, flying immediately to Buenos Aires in a desperate bid to learn what was transpiring in the holocaust beyond the border. While he realized there was not any hope of him reentering Chile, at least for a time, he had no sooner set foot on Argentinian soil than he was told he was not welcome there either.

Argentina, without a president, was cautiously awaiting the latest election of Juan Peron and his wife, a few days hence. Officials of the government, many of whom not only knew Hector Lomolin as an esteemed physician and prominent member of Chilean society but as a warm acquaintance as well, did not know if the military leaders in Santiago viewed this man as friend or foe, and they were not about to prematurely compromise sympathies with the new junta.

There was a fresh pie to dissect, and their plates were at the ready.

Hector was held in a small room at the airport while the authorities nervously awaited the next scheduled flight out, a feverish hour spent calling everyone he knew, both within and without the government.

Everyone was inexplicably "unavailable" except for one man, an archbishop who had once stayed in the Lomolin home. He met all of Hector's questions with silence. Only when Hector lost his composure and damned the apostle was he told his land had "become a hell on earth that only our all-seeing God shall witness."

Hector said he would go to Rio and renew his efforts there; at least they would be more neutral, more compassionate, more civilized. With this the archbishop castigated him as a naive fool who had walked the world and seen nothing. There were no nations of neutrality, only those who shut you in or shut you out. Brazil would be a good deal less tolerant of his presence than where he was sitting at the moment. Where was his wife? Hector told him, in New York.

In a rising response that was little better than contemptuous the archbishop advised that, "The Americans are the least neutral of all. In this they are *le patrón,* my infant son!"

Hector's thoughts were chaotic as he hung up the receiver. He took his nitroglycerine.

Events would prove the archbishop to be something more than a prophet.

In Rio it was immediately apparent the Brazilians were primed to expect him. As soon as the plane taxied to a halt and the ramp put down, an army officer and some men in civilian attire came aboard. They approached Hector and ordered he remain seated. The other passengers filed past with ghoulish glances, certain the harried but distinguished looking gentleman must be an international criminal of imposing stature; not only had he been put on the plane by the military, but now was being kept aboard by yet another military.

Hector Lomolin Vilela was an entirely apolitical Chilean citizen of fifty-seven years, hindered by chronic angina pectoris, his existence centered on the art and dissemination of medicine at the Lomolin Clinic in Santiago, for which he had been honored by colleagues throughout the free world, and even beyond. To regard him as a threat, as a subversive, was preposterous. Indeed, to regard Hector Lomolin as anything but a dedicated man of healing would be a distortion.

All of Hector's pleas and protests fell on deaf ears. The flight was scheduled on to Mexico City and he was to go with it.

When he attempted to free himself of the confines of the

seat, the officer broke two of his fingers, slammed his head against the window, and removed his nitroglycerine tablets.

On the passage to Mexico he was dutifully ignored by the flight crew and, at their intervention, by his fellow travellers. Despite visible injuries and the crushing pain in his chest, he was refused medication, food, and water. He was not allowed to go to the bathroom.

At that time the Chilean generals had declared their country in "a state of siege," as applied in time of war, and an entire continent was oddly hostile to anyone holding a Chilean passport and not in military uniform. The Lomolins were to later learn through the International Red Cross that Brazilian police were at that very moment standing alongside the Chilean interrogation teams in the National Stadium in Santiago, participating in and instructing in the beating, torture, and murder of hundreds of political prisoners. Some of whom were Brazilian citizens.

Chile had been a country with the largest proportion of middle class in all of Latin America.

Upon arriving in Mexico City, Hector spent a month in hospital recovering from the heart attack suffered on the plane. Surrounded by his cage of bottles and tubes he focused his energies and, together with Isabelle, set in motion the program of assistance to their compatriots that would become the largest sanctuary of its kind.

The Lomolins lived with George's father and mother for months after Hector was released from hospital. Some land was donated by the Hidalgos and they had a clinic built, then an adjacent dormitory for those victims still in transition, finally a communal farm was acquired to complete the cycle of mortal restoration.

The Lomolins assumed all operating expenses, accepting donations reluctantly. George and his father had to prevail upon them to take offerings.

The compound at the edge of the city arranged for and made welcome all manner of human flotsam discarded by the generals in Chile.

Some of these were whole and merely displaced. Some were splintered and disfigured and yet able to be mended. Some were horrific distillates of humanity that would exist the rest of their days as breathing bags in a bed. Some were partial shadows that would fight the life left in them until they faded to a statistic . . . a statistic Isabelle faithfully entered in a log with a brief adumbrate ending with the relentlessly accusing postmortem, *Why?*

Another log, infinitely more voluminous, listed the dead witnessed in Chile by the survivors. Those entries were still being made. Isabelle was not optimistic of their slackening.

Isabelle Lomolin had always been the keeper of the candle to her husband's keeper of the flame. Once, when George was a child, Isabelle had gone to visit them while Hector remained in Santiago, and he had found it necessary to borrow pocket money from his employees because he had never learned to make a bank withdrawal.

Such interdependence was typical of the union. It was Isabelle who had always monitored the prevailing flux of their government's fortunes, and had therefore seen that their personal monies invariably found deposit in Liechtenstein as soon as taxes were paid—as had the respective generations before them.

In the years since 1974 George could only speculate on how much that fund had been depleted by their philanthropy. The calculations alone would be exhausting.

Hector and Isabelle always paid, in currency, in passion, in pieces of themselves. The toll since that early September day had been catastrophic. Each day of the hundreds of days had seemingly aged them years, while George watched helpless and impotent, the nobility of their Sisyphean labors rendering him awed and humbled.

"Their tragedy has been complete, my friend," he summed up. "Now they live only to aid those who have been tortured. Were it me in their place I would have succumbed to the howling vacuum of futility long ago. There have been times I nearly did."

Misery made a deep mask of his face in the shadows. He looked weary. Dusk was closing the trees in behind him.

"I'm ground down, Goddamn it," he said, slumping visibly.

Holland motioned him to sit down. He poured him wine, but George left the glass in its place.

There was a long silence.

"They don't sound like people who would commission a man killed," Holland contemplated. "Not even someone like your Doctor."

George took a deep breath, his composure returning. "They have not been, not for sixty years. Quite the opposite, in fact. But, The Doctor and his grim science has changed that. It comes late in life for them."

"Come, now," Holland insisted, "this man's been doing this for at least twenty years."

George was stopped by the assertion. He looked at Holland, never sure of the man. "Exactly how much do you know about him?"

"I know there have been attempts on his life before," Holland offered.

"None that even came close," George protested. "And none in recent years. They were the spontaneous acts of amateurs, without so much as a chance of scratching him."

"The Mossad can hardly be termed amateurs, George," Holland stated flatly.

"Certainly not," George conceded, again caught unawares by the knowledge thrown down. Holland excelled at this. Any of the previous times he had raised the topic Holland had met it in silence so inhibiting as to preclude discussion. "But it was an isolated attempt. They failed miserably."

"This thing with the Lomolins," Holland said, "I take it The Doctor was involved in what's happened in Chile."

"He structured and implemented the entire program of political torture that exists to this day," George explained. "The generals, in league with the Americans, had him waiting in a ship offshore for the full month of August while they prepared for the coup. With him was a group of Brazilians he had already trained. By the evening of September eleven the prisons and stadiums, even private houses appropriated for the purpose, were full of prisoners. It was then The Doctor went to work in earnest. An infinitely small number of those detained posed a threat, of course, as that is never the point of the exercise. The purpose is to instill a fear so pervading that it enables power to be marshaled and held without opposition. The quintessential terror tactic."

"Mmm," was Holland's only reaction while he waited for him to go on.

"He still returns there twice a year, or whenever they summon him, to instruct new interrogators and to refine the methods of those previously indoctrinated. They have him on retainer, you see, as maybe fifteen other countries do. The rest pay him the stipulated tariff. Some accept his services as part of foreign aid payments. By all accounts he is a fabulously wealthy man."

"Mmm," Holland repeated. Money failed to hold any great interest for him, other than the interactions it provoked in the motivations of others. Beyond his work, he had little use for and even less desire of it. He knew, certainly, that those such as The Doctor were motivated by forces far removed from mere currency.

"A great philosopher," Holland muttered, in the manner of verdicts long since reasoned.

"Absolutely," George said bitterly. "Karmic. Are they ever anything but?"

The coals of the fire were faint. Off to the west slivers of cloud reflected persistent sunlight, while here in the cove the night had smoked all that surrounded the two men.

A breeze reached them and made amiable sounds with the palms. George welcomed it. Holland swabbed butter from the skillet.

"He's shielded as well as any man I know of," George said. "As well as Arafat or Marcos or Qaddafi. Even better than Kissinger. His protectors are the powerful, as you could imagine, who need him for his expertise. But there are also the implications of what he knows, and about whom. Twenty some years in the service of despots the world over tends to impart some specific influences. They need him alive."

"I understand," Holland said.

George rose with his glass and brushed sand from his legs.

"Do you think it possible? Hector has his doubts it can be done at all."

"Let's put aside the clichés about impossibilities," Holland said, admitting, simply, "I don't know."

"Then you agree a successful assassination is unlikely?" George said, intent on reaction.

Holland's was a gesture of near indifference. "Your godfather may be right, my friend. From what little I know, relatively speaking, it's more likely to get to the others you mentioned than it is your Doctor."

George was uncertain what Holland's detachment signified. He thought, if Holland doesn't know, who does? The journalist felt the first pangs of dejection as he walked to the water and let it ride over his feet. Above, stars were everywhere, brilliant and aloof from all that was earthbound and soiled, holding all the optimism so elusive below.

Holland was collecting the remains of the meal when George turned back to him.

"Still, how much would an attempt cost? In today's marketplace?"

"Commensurate with an untouchable. The fee would be top dollar." His tone was that of commerce. Bland, indifferent, without sufficient import to stay his chores. "About five hundred thousand American dollars."

"I see," George considered.

"The three of you are willing to pay that merely to kill a symptom?"

"We'll meet the expenditure," George confirmed, passing the insinuation. "Although, I would assume the sum myself. The Lomolins' funds are better served by the clinic."

Holland appeared to be thinking. He had a habit of drawing his thumbnail slowly across his upper lip. George had yet to see the hand waver in the time he had known him.

"Will you do it, Holland?" the journalist asked abruptly, no longer able to hold the question.

Holland did not answer at once, instead plunged the skillet into wet sand twice, then scoured the abrasive stuff against the metal. The sound grated on George's teeth and made his hands close at his sides. Finally, Holland stared across at his friend from where he was kneeling, a look that was benign and final.

"I'm not in need of half a million dollars, George," he said, quietly.

The rejection hung in the air like a weight. So there it was, George thought, heart sinking, fears realized. Eight years scratching for a purpose, for an answer. Five years accepting this as the only solution given them. Finally, inevitably—only forty-eight hours ago—the Lomolins accepted the like conclusion. He had felt such relief then! Such purpose! The moment he had cherished but had long since resigned himself would never come, had been at hand. Yet, it seemed had never been. The warning to Hector and Isabelle came back, haunting; Isabelle scoffing, "You're saying this is an assassin who discerns whom he will kill or will not?" Now they would know it was true. The fee was a number to Holland, no more. His interest was purely in the reasoning. Motivation had failed to meld here, on the Cayman beach.

The dread felt on the plane had been prophesy.

Holland finished gathering the utensils, took them into the house and came back for the unopened bottle in the pit, offering it graciously to his guest.

George shook his head.

"I'm going to bed," Holland said. "Anything you need?"

"No, I'll be fine."

"Will you sleep?"

"I'll go for a stroll first," he said, looking up the barren sand, now lighted by a high slim moon. "That will help."

"Walk in the water," Holland advised. "It'll help more."

It struck George as a strange thing from Holland. The man could sleep soundly through two hours of Cong shelling. George had seen him do it, while he and all those around lay wide-eyed, wondering if the next round of incoming would be for them.

"Yes, I expect it does," he thought aloud. "I'll watch for Quasimodo."

"Don't bother," Holland said, turning for the house. "He'll see you first."

Holland was right. The fish did not make an appearance. George walked halfway to the point of the cove, dragging his legs through the ocean as he followed the beach.

His first strides were forced, out of dejection, whipsawing awkwardly through the salt water, his thighs knotting with the strain. Fatigue came eagerly, in waves, satisfying in its lenitive powers.

When he returned it was to note a beach clean where the fire had been, and the hole for the wine. The same for the spot where Holland had scrubbed the skillet. Upon kneeling to look closer, he was unable to detect the least markings. Footprints were absent, even leading to the veranda.

He went to the door.

In one of the rooms, Holland was sleeping on a coco mat.

Then he remembered about the absence of footprints at night, from his times here before. And there were the strands of tiny shells now hanging in the doorway. The habits of living carefully. Not without reason.

"George," came out of the darkness, the sound unexpected and causing him to jump. "I can remember when you thought there were no provocations to justify the taking of a life. The sanctity of it and all that."

George collected himself, straining to see into the room. "I feel I was wrong," he said without difficulty. "I came to think as you. There are those who shame us all and must be held accountable for what they do. They never are."

"If I'm right in assuming the Lomolins' first exposure to this torture was the coup, I'm wondering why it's only now they want him dealt with."

"It was a cumulative thing, I suppose," George said. "They see so much every day. But, I did want you to hear their reasons for yourself. Isabelle wished to meet you before you proceeded."

"With you involved that would hardly have been necessary," Holland stated flatly.

"I knew that as a matter of course," George acknowledged, "but I thought you would trust my initiative precisely because I was involved."

Holland did not respond. He lay in shadows.

The journalist stood a minute or two, waiting, then went to the hammock and slumped into the netting. For an hour he listened to the quiet.

At three, Holland passed his sleeping guest and entered the water.

Quasimodo was at his place. They did not take up their usual pace to the reef. Instead Holland glided leisurely, diving frequently to dawdle near the bottom. And when he walked the spit of sand and coral, he stayed longer.

George wakened at the first feelings of light, seeing the lone figure far out, seeming to the eye as though he were walking the glassy surface itself. The form was silhouetted against the new morning, framed by the sun as it rose, making the silhouette glow and flame until George could no longer watch.

The incongruous musing of an assassin walking his fish

came to him, as it had once before. This time the amusing side of it was lost.

When Holland returned George told him of his decision to catch the morning plane home. Holland nodded without comment.

Santiago came shortly after and shared breakfast with them. Then he prepared his boat to take George to the airfield.

The men stood on the beach and clasped hands, a Mexican journalist granted a piece of potentially deadly knowledge and the American whose profession provided that fatal fascination.

"You were right about the walking stick," George offered, the last thing he could think to say. "Santiago thought it perfect."

They waded to the boat.

A few minutes later Holland had his cove to himself once again. He began washing clothes.

Santiago was back at noon. By then the day was clouded over and there was a modest chop rising inside the reef. The clouds were toying with the Islands; not sober enough for rain. Santiago observed that the drought would go on.

In the house Holland put a shallow pan of water on the propane plate and two cups on the table next to the foil of tea.

"Will you fix the tea while I get washed and packed?" he asked the old man.

"Sure, mon," said the elder. "Where's dat Artie Shaw?"

Holland reached into a cookie tin and produced a cassette, snapping it into the player, then took a bar of soap and went outside to stand under the barrel.

When the water boiled Santiago shut the blue flame and generously sprinkled the black tea directly into the bubbling liquid. They liked their tea hoary.

Santiago listened to *Stardust* while the tea steeped. The pair of telegrams lay discarded on the table at his elbow. He ignored them, had not read them. Instead he chastised himself for not getting the baseball scores in town. Holland had probably tuned his radio to his beloved Yankees in any case. Santiago had listened to *Gunsmoke* on the Miami station.

When Holland reentered, his skin was already dried by the offshore breeze. He towelled his hair, then cut two lemon rinds. Santiago poured the brew through a silk swatch onto the rinds.

After the tea and the packing and the conversation they locked the house and put Holland's things into the baskets on the bicycles. All he had was a roll bag and a photographer's case, the shiny metal specimen generally used by devotees. His passports all said he was an accountant.

Somewhere Holland had read how the wife of the Shah of Iran required three jet airplanes in order to travel: one for herself, one for her entourage, one for her luggage. It was said she did much for the poverty stricken in her country, and was expected to be named to the list of best-dressed again. He had also read, in *Le Monde,* the Shah's confirmation that political torture was not altogether unheard of in Iran.

Santiago waited while Holland took his sandals off and walked into the ocean to the edge of the shelf, the water marking his cotton trousers. There was little point in hiking them up. The material would dry before pedalling half a mile.

He was looking for Quasimodo, although knowing it was unlikely the sea bass was about. It was too warm in the shallows during the high day. The fish would be sleeping out beyond the reef.

But he looked anyway. And spoke softly to the sea.

"Have you any plans, Quasimodo?" he said, standing straight, shielding his eyes from the glare like diamonds, and filling his lungs with liters of salt air. "If you do, now is the time. I'll come back if I can."

Quasimodo would swim alone tonight, in faithful vigilant circles.

Holland went to Santiago and the bicycles.

"Hey, mon," Santiago chided him, "if fate sits you next to a beautiful tourist on de Cessna, you bess don't tell de womans you talks to fish, eh? Take it from dis old Copm, she won't understand. And dass de truth, darlin."

Holland laughed easily, then started his bicycle away from his cove.

Just before they reached the pines Santiago noticed him look back over his shoulder, once.

He was leaving his place, his home built over the mass gravesite, his jewfish.

•4•

Clement Moloch entered the room like a dark thought, made more so by the demoniac hood enshrouding his head.

He brought up the rear, the last of a group of men making up an even dozen. They were a curious collection, all dressed casually, and a majority of them carrying the civilian dress badly—as warriors will when occasion causes the shirking of uniforms. Officers, particularly officers of high rank, feel castrated when not bedecked in the braid and brass of authority. It makes them mortal, or at least to appear so. How were the citizenry to know their place when the general staff were without their clustered robes? When this was over they would be reconstituted by their uniforms, and they took frequent consolation in the anticipation.

Most were professional soldiers of one description or another. Others were physicians, although all had some medical training, if only the rudiments of first aid treatment. Security of the state was supposed to be the common denominator of the gathering.

They shuffled and talked in the hushed tones typical of exchanges that follow enlightening demonstration. Dialects were mixed, largely Arabic and Farasi, a sprinkling of Persian. Some of the men were silent, heads hung with absorption, trailing the residue of shock.

Moloch closed the door behind him, shutting out the racking sobs beyond, and walked purposely to the desk at the head of the classroom. It was not a classroom actually, but a space converted to make do in a barracks building at a military base in a Middle East country of sand and oil pools.

He spread his hands on the desk and waited patiently for his alumni to take their seats, thinking that middle-aged dragoons were more annoying in tardiness than were grade-schoolers.

The only one with a hood, Moloch's other garb comprised a clinical smock over white linen suit pants, these reaching to tan shoes displaying a rich sheen. Only his hands were exposed. His stoney gaze fell to them. Saliva matted the hairs on the back of one. He took a cloth and scrubbed at it intensely, making the arteries vivid. He hated his ruddy hands. The two extremities were absurd blocks of rare beef, the fingers pigmy things, fleshy enough for dimples, the knuckles making the rest look like tied-off sausage pasted to a dumpling.

Not the best digits for the arsenal of medicine.

Once his wife had gifted him a pair of open-fingered driving gloves, but when he pulled them on he found they covered the whole of his fingers. Besides that, they split. She laughed. He was furious, shouting that it was a cruel trick and he should bash her for it. Instead he threw them in her face. Her wronged expression of fidelity was as counterfeit as the gloves, failing to fool him. Or so he divined.

She was not the first to ridicule his stunted claws. There had been the episodes at every school he attended, from Wellington to the Paris Faculty of Medicine, even to the University of London Institute of Psychiatry. They would snigger and deride his "shortcomings" every bit as zealously as they would a dwarfish penis. At Wellington that sort of thing was to be expected, considering they were just snotty British twits anyway—and he was blessed to be Welsh—but surely they should have known better at the London Institute. The lessons of the lecture halls were often countered by those of the common, and were therefore all the more profitable. But, in consequence, it did spur him to leave the Institute before he was anointed by degree. In later years he obtained a doctorate in psychology, elsewhere, and though it was politically secured rather than academically earned, he was as expert in the field as any legitimately qualified master.

"Gentlemen, please," he carped, his voice bated somewhat by the slash in the hood. "Shall we get on with it?"

The buzz of conversation slackened. The stragglers went to the desks fanned in front of him. One desk was exiled to the rear, for the two who did not speak English and therefore required a translator. They spoke Swahili. Their skin was black, the only ones there. On the first day the interruptions had disturbed Moloch and he ordered the routine be moved to a proximity less encroaching. This did, of course, raise the predictable hackles. A small scene ensued, quickly resolved by his stalking from the room and not returning until a prescribed decorum was advanced and adhered to.

All too often he found soldiers who could discipline with dispatch were something less than keen when the posting was turned on them. A natural enough malady of the new geopolitik, he judged.

The seminars had been orderly and productive every day since, but the whispered gibberish irked him still. The incompetents, all they needed do was arrange for headphones prior to his arrival. After all, it was hardly the first occasion for his being there.

Clement Moloch demanded order in the seamless sphere that was his place, a world constantly besieged by trespassing fools. A vastly superior being, no less so than in his own eyes, he at times regarded genius as the thistle crown some had to endure, the distinction being in how well the thistles were worn. He was secure, beyond any pale of doubt, in the belief that he wore his exceedingly well. A fond phrase was, "Who knows better his worth than the self best able to assess it?" Who, indeed.

He waited for the pens to poise.

Outside the windowless room the snapping of flags could be heard in the dry, dust laden wind called the *Ghibli*. The wretched thing had been blowing for three days and nights without respite, sometimes blocking the sun itself. Last night his wife had shaken her dress and the sand could be seen on the carpet. More astounding was the sound of it falling on the marble of the bathroom when he flounced her undergarments. She had spent the day shopping in the bazaar. At dinner she told the children that, were it not for the oil, the country would be a good place for Britain to dump her garbage. The children thought it smashing, and told the attendant. The attendant had smiled graciously, the simpleton, just the way the interpreter was smiling now.

The pens were ready. Finally.

"You won't need the pens," he said sharply.

There were audible sighs. Pens lowered. One fell to the floor. He glared at the perpetrator from the crypt of his hood, his eyes flinty grey chips.

"Now then," he began, jutting an arm in the direction of the door they had just passed through, "you have seen once again how expedient are the simplest forms of psychological manipulation. Contemporary human species insist upon covering the body; so be it. Remove the covering and we peel away the first line of defense. That's it. What could be more elementary? Think about it, gentlemen. I insist. Envision yourself, stripped, naked, without a stitch . . . in the hands of your enemy."

His practiced eye watched the infirmity sprint across the faces, faces of powerful, arrogant centurions. Although he had been battering them all week with the same textbook tactic of stripping their prisoners as a first step, they never failed to shift in their seats when he repeated it. But then, where was the covering of the body more sacred than in an Islamic society.

The ploy was one they were uniquely equipped to grasp.

"Remember, again, as I did with the woman, we demand that she—*she!*—remove her clothes. Only as a last resort does the interrogator do this for her. If the prisoner refuses, the interrogator tells her in a calm, civilized manner what will be the consequences. Firmly, graphically, but no need to shout and carry on like aborigines. In the simple act of having the woman disrobe herself, the interrogator has annexed the native will to cooperate. As well, her dignity has been eroded at this earliest stage by her own hand, thus depriving her of feeling she was denied choice by reason of force. An important distinction. An auspicious beginning. We pull the string, you see, not the tit.

"With the male it is quite the opposite. Force is implemented at once, his clothing is torn from him. This way his manhood is assaulted, his virility put in question. The male will always resist. Without his clothing he in fact feels defenseless to a degree greater than the female. You have seen this a number of times these past days. No need for me to dwell on it, now is there? But do not forget: Without clothing your prisoner experiences a profound vulnerability; keep them bare at every opportunity then and you will heighten the effectiveness of all that follows. Right. Questions, gentlemen?"

The pattern continued. There were no queries on nakedness from the Moslem audience. They were sick of hearing it.

Of course, his intent went beyond the mere affirming of an exemplary principle. The effect he had been pursuing throughout the week was an appreciation of basic psychology as a working stratagem in reaching their desired purpose. If they could accept the premise it would mean he had made progress with them.

He had harped over and over: Maximum accomplishment via minimum violence. Anyone could wield a club. That took little finesse, less imagination. But to elevate stress by dissecting the mind, until the prisoner was broken, well, that was an art. If only he could find more who were capable of comprehending. These, most of whom commanded scores of interrogators in their service, had the inherent authoritarian predilection for force as a means to all ends. Whenever he suggested they were degrading and brutalizing themselves by resorting to their crude instincts, he saw the notion going beyond their ability to fathom, and what better should he have expected anyway. Few inroads were to be made into the military mind this trip, or any other as far as that went, and so he was not about to exhaust himself on these Calibans.

"Enough of that," he decided, scanning some papers on the desk, pausing when he came to the list of pertinent literature he had drawn up for them. Titles were imposing: *Role of the hypothalamus in the sexual behavior of mammals; Advances in neurology, International Symposium on pain, Volume 4.* There were quite a number of reference titles, and though hardly papers conceived of as fodder for this work, they nevertheless proved useful in a general way.

Bah! These minstrels would better understand a treatise on moral probity by Richard Nixon, he decided.

He balled the paper, needing both hands, and flung it into the medical bag that served as a catch-all.

"Let us get back to the topic of the day," he said, taking up where he had left off earlier, "that being the prospect of released prisoners possibly coming under examination by one of the crusading groups of foreign moralists. I can scarcely think why this should concern any of you gentlemen, but, unlikely as it seems in contemplation, the question has been raised by our worthy friend and we do want to be thorough, don't we?"

He gave an admonishing nod toward a roundly deflated police general seated to his left, the third such censure of the day, he not being one to cancel a novice indiscriminately.

"In any case," he continued, "there are certain ratios of detainees which must be set free—in a manner of speaking—in order to provide a further deterrent to those who would oppose authority; we all recognize the necessity of this. As to the proportion to be set free versus those to be terminated, this is subject to variables of time and place, level of general unrest, purpose to be served, among other considerations, and I leave those aspects to your discretion. However, let me say this, it is rather inappropriate to release prisoners who have been unduly disfigured by their experience, besides it being quite unnecessary. Each of you has an infinite range of procedures at your disposal that are difficult if not impossible to detect once completed. Use them."

Looking as though he were a schoolboy primed with questions, the bowed police general shifted to speak. Moloch turned, hands in a prayer pose, his glare instantly quashing any inkling of rebuttal. They stared for a few moments, then the man passed a hand in his hair and commenced to study his cuffs. Moloch, satisfied, moved his attention away.

"Energy shortages notwithstanding," he went on, his implicit bow pleasing to his listeners, "the application of electricity is still efficient for those who do not have the patience for more subtle procedures. If you adhere to the table of amperages I have provided, you will find any skin searing is of a minor nature—even at the upper reaches of the scale—difficult to detect after a few days of healing, and even more difficult to isolate in origin. The markings can be dismissed as blemishes in most instances. But, of course, the body has conveniently provided a variety of orifices that effectively conceal even excessive levels of current, amongst other things."

The blunt end of a pencil was then raised to the hood

where it covered the front of his skull, leaving no doubt that he meant the part of the forebrain that served as a nervous center for primitive physical and emotional behavior.

"Irregardless, the hypothalamus will retain the message long after boundary tissues have revived themselves. Temporary asphyxiation is appropriate as well, leaving no trace. Monitor your subject's pulse while the breathing apparatus is submerged and you will suffer no accidents. But do not use gasoline or other toxic substances in these cases, or else ancillary evidence will remain.

"Drugs are also particularly suited to this category, only hindered by the somewhat more controlled conditions they dictate. My own recipe of taquiflexil and sodium pentothal, which some here have used, is an example of this. For those not familiar with taquiflexil, it is a derivative of curare—the vine extract first used by Indians on poison-tipped arrows. It induces muscle contractions sufficiently severe to prove fatal unless administered prudently, even then it is necessary to keep the subject alive in an oxygen tent until a dose of sodium pentothal can be injected, thus invoking a relaxed semi-conscious euphoria ideal for interrogation, or what you will. The adventure is castastrophic to your candidate, I assure you, and one not easily forgotten. Those of you wishing particulars in respect to dosages and the like can speak up when we are through."

The concrete block walls and corrugated steel roof of the building soaked up the droll wordings of menace—words that, if heard by ears not understanding of the language, would sound every bit as vital as instruction in appliance repair or lumber yard audit.

There was not much life to a dissertation on just that very subject.

Just then a foreboding rumble reached the room, knifing through the concrete and shaking the air with a booming resonance. Moloch looked up at the trussed metal roof and saw seams of dust vibrate loose and fall in curtains.

No one moved. They knew what caused the din. A tank, maybe two, Cyrillic lettered T-54s, had lumbered by in a close passing of the building. Moloch was reminded of where he was: a military installation where soldiers went on maneuvers in tanks and trucks and AFVs to play war games.

The thumping subsided. He eyed the dust warily as it came nearer.

His handkerchief sailed, Satchmo style, the blessed stuff running riot with his allergies required an incessant stabbing beneath his hood with a flurry of stoppers. At day's end his pockets were stuffed with discarded cloths.

Stupendous oil revenues and the heathens didn't even have the common sense to filter the air properly, he thought. Well, at least they knew better than to dole it out to the parasites, as England would do now that she had her own petrol screw. The building had a Russian-made air-conditioner and it failed to function appreciably better than a paddle-bladed ceiling fan. Thank goodness the Official Residence had its air processed by a unit of American manufacture or he would have been unable to sleep at all, much less as soundly as he usually did.

When he finished placating his passages he took stock of his audience, they waiting on him with fixed anticipation.

Clement Moloch, the irrefutable Grand Master of a torture cartel truly international in scope, the progenitor of the most innovative and sophisticated of techniques, the supreme authority on fear plumbed for political and ideological purpose, was not comfortable with verbal theorizing, preferring instead that sheer brilliance be illustrated by empirical demonstration. Choose the prisoner; break the prisoner. See Spot run. The challenge was in the doing, not the telling, and he longed for the rigors of application in place of the tutoring of callous melon-thumpers.

Here he was in this godforsaken wasteland with the tools of order and stability, and all they wanted were quick and dirty perversions of his wares.

True, he would readily acknowledge that his was not a nice place to visit; a darkness filled with running feet, screeching brakes, revolver shots, and the screams of torment from a thousand prison grates. But what simple fool could deny the urgency of his mandate, the insatiable clamor for his repertoire of remedial terrors. He knew the answer to that one. History knows the thumbscrew. Man plans; God laughs.

"Continuing on in this theme," he persisted, "prolonged isolation; deprivation of sleep, food, light, darkness, and so on, should be mentioned, although these require a time frame that is not always realistic. The sight and sound of relatives or fellow prisoners being interrogated can be utilized, though one should not then release any two prisoners who have witnessed the same events. Humiliating the prisoner in a sexual manner works exceptionally well with some individuals, especially in the presence of others, and their vanities will often prevent them from telling of it after. This reflects the experience of the Danish medical team that interviewed and examined the Greek and Chilean refugees. In fact I am quite familiar with the findings of these meddlers and I can assure you their conclusions were hopelessly vague, with absolutely no evidence conclusive enough to serve any useful purpose, their detailed medical and neurological examinations of so-called 'torture' sequelae producing nothing more than self-serving supposition."

Because the discourse was leaden to his own ears, so labored by past repetition of the same essay, he decided to inject some belated theatrics to this afternoon session; some arm waving, some hooked thumbs, some closely watched faces. He orbited about the desks, causing heads to swivel after him, eyed notes cryptically, stood beside the interpreter—behind the others so that they had to turn full around.

"I could go on, but I know that none of the gentlemen in this room needs bother himself with interference from within his own country, or indeed from his neighbor. And in the event a freed prisoner were to somehow make his or her way out of the country and into the hands of one of these groups, the sum is nothing more than blind hysterics at best. What possible consequence can they be to men in your positions?"

He went to his desk and stood on the chair, rising over his listeners, his bagged head lending the appearance of an unfinished sculpture.

"Consider Chile," he proposed to them, "who has thrown it back in their faces. Like you, Pinochet has done what he must for the greater good of his country, and has told them he does not have time for their sanctimonious ravings about human rights and the sanctity of life. You must keep in mind that Chile does not even have oil."

They responded on cue, exchanging imperious glances and seeming as though they had discovered their chairs were suddenly more comfortable. Smiles were absent though, considered bad form. Partners in power could smirk, but too brazen a camaraderie was suspect in the political puzzle of the Middle East.

Moloch swept from his chair and hammered the desk with a flourish.

"Uruguay, Brazil, Argentina, Spain," he cried. "What sanctions were taken against them? How have they suffered? Did the capitalist countries curb investment of their business sector? Did they curtail the aid programs? Did they stop the arms shipments? Certainly not. One need only remember who put the regimes in place to begin with.

"Let us not overlook the Soviet Union, where they know how to deal with opposition with expediency. They just clap the more bothersome agitators in the insane asylums and forget them. Now that, I submit to you, is efficiency. The Russians could care less what they are accused of, and by whom. Let them say what they will. Only an idiot listens to the dog's bark."

His voice moderated and his dramatics waned as quickly as they had risen. He knew, as all accomplished orators knew, the value of rapidly contrasting moods while telling your audience precisely what it was they wanted to hear. So now he spoke quietly and made them strain to hear it, dropping an octave in tone.

"Each of you is responsible for the security of your country and the good order of its citizens. To that purpose, I give you the staples. If you bother yourselves with foreign cause-seekers you will do your countries a grave injustice. Recognize them for the nuisance they are, and get on with the job."

And with that the entire question of scrutiny by those pledged to differing ideals was summarily dismissed. To him, and the rulers to whom any means of holding power was acceptable, the proposition of curtailing their activities because of the scattered bleatings of a few self-righteous messiahs was folly. He had spent a good portion of the day on such foolishness, that was enough. It was time to get back to the agenda of snuffing out dissent.

And if rough trade was what they wanted, he would give them rough trade.

"Alright," he said, clapping his hands before him, ready

to plunge with fresh enthusiasm into a selection of techniques new to most in this group. "Even the layman knows how marvelously efficient the kidneys are in flushing wastes from the body and keeping the crucial chemical allotments in balance. But, like any delicate organism, we cannot ask too much of them. If, for example, a person is forced to ingest water faster than the kidneys can excrete it, some of the fluid will automatically drain off into the lungs, causing the person to slowly suffocate from within. Call it internal drowning if you will. However, let me illustrate the significance of some variations in a controlled condition."

With a generous sweep of his arm he invited them toward a door to his right, to the room he had been using to implement his teachings in controlled conditions, beyond that a room of cells where civilian prisoners were held for his access.

But, before he had taken more than a few steps, the opposite door opened and the head of one of his aides appeared. Brian Randolph beckoned to Moloch.

"Bloody hell," Moloch muttered, turning to the now eager officers. "Go right on, gentlemen. I'll join you shortly." Singling out an older officer, he added: "General, choose a subject for us, would you? So that we are not held up."

Moloch strode to the outer office where his three aides were stationed, closed the door, and slipped the hood from his head. Whatever sinister implications the hood lent were gone with its removal, leaving a full, hearty, solidly-boned face without a hard line to it. Pink, like his hands, the skin had the pronounced luster of vitality that seemed a birthright of all raised on the windward side of the British Isles. His cradle of dense white hair and his blended countenance could have made him a kindly November Santa Claus such as hired by department stores, instead of what he was.

On the desk were the makings of a card game and two partly-consumed Coca-Colas, bottles slashed with arabesque markings. The two who had been playing were standing, ready to do his bidding, while the third, Ray Crosetti, sat in a chair in the corner with an ancient copy of *Look* magazine in his lap. On the cover was an astronaut, with the caption: LEAVING FOR THE MOON.

Randolph was a giant man over six and one-half feet tall and as craggy as a breakwater, a specimen able to intimidate by sight alone. Yet his size was less practical than fortunate, useful for those who persisted in equating mass with might. Professionals knew better. Crosetti, at little more than half the size, spindly and sallow, was much the greater threat because of his will. Professionals knew that, too.

The three men were as much a part of Moloch's routine as his toilet kit, all having been previously employed by the Central Intelligence Agency, trained specifically for this work. He had hired them away and paid them now himself, handsomely, because they were the best he could find and were charged with his protection at every minute of his—and their—lives. Their lot was a measurable improvement over the CIA, and, though not for that alone, they were voraciously committed to him. Theirs were the finest of accommodations as Moloch flitted from country to country. Meals were supreme, because his were. Travel was by private or military jet, or first class in commercial aircraft. Their rooms were next to his own when home on the estate. At most times their number was supplemented by security agents of the country they were in, making the task considerably less demanding. Crosetti and Randolph had been with him almost a dozen years, the third man seven.

"What is it, Brian Boy?" Moloch asked, using the tag he habitually addressed to Randolph.

"Mrs. Moloch, sir," Randolph answered. "She's outside with the children and wants to see you."

Moloch frowned, displeased at learning the reason for the interruption. He put a finger to his lips, considering, then pointed it at the third man. "Jack, find someone in authority. Tell them to stop driving their ruddy tanks up against the building, will you?"

"And find some asshole who knows how to turn off the sand," Crosetti added, his brow squeezed with migraine.

Moloch went to Crosetti and gently put the back of his hand against his temple. "We can do without the poor language, Raymond. Would you like an injection?"

"I'll beat it," Crosetti said acidly, Moloch recognizing the blur of masochism he knew to be there. "It could be worse."

Moloch patted his shoulder, left him and walked to the door.

"How much longer?" Crosetti asked him.

"Three, perhaps four days," Moloch said, opening the door an inch or two and looking outside. He saw a Citroen limousine a yard or two away, wind-driven sand raking it with the sound of rain on a tin roof. His children waved at him with their faces pasted to the window, smiling, a boy, nine, and a girl, eight. He waved in return, closed the door.

"Ask Margaret to come in," he said to Crosetti, "then wait in the car until she returns. Tell the children I'll see them at dinner tonight."

Crosetti got up from his chair, taking the Ingram M-10 machine pistol with him. He stopped, remembering the Ingram in his hand, and passed it to Randolph. Then, from habit, he reached under his shirt and absently fingered the Walther at his waist. Satisfied, he buttoned his shirt at the neck and went outside.

Randolph waited until Margaret Moloch appeared before going through the other door, leaving them alone. Both exits to the place were covered then, merely their combined function performed on reflex.

Margaret Moloch was a woman who took faithful excursions at two-year intervals to Rio de Janeiro, with Moloch's sister, for face peelings and various pruning tucks here and there, and therefore appeared thirtyish instead of fiftyish. The fetish with face had commenced with the arrival of her first child and was somewhat of a trade-off agreement struck with her mate. He wanted the children more than she. The risk was hers, probing the limits of what a man could ask of a woman, but in turn for allowing him to impregnate her she was granted these forays back into youth. Broad in pelvis and perfectly tilted for conception and carry, she'd had much less trouble dropping the infants than Moloch knew, therefore besting him in the bargain. He had his heir; she had the kindest cuts.

As a psychologist he had known what to expect. The preening, the care not to smile too spaciously or squint at the sun or frown too deeply. The wardrobe revamped for flattering fit; more imaginative lingerie that stretched, too sheer for seams. The escalated sexual appetite. All too predictable for him, but still interesting to observe close at hand, and not without its spurts of adventure.

Margaret remained a matron beneath it all, despite whole whacks taken from her Rubens architecture. For she was the Welsh lass that his own father had delivered in the cottage next to their own, who had held his hand and wept with him when his father ordered he bury his dolls in the meadow on his fourth birthday, and who had betrothed herself to him after the ceremony. In intellect, they were magnets of opposing poles, but he knew very early that that was a proven catalyst in matrimonial accord. If anything, they were more devoted now than they had been at the doll burial.

She bent to him, because she was the taller, and they kissed the void beside each other's cheek.

"Dearest," she said.

"My dear," he said.

Her glance, poised with covenant and mindful of interest attended in reverent order, went past him to where she knew he was occupied. To her husband's place of business.

"How is your day?"

Moloch shrugged. "Satisfactory, no more. How are the children getting on?"

"They're bored stiff as day old porridge, you might know," she said, inspecting the meager features of the office, "but—and God bless them—the little souls are bearing up wonderfully. It's just that they can do very little of anything outside because of this maddening wind. The sand can blast the skin away if one isn't careful."

He nodded understanding. "Surely there are enough diversions to keep them busy at the Residence . . . any number of games rooms . . . they can swim in the pool. Oh, and there are motion pictures, did you know? The Colonel told me . . ."

"We saw them," she interrupted curtly. "None in English. Walt Disney dubbed in Arabic was uproarious for all of two minutes before they started screaming for the sound to be fixed. Somehow it's not the same, now is it, Clement?"

"I suppose it isn't," he allowed.

"And everywhere those young girls," she said. "Some

of them are mere children. I suspect even they are concubines."

"You're speaking of customs that go back centuries, Margaret," he cautioned her.

"That does not make it correct," she countered, "any more than Waterford crystal and brocade love seats make a visionary of a common thug. I do hope you're not suggesting it's a suitable atmosphere for our children."

"No," he said, moving away from her and putting a clenched fist to his forehead in a display of torment. "But I pleaded with you not to come. I don't know what got into you. I said that I wouldn't be responsible . . ."

"Yes, yes," she said abruptly, but following him and lifting his fist from his forehead, kissing him there, tipping with her tongue before drawing away. The tongue touching was another of her post-renaissance affects that annoyed him. "An avid camp follower I am not, and have never been. The lesson is yours, my darling."

"You'll forgive me if it provides little consolation now that we are halfway around the globe, Margaret," he said, wanting the lesson sufficiently ingrained that it would not again need refreshing.

She clutched his arm persuasively. "Could we take the children home then?" she ventured.

He took his arm away deliberately, feigning astonishment at the proposal—though knowing all along it was her purpose in coming. "Why, that is completely out of the question," he retorted. "An enormous amount of work remains to be done, and without an hour to spare. Surely I needn't remind you that the same rabble is loose here, and they do not work to a schedule submitted for our approval."

"Oh, I realize how these people depend on you," she allowed, "and I know how critical your work is, but you did give me your word you would take this month to rest at home. You've been promising for a year, and here you are spending the first half of your month in this horrid place."

"I tried to beg off," he protested. "I did, you know."

"With precious little conviction, I must say." She circled him as she would a mannequin. "Look at you. Soon you'll resemble the gaunt scientist who wastes away in his laboratory with his mice. You've abandoned any semblance of regime, you're not eating properly, and you're definitely not sleeping adequately. Why were you so late to bed last night? It must have been past two."

"Gad," he growled, piqued by the memory of it, walking in front of her and wringing his hands. "The Colonel, ever the gracious host—or at least following instruction from whatever high priest of decorum he has lately imported—insisted on chess, except the man is hopeless at assimilation and anticipation, which scarcely augurs well for a military ruler, and if I failed to humor him the games would be over in a matter of minutes. He would get hemmed in with monotonous consistency, at which point he would become livid and demand a restart so that he could compose all of the same moves once again. Then it would only do if I saw his collection of pornography, a staggering profusion of really dreadful stuff."

"Surely he could see it was hardly grist to interest you," she said, knowing it to be true.

"Not at all," he explained. "I had to speak up, and I think he was quite wounded. Though they don't like to show it, you know."

She took his arm again, stroking it this time, working her wiles in the mistaken belief she was winning him. What she did not know was that the burlesque he related was genetic to the despotic characters who employed him, and his being subjected to such behavior was not uncommon.

"You see?" she said hopefully. "This has been no great delight for you either. You do need a rest desperately. Let us go home, today, when you're finished. Please?"

"Impossible," he shot back. "A minimum of three days is required before I'll be through. Besides, the Colonel's holding a reception for me this evening."

"Oh, joy," she chafed, wheeling away from him and flinging her pocketbook to the desk. "Endless toasts by illiterate gunmen whose fronts are covered in crackerjack medals. A striking spectacle if one enjoys the circus. How nice."

"You needn't attend, my dear," he offered, skirting the sarcasm. "Few of the officers have brought their wives along, and I'm certain the Colonel will understand."

"You may be equally certain I will not attend," she advised. "Regardless of the fact he understands or not."

When he went to her she turned her back on him. He persisted, putting his arms around her, eager to reach some ready accord, not forgetting the waiting officers. "I have an idea. Why don't you take the children and go on to Europe. I'll join you there as soon as I can break away; perhaps two more days would be enough. We'll meet in Rome. You could shop for clothes."

"Rome is old," she snapped.

Stunned, he uttered, "What?"

"Oh, don't be that way with me, Clement. I know that's the attraction, but not all of us are enthralled with crumbling ruins."

"Milan, then. You adore Basile."

"They don't understand me there anymore," she said sullenly. "No, the children and I will wait until you're finished and then we'll go home together." She turned in his arms to face him, pressing her rigged parts on his. "But you must promise you'll stay the rest of the month at home. I've arranged a few formal gatherings and I won't stand the embarrassment of cancelled invitations again."

"That won't be necessary, my dear," he soothed, stroking her flanks. "You're right. I am tired and in need of a rest, two more days, then."

"That's better," she sighed, kissing his cheek.

He retrieved her pocketbook and walked with her to the door.

"Shall I assume you're having dinner at the reception?" she asked him, her hand on the knob.

"What . . . ?" he said, his thoughts already diverted. "Oh, yes. But I will come by for a cocktail before. You're sure you wouldn't like to accompany me?"

"Quite sure," she confirmed with a bleak facsimile of a smile.

With one hand fastened to her breast and her head lowered to thwart the wind, she stepped outside.

The dust made Moloch sneeze. He heard the Citroen's door open and close, the pitch of the engine change.

Crosetti appeared a moment later, shaking sand from his hair. Moloch was already in motion. As he dashed across the empty classroom, he tossed over his shoulder: "I've decided we'll return directly home in the morning, but we'll keep the fact to ourselves until then. Right?"

Randolph and Crosetti stood at the office door. "Right," they said in unison, accustomed to the logistics of vague itineraries, and too disciplined to question decisions of domestic origin. As well, recent years had provided scant challenge for the industry of shielding Clement Moloch and they saw nothing to suggest the altering of that favorable condition.

The man known as The Doctor went to his labors with a visible urgency that belied his time of doing it, the hood descending once again as he passed into the next room.

A muffled cry was emitted before the door sealed it off.

They had started without him.

•5•

Holland slumped in the sumptuous leather of the car and watched the people of Mexico City drift past the moving window sill. He wore a navy blue windbreaker with the imprint of the New York Yankees on the breast. Between his knees, on the floor, was the camera case.

The crabbing ache was back, this time in his left arm below the shoulder. Not really enough to be called pain, the sensation more what one might refer to as legacy. A long time ago a bullet had entered there to mush itself on the bone, spaying some nerves, leaving others disheveled and susceptible to remittent inflammation. He never knew from where the ache would come, for there were many sources to choose from and sometimes the debility would roam far from its origin. The last time he visited his physician in Lucerne, the consensus was that as his age advanced so would the effects of the damage advance, until eventually the condition would settle into permanence. The physician felt he should advise of the possibility of some disablement. Perhaps in the mid-forties or early fifties. Maybe.

Somehow Holland did not think it an eventuality to give him pause.

He straightened the arm and rubbed the spot, looking

aimlessly through the side window. Some of the people walking the sidewalks would occasionally take notice of the car as it passed.

"What kind of car is this?" he asked, turning to George Hidalgo.

George glanced away from his driving, surprised by the question, but remembering how Holland was with automobiles. "It's a BMW," he said. "Do you like it?"

"Very comfortable," he said. "The people in the street like it. These are the ones they call 'Bimmers' in Europe, aren't they?'

"The same," George confirmed, amused by the expression.

Ahuehuete trees lined the boulevard, their broken patterns of shade marching across the hood and windshield like a silent film strip. The day was warm and the pedestrians looked it.

Holland had called George that morning, early, before Mass, and said: "Let's do it."

George was jarred by the call, by the knowledge Holland had left his island only hours after he himself had, and by the fact Holland had been in the city more than a day before contacting him.

When he departed the island he was resigned that Holland's mind was made up. Nothing more could be said. Yet, in retrospect, George knew that once Holland had changed his mind—whenever that had been—his pattern in coming here was typical. Holland granted little to anticipate, less to predict. He travelled alone. He was simply there, or he was gone. As elusive as the shadows dancing on the car.

The conversation had been brief. He would meet George in Alameda Park, next to the Palace of Fine Arts on Avenue Hidalgo, in the late afternoon. George would take him to the Lomolins.

Holland had been waiting at the appointed hour, sitting on a stone bench, smoking his pipe.

Now, the traffic was heavy as they made their way out of the downtown area. Throngs of workers returning home were countered by those converging on the city for dinner and an evening's entertainment, all squirming to claim and discard the same bit of ever moving space as they completed the cycle of daily shuttle.

Inside the car, the conditioned air swirled about with Teutonic efficiency. Even so, Holland noticed that the steering wheel glistened whenever George moved his hand away.

"I've never known you to be interested in photography," George said, indicating the aluminum valise at Holland's feet.

"I'm not," Holland said. "It's one of the easier ways of carrying a gun through airports, is all."

George, puzzled, asked, "How is that done?"

Holland elaborated without diverting his attention from the procession of commuters, explaining that the scanners were unable to penetrate the metal skin of the case, making it necessary for the inspectors to open the case if they wanted to be bothered. He habitually waited until the last minutes before boarding because most passengers arrived then and there was the predictable reluctance to impede them with lengthy searches. The gun itself was partially disassembled in two wedge-shaped compartments under the case's hinges and lock, providing balance. In the event the inspectors did take a look, all they could see were a camera and lenses neatly tucked away in their foam pockets, just as they were supposed to be. The shutter on the camera operated, and the lenses had glass in each end, but otherwise they were gutted to help compensate for the weight of the gun. Pressing on the foam would betray nothing, it being epoxied in to prevent them simply lifting it out.

"I see," said George, finding the details fascinating. "You've never had them find it?"

"No," he said. "But I should also mention I don't take the case on as hand luggage. It goes into the cargo hold."

"I don't understand though," George pressed. "Guns are easy to come by. Why not just buy one when you get to your destination?"

"Buying a gun entails needless exposure, especially when the idea is to be as autonomous as you can. More importantly, the gun has been modified to suit. I don't like to be without it."

George felt cautiously rewarded that Holland was allowing even a fleeting glimpse of his craft, the first time he had done so to this extent. He hoped there would be more of the same, yet knew that was unlikely. "It sounds as though it's a special gun," he speculated, aware that Holland had originally been posted to Vietnam as a weapons specialist. "I'd be interested in seeing it one day."

"You're welcome to," Holland offered, "but you'll be disappointed. It's still a revolver that fires six rounds of decent caliber. If you expect exotic trickery, there isn't any. Just a refined piece."

They passed beneath another massive stone sundial on the facade of a building, the second Holland had seen in three blocks.

"Any ideas where to start looking for your Doctor?"

"Better than that," George replied quickly, anxious to have Holland know he had been busy and was not without resources of his own. "I know exactly where you can find him. At home, in Guatemala City. I telephoned there this morning after hearing from you. It was confirmed he's there. We're not certain, but he may be there another two weeks, maybe three. You see, he's seldom home more than a few days at a time, and that's why I came to see you when I did; it seemed that fortune was about to come in our favor."

"I can think of better places to have to go after someone than Guatemala. I suppose he makes his home there for the usual reasons."

"Definitely. The political climate's ideal for someone like him, just as it is for Mengele and the Nazis in South America. They're secure in the same beds. As well, the CIA has the run of the place, and the local office looks after him like a mother hen. Another reason he lives there is his allergies, apparently the climate is perfect for that too."

Though it was not apparent on his face, Holland's mind was working rapidly, beginning to sift the initial pieces of information. Whether George knew it or not, the most auspicious place for an attempt was usually in the general proximity of the objective's home turf. A routine was to be expected to some extent, because of the familiar surroundings, and vigilance was generally more lax than it would otherwise be. Perhaps. With a quarry the stature of Clement Moloch almost anything could be expected and almost nothing could be safely assumed.

Nevertheless, The Doctor was human. With Holland, that was always a strike against.

"Who fed you the information this morning?" Holland wanted to know.

"Max," George answered. "Maximiliano Ortiz; an uncle on my mother's side. I'll leave it to you, but I think he could be of great help, and he's willing. He knows the Lomolins well. Nothing happens in Guatemala that Max doesn't know about. You'd like him."

"It'd be more important I trust him," Holland suggested.

George looked at Holland directly, offended by the remark. "I have no reservations, Holland, none whatsoever. You could trust him with your life." Then, realizing what he had said, "I mean . . . well, you know what I mean."

Holland smiled briefly, then pointed a finger ahead so George would direct his attention back to the road.

Holland was apprehensive to a fault when riding in automobiles, probably because his own driving was scarcely better than adequate. George wasn't much of an improvement, but then, almost anything was an improvement on Holland's ability. George knew, and virtually refused to go anywhere with Holland at the wheel.

"What's he do for a living?"

"Max is a businessman of many interests," George explained. "His import and export firm is the biggest in the country, everything from earthmovers to teapots. If there's anything you require, I should imagine he could provide it, including information. Needless to say, I haven't told him anything, assuming you want things kept to ourselves and the Lomolins."

Holland did not respond. They stayed silent as the car crawled along in the jam of vehicles. Holland put his head back on the seat and closed his eyes, his pipe empty in his mouth.

At the first opportunity, George wheeled impatiently from the boulevard and sped up the less congested side streets, charting a secondary course of hurried turns and unhindered stretches.

Holland's eyes opened. Shops and carts and people on bicycles were flashing by.

"Uh, George," he said tentatively. "Let's not crash."

"I'd know these streets in my sleep," George responded confidently. "Besides, this isn't at all fast for a car like this."

It was a mystery to him that George, who was a fine

pilot, was somehow powerless to apply the same skills to land-based transport. Flying was a long-established pastime of George's. He had a particular passion for helicopters—supposedly one of the most difficult of kinetics to master—and when first married he had spent four hours a day for months on end learning the intricacies of flight on the vertical axis, until ultimately able to chase swallows and to impress the professionals at the Naval Air Station at San Diego. Holland had flown with dozens of 'copter jockeys in Vietnam and Laos and Cambodia; none were better. Why it was then that George guided automobiles so deplorably was beyond him.

"Have you anything in mind yet?" George asked him.

"Too early. There are always a few options, but the rest has to be played by ear. I'll want you to tell me what you know about him. Everything you can think of."

"I've already prepared for that. This morning I gathered my material and started making notes. We can go over them tonight if you want."

At once it occurred to Holland that George should not have made notes, then he realized George had been stalking Moloch for years. With a pen.

"Have you begun your book yet?" he asked, watching the speedometer.

"No," George admitted dejectedly. "I suppose I know it won't do any good anyway. What you do seems the only thing that ever works."

Up ahead, a street vendor, apparently left with some turned melons at day's end, was throwing them into the middle of the road for cars to run over. By the time Holland pointed and George looked, it was too late to slow.

The great Bavarian went skating through the melons with the brakes on full and the wheels cranked on a trajectory as true as a crazed missile, headed straight for the line of parked cars. Only a few feet from disaster, the tires shed the last of the melon meat and caught the pavement, jerking the BMW back on track.

George swallowed, his pace slowed considerably, and looked over at his passenger.

Holland remained with an arm extended to the dash and his other hand gripping the armrest. The knuckles were white.

"Sorry," George apologized. "I'll go slower."

"Do that," Holland agreed, looking for his pipe on the floor.

They continued in silence for a while, leaving the central area and going north on the Periferico expressway, past the race track and the El Toreo bullring.

As they approached the immense slab monuments marking the southern limits of suburban Satellite City, Holland turned to George. "In your material on Moloch, do you have any documented accounts of what he's done and who he's done it for?"

"Yes," George said emphatically. "Quite a lot. All of it true and authenticated beyond question. Why do you ask?"

Holland pondered it a moment, his expression holding the first promise to be evident to George. "I'd like to see them. As I recall, you said the press doesn't show much interest in stories like that."

"Right. The public doesn't want to read about it unless the victim is 'news,' or there's a focus or a twist to catch their imaginations. Every act of torture is ultimately an understatement of the next or the last, we know that, but there are still things done there that cannot be known here. People simply don't want to know, or they refuse to believe they happen. It's grotesque, but today even the news has to be entertaining, and the editors know it. Besides which, it's damned hard to sustain indignation when everyone knows nothing is done to stop it."

"Interesting," said Holland. "I was thinking about contingencies, and that might prove useful. We'll see."

George nodded without speaking, wondering what he meant.

Holland said no more. He was looking at the monuments jutting into the early evening haze, and thinking now about what he knew of Guatemala.

He knew the country had a legacy of violence unrivaled in the western hemisphere, its people steeped in bloody conflicts between tyrannical regimes and bands of revolutionaries in the wild hills and steaming jungles, either side being little better than rank predators preying on the same countrymen. Laws were not of the land, but of convenience, and guns and razor-edged machetes were as abundant as teeth. Lives were spent cheaply. The parting of a throat was as orthodox a conclusion to political discussion as it was in a sporting argument over a whore.

Six million people were clustered in a country the size of the state of Tennessee, half of them pure-blooded descendants of Maya Indians, the other half a volatile extrusion of Spanish and Indian called *ladinos*. Each hated the other as a rite, and practiced hostilities at every opportunity. The *ladinos* said the Indians were Christians in the churches and pagans in the fields. The *blasfemias* the Indians reserved for the *ladinos* were uttered in eighteen local dialects in addition to Spanish. Even the ground beneath was riotous, frequently disposed to horrendous earthquakes, fuming volcanos, and torrential floods.

Transcending all of this was one of the bitterest of ironies, that to be found in the knowledge that the country was once the fountainhead of perhaps the most glorious of cultures—the great Mayan civilization. Grand Maya ruins of pyramids and temples and palaces and courtyards stood shoulder to shoulder with magnificent Spanish colonial architecture, and irony was compounded even in the steady plundering of tombs and sculptures by looters who sold the past in New York and London and Paris.

Everyone and everything provided inspiration for suspicion in Guatemala, and justly so. That very ambience was quite possibly the compelling reason for The Doctor's residence there, providing a natural screen for all who would threaten. The contemplation was a good deal less than welcome to Holland.

By the time the monuments were lost from sight, Holland had settled on an initial course of action. That it involved a measure he had never before implemented did not unduly disturb him. His was a free-form pursuit with few conventions, and Moloch represented the doctorate of assassinations. He was beginning to warm to the task.

• 6 •

The clinic was cloistered deep within the perimeters of working farmland owned by the Hidalgo family. Bolstered on all sides by fences backing on fences, and by the farmers and families who tilled the land and lived on it. One central gate, manned by two armed attendants, gave access to the vast property. Another guard stood at the entrance to the grounds of the clinic itself.

Each waved the BMW through upon recognizing the familiar face of George Hidalgo.

Holland made note of the security. "What's that in aid of?"

"You've heard of DINA?" George returned.

"The Chilean secret police. They'd bother you here?"

"Not so far, or at least not that we've been aware of. However, Pinochet and the Generals don't hesitate to send DINA agents after those who displease them, anywhere. DINA were the ones who killed Letelier in Washington."

Holland knew that Orlando Letelier had been a former Foreign Minister and ambassador in the Allende government who found freedom after the coup and dedicated himself to vigorously opposing the junta. Ultimately the junta grew weary of him. His moving automobile was blown apart by an electronically-triggered bomb within sight of the Chilean Embassy in midtown Washington, D.C., in September of 1976.

"They may have had a hand in," Holland clarified, "but the job was pieced off to Cuban exiles from Miami."

George looked across at Holland as he brought the car to a halt in the parking lot. "That has been the rumor. Are you sure?"

"Uh-huh."

"And the CIA?"

"Does a bear go in the woods?" Holland said. "A former government minister is shredded on Embassy Row in the capital of the Free World and the combined security forces of America can't even find a few Cuban dumpers? A few Cuban dumpers who couldn't get to page one with remotely-detonated explosives? Shit."

His tone was not precisely one of irritation, but of shop talk made prosaic by a clarity of origin that was brutal. Questions undeserving to be. To George it was as natural that Holland know the tidings of his trade as it was for himself to know the recent nominees for Pulitzer Prizes in International Journalism. It came with the territory, and was not for him to question.

"Pinochet recently announced the disbanding of

DINA," George advised, "although in reality he simply changed the name. Window dressing to appease the critics."

Holland removed his baseball jacket before getting from the car.

"Whatever name they're using, I doubt you and the Lomolins are in their good books," Holland reasoned. "You ever suspect they were watching you?"

George shook his head, though not as surely as Holland would have liked. "I've wondered, I admit that," George said. "But, no, I've never actually caught anyone observing me. Of course, I'm not very adept at that sort of thing. We've taken precautions from the outset though, such as having the clinic and our homes swept for listening devices every few weeks. I assure you I've been extremely careful since we decided to contact you."

"Alright," Holland said across the roof of the car. "But, look, George, remember that outfits like DINA and the CIA have paranoia that you could never get, motives that have no relation to reason, and they have none of the restrictions you do. If you keep that in mind from here on in, you won't go too far wrong. Neither will the Lomolins. If you think it's necessary to point that out to them, do it."

"As a matter of fact, I didn't feel it was necessary," George replied. "But we talked about it anyway. They understand. And I should tell you that Moloch won't hesitate to call in the DINA if he thinks he needs them, or any of a dozen like them that he can call on."

This failed to elicit a reaction. They started for the austere single-story building.

A hospital quiet was appropriate to the place. Grass and trees, shrubs and flowers were abundant and lush, being cared for even now by men and women who were obvious patients from their dress. Others sat about the lawn in small groups, talking quietly, reminiscent of the chains of war. Some waved across at George. There were a good number of children too, some very young.

"I didn't expect to see children," Holland said. "Not so many. Are they here because their parents are?"

"I wish they were," George said, watching Holland closely. He knew he was fond of children. "But we don't have enough room for that. They're here as patients."

Holland continued to look at the children and kept walking.

"Children aren't exempt, you see," George elaborated. "On the contrary, they're often tormented in front of their parents, other members of the family. The interrogators will molest children as young as eighteen months. Sometimes they'll give them to the soldiers for sport."

Holland waited until they reached the building, and said, "Ain't life grand?"

George thought it fitting.

Unlike most infirmaries, the Lomolins' clinic had walls stamped in bright bolts of color instead of the customary creams and whites of antiseptic sobriety. One whole wall of the central corridor had been reserved for the creations of the youngest patients. On it were sprawling suns of orange, pointed houses with grass and trees and smoking chimneys, dogs and cats and stick figures. George explained that these last often represented the child's family. Isabelle had once told him the children would ask her if they should depict members who had died. She encouraged them and had them sign their work.

A section nurse looked up from her post and smiled at George as they went by.

Upon turning a corner they saw Hector and Isabelle Lomolin waiting at the end of the corridor. They came forward. Introductions were made and a few words exchanged.

Hector was so frail as to appear infirmed himself, while Isabelle had a face of striking character much like her husband's, but fuller, rounder, more assertive, and less searching. Her stern shoes rang of efficiency; his shuffled with crisis. Her voice made pronouncements crisply; his questioned tentatively. Still, as George had said, each complemented the other perfectly.

George was relieved when Holland's initial remarks were civil and reasoned. He knew only too well that Holland at times opened with comments sufficiently extraneous or provocative to disconcert whomever he was speaking to, thereby facilitating spontaneous insights—and establishing a lingering unease to all that followed. It was a ploy of verbal manipulation he employed judiciously, never when respect was a foregone conclusion and seldom when the recipient was deemed likely to see what he was about too readily. George speculated on which applied this time, concluding that perhaps both did.

Hector ushered them into his office. What furnishings there were cast the impression of being hastily assembled and decidedly impermanent. The only warmth came from the Lomolins. Holland found it odd. And said no to refreshment when asked.

He did the same when a chair was offered, saying, "I'd prefer we talk outside, if no one objects."

Uncertain glances were exchanged.

"You needn't worry . . ." Hector started to say before George raised a cautioning hand, Holland's stipulation fresh in mind.

"I'm sure," Holland said pleasantly to Hector. "But, the grounds are lovely and it is a nice evening."

"Very well," Hector said, a bit perplexed as he rose from the chair he had just settled in. His misgivings at meeting with a man like Holland were apparent. At sixty-three, his life's work was diametrically opposed to what Holland's was at half the age; a distortion he was incapable of concealing.

A cursory appraisal of Isabelle Lomolin betrayed none of the same to Holland. He smiled to himself, satisfied that his first impression of her was holding. He liked the woman.

"We have a garden right here that is suitably private," she proposed. She opened glass doors and led the way without waiting for consent.

The rock garden was framed by a shooting cedar hedge and wisteria vines that did indeed lend privacy. Because the garden was on the west side, late sunlight was slanting in, catching the small central reflecting pool banked with fragrant portulacas.

They took seats at the table where Hector and Isabelle had their lunch each day, a setting that was almost certainly sabbatical at those times.

"Our hospital is not very imposing," Hector said, "but it is safe."

"You're probably right, Mr. Lomolin," Holland said. "On the other hand, there are many ways to listen. When we arrived you told your wife I didn't look at all like a killer."

Hector was startled. It was true he had said that, but

Holland had been at least five meters away and couldn't possibly have heard.

Isabelle smiled at Holland. "You read lips," she said.

"On occasion," he admitted. "I took the comment as a compliment."

Hector seemed even more muddled. "Lord knows what I was expecting," he said. "I confess I still have many reservations, not the least of which is our meeting this way."

This last was directed at his wife, though not unkindly.

"We are effecting the death of someone, and that in itself is a terrible contradiction for us," she said to him, but by way of explanation to George and Holland as well. "If we are not sealing the fate of The Doctor, then possibly of yourself, Mr. Holland. For that reason I thought it necessary that we explain why it is we have finally chosen this course."

"I understand," Holland said.

There followed a short silence. Holland took the opportunity to dip his pipe in his tobacco pouch. Isabelle waited on Hector. He cleared his throat.

"Myself, I am not sure how well I can explain," Hector began. "There are so many reasons. I said that our hospital was a modest one, Mr. Holland. It is more correct to say that is how it began, because it is no longer so. More than seven thousand have been patients in the precious time we have been here. Eighty-three were mutilated to such a degree that they died here. A further twenty-seven were so tormented by the contagion of memory that they took their lives after leaving. Two years ago they began arriving from Indonesia and the Philippines; last year from Haiti and Uganda and South Africa. Now, well, you can name it.

"At first we thought of our work as a temporary measure that would not be necessary once sanity returned and these people were brought to justice. But, nothing is done to stop them. None of them are made to account for their wretched atrocities."

He leaned forward and put his hand on George's arm.

"George has been a wonderful ally; more than we deserve. We have spent five years scurrying from country to country, from council to commission to committee, from senates to tribunals to chambers to churches. The dais swim in my head. The ranks of so-called human rights organizations is a catacomb without end, believe me. There are so many! Isabelle calls it The Industry of Fraternal Pathos. There have been times when I was convinced the labyrinth had been assembled by some crazed Caligula for the single purpose of wearing away so much as the notion of retribution. The Doctor himself could not have been more enterprising.

"They welcome us to smother in their cloaks of humanity, bending intensely to listen and commiserate, using a sanitized vocabulary where systematic political torture becomes 'unpalatable excesses.' The body of a nineteen-year-old Kurdish student in Iraq is returned to his family with nine nails driven into his body, an eye gouged out, and his penis severed. To them this is an 'unpalatable excess.' One can't help wondering what it takes to make them choke. To make them stop it."

His voice trailed at the end until it was barely more than a plea. Then his anger rose crimson under his skin again. He clenched his fists. His arms trembled.

Isabelle turned her attention to Hector, worried for his heart. He settled noticeably when her hand covered his.

After an interval, he went on.

"The panacea is always the same. More inquiries, more delegations, more conferences, another Commission or Special Committee to compile reports and table resolutions and shuffle the papers. For us, there is no illusion to it anymore. And no hope. We have run every course of reason, sought every established procedure for judgment, pleaded like beggars for so much as a gesture of penalizing the butchers. We have exhausted them and they have exhausted us. The Doctor's science spreads like plague with every minute the moralists debate in their comfortable committees."

"Please understand, we are not vengeful people," Isabelle said quietly to Holland. "We wanted so much to believe something would be done. At this time our society is better able to administer justice than it has ever been, yet we administer less with each passing hour. The Fraternity, as I call it, whines about the black abyss we are descending into but is satisfied with rhetoric and debate and hushed censure while the heads roll and the blood runs."

Holland saw that George was increasingly disturbed by what was being said and by the anguish exhibited in his godparents, until finally he got up and began pacing. Holland found the discourse interesting for its eloquence but predictable for its content. About what he had expected.

Hector sighed heavily. "The sum of our collaboration has been complicity. We are shamed that the price of our naivete has been so heinous. If we can still The Doctor's hand, that will be enough."

"Giving the devil his due will always jostle the angels," Isabelle whispered.

"Besides The Doctor," Holland said, tamping his pipe, "have there not been any reprisals against the people engaged in this sort of thing?"

Hector's gesture was futility itself. "Not to speak of. Oh, once in a while a father or some relative will try taking things in their own hands, but they are virtually helpless and are quickly dispensed with. There was a case in Uruguay a few years ago. A man named Mariani was an official of the U.S. Agency for International Development, stationed in Montevideo. He was shot shortly after a police official implicated him in a newspaper interview as a specialist in torture training. The conjecture is that he was murdered by American agents because he was enjoying his publicity too much and they began to view him as a liability. There is an inflatable device used to increase pressure on the chest during interrogations, eventually crushing the rib cage. It is known as the 'Mariani Vest.' He is credited with its design."

A squadron of pigeons fluttered noisily into the garden to alight on the gravel pathway. Holland could hear a tractor a distance away, probably in the fields, and could make out the sounds of children playing on the lawn.

"What about the trials in Greece?" he asked. "I remember reading about them."

"You may have even been reading my articles," George speculated, resuming his pacing. "I was there, so I'll tell you what a vulgar mockery that was. Every trial without exception resulted from private lawsuits brought by the torture victims themselves, not a single one brought by the state. Of the 150 officers and security police implicated, only 28 were recommended for trial. The Court of

Appeals searched its soul to the extent that 16 of those had their charges reduced from felonies to misdemeanors. Three security police were released by the court before their trials could begin. The Chief of the Athens Security Police was named as a torturer by Amnesty International and the Council of Europe and a dozen victims. He was released with a fine that was less than for a traffic offense."

Holland smiled knowingly. "I don't remember reading that. Why'd they bother?"

"You didn't read it because it wasn't considered news," George stated flatly. "And they did it because the Americans told them to. Everyone knew the U.S. had been behind the military takeover and had pulled the Generals' strings from the beginning. So when the torture stories couldn't be suppressed any longer, they decided the Greeks should hold a trial as a public relations gesture. I'll tell you something else. At the trials the victims testified how they were taunted while being tortured, the soldiers saying, 'The Red Cross can't help you now . . . The Human Rights Commission can do nothing for you . . . Tell them all, it will do no good, they can do nothing . . . The United States supports us and that is all that counts here.' That's all part of The Doctor's repertoire. He taught them how to integrate the impotence of the human rights industry into the torture process, mocking them, just as he's done elsewhere."

A bag of grain rested near the office doors. Holland got up and brought it to the table. Isabelle nodded and he began tossing it to the birds.

"You're American, Mr. Holland?" Isabelle asked him.

"Yes."

"It has been necessary to mention the involvement of your country in these instances," she explained, without the slightest rancor. "Unfortunately, that is unavoidable. You may know that the United States has been the foremost exporter of this misery. We wish it were otherwise. I hope you understand."

Holland did not look up from feeding the pigeons. He was dropping the seeds and broken corn near his open sandals, making the feeders come close. Sometimes they pecked at his toes instead.

Isabelle could see from where she sat, expecting he

should flinch. The demeanor projected was uniformly serene and belied any of what she knew he must be capable of. If there was murder in his heart, it was of a kind she had never seen.

"The fish may stink from the head, Mrs. Lomolin," he said eventually, his voice giving up nothing, "but that is its nature. They all stink. The larger ones just stink worse. It really doesn't matter."

The garden was quiet for a few moments longer. They expected he might say more. He did not.

As always, one or two pigeons were more aggressive than the rest. Plenty of food was about, but they left it to encroach on others. Holland patiently bounced single kernels from their wide backs until they got the idea. They tilted their heads and blinked at him warily, then ate where they stood.

"I think your reasoning is clear," Holland said, taking his attention from the birds. "I'm willing to proceed if you are. I'd like to get on with it."

Hector and Isabelle looked for resistance in each other, and saw none. George returned to his chair.

"George has declined to tell us what your fee is," said Hector. "Should we assume you'll want half now and half when you are finished?"

"I'll discuss the fee with George when I'm through and if I'm successful. Until then I need expenses only. George can provide that."

"The risk is enormous," Isabelle said. "Surely there has to be some payment even if you find you cannot do it."

This time there was a reaction. Scant, and gone at once, but a reaction.

"There'll be a way," Holland said. He rubbed his left arm.

She could not mistake his meaning. She said, "Yes."

"You'll have to remain absolutely silent," Holland directed. "Don't even discuss it between yourselves. If something unusual happens, tell George at once. I'll do what I have to do through him. The less you know, the better for all concerned. That will include George as much as possible. Agreed?"

"Yes," Hector said.

Holland swept a deliberate look past George and said to the Lomolins: "Can I trust Mr. Ortiz if it's necessary?"

"Certainly," Isabelle answered readily. "Do you want us to speak to him?"

"Would that be necessary?"

"Not at all," she said. "George needs only to tell Max of our involvement. He has every confidence in George that we do. We have talked of The Doctor many times and Max will not wonder about it once he's told. How soon will you go there?"

"It's important to move as quickly as possible." He scrutinized each of them. "I have one request. Something that may be difficult on short notice."

"What is that?" asked Hector.

"A woman, preferably with young children, who can act as a wife while I'm watching Moloch and seeing what can be done."

The effect was predictable. Hector and Isabelle appeared stunned by the proposition. Even George was caught unawares.

"My word," Hector murmured.

"Something like that never occurred to me," George said.

Holland went purposely on. "She'd be needed for a few days only, maybe a week at the outside, and I'd put her on a plane before I went ahead. She'd have to know I'm there to observe someone, of course, meaning you'd have to know her well and have complete faith in her."

"Forgive us, but we were unprepared for this," Isabelle said. "Are you sure this is necessary?"

"If we were talking another place, probably not," Holland said. "I'd much prefer to work alone, I think you can appreciate that, but as soon as George told me Guatemala I knew what to expect. The whole country's his personal preserve and anyone who looks out of place is immediately suspect for any number of reasons. Guatemala isn't exactly a tourist trap, ruins or no ruins, and it's even less so since the earthquake and the hassle over Belize. I'm Anglo, no mistaking that, and if I go in there alone and get somebody's interest up they'll be watching me closer than I can watch Moloch. There are things I have to know firsthand, otherwise I might just as well stand in the street and throw rocks at him."

"Then you want the woman as a foil while you're getting your bearings?" George asked. "Nothing more?"

"Uh-huh. Your own reactions tell you why. Not even someone on watch takes much notice of a man travelling with his family, and for certain they don't see him as a threat. The Russians and Palestinians have been doing it for a while, although not many know about it yet."

"Nevertheless, you are asking us to put a woman—and maybe her children—in jeopardy," Hector protested.

"If that were the case, I wouldn't consider it," Holland said. "I'll be frank with you: At this point I have no idea how I'm going to get close enough, but if I didn't think I could find a way to get to him in his own backyard I wouldn't have come. Make no mistake, for Moloch to be alive at his age and with his history means he didn't come down with yesterday's rain. It also indicates he knows more about my business than I know about his. The thought doesn't particularly appeal to me, but I'm not about to ignore it either. Until I see what's open to me I have to play it the way I see fit. This is it."

The reasoning seemed to assure Hector somewhat. He spread his hands on the table before him. "Your credentials are not in question," he said. "I'm satisfied that George's confidence is well-placed. You have mine as well. We will do everything we can."

"And you have my word the woman will be perfectly safe," Holland responded.

"I know she will," George said. "What about Mariana? I could ask her, and I think she'd be willing."

"No," Holland said without hesitation. "Not Mariana."

George chose not to press it. The complications were known only too well to each of them. Mariana was, at the same time, too close and too far removed.

"You must tell us what you require," Isabelle said.

"Ideally, a woman who speaks English and Spanish, who has a child less than ten years of age, and who wouldn't be out of place in expensive surroundings." To the Lomolins he said directly: "A woman from your country would probably be most suitable. If she could recognize Moloch, that would be a bonus."

"I see," said Isabelle thoughtfully. "There are many widows from our country living here now. They would not hesitate to help us, I'm certain of that."

Holland went back to feeding the pigeons while they gave it their consideration. The sun was gone now and the garden was cooling in shadows. Isabelle draped a sweater over her shoulders.

"There is Helené Alarcón," she said. "She has three children, but she could take the youngest boy and leave the others with us."

Hector shook his head. "That would not be wise. Helené is still in the care of Doctor Berman." He turned to Holland. "Doctor Berman is a staff psychologist with the National Medical Center who donates his services to us. The problem with this woman is that she saw too much of Clement Moloch."

Holland nodded.

George mentioned another name. This time it was Isabelle who rejected it, saying the woman's husband had been a prominent member of Allende's government and that made her unsuitable. Holland felt better for the perception of her logic.

"We could go through our files tonight," Hector suggested. "If we had some to consider by morning?"

"Wait," George said, his face flush with promise. "I have the one. She's perfect. Rhiana Rhead."

A cautious optimism registered on Isabelle and Hector.

"Perhaps," Isabelle said.

George used his fingers to emphasize the woman's qualifications. "Rhiana has everything Holland specified and more. Her daughter is five. She knows The Doctor on sight, and would certainly do anything to help stop him. She even knows Max, who adores her. And if I'm not mistaken, she's in the city at the present time."

"Rhiana was here today, as a matter of fact," Isabelle confirmed. "She left at four o'clock to take Sarah to her violin lesson. You may well be right, George, the more I think of it."

"You're forgetting that Rhiana is a very astute woman," Hector said, retreating to his familiar pessimism. "She would know what we are about the minute we said what it was we wanted of her."

"Well then, if we came right out and told her," George said, presenting it as a question to Holland. "Has that been ruled out?"

"Again, that depends on what you know about her and what the collective judgment is," Holland said to them. "You tell me."

"Obviously it is not a simple task to assume the role of wife to a perfect stranger, and to somehow have her daughter play the game too," Isabelle reasoned. "Even if it is just in public and just for a few days. The only way is to tell Rhiana what our intentions are immediately. I know she will do it. We could not do better for you, Mr. Holland."

Holland isolated his attention on Hector. "How is it you know this woman?"

"Her family was originally from the north," Hector explained. "They came to live near us when she was very young and we became close friends with her father and mother. Rhiana was the only child. She practically grew up in our home. Her mother died when Rhiana was about twelve or thirteen and she spent more time with us after that. And, as Isabelle said, she does volunteer work for us here four days a week. We often have dinner together. We are all family here, you understand."

Now Holland directed his question to Isabelle. "Why does she feel as you do about The Doctor?"

"On the day the military took over there were mass arrests—tens of hundreds," she said. "Rhiana was arrested with her father and her husband and taken to the Chile Stadium in Santiago. She was five months pregnant with Sarah, after having had great difficulty in conceiving. Her father and husband were taken away to another part of the stadium, leaving Rhiana alone, but there were some friends there and they looked out for her and kept her hidden away as much as they could. After three or four days she was released and was smart enough to go directly to the Swedish Embassy, which provided her asylum. We then arranged to have her come here, and did not tell her about her father and husband until after the baby was born. They had been tortured to death by The Doctor on the same day Rhiana was let go."

"She can identify Moloch?" Holland asked.

"She saw him each day in the Stadium," Hector confirmed. "The prisoners were crammed like fish in a net and he would take strolls as a respite from his labors. Some of the prisoners knew what he was right away. Some never knew."

"How long have you known her?" Holland asked of George.

"From my first visit to Santiago." He smiled. "Patrick and I were enamored with her for as long as I can remember and used to fight over who she would marry. Unfortunately, the boy she eventually did marry lived there and could spend the whole year courting her, we only had the summers. Rhiana has had a tragic time of it, but she's resilient and determined and completely devoted to Sarah. If it were me, I wouldn't hesitate to take her with me."

"I gather she's attractive," Holland concluded, though not with optimism.

"Very much so," Isabelle said.

"That isn't good," Holland said. "A woman who attracts attention to herself might be worse than none at all. I should have mentioned that."

"I see what you mean," Isabelle said. "Rhiana is a striking woman, true, but it comes from the grace of breeding, not from any artificial means. Her mother was Swiss, you see, a beautiful, elegant European lady, and her father was a native Chilean with the traditional strong will and latin temperament of our people. Rhiana enhanced those qualities by finishing her schooling in Switzerland and America, and you would find her to be exceptionally capable, I'm sure. Her bearing brings admiration, Mr. Holland, not whistles."

George nodded his agreement. "Isabelle's right, Rhiana won't draw the attention you're talking about. She's also four years your senior, but looks considerably younger."

"You said something about expensive surroundings," Hector said to Holland.

"We'll stay in the best hotels and spend like the carriage trade," Holland replied. "It's just another way to alleviate suspicion. Does that raise any problems?"

"No," Hector said. "Rhiana's family had wealth, although it was earned by her father while she was still of an age to keep her values. You would have no worries on that account."

"Can you speak to her tonight? In person?" Holland asked.

"Yes," Isabelle answered.

"Don't tell her any more than you have to, and try to get her answer right away. I won't want her to see me or know of me if she's not sure, or if there's any chance she'll change her mind."

"Of course," Isabelle said. "And if she agrees; what then?"

"I'll meet her tomorrow with George. Tell her she'll have to be ready to leave with her daughter anytime within the next forty-eight hours. George will call later to see where we stand. There won't be any more contact between us once I leave here tonight, so I have one final question."

"Yes?" Hector asked.

Holland took deliberate stock. "You're certain you want this done?"

"If it means we must go to hell for what we do," Isabelle said quietly, "it will be a better hell than to do nothing. Yes."

They got up from the table. Holland looked around without specific cause. It was now dark enough to have tripped the light-sensitive switches on the floodlights at either end of the grounds. Swallows swept the dusk for flies. The lights of the city were showing from the south.

"You have some pain, Mr. Holland," Hector observed. "Can I offer assistance?"

Now it was Holland's turn for surprise. George and Isabelle had missed what Hector's practiced eye was able to detect during the talk. They looked at Holland expectantly.

"Thank you, no," he said. "It's nothing more than an ache that comes and goes."

Hector complied with a yielding gesture.

Instead of returning via the hospital itself they went through a parting in the hedge toward the parking lot on the far side of the building. George went ahead with Hector.

Isabelle knew acute defeat, for she took a deep-rooted pride in her ability to read personas, to decipher reflections and riddle defenses. And yet Holland was slipping away untouched, like a photograph that faded, taking with it tracings never defined; a crisis of illusion.

Never before had she been so thoroughly frightened and made utterly secure at the same time. She prayed that The Doctor was finally matched.

"It is redundant, I know," she said, "but you do know what will happen if he catches you."

Holland nodded.

"Don't let him. Rhiana will go with you, Mr. Holland. Be careful with her and with Sarah, please."

"They'll be fine," Holland said to her.

Isabelle wondered from where his intelligence sprang and what it was that sustained it. Where had he been? What had he seen? What had he done?

"I would be grateful if we could talk once this is over," she said. "But I imagine you do not do that."

"No, I don't do that," Holland said.

He was, Isabelle realized, outside looking in. But how did he get there?

"Then I hope you will change your mind at some time. And I wish you good fortune because I want you to have it."

Holland thanked her.

The Lomolins stayed at the corner of the building while Holland and George continued to the car.

Hector straightened his arms, rocked back on his heels and looked up into the darkness.

The swallows left trails like blots of ink.

"Bats," he said.

"Does he still not impress you as capable of killing?" Isabelle asked him.

Hector checked that Holland's back was to them. "Who in the world knows what to expect? We are so out of our element in this dirty business. Thank God. I expected him to stink of death, but he does not. And it is refreshing that he does not appear to take himself as seriously as he might. Perhaps if he did I could be more confident. So, yes, to me he does not seem any more a killer than does George."

"Then I think you are quite wrong, my husband. *Sui generis,*" she said, her closing valuation.

The car drove from sight, quiet except for the squibbing of tires on gravel.

Holland had not gotten into the car until George started the engine. No one noticed.

• 7 •

They returned directly to the city, where Holland took a room at the Casa Blanca while George went on to his villa to retrieve the material on The Doctor.

The hotel afforded a secure site for the intense learning exercise Holland would assume in the next few hours and he did not want to chance a location that could possibly be under surveillance. For the same reasons his activities in Mexico City were to be limited to as brief a span as the essentials allowed. The premise was simply that the less he was seen in the company of George or the Lomolins, or even the Rhead woman, the better. They were known here, each to a varying degree, and the raising of even a spontaneous curiosity was to be avoided. Get In and Get Done and Get Out was a commonly held tenet in the murky trenches of unsung battlegrounds.

George was ravenous and had a meal sent up to the room. Holland limited himself to some fresh fruit washed again in the sink, knowing his digestion was slowed by the altitude and that unfamiliar foods at unfamiliar times were not prudent until he became acclimatized to the new bacteria. He was nothing if not thorough in such ancillary precautions, but despite the potential for hilarity, even an indiscretion as eternal as diarrhea could get a person killed.

When George finished his meal he began relating everything he knew about Clement Moloch. The extent of his knowledge was considerable, as Holland suspected it would be. The man was a journalist, and information was his forte. He took pains to specify all that was unsubstantiated or merely speculative, and even then there was much that was not central to Holland's requirements. Holland listened with rapt attention, head bowed and arms crossed. The gnawing in his arm and shoulder had dissipated.

At midnight they ordered coffee. George placed the call to Hector and Isabelle. He spoke briefly, staying clear of names or places.

Rhiana Rhead had consented after some discussion, having the anticipated fears and reservations—principally in respect to her daughter. At first she had proposed she go without the girl, but then agreed to taking her once she had received convincing assurances from the Lomolins. George displayed relief at the news.

When he hung up he said that Hector wanted Holland to understand that Rhiana wasn't . . . well, the way Hector had put it was that she was not a Shakespeare widow.

Holland responded by saying it didn't matter if she was, his interest was in Moloch. He added that, while Hector's chivalrous instincts were laudable, they were hardly applicable under the circumstances.

George assured him that he had told Hector the same.

They went on with the dissemination of knowledge, Holland injecting questions at a Socratic pace. By three George was too tired to continue. He fell asleep on one of the beds while Holland dozed for a while in the chair and then left the room to stroll The Reforma, Mexico's most handsome street, lined with wide sidewalks covered in greenery and studded by memorials to everything from Aztec emperors to the huntress Diana.

He walked as far as the Independence monument, mulling over what had been learned from George. There he sat next to the *glorietas* and watched the sun come up. It was a propitious time for decisions. The ones he arrived at came easily.

George was shaving when he got back to the room. He showered while George phoned for breakfast and listened to a news broadcast. The news was the same as yesterday's and tomorrow's George quipped as they sat down to eat. Except that the Yankees had lost to an expansion club the night before. Holland grimaced and reminded him of the fate of messengers bringing ill tidings. They laughed.

Again Holland ate sparingly, moving George to wonder aloud how he sustained himself on so little sleep and nourishment. Holland peeled three oranges and one hard-boiled egg and related the latest entries in the agenda to assassinate. George listened intently.

He needed some papers for himself, Holland said, more a formality than a necessity, but just in case. A Mexican driver's license and a Guatemala tourist card would suffice. They would use the name Tyler and their guise would be as newlyweds, Sarah being the child of Mrs. Rhead's previous marriage. This would account for the name Rhead. In all likelihood she would have a Mexican passport, but he wanted George to confirm it. Only Panama and Nicaragua required one, anyway.

As it happened, George had anticipated him. There was a printer who had filled the needs of the various Hidalgo interests for twenty years. As a rule the man declined to do illegal work, not like many in his field, but he never hesitated to accommodate George when asked. As a journalist there were certain investigative assignments where a false I.D. was useful, and the printer, knowing George's profession and admiring the family, did not question the need or mention it after. George even had a blank Mexican passport, for which he could take and develop Holland's photograph himself, therefore negating the necessity of contact between Holland and the printer. As for a marriage certificate, that was child's play. The entire process would take only an hour or two. Holland was pleasantly surprised by the initiative.

He also wanted George to lease a helicopter immediately, one large enough and fast enough for the quick foray into Guatemala, and thereafter to be kept on standby until Holland told him it was no longer needed. George protested that he already had such a craft in his ownership, but Holland was adamant. The helicopter should be leased in such a way that it could not be readily traced to George. It took but a moment for George to grasp the intent. Every Mexican businessman had a variety of shell corporations that were intentionally impractical to decipher, to this end his father had a wide choice of entities the helicopter could be rented under.

Next, they discussed locations in Guatemala; one for going in and another for coming out. The first had to be in reasonable proximity to Guatemala City, away from prying eyes, and practical for Maximiliano Ortiz to meet them with a car. George knew the place at once. Max had a weekend retreat on the shores of Lake Amititlan, only seventeen miles from the capital. The second location was not so easily selected because of the more exacting standards imposed by Holland, demanding that it be remote and absolutely private . . . preferably where no one, not even Indians, would go for months or even years on end . . . and yet not too far removed from a road of some description . . . and a place that George could spot from the air.

Once again George was able to contribute his analytic approach, having brought with him some highly detailed topography maps. They studied the grids and traded assessments for more than an hour before settling on a place that would do. George had been there before, though a long time ago, and was confident he could find it again. Holland determined that they should make a dry run over it anyway, on the way into Lake Amititlan, thereby leaving nothing to chance. George agreed, confident in the concise simplicity of all that Holland said. In the act of beginning, Holland began to close.

Distances and speeds and times were all calculated in their heads, not once resorting to pen and paper. An itinerary for the following thirty-six hours was chosen.

George placed a call to Guatemala City and found Max Ortiz at his office. The older man declined to question what must surely have sounded a quirky rendezvous proposal. Holland could detect the man's delight upon learning George was coming the following day with Rhiana Rhead and her daughter. The entire exchange was completed in a minute, much to Holland's satisfaction.

It was then that Holland outlined the conditional device he had formulated in his own mind, a scheme that could be put into play by George from his end with only a predetermined sign from Holland. The ramifications were evident, the scope devastating but wildly enticing too, especially to someone like George.

Another hour was taken up with the briefing on Rhiana Rhead and her daughter, so Holland could predispose himself to the temporary union. Mrs. Rhead was to be granted no such luxury, George receiving instruction to disclose only what was imperative and at the same time expedient.

George enjoyed talking about the woman, Holland noted.

When George finished he phoned Rhiana and asked if he could take her and Sarah to meet someone in the afternoon. She knew, and complied.

A specimen signature of Holland's new surname was put on a blank file card that George took with him when he left, as well as removing everything he had brought with him except for the maps. Those, Holland pored over for the balance of the morning.

At two o'clock he went out into the bustling streets and scouted the markets until he found one that sold kohlrabi, buying a couple of choice small ones. In another shop he purchased a penknife for 30 pesos and peeled the green-skinned cabbages into a refuse container, discarding the knife after. He ate the kohlrabi as he walked the two miles of The Reforma toward Chapultepec Park. On the way there was a bar open to the street and he ordered a beer.

When he came out there was a boy and a girl sitting at the curb smoking grass, knapsacks beside them. They looked to be late teens or early twenties, American, wearing cut-offs that were bleached and frayed, their feet bare. They spotted him and came over before he could get away, smiling as though they had seen a friend from home. Holland did not know them.

"Oooh, hey! Yankees!" the girl said, pointing at Holland's jacket and doing a cheerleader bounce on the sidewalk.

It was true, she reminded Holland of a cheerleader, circa 1950's, spinning and cartwheeling on the football turf of New England autumns. And of powder-blue sweaters over black chino slacks. And Johnny Stompanato. And James Dean and Donald Turnupseed and Cholame.

"All right!" the boy exclaimed, holding his hand up to slap Holland's.

Holland watched the Harvard Business School ring come down.

"Remember the Alamo," the boy said with the slap of palms.

"You say that too loud or too often, Harvard, and they'll cut you a new asshole," Holland advised him.

"Oh, yeah. That trip," the boy said, glancing around like a thief. "Sorry, folks. Take a joke."

"Hey, ain't this some bitchin' country though," the girl said.

"Qué?" Holland said.

"Cheap seats . . . Hot food . . . Don't have to do a wall-search every day cause it's always warm enough to throw a roll on the ground," she elaborated joyously. "Like that, you know?"

"Yeah, it's magic. Enjoy," Holland said. "I'd rap, but, I gotta walk, you know?"

"Oh, yeah, hey, we're just real ripped to see a civilian," the boy said, noting that Holland was not overly thrilled. "Uh, hey, man, you got any loose change you can spare a fellow gringo? We're tapped, man. Tapped out."

A decade from now the boy would sit in the Indian River Yacht Club and talk securely of first-class minds, and not be any nearer to seeing himself than he was now. The girl would live in a cookie-cutter house in the tracts of suburbia with plastic ducks flying across the kitchen wall and be into missionary sex and natural childbirth and meaningful relationships on tennis courts.

Both with someone else, both clinging to memories of youthful trampings in foreign fields. Their Great Adventure.

Holland gave them ten American dollars.

"Oooh, wow!" the girl said, grabbing his arm and applying her breasts, firm as purple plums. "Down here that'll last a week. Fucking A, man."

"Yeah, thanks, man," the boy said. "Really."

"Compliments of Yankee Industry," Holland said. "Really."

He left them, walking in the direction of the park, his freedom precious and exhilarating, once again clear of fellows who were gamy.

In the bedroom of her villa in the Zona Rosa district, Rhiana Rhead sat at her dressing table and brushed her hair relentlessly, stroking to her shoulders with obsessive motion, having made the perfectly centered part with a comb a full thirty minutes before. Her arms were weary. Still she kept on.

She was not looking in the mirror, but at two framed photographs on the table in front of her. One was of her husband, the other of her mother and father crushed together in ecstatic embrace on the day her father had first discovered his dreamed of copper deposit in the mountains of home.

The photographs, and the watch on her wrist, were all she had been able to take with her when she fled her home with Sarah, and then Chile itself. Thoughts of the three in the pictures were constant, but when she brushed her hair the act became an intimate, erotic, desperately private ritual to share with her husband in her mind's eye. Agustin had worshipped her hair and had never tired of telling her so, teasing her that it was the inspiration for his passion and he would sooner she neglect him than her hair. When they made love he would put her hair in his mouth, moving his hands in it. On the occasions when she had her hair cut he would insist on being present—the jealous guardian—and would arrange his business appointments to allow for the clipping. Their secret.

He was the heart of her and he had been cut out.

Unable to bear looking at the photograph longer, she put the brush down, reluctantly, beaten by being alone.

What would he say if he knew what she was about to do? It was the question she had spent the night with. He would storm at her about the depravity of hands raised in anger and would extol the nobility of the turned cheek, she was certain of that. That was so like him too. But it was theory; a code for Camelot. Today he was dead, butchered without regard or dignity. Now she was left . . . and Clement Moloch was left . . . and they were left with this killer that Isabelle and Hector and George had bought to do what no one else would, or could.

Sarah came into the room, and stood to have the bow on her blouse tied.

While Rhiana was looping the cloth the child said, "You're crying, mummy."

"Just a tiny bit," Rhiana said, smiling for her.

"Are you happy-crying or sad-crying, mummy?" Sarah asked.

She had been taught that crying was a perfectly acceptable emotion to have whenever the need was felt, except in anger, and therefore the child cried somewhat less than other children. She cried at disappointments with herself, or with joy, or when Rhiana did.

"To be happy, my darling," Rhiana said, hugging her briefly. "Did you take Annie next door to Mrs. Fuentes?"

Annie was a stray kitten that had adopted Sarah in the Thieves' Market a few weeks before, now a fixture of the house and virtually inseparable from the child.

"Yes, and I combed her first so she wouldn't fall on Mrs. Fuentes. When will Uncle George come to take us to the park?"

Rhiana looked at the Cartier tank watch, the last birthday gift from Agustin. "In a few minutes, I expect. Uncle George is very prompt. Are you ready?"

The little girl nodded with anticipation. She loved the park. "Should I like our new father . . .", then, annoyed at her mistake, ". . . my new father?"

"You must decide that for yourself, dear," Rhiana said, picking Annie's fur from Sarah's dress. "If you don't like him, I'm afraid you'll have to pretend you do anyway. It's only a game, but it is a very important game that *abuelo* and *abuela* Lomolin have asked us to play. We are the only ones who will know. Uncle George says he is his close friend and a good man, but if he frightens you, I want you to tell me. Will you do that?"

"Yes," she answered obediently, gazing at her father's likeness. "But he won't frighten you, mummy, or Uncle George wll be angry."

Rhiana hesitated, wondering what would prompt her to say that. George Hidalgo had taken her to dinner perhaps six or eight times in the years she had been in Mexico, sometimes with Mariana and Sarah, and there had been a few holidays at the Lomolin home. The relationship was, as all knew, purely one of infrequent evenings spent in the company of friends, late night talks touching on common sorrows, a drink shared, kindred kisses on the cheek as one left for home. Sarah was, by the grace of God, a brilliant child, but had she perceived an affection that Rhiana had not even noticed herself? Or, more probable, was it the fantasy of a child without a father?

"That's true," Rhiana assured her. "Now be a busy lady and gather up the books for the library. Put them in the tote bag and we'll stop on our way home."

Sarah scurried from the room, braids and ribbons flying, leaving Rhiana to question the sanity that compelled her to return books to libraries at a time when her entire existence was converging on a revenge finally realized. Though it did clash of irrationality, the books *would* come due while she was away, and an insurance premium, a dress ordered for Sarah would arrive, and she had promised an outing in the country for some of the children at the clinic. Her phone had been busy this morning. Sarah learned the more lasting values by example, but Rhiana did not delude herself in thinking that was her only motive.

The discipline was needed for herself, for stability, now more than ever.

When the Lomolins left the evening before, the prospect of sleep was out of the question. She had lain beside the sleeping Sarah and been able to think with a clarity that had eluded her since the deaths. By morning she was limp but composed within, and as sure as she could expect to be.

Despite the qualification, it was safe to assume that Sarah would not be frightened, not knowing why she should be, but Rhiana was frightened herself.

She busied herself with articles on the dressing table, putting away the hairbrush and what few cosmetics she used. She kissed the photographs and had to wipe the fresh lipstick away with a tissue. She then put them both in a drawer, facing, the first time she had taken them from sight since she had been in the villa. She crossed herself.

George Hidalgo's knock sounded a moment after and Sarah could be heard running on the carpet. Rhiana got up and smoothed her skirt, and took a deep, sharp breath as she closed the drawer over the photographs.

"Do you speak Swiss?" Holland asked.

Rhiana did not reply for a moment, then said, "How should I address you? George said your name was Holland, but didn't say which it was."

"It's the only one I have. But to answer your question, Holland will do as a first name." He knew George would have already explained the cover of recent marriage, the alias of Tyler, and the business of the papers.

"There isn't a Swiss language as such," she said. "A dialect called *schwyzertütsch* is popular, but I can't speak it in any event."

They were in a small rented rowboat on one of the park's artificial lakes, a suggestion of Holland's that thrilled Sarah and assigned him some initial favor with her. George had left as soon as he brought them together, saying he would return in a couple of hours.

"If you don't mind my asking," he said, "What was your mother's maiden name?"

"Padovani," she said. "My mother was Swiss-Italian, rather than Swiss-German."

"A lovely name. So is yours. I've only heard it once before."

"Thank you," she said. "It was my grandmother's."

"I thought it might be."

"You knew there wasn't a Swiss language," she said stiffly. "Why did you ask?"

"I'm sorry," he apologized.

"Did you learn whatever it was you were after?" she challenged him. "Or should I prepare for more of the same?"

"It won't happen again." His sleight of word had not worked. But then, in its way, it had.

Holland had put the oars up and the boat was drifting. Chapultepec Park could easily rival London's Hyde or New York's Central, and, like those, had a charm of its own, lent in part by the antiquity of sections as much as 700 years old and by the Castle on the high Grasshopper Hill and the picturesque red mill. This afternoon the heavily treed expanses were open and uncrowded, being crossed mainly by children. Sarah sat between her mother and Holland, trailing both hands in the water, and sometimes looking wistfully at the children on the shore.

"You're right," Holland said eventually. "We should be using first names and getting used to the terms of a couple just married."

A rowboat was not the ideal setting for a skirt. But Rhiana sat with her reed slim legs together as one, folded neatly and tucked to the side.

"And what exactly are the terms, Holland," she said, leaving little doubt the name was used as last this time.

One of Sarah's braids dipped into the water and Holland handed Rhiana his handkerchief.

"We'll act as mature people who married, no more and no less, so you'll be relieved to know we won't be pawing at each other and nibbling ears over dinner. We make a family on an excursion to a neighboring country to visit a friend and to look around at the ruins and the architecture and the markets, just as tourists do. In public we'll appear as what we're supposed to be. And in private as much as we can without being foolish."

Only a few feet separated them, yet they might as well have been in different latitudes. Rhiana did not admire what he was. The distance was established and notice given.

"Max Ortiz will expect us to stay in his home," she said purposely. "He'll be offended if we don't. My father knew him for years. They did business together."

Holland was amused. In the Latin culture everyone was related or conducted themselves as though they were. Like the Jews. A trait to admire.

"I know," he said. "George told me. But until I see what the situation is, it's better we decline."

Rhiana at first thought it odd he did not wear any jewelry, not even a watch. Then she remembered the espionage novels she had read, the sneaks inevitably having the labels from their clothing missing.

"Where do you plan on staying, then?" she asked him.

"Let me put your mind at ease, Rhiana," he said, applying her name amicably. "We'll take a double suite in a hotel, but the three of us will sleep in the same room. I'll sleep on the floor. You needn't worry on that account."

She was sure he was stripped of labels.

"I appreciate your sentiments," she said, "but you're not about to put my mind at ease. And I hardly think you need go to the extent of sleeping on the floor. Or do you have some sinister aversion to twin beds?"

He smiled. "Lighten up, Mrs. Rhead. I'd sleep on the floor even if I was alone. I always have. Write it off to an eccentricity if that makes it more acceptable."

Sarah had taken one of the books from the tote-bag and was flipping the pages, mindful of the talk of adults.

"Why do you sleep on the floor?" she asked Holland, unable to still her curiosity.

"For me, it's comfortable, Sarah. If you've always done it you begin to wonder why everyone else sleeps in beds."

"I don't," she said.

The book was too heavy for her and it slid from her hands, striking the water.

Holland swept the book up before it was fully submerged, holding it aloft, dripping. The motion was rapid enough to startle the child and cause her to draw away. Holland steadied her with his other hand.

Rhiana watched, learning.

The author's name was at the top of the book's glossy jacket, as prominent as the title itself. Sarah looked at it, saying plaintively, "Gore—"

"It's alright, dear," Rhiana soothed. "It was an accident."

"No harm done," Holland said, sponging the moisture away with his handkerchief.

"Holland doesn't frighten me, mummy," Sarah said.

Holland and Rhiana exchanged glances.

"I'm sorry, mummy," Sarah said.

"Hush, dear."

"I mean I'm sorry about the book."

"I know."

Holland handed the book back to Sarah.

"My kitten's coming apart," she said, turning in the seat to face him.

He was dismayed by the comment. "Coming apart?"

Rhiana explained that the kitten was molting. They laughed together, Sarah mischievously.

Holland gave his attention to the child after that. Rhiana suspected it was to escape their verbal fencing. That he seemed enchanted with Sarah was not unexpected, most people were quickly caught up in the spell of an exceptional child, others were intimidated and didn't know why. Somehow he knew the secret of speaking to her as an adult, even if it did not always work. When he asked about her violin lessons Rhiana told him they were using the Suzuki method, whereby a child learns to play an instrument at two and by eight is an accomplished musician. Holland professed ignorance of the practice and drew them into a mutual discussion of the details before Rhiana realized how smoothly he had done so.

Later, they slowly made their way toward the polo grounds, stopping at the miniature train so that Sarah could ride. Holland bought her a cluster of balloons but she did not show much interest until he tied them to the collar loop of his jacket and closed the zipper midway to his neck, causing the balloons to float the jacket up in an absurd posture. Sarah laughed and he gave her the balloons and she skipped ahead with them.

As he tied the balloons Rhiana had seen that his jacket did indeed retain a label in back, leading her to temporarily abandon assumptions that were amateur.

She hoped George would appear soon.

At the polo field they sat on a bench and followed some players as they practiced their mounts up and down the grass. Sarah stayed nearby on a raised knoll so she could see to better advantage.

"I'm told you're an excellent horsewoman," Holland said conversationally. "George claims that when you were Sarah's age you could ride a pony bareback on the dead run."

She looked at him, the statement sounding original. "George has a far better memory than I. When I was younger I was . . . a . . . oh, what do you call it . . . ?"

"A tomboy?"

"Yes, a tomboy. Poor papa had fits. I miss the horses, now that you mention it. I've only ridden once or twice since we've been here."

Holland crossed his arms and observed the animals galloping up and back in wind sprints, lathered in the sun. "The Sport of Kings," he mused.

"I used to think so," she said. "Now I know the sport of kings is torture. We learn."

"You think so?"

"Don't you?"

"I meant learning."

"Your professional detachment—if that's what it is—becomes you," she said coldly. "Foolish me to expect it would be anything more than a job to you."

"You want him very badly."

"More than you, and as much as anyone. But don't bother yourself, Mr. Holland, I won't do anything rash. The others have left that to you. So will I."

"Holland," he said.

"Holland," she repeated.

"*Can* you play the part?" he asked, regarding her directly.

"I'll do what's been asked of me, but I won't pretend that what you do is measurably better than what he does. As far as I'm concerned it's a matter of lesser evils."

"Let's not forget expediency."

"Have it your way."

"Get it out of your system before we go, Rhiana," he advised her calmly. "There won't be any time for it once we're there."

"You'll be satisfied," she said. "After that the question is yours. We'll see what you can do."

From the corner of his eye Holland saw the BMW nearing. Sarah ran to meet it, trailing the balloons.

"So far I'm overwhelmed by the confidence everyone has," he said absently, rising with Rhiana to walk to the car.

George got out and took Sarah's hand. He said everything was set. He said he was ready whenever they were.

Rhiana nodded.

Sarah reached to hold Holland's hand, joined then to both men.

Holland declined to share the car with them, excusing himself by saying he had some things to do and would meet George at the hotel later.

"I thought we'd have dinner," George said.

"Please do," Holland said. "I've got to round up some hardware."

"Is there anything wrong?" George asked.

"Everything's just lovely." Then he smiled and added, more to Rhiana, "We attack at dawn."

She gave him a withering stare as she got in the car.

Sarah waved. But Holland had already started across the polo field. Rhiana gently stayed Sarah's fluttering hand.

•8•

In his bed in his estate house outside of Guatemala City, Clement Moloch's dream was lurching into nightmare.

He had worked late on his papers and afterwards had his customary hot cocoa before turning in, tired. At first he had merely slept, without dreaming, but then the descent into dreams began, burrowing down to familiar haunts.

Birkenau. Nazi Germany. October of 1944.

He was winging into the camp that was a satellite of Auschwitz, in the desolate region of Silesia, past the towering smoke huffing from the crematoriums, the flames of bonfires below him in the Avenues, and death rattles filling the ears.

Recently the entire ghetto of Riga had been fed to the incinerators on a single day, a day pummeled by a savage rain. In only a few weeks, in November, orders would come from Berlin to shut down the exterminations for an unlimited period; the Russians were coming too close. But until then the fires would function to capacity. On the most productive days 20,000 would whiff the Cyclon B. Twenty minutes later their bodies would be pulled apart and taken to the steel trolleys in front of the flames, and in another twenty minutes the ashes would journey by truck to be thrown into the River Vistula. The camp's electrified barbed wire enclosed more than 500,000 prisoners.

Moloch found himself wandering in the women's Camp Hospital. It must have been morning, he reasoned, because the incredibly filthy mattresses had been cleared of corpses. Nurses were busily scouring the dull grey bricks. The women had not been fed yet. They were all naked, without even a stitch in their hands. Moloch knew what that signified. He had arrived just in time. He was to be privy to a selection. Immense pleasure was to be derived from selections. Perhaps, out of deference, they would allow him the courtesy of participating.

Just then a woman came running.

They're coming! Mengele! For a selection!

An indescribable pall of fear came over the place. Wailing and crying sent up a clamorous concert that shook the walls. Women were falling. Others threw themselves against the walls and floors. Many were shaking uncontrollably, holding onto their shaven heads as though to an anchor. Some went on all fours to empty what little was in their stomachs. Moloch's heart stirred warmly at witnessing such complete subjugation.

He moved amongst them, unhindered by barriers in the world of sleep, observing intensely and studying clinically from the privileged position of seeing without being seen. There were women of every age, beauteous and unsightly, towering and squat, glowing and ravaged. Nationalities on display were Polish, Czech, German, French, Greek, Russian, Italian, Dutch, Belgian. Little better than half were Jews, if that. Every infirmity imaginable could be seen, from broken limbs that had never been tended, to running boils and discolored swellings. Without exception, all had the itch.

Moloch took his time looking over the squalid spectacle.

When the SS soldiers thundered in, the din the women were making diminished considerably. The SS were followed by the doctors and nurses. And then Josef Mengele strode with haughty indifference into the room, pausing while an orderly knelt before him to remove his mud-encrusted boots and replace them with shiny clean ones. Another orderly stood with an armload of freshly buffed footwear for the various changes Mengele would make on his rounds of the camp. The name Birkenau meant Birchwood Field, and at most times of the year the Avenues between Blocks were a quagmire of mud and wastes which the stylishly impeccable Mengele detested. It was for that reason he insisted on the boot change at each entrance of a building. Tightly belted into his uniform with the gold rosette at the collar and the medical corps armband on the sleeve, it was unthinkable for him to be seen by these dregs of humanity in anything but immaculate visage.

Clement Moloch was thrilled, as he had always been, to see a personage who would form some of the cement of history. Born on the banks of the Danube thirty-three years before, Mengele was now the Chief Medical Officer of Auschwitz–Birkenau, and he would most definitely form a long and colorful history.

Behind Mengele came his mistress, the young and nubile Polish Jewess, Wilma. For a moment Moloch thought it odd that Mengele would flaunt the relationship so openly, but then remembered how late it was. The war was closing and discretion was becoming superfluous.

Mengele looked down at a chair, swiping fussily at it with his gloves before deigning to sit. He was whistling an operatic aria by Wagner.

Without further ado he initiated the selection. The naked chorus of women was forced to file past one by one. His selections were made silently so as not to interrupt his whistling. He pointed with a red pencil. When he gestured to the right it meant the crematoriums, to the left life—for a while longer. Even this was done with a flair Moloch admired.

Moloch continued circulating around the women with a critical eye. A remarkable transformation had taken place among a number of them. They stood erect with their heads elevated and their shoulders straight, their stomachs flattened, and their breasts jutting. Here, at the brink of their existence they were going to face the red pencil with pride and defiance. Moloch was incensed. They were nothing but soiled scraps of an inferior order, scarcely deserving of the time it took to be rid of them. How dare they make pretenses! He would show them. Committing them to memory, he would go to the front of the line and point them out to Mengele.

Some of the women displayed more animal sense. They rubbed their bodies vigorously and pinched their cheeks to give them color. They spit on their fingers and tried to take the dirt from where it was crusted. They practiced their smiles. The selection would spare some of those who appeared healthy, or enticing. Moloch approved of that kind of cunning. Let them live a week or two more. Let them work. Let them serve.

There was a commotion at the head of the line. Moloch went to see.

A woman, condemned to the right, had spat on Wilma. An SS clubbed her senseless with his rifle butt and dragged her outside. A pistol shot came back through the door almost immediately. Mengele's pencil went on without pause. Another *Kapo* was busy entering the matriculation numbers tattooed on the prisoners' left forearms.

Standing before Mengele now was a teenaged girl.

She was budding, but her stomach was more pronounced than it should have been. Her attempt to cover the swelling with her hands had failed.

Mengele asked her if she was pregnant. Her reply was muted. Moloch moved closer, to hear.

Mengele struck with his gloves and asked her again. She nodded, her face crimson with fright and humiliation.

Who was responsible? She said the SS. Mengele heaved his head back and laughed. You mean to tell me an SS would lay with tripe like you, he said. Is that what you would have me believe? If it were me, I would have thrown you back. He glanced at the soldiers by the door. The glance was an order to laugh, and they did.

Mengele's lips twisted with amusement. He demanded the intimate details be recounted in full. The girl complied, unable to look at Mengele, her face averted, her whispers barely audible.

When she was through, she said she wanted to die.

As you wish, Mengele said agreeably, as if there had been any doubt. His pencil flicked to the right. That's life, isn't it, he joked to Wilma. Her reaction was a disinterested shrug.

Then Mengele's gaze was fastened on Moloch.

Mengele stood bolt upright. You! he bellowed at Moloch. You! Come here!

Moloch was momentarily confused. He had been certain he could not be seen, but now every eye in the place was on him. His intention was to speak to Mengele at *his* choosing, not Mengele's. They were two masters in the midst of cattle and a certain protocol was to be afforded him, not the affront of shouted You's! Mengele should know he was not one of them. It was all very strange.

He hovered nearer to Mengele.

You're a man, Mengele accused. This is a women's hospital. How did you get in here?

Before Moloch could answer, Mengele's hand, like a rubber band, snaked forward and dove down the front of Moloch's trousers.

Mengele drew back. You *are* a man, he said. I thought maybe you were a clown. We even have them here. We have everything here. He swept an arm about generously. This is my vineyard, he said.

Josef, it's me, Moloch said. It's Clement.

Should I know you?

But, of course.

You look to be a Limesucker to me, Mengele said, walking around him, his boots tapping the bricks, cleats on toes and heels.

I'm Welsh. You know that.

The oldest race of the British people. You *are* British then.

Not British, Moloch protested, puffing with outrage. I won't have that.

You won't have that! Mengele mimicked, stealing his outrage. Do you know whom you are addressing, Limesucker!

Josef Mengele, said Moloch. Gentleman of rank, born of privilege. Physician. Philosopher. Appointed to the Institute of Biological Heredity and Race Hygiene at Frankfort. SS Section Leader and Chief Medical Officer of this superbly efficient installation.

Who are you, then? Mengele demanded.

Moloch inflated himself to full stature and asked if they could talk with a measure of privacy. The SS jabbed him with the rifle barrel. Moloch slapped at it. Mengele motioned the SS away and drew Moloch to a far corner of the room. The women formed a half-circle around them, clustered like moon-eyed livestock at a salt-lick. The SS kept them away.

I'm Clement Moloch. In literal terms, Clement means mild or merciful. Moloch; now that pertains to a deity, mentioned in the Bible, whose worship was marked by the burning of children offered as a propitiatory sacrifice by their parents. More simply put: Anything conceived of as requiring appalling sacrifice.

Don't dare be insolent with me, Mengele warned.

Oh, heaven forbid, Moloch said quickly, I hold you in the highest esteem. In time we will become friends.

Time? You do not have time. Mengele reached for Moloch's left forearm and yanked the sleeve back. There, tattooed on the suckling pink skin was a matriculation number and the infamous letter L. It stands for *Leiche,* Mengele said. That means "corpse."

It's a mistake, Moloch said. It isn't there. Listen carefully: The war will be over in a few months, but don't worry, you will get away and live a long and prosperous life in the company of friends and countrymen.

Who wins? Mengele put to him.

You lose, Moloch said carefully, but only the war.

We cannot lose! Mengele erupted. *Look what we have done here!* He slashed Moloch's face with his gloves.

Of course Moloch felt nothing, so he was able to contain his own rage. Still, it was all very strange. No, you don't understand, Moloch said patiently. Only three months remain before the Russians will be here. You will send Wilma to Warsaw—you should do it now, but you will wait—where she will get false papers for you from the Jewish mafia. In January you will get away clean and go to your home in Gunzburg where your family's wealth and influence will keep you free of the Americans until '51. By then the bribes will be too costly and you will find it necessary to cross to Italy, then to Spain so you can board a ship to Argentina. The ODESSA will have set up escape routes, you see—

What is this ODESSA? Mengele interrupted.

Moloch shook his head. For pity's sake, Josef. It is the secret group the SS will form to aid the surviving members. Your own funds—from your family and from your transactions here—will be instrumental in much of its work. Hitler and Himmler will not survive, but Eichmann and—

Forget them, Mengele interrupted again, coldly. Tell me about Argentina.

Peron's administration will make you welcome, of course, for a price, and all attempts at extradition will be turned aside by them. The Dictator's fortunes will ebb and flow like the tide and there will be times when you'll have to cross into Paraguay to wait events out, but the waters will always clear in your favor. In time you will live under your own name on Vertiz Street in Buenos Aires and you will even become a Director of your family's machine factory there. However, I must warn you it will not always be smooth sailing. In the spring of '59 your wisdom will take you to the more secure shelter of Paraguay, this because the government's hold there is not so tenuous, and they are, shall we say, more receptive to the unique nature of your particular talents. They will issue you naturalization card Number 809 and grant you citizenship in November of that year. You will purchase a villa south of the capital in the village of San Antonio, as well as a gentleman's ranch at Puerto Stroessner. It is there I will visit you from time to time.

Mengele was mesmerized by the mysterious odyssey that was supposedly ahead of him. He kept wringing his gloves in his hands while he listened. For what reason will you visit me? he asked Moloch.

Why, to pay homage, Josef. In the halls of authority you will become a legend of gigantic proportions. There will be books written about you, and motion pictures made. The craven will call you the Angel of Death. We will become fast friends because we will both do work for the governments around you, although naturally you will not be availed of the freedom to work as widely or travel as extensively as I. But, in Paraguay, for instance, there will be much for you to do. The peasants and Indians will form clandestine trade unions and lay claim to farms needed by the landholders. Our help will be requested to deal with fifth columns of scum like this. It is the security of the State which is of supreme importance to men like us, men who are capable of destroying the State's enemies—just as you've done here. Ours is the work of knowing. There will be successful trips to Germany itself once or twice. To Egypt and Italy, Spain and France. Happily, you will give me the pleasure of your company at my home in Guatemala a time or two.

Guatemala? Mengele said distastefully. And Paraguay? I think not.

Oh, yes. Moloch smiled assuredly. You cannot imagine what the world will be like. There will be almost no discipline to speak of. Anarchists will run wild in the streets and spit at their leaders. Measures will have to be taken. They will call on me. The means of travel and communication will be so sophisticated I will be able to do as much in one month—and in a dozen countries—as you are able to do in one place in one year.

Your mind plays outlandish tricks on you, even for a Limesucker. Your assumptions are preposterous.

That would be a grave mistake on your part, Josef, Moloch advised him.

The tableaux you have taken my time with would shame a Gypsy. You do know what we do with Gypsies, don't you? You pretend to know everything else.

I ask that you do not forget my station, Moloch said. I am as good as you.

Now you have really lost your senses. You are not.

I am. Moloch was trying desperately to get away, grasping for the conduit of levitation, the ascending stuff out of nightmares.

Mengele's ectoplasmic hands somehow got hold of him and would not let go. In an instant the SS were there, holding him firm. He thrashed in the way he had seen beached fish. He could not get free.

Mengele gave a terse command to the SS: Take the Welsh Rabbit to Block 25 without delay.

Moloch screamed.

Block 25 was the anteroom of the gas chamber. Josef was making a terrible mistake.

Clement Moloch rose screaming from his bed, showering perspiration, his mouth bloody from gnawing his lips, his wife's hands on him. In his poisoned thrashing he bit her hand. As a last resort she threw her body on his.

Tears streamed from his eyes. His chin shook. He called her vile names and kicked out at her bare legs. He called her Mengele.

When his senses were again in hand she sat on the bedside and held his head to her breast, passing the glass of bitters he kept on the nightstand.

"It's been at least two years since you've had that dream," she said, dabbing at the blood.

"I don't remember," he lied. How could he forget. The periodic nightmares had come ever since his first pilgrimage to Auschwitz, when, long after the war, the gates had finally been opened to the public. They started then, not when he had belatedly presented himself to Mengele in Paraguay.

Suddenly he tore at the left sleeve of his pajamas, yanking the fabric away. He slumped, nearly slipping from the bed. The skin was clear of ink. No L, and no number.

"That too," Margaret observed, arching an eyebrow. "I've never been able to make the connection. We were in London throughout the war. It's very strange. You generally have the dreams after visiting Mengele. Have you seen him recently?"

"Not for a long time," he said. "Maybe I should." He got up and shuffled to a cabinet, pouring himself more bitters. The door to Margaret's room was ajar, a lamp glowing by the bed. When he looked back he realized she was wearing one of her infuriating silk seducers that scarcely dropped to the leg. "Picking at dreams as if they were carrion is only a business to make money, Margaret. People dream. Scores of people who only saw Auschwitz as we did, as tourists, will dream of it."

"I dare say." She began straightening the bedclothes, some of which lay on the floor, deliberately presenting her backside to him.

"Did you ever wonder that the majority of our monuments are tombs?" he said, seeing the ample globes.

"The linens are soiled," she said.

"I was perspiring, Margaret, after all."

"*Soiled,* dearest."

Mortified, he looked down at the front of his pajamas. "Oh, my God," he said.

"The linen will have to be changed." She said it with no more opinion than that necessary for a simple domestic decision. She turned the sheets out, then lifted his robe from a chair and took it to where he was standing at the cabinet. He shrugged into the garment while she held it and looped the belt for him. From the looping of the belt she moved skillfully into an embrace.

"I'll draw a hot bath, dearest," she invited, "and then you can make yourself comfortable in my bed."

His expression disbelieving, he struggled away. "For heaven's sake, Margaret. I have had a bad night. Go to bed. I've work to do. I'll see you at breakfast."

She went pliantly from the room and closed the door. Moloch changed to fresh pajamas and donned his robe again. There were a few hours before dawn and he could get some work done downstairs, in the locked room. The aftermath of his nightmares always proved fertile, somehow facilitating his powers of recall. Besides, he was meeting his sister, Claire, tomorrow. It would be a busy day for a change. He despised his holiday Margaret had inflicted upon him. Soon over though, thank goodness.

In the corridor outside the room, Crosetti stood with his ear turned to Moloch's room. Clad only in undershorts, he held the Ingram M-10 machine pistol in hand.

He had heard everything. Moloch's opening screams had driven him from his bed next door to Margaret, and the slower Randolph had joined him in the corridor. They recognized the cause right away. Crosetti sent Randolph back to his room, offering to wait it out himself.

Moloch would give him proper hell for being in the hallway in his scivvies.

A secret smile spread when he overheard the last exchange. Margaret had run true to form. Amorous at the worst of times. So had Moloch.

He'd almost laughed out loud when, in the Middle East, Moloch had told him about the sand Margaret had spilled from her clothes. Crosetti knew only too well why. The mare had had her driver in the desert. Not the first time, or place. Crosetti was sure Moloch knew of her stolen moments. The knowledge lent him a degree of control. If nothing else, the scattered infidelities gave him a respite.

Once, in the car, Crosetti had taken her himself. Once was enough. In all thoughts thereafter he referred to her in his own mind as Margaret DeadFuck. Not like Claire, who had every talent with those impulses lacking in Margaret.

The door swung open and Moloch went bustling past him, not even bothering to look his way.

"Not to worry, Raymond. I'll be downstairs," Moloch informed, padding off down the marble hallway of his estate.

•II•

HOBBIT COUNTRY

The terror commenced with the arrival of the prisoners in the stadium (Chile Stadium in Santiago). They arrived in army buses, in vast quantities. The reception was formed by hundreds of soldiers and policemen, who placed the prisoners against a wall in front of the stadium, continually beating them with hands, feet, boots, gunbutts, etc.

Once done, the prisoners entered a kind of hall, where they remained several hours lying face down with their hands behind their necks, without being able to move. In this position the continuous blows produced spasms throughout the body; after a few hours one was unable to move, remaining completely paralyzed.

From here, many were taken directly to the interrogation and torture rooms, or to the basement where many met their death. The great majority were led from here to the gallerys and sports center of the stadium and to the corridors, once the capacity of the stadium was heavily surpassed. In the galleries and sports center approximately 6000 people were massed together, the majority of them in a pitiful condition because of the violence with which they were treated and because of the following conditions.

During the five days that most people remained there, they were given no food except for a small cup of cold coffee.

As the majority of prisoners had been arrested at work or in their homes without being permitted to clothe themselves adequately, as they were given no type of shelter and were obliged to sleep on the bare cement of the galleries and corridors, people suffered the consequences of intense cold which were reflected in pulmonary diseases.

During the five days it was almost impossible to sleep, given the conditions of overcrowding, cold, hunger, tension and terror with the expectation of interrogations, and the pain provoked by the beatings.

At moments when the tension rose, the commanders or-

dered soldiers to open fire with their arms inside the stadium; throughout the bursts of fire the prisoners had to lie down one on top of the other, creating a situation of general panic. Some of these bursts of fire lasted for several minutes while soldiers shot at the roofs and walls with machine-guns, rifles and pistols, creating the atmosphere of a battlefield. This was repeated for all the time that we remained there.

All this tension generated a despair and unbalance so great that some resorted to suicide protests.

A worker who was being pushed by a soldier with his rifle, reacted, as a result of which he was beaten by soldiers and officials. Meanwhile the camp commander appeared, ordering that he should be more heavily beaten and transferred to the basement where tortures and executions were carried out. In this situation, the worker, terrified, tried to free himself from the soldiers—an act which caused the camp commander to intervene personally —they beat the worker until he died; not content with this, the commander (a colonel) took out his pistol and shot the body. All this happened before the eyes of 6000 people who were heaped in the sports center and galleries.

A youth of approximately 16 years, who had become completely unbalanced by this situation, was wandering through the galleries shouting illogical things. This began to create problems of discipline for the soldiers. After two days they found a solution. They allowed him to go to an isolated corridor, where a soldier on guard stopped him violently by hitting him with his rifle barrel, which frightened him and caused him to cry out. At this moment the soldier, who was only a few feet away, shot him in the chest and caused instant death. This execution was also witnessed by many of the prisoners.

Another worker, also unbalanced by the situation, threw himself from the gallery to the sports center and remained unconscious for a few minutes. A few minutes before, he had suffered an attack of nerves as a result of which he was transferred to the upper corridor, where they gave him some drugs. He was taken unconscious from the sports center on a stretcher to the basement, where he was killed by pistol shots shortly afterwards.

A man who was on the upper gallery of the stadium

shouted 'down with fascism' and hurled himself to the lower gallery where he remained unconscious for several minutes. The 'black berets' arrived immediately and took him by his feet, dragging him head down, and beating him on the head with rifle butts and bayonets. The man was already dead before they arrived at the steps leading to the basement, though this did not prevent them from shooting him in the head.

In one of the galleries a prisoner shouted 'down with the fascist assassins.' The commander personally took hold of the microphone and asked who had shouted. The prisoner got up and announced that it was he, at which the commander ordered him to 'come here.' The prisoner walked towards the corridors and shortly afterwards one could hear the shots that ended his life.

During all the time we were in the stadium, lists of names were read out calling prisoners for interrogation in the basement. The prisoners descended by the stairs leading to the basement, and after a few moments one could hear the shrieks provoked by torture. Moreover, one could hear throughout the stadium the noise caused by the beating in the basement, which contributed to the tension that brought many of the prisoners to a state of hysteria approaching madness. The climate of tension even affected the soldiers, who, after some days, addressed themselves to the prisoners and tried to calm them, confessing that they too were affected by the tension. This tension reached such a level that, when the commander talked of peace and calm in one of his speeches, he was mechanically applauded by the prisoners, thus creating a surrealistic picture. This applause represented all the protest or impotence of the prisoners faced with terror and violence.

Many had to be treated in the infirmary in the basement of the stadium. That made it possible to see clearly what happened there:

A 'Dantesque' place . . . naked corpses . . . with the stomach wrenched open by bayonets . . . carved up . . . mutilated by the blows of rifle butts . . .

Apart from the basement, some bathrooms of the stadium were used as places of torture, principally when they were dealing with groups of people who needed to be beaten and killed . . . and because of the violence with which the soldiers acted one could see blood and flesh on the walls and floor of the bathrooms.

—From the testimony of a group of political prisoners to a delegation of official foreign observers, describing conditions in one of the ad hoc detention centers immediately following the military coup of September 11, 1973.

There were a great many of these improvised detention facilities all over Chile, the Chile Stadium being one of the smaller, having been originally constructed for basketball and similar pastimes.

•9•

The Saturday flight into Lake Amititlan went off without incident, George setting the helicopter down with ease on the great expanse of lawn behind Max Ortiz' weekend retreat on the lake front. The house was a Scott and Zelda Fitzgerald setting and their arrival was followed by lunch with Max in the screened veranda looking out to seething volcanoes across the water, the meal served by an elderly Indian couple who cared for the premises.

At first the atmosphere was shot through with grievance, no one except Holland knowing quite how to behave. On the one hand was the coming together as a family, hugs and kisses and arms snugly entwined, on the other the stranger in their midst, thrust on them by a vile milieu. Pleasure was tempered at every turn by the reason for being there, the awareness skipping back and forth between them as if it were a contagious twitch in the skin. Laughter and snatches of reminiscences were cut short by guarded glances at Holland, and each other. Only Sarah was exempt, because she did not know the real reason they were there, and because she had been so excited by the helicopter ride. In addition, they could not talk in front of her, so Max's questions had to wait, painfully.

Max, as George had predicted, had a gregarious charm impossible to resist. A man who had never married, Holland guessed him to be in his late fifties, a short rotund man with a hairless pate, a gently smiling cherubic face, and quick lively eyes. His adoration of Rhiana was abundantly clear, reminding Holland that he had known her from a child and thus had seniority. And within minutes of their touching down, he made it equally plain there was nothing his nephew could ask of him he would not do.

Observing from the fringe, it occurred to Holland there was an outsized band of casualties in a group so small as this. George's brother, Patrick, had been murdered; Rhiana's husband and father; Sarah's father and grandfather. All had been known to Max, and therefore he had sustained his losses too. An inordinate amount of violence had already visited this union, and more was to come.

From the beginning Max pretended Rhiana and Holland really were married or, at least were lovers. Rhiana did not exactly resist, but for the first hour it was apparent she was uncomfortable with the ruse in front of Max and George. However, shortly after that she slipped acceptably into the pretense, and by the time lunch was finished the byplay between her and Holland could have fooled most observers.

After lunch the men went aside, George to do the bulk of the talking. Max's suspicions were confirmed in full, his queries to both George and Holland being concise and pointed in a manner befitting someone who had as complete an appreciation of the undertaking as could be expected. He was at their disposal and they only needed to tell what they required of him, adding that in good conscience he could not dispute their rationale. George stated that anything that might be required was up to Holland now. Max seemed satisfied with Holland's explanation after asking about Rhiana and Sarah. The exchange lasted less than half an hour.

Holland shook hands with George and then walked clear of the wash as the Hughes rose in an unfettered arc and darted swiftly into the mountains to the north, the jet engine whining off into silence. Sarah ran across the grass with her arms raised wide as though she had just released a bird to the sky. Holland promised her George would take her for another ride when they returned to Mexico.

Before leaving the lake Max insisted that Holland take

a spare set of keys for the house, and instructed the elderly couple to make them comfortable in every way if they should appear without him. On the drive into the city the car passed Indian women carrying baskets and water crocks on their heads, men leading donkeys burdened with produce, and modern industrial plazas bearing names like Coca-Cola and McGregor Clothing. Holland sat in the front seat with Max, who advised there was a bullfight the following afternoon at four and Moloch had purchased tickets for it; a rare event this time of year, and one of the few chances Holland would have of seeing the man outside his estate. He could arrange seats if Holland wished. Holland said yes without hesitation, and without asking Rhiana. She stared at the back of his head, then out the window.

The Sheraton-Conquistador was a hotel whose decor could as easily have put it in Spokane or New Orleans, suitably situated near the center of town and only a brief walk from the main shopping district. From the hotel balcony the city spread out low and flat below, broken only rarely by the odd jutting apartment or office building, the long straight streets cutting a neat patchwork across a plateau almost a mile above sea level. The air was thin and sharp and clear, giving Holland and Sarah an ecologically approved view of familiar billboards. Sarah was quick to point out McDonald's, moving Holland to make another promise.

Rhiana stayed in the room, unpacking and hanging garments in the bathroom. She called Sarah in and said they would both soak in the bath, if that was alright with Holland, after which Sarah would take her nap. Holland told her to go ahead, he was going downstairs for a drink before Max came back to take them to dinner.

Rhiana laid her hairbrush out, and went into the bathroom with Sarah. Holland anticipated that the door would be locked. It was, almost as soon as closing.

The sound of the bathwater running afforded him an opportunity to assemble his revolver; as good a time as any, and no telling when it would be needed.

He put the camera case on the bed, snapped it open and placed the useless photo paraphernalia aside. A few twists of the tiny screwdriver affixed to a key chain removed a number of watch-sized screws hidden under the foam lining, and seconds later the gun's organs were melding with skilled dispatch.

Having begun life as a quite ordinary Smith and Wesson Model 57 revolver in .41 magnum caliber, the firearm had then undergone more than a hundred hours of work in order for it to suit Holland's exacting standards: fitted with a custom five-inch barrel, muzzle vented and sufficiently heavy to reduce recoil; a rib dovetailed to the barrel for its full length and then locked by four Allen screws; cylinders fitted and indexed for precise alignment; buffed frame for cylinder closing; ejector rod lapped and fitted; lightened rebound slide spring; hammer shaved to negate cocking, as well as to prevent snagging on clothing; an S-shaped mainspring to lighten and smooth trigger pull; combat wings and a quarter-click rear sight; stock and cylinder release latch modified to more readily accept the use of speedloaders; the metal finish glass-beaded to a dull satin in order to cancel glare. However, beyond these modifications, the gun's most distinctive feature was its conversion to exclusive double-action, thereby suspending any need to cock the hammer, and eliminating the two-stage pull and backlash in the trigger. Thus crafted, the revolver became as fast and as accurate as any for use in the field.

Also in the case was a silencer. Silencers by their proper designation are called "suppressors," most being woeful devices severely hindering the effectiveness of the firearm they are coupled to, restricting the bullet's velocity as well as adversely affecting the accuracy because of vibrations. They are deplored for fouling the gun barrel with spent powder, many not suppressing the report of the gun so much as redirecting the noise indiscriminately. However, the suppressor Holland employed was the latest in applied technology and not only did all that a suppressor was designed to do, but in practice actually enhanced the velocity of the bullet passing through its titanium embrace. Larger and more cumbersome than its pretenders, Holland carried the device only when its use was anticipated, knowing it to be the standard of truly professional practitioners—as few as there were of either. When it came to the tools of his trade, Holland was pragmatic to an extreme.

He still held the gun as the bathroom door opened.

Rhiana stepped out in her slip, saw him, and turned to go back.

"It's alright," he said, moving his attention back to the gun. "You're dressed. We can't hide from each other."

"I thought you'd gone," she said.

She crossed to the dresser and picked up a bottle of bath salts. Her hair, pulled back before, sleekly, now hung loose and heavy, shining in different planes. She watched as he tightened the last of the Allen screws atop the barrel.

"You said you wouldn't need that until we were gone."

"That's the way I see it," he said.

"You want to feel whole, is that it?"

"I can't force you to relax," he said. "You're as tight as a circus wire. It shows."

"I know it does." She looked at the window. "He's out there. This is his place. There's Sarah. Try to understand what that means at first."

"I know," he said. "Do what you can."

He had not looked up. Now he did as she walked away from him. He saw that she wore nylon stockings with seams.

He finished assembling the gun and then went downstairs. He ordered a bottle of Bohemia beer and flipped through tourist brochures picked up from the lobby desk.

"You'll see it around this next bend," Max said, directing his speech to the rear view mirror as a courtesy to Holland, seated behind him in the car. "I won't slow too much or it will look suspect."

Rhiana, in front with Max, darted a glance at Holland and then directed her attention forward again.

It was late evening, the light failing. After dinner at his home, Max had offered to drive Holland past Moloch's estate so he could get his first look. Rhiana said she wished to go along, and so they waited until Sarah was put to bed in one of the guest bedrooms by Max's housekeeper. Holland would have preferred that Rhiana wait for them, but decided it was a point better not made just then.

"They likely to see us drive by?" he asked Max.

"Undoubtedly," Max answered. "His is the last place and the road only goes a short distance past before ending in the trees. They'll wait to see if we drive back too."

"You'd better put your lights on then," Holland said.

The estate loomed into view as they rounded the curve, dominated by high stone walls crowned with wrought iron grillwork, only the steeply pointed blue roof of the central building seen above. The compound dominated a portion of ground rising above that around it, somewhat reminiscent of the battery sites of medieval England. Holland estimated the enclosure took in two acres or so. When they passed the gateway facing the road he saw it was of narrow-cut beams fronted by massive iron hinge plates, as high as the stonework and topped by iron as well. Lights atop the walls directed illumination inward. The overall impression was of an impregnable structure inspired for the security of wealth. He had seen similar in Falls Church and Palm Springs and Geneva.

"The whole front courtyard is sealed in shiny black asphalt," Max said. "Not even space for a fruit tree or a flower bed. On the other hand, the house itself has a lovely gambrel roof and leaded windows all round, but it all looks down on this depressing parking lot. Why he did that, I'll never know."

"Moloch's allergic to dust," Holland said.

"Ah," Max nodded. "And this road too is the only one paved for miles around. They listen to his whims here."

"I don't doubt it," Rhiana said.

True to Max's description, the road terminated in a dirt patch a few hundred meters beyond the estate. Max circled the car and retraced their tracks, once more keeping his pace steady as they went by the residence.

"I'm far from an expert," Max said, "but I think it would be next to impossible to get inside, if that's what you have in mind. There's all manner of electronic gadgetry to prevent it."

"How do you know?" Holland asked.

"An acquaintance owns the company that installs such things. Moloch has his continually updated, just the way the embassies do. There are alarms inside and out; an ultrasonic motion detector, and electric beams—but even that has been changed to something more elaborate. The name escapes me, but I wrote it down . . ."

"An infrared pulsing photoelectric beam?" Holland offered.

"Yes," Max said. "That's it."

"What about closed-circuit TV?" Holland asked.

"That I don't know," Max said.

Rhiana turned in the seat. "Can you get past what is there?"

"I doubt that I'd want to," he said.

The answer was not the one she expected. "But if you wanted to, could you?"

"It depends. Probably."

As soon as he'd said it he wished he hadn't. In the gloom he thought he could detect a dryness in her face, he couldn't be sure. What came to mind was the time he had sat for hours in the lobby of the Danieli Royal Excelsior Hotel in Venice, next to the Doge's Palace, and waited for a woman to enter who could match the enchantment of the room. For him, the room—a hotel lobby—was one of man's more handsome creations in veined marble, and by his scale only women could eclipse grandeur that came from the earth. None had come near to then, nor in all the time since.

"How?" she said.

He took his time before answering, contesting her look. She was more in control now, not the way she had been in her slip. He decided she would complement the Danieli, even humble it when she turned a certain way. The conclusion was unavoidable and vaguely unsatisfying.

"Ultrasonic motion detectors are used inside," he said. "They look like stereo speakers. Depending on the equipment he's using, you might be able to crawl up while staying out of range and simply unplug it. If not that, the built-in delay mechanism can be taken advantage of by running straight up and unplugging it before the alarm is tripped. Naturally, there are variations."

He looked out as they passed the first crossroads on the way back into the city, Moloch's ground being outside the city's boundaries. It was dark now. But Rhiana wasn't about to let him go so easily, he knew that.

"Max mentioned another device," she said. "Can you beat it too?"

"The difference is implied by the name: The beam is infrared so it can't be seen by the naked eye, and is pulsed at irregular intervals to complicate attempts at fooling it with a substitute beam. It can be located by using infrared glasses, and from there the principle remains the same;

you get at its source and shut it off. But the main asset of any of these is that the intruder not know they're there in the first place. Once that's known it's merely a matter of predictability."

Rhiana looked down from him. "I see," she said. "The people inside are what you really worry about. The human factor is less predictable. Is that it?"

"My compliments," he said.

She turned away. Max smiled back at Holland, then at Rhiana. Rhiana let it settle without further prosecution.

Max, an observant man, had noted the chilling curtain Rhiana had erected between herself and Holland, recognizing the formal contempt as early as that morning at the lake. At dinner, his expression and gestures to her were clearly meant to moderate. The relationship was daughterly then, an implied reservation to challenge the mercurial emotions of youth. This is not the time or place for judgments, Max seemed to be saying, and when it happened Rhiana took heed, if temporarily.

Holland caught headlights coming up quickly in the rear view mirror. Max saw them a moment after.

"Look the other way," Holland said to Rhiana.

The car, of American manufacture, shot by them at a rapid rate, the driver's face a ghostly blur as it swiveled in passing.

"One of Moloch's bodyguards," Max said. "It must be his night off."

Holland regretted not being afforded a better view of the man's face; knowing Moloch's inner circle was almost a prerequisite. His thoughts were read by Max. "I could try to follow him but I'm reasonably sure of his destination. He's the one I told you is having an affair with Moloch's sister."

Rhiana paid attention, having been excluded from the before-dinner discussion between the men.

"Don't follow him," Holland said.

"I can take you a different way if you want to see where she lives," Max said.

"Alright," Holland accepted. "You told me Claire was only a few years younger than Moloch. The driver of the car looked a lot younger than that."

"Correct," Max said. "But she doesn't look her age at all and is a fine figure of a woman. She must take exceptional care of herself, although I'm sure she's had cosmetic surgery too."

"You've met her, then?" Holland asked.

"At a dinner party Moloch's wife gave for some local dignitaries a few months ago," Max said. "I went out of curiosity and on the chance I might have something to report to George. When we were introduced I mentioned that I hadn't seen her about the city before. She said she had been here only a few months, that making it about a year at present. I asked if she was taking up permanent residence—I confess I was thinking of romance myself," he laughed, "and she answered that her intention was to eventually move on."

Holland leaned forward. "You're saying she wasn't introduced to you as Moloch's sister?"

"Oh, no," he said. "It was only after I mentioned it to George that he was able to find out who she was. Didn't he tell you?"

"No," Holland said.

"What happened to your ideas of romance, Uncle Max?" Rhiana asked him.

He laughed again. "At my age one has to make the best of these opportunities, but she was a cold fish, very guarded. Maybe she only likes the English, who knows? I tried, but she kept her distance and was mindful of what she said. She only stayed for one drink, and when dinner was served she was nowhere to be seen. Since then she's always in the company of Moloch's henchman. I think the only time she leaves her apartment is when they have dinner. Oh, and a strange thing, they sometimes go to a bar in the rough part of town. It's a place where they break bottles over each other's heads and get the knives out."

By now they were well within the city, moving in sparse traffic on a broad thoroughfare lined with modern office and apartment towers. Further along, Holland noticed a gap where the pilings of a building had been picked clean, evidence of the country's last earthquake.

"Do you think Moloch knows about the affair?" he asked.

"I don't see how he couldn't," Max said. "No effort is made to conceal it. You can see for yourself. His car is already parked in plain sight."

Max nodded toward a glass and aluminum building of

eight stories they were about to pass. The American automobile that had barreled by them earlier was now sitting empty in the building's circular drive. This time Rhiana didn't have to be told to avert her face.

"The distinct impression I get is that Moloch is not as close to the members of his family as he might be," Max said. "I suppose that's predictable though."

"I'd be astonished if he was," Rhiana said.

"Enough?" Max said to Holland.

"Uh-huh. We'll get Sarah and go back to the hotel, if you don't mind."

"What has all of this to do with . . . well, with what you have to do?" Rhiana asked him.

"Probably very little," Holland said. "I have to know who the players are, that's all."

"We've all known from the beginning how elusive he is," she said. "It's practically legendary. I should think the obvious way to overcome that is to shoot him from a distance with a powerful rifle. Or is the obvious considered passé in the latest state of the art?"

"Rhiana . . ." Max cautioned her.

"Please, Uncle," she said. "The Doctor isn't your city's only expert at killing now. Supposedly there's another Ace on the scene. As I won't see how one dinosaur finishes off the other, I think I'd like to know how these things are done in such heady circles."

"I don't want to know," Max said.

"Then I must be more primitive, Uncle," she said. "I do."

Her attention reverted to Holland. He was watching the lights stream by, reflecting on the window like fleeing klieg lamps. He was thinking that, given a choice, he'd just as soon have her call him "Ace" instead of a dinosaur.

"These things aren't done that way, Rhiana," he said finally. "Despite what you read and what you see in the movies."

He considered adding that the state of the art—as she put it—hadn't changed since the dawn of creation, other than by way of the implements, but that also was too obvious and would only provide her another opening. Besides, experts in any endeavour were only experts so long as their expertise worked.

"I see," she said. "Then perhaps you'll see fit to tell me how these things are done sometime before I leave. We already know how he does it."

Holland remained quiet. He would have liked to smoke his pipe. Max came to his aid. "It probably doesn't matter, but Moloch has been visiting her almost every morning since his return. I drive this way to my office and I couldn't help noticing."

"What time would that be?" Holland asked him.

"Eight-fifteen," he said.

"My," Rhiana said, "a man visits his sister after being away. She becomes more of a threat with each passing moment."

Max wagged an admonishing finger at her below the seat top, where Holland couldn't see.

The balance of the drive to Max's house was made in silence.

Rhiana lay on her back, one hand squeezed midway between her thighs, the other caught under Sarah sleeping beside her in the bed. That hand felt adrift and numbed by not having moved for the best part of an hour, even though she knew from long experience she could draw it out without waking the child.

The other hand was jammed between her thighs for warmth, not because the room was cool, but because she felt such fear that her bones might well have been casings of ice. Yet she knew there was nothing to fear in the room, with the possible exception of Holland, lying like a pet dog in the darkness in the middle of the floor. But she didn't know yet where to place her fear of him. No, it was the outside she feared, The Doctor asleep in his house with its gambrel roof and leaded windows, and the thugs there with him.

She had anticipated fear from the time Isabelle and Hector had come to her, but she hadn't been able to prepare for a fear as deep and persistent as that she had felt in the Chile Stadium. Nevertheless, it had coursed through her all day, mounting now. Firm in her mind at the day's end was the conviction that if she and Sarah should find themselves in danger they would also find themselves utterly alone, save for Max. Holland would desert them in an instant, she was sure.

Before sleeping, Sarah had sat in bed and stared at Holland on the floor. He didn't cover himself or recline on a pillow, but simply stretched out in an aged pair of corduroy pants and frayed flannel shirt. He told Sarah they served as his pajamas and had for a long time. That had initiated a light bantering between them, laced with trivia he knew would enthrall her young mind, one such item an account that men's trousers in the eighteenth century had buttons in front and a drawstring in back so that one size fitted all. Sarah had wanted to know more, until Rhiana had insisted she sleep.

Rhiana turned her head to look at the clock on the bed table. The first day was gone. She would count the days until she could leave with her daughter. From the clock, she strained to see if Holland were still there.

"You're awake?" he said, low enough to keep from disturbing Sarah.

"Yes," she said.

"I've been thinking that I'd like to see if Moloch visits the sister in the morning. Can you be ready?"

"Yes. Sarah wakes early," she said, thinking that she herself would not likely sleep at all.

They lapsed into silence.

He had infuriated her repeatedly during the day, so smug and certain, his damned intrepid silences, his studied campaign of pompous detachment. The pat routine repelled her. Any fool could converge all lines of reasoning into blood lust. Still, she should not have spoken to him that way—how unpredictable was he?—and surely not in a way that allowed him to win purely because he was so contemptuously uncaring. Her condemnations, when not challenged, made her feel more the fool, when it should have been him. Agustin would have been ashamed of her, angry. Her father, disappointed. Her mother mortified by her behavior. And Max, as sweet as any man could be, was too kind to intrude, and so suffered. She had to stop herself but her fears robbed her of trust in herself.

"Do I have to go with you to the bullfight?" she asked him. "I hate them."

"They don't thrill me much either, if it's any consolation," he said. "But I need you there."

"Max can point him out as well as I can," she said hopefully.

"I want you to do it."

"Not Sarah then. I won't take her there."

"No," he conceded. "She doesn't seem to mind staying with the housekeeper, but the rest of the time I want her with us."

The housekeeper. Rhiana remembered that afternoon, when she had gone into the kitchen to see Rosa. The woman was peeling vegetables, but had jumped up and showered her with compliments on her marriage, truly happy for her. Startled, she had almost corrected her. Rosa, so attentive at dinner to what she thought was a loving match, caused Rhiana to finally lash out at him in the car.

"Do you want to go home?" he asked.

"I . . . Do you want us to?" she said, the question coming to her like an ambush in the dark.

"Not that," he said. "I meant Chile. If it changes."

"No, never," she said. "They've made my country into a graveyard. For some of us that will never change."

She didn't expect that he would understand, a man who peopled graveyards himself, and whose country had made hers a pyre.

Wearing his tweed jacket with elbow patches, smoking his pipe, at dinner his manners had been impeccable. He even recognized one of Max's paintings—a Laurencin. Who was he fooling? Who but himself? After all, working against the image was the rage, and the fact that he did it with understated perfection was a shallow distinction to her. Try as he might, he was inseparable from the pursuit of death, at least in her view.

Sarah stirred in her sleep. Rhiana's arm was almost free now. She turned on her side herself, away from Holland and nearer to her daughter, a shield by instinct, for their preservation.

The first day was over.

• 10 •

The bullfight brought about in Holland a black mood perfectly suited to his own contest. Not that the sordid exhibit being played out on the sand below was itself in any way a contest, any more than a car wreck could be construed an Olympic event. Few things incensed him to the extent he allowed the emotion to linger, but this garish pageant was doing so admirably. Worse still, Moloch had not yet made an appearance. Holland, in union with Rhiana and Max, was beginning to question whether the object of their being in the plaza was going to show at all.

As an act of diversion he packed and lit his pipe. Rhiana, seated between him and Max, turned her face away.

"This bother you?" he said, meaning the pipe.

"It's the matches," she said.

He arc'd the sliver over the heads into the aisle. The dank air in the arena had stirred her way, carrying the sulfur with it, and he understood that the sharp smell could be offensive at full force.

When they had first taken their seats in the favored *sombra* section, because it was shaded during the sunny days and therefore sought by those able to pay more, the men had turned to look and admire and to elbow the companions next to them. In an audience predominantly male there was a good representation of women worthy of watching, but none to rival Rhiana, and she was accorded brassy attention, even from the cheap seats far removed. Holland had ignored it, or tried to, though not as effortlessly as she did. He was reminded of a comment once made, perhaps by George, he couldn't be sure, to the effect that the bullfight was taken as a sexual stimulant by some, who found a powerful erotogenic current present that clearly made them smolder, until, as he'd put it, "they sprinted home to fuck their brains out." Holland reconsidered; George wouldn't have put it that way, it must have been someone else.

Although they had purposely not arrived until after the opening fanfare, Moloch could not be seen in the crowd, Max having carefully taken seats that were higher up in order to ensure they would be looking down on him. Rhiana had hoped he would be there, meaning they could then leave. Only Max cared to see the fight, if she was to believe what Holland said. Moloch's absence was disturbing, not the least because it meant they had to await the first bull.

The bull ran from the corridor into the flat open space, a pit in reality, its hide rippling as it twisted gaily and kicked its hooves out behind. A groan floated on the crowd who knew at once that the animal was a false pretender without heart for the entertainment of dying. Spit and scorn set the tone for the afternoon, fitting skies that threatened of rain. The bull stopped then, almost skidding to a halt, maybe smelling old blood, or maybe just realizing he was alone and there was no grass here, no steers and no Judas bull, nothing but two-legged tormentors in tiers that trapped him. The toro's expression went from blank to open conjecture. Out came his tongue to sweep his snout.

Little did he know what lay ahead, Holland thought while he looked at the toro, and wanted to say it, shout it, shoot it from a gun. Let the malignant collection hanging from their seats pick two from their ranks and send them into the pit to flog and cuff each other to extinction in any way they saw fit, if they so desired, and so long as they provided amusement, of course. That brand of spectacle he could encourage and applaud and put his money on; there would be a fragrant sweetmeat taste to the decay then, a pungent logic germane to the human condition. But otherwise leave the animals to themselves—they were so much more the intelligent anyway. Were it not for man, the shy bull would have been in a meadow contentedly snipping delicate clovers and breathing air empty of the stink of people.

The fight was slow and inept and undeserving of the name. Not one "Ole" came forth. Both the man and the toro were young novices and only capable of making the other look awful, the bull retaining what dignity was in evidence.

Moving his cape as though he were pitching turds from

a shovel, the torero's knock-knees played like castanets with every pass. He was unable to draw the stunted horns anywhere close to his torso regardless of how he whirled and stunted, his motion with the cape a jerking off rather than a synchronized leading, his posture more indicative of a severe bowel restriction than something supposedly held classic. On one occasion the bull took the cape away on his horns and then tried to chew it, spitting out small red Christmas stickers of cloth. The crowd yammered and boo'd, made fists and slapped their forearms. His detractors grew by the moment. Today the plaza was his poorhouse, the imagined illumination of bullfighting engraved in the manure of the arena.

At about six hundred pounds, soon to be dead weight, the bull was three to four hundred pounds short of what it could have been. Its most endearing quality was an indifference to charge the red banner. According to one expert along the row this lamentable attitude was due to the animal's antagonist being a southpaw. Holland was tempted to ask him how or why the bull made the distinction.

But the contest went on, and on.

"A deplorable match," Max said, Holland unsure if he was drawing from past observations or not.

A breeze came up with the signal of rain on its breath, Holland wishing he had worn more than a shirt. He rolled his sleeves down.

In front of Rhiana a man was shouting in Spanish, calling the torero a "peon with a little prick." Now that, Holland considered, the critic might be drawing from past observation. Max tapped the man's shoulder and asked in a genial way that he be careful with his choice of language. The man said something that Holland missed, then gestured insolently. Max spread his hands helplessly and sat back. Rhiana smiled her gratitude, telling him not to fret on her behalf. Max kissed her hand.

Across the way in the *sol* bleachers money was changing hands in wagers and coca leaves were being chewed languidly. Every once in a while someone would stand to heave a bottle down. Below, in the first row, two louts stood to display their sentiments by pissing over the barrier, and were hustled away after a delicate skirmish with a policeman.

"If he doesn't come soon I'm going to leave," Rhiana said.

"Wait," Holland told her. "It'll get even more civilized."

"You've been to these before?"

"Once."

"I should have known," she said. "A few more minutes, that's all."

Down in the dirt the aspiring matador was trying to kill the beast, going about it with all the flair and inspiration of a mud turtle in heat. The gallery laughed to tears, getting a bellyful of the buffoon's blunted exertions. The first sword had struck bone and broken, apparently the steel as defective as its pilot. The torero loped to the barrier for another, his knees clashing all the way, the bull heaving its massive head and sniffing the blood from the bad stabbing.

Max looked over at Holland and made a face toward the ring, holding his nose between his fingers.

A second *aviso* sounded before the torero chopped the next sword over the horns and deep into the shifting meat. But the blade went awry, its aim intoxicated by frenzy, missing the ripe organs and plunging into a lung. Instead of staggering, the bull coughed, vomiting blood, dumbfounded by what was happening to him.

The man in front yelled that his grandmother killed chickens better than this loco pimp did a bull. Next to him a man fired his cigar at the torero in disgust, or maybe at the bull, incensed at paying for such a poor performance. This afternoon, all things were possible.

Dragging its feet, the bull lagged along with steel filaments sticking up, bloodied from its midriff forward, looking for a way out. The mortified torero skipped along beside as if he were delivering papers and tried to wrench the sword free for one clean thrust before the third and last *aviso*. To have it blow with the bull still alive was a disgrace. By fumbling the kill even worse than he had the play, he was turning a dull display into a stinging fiasco.

A mercenary ran up and booted the animal in the testicles with all the energy he could deliver, eliciting an "Ole" from the stands.

"Oh, God," Rhiana cried, closing her eyes.

Still the bull did not go down. But he wavered, and vomited more, and didn't have the strength left to kick back. So the peon kept on booting until the torero, shamed even with himself in the end, stepped up to shoo him away.

Even a great writer or two had perverted his gifts by squandering praise on the *corrida*. Holland had read them and been unable to deny their skills, yet he wondered what they were so deprived of in themselves that they needed this. Another, more a sullen jock-sniffer than an authority on hostilities, had vented one of his interconnected holes to say that the bullfight was nine-tenths cruelty but a triumph even for that. Holland considered, given the man's limits, his proposition was quite likely obligatory in his cramped domain. But then, the rape of Europa was never as squalid as this.

A wineskin came down and slapped the bull's hide just as his legs set up a final trembling, betraying him at last. the great limbs shook like saplings in a gale until inevitably he keeled to his knees and over onto his side. The arena was enveloped in sighs of relief, followed immediately by hooting and ridicule, drowning out the last *aviso.*

"Finally," Max said, lifting praise to the heavens.

"He's not dead yet," Holland said.

"You must be joking," Max said, looking.

The bull, defiant now in death, was sweeping its head to and fro in the dirt, lifting an inch or two with excruciating difficulty.

Rhiana was staring resolutely into her lap.

Holland took her elbow. "Look at this," he said.

She didn't move.

"This is where the fight comes in," he said. "Look."

She shook her head.

"You can learn something here," he said. "You said you wanted to know."

She looked up, at him, then at the bull.

The bull had the great weight of its head raised, steadied by a horn.

"There's the fight," Holland said.

"Stop," Rhiana said.

The beast's lungs swelled like a bellows, fanning blood on the sand as he drowned inside.

"He's not ready yet," Holland said. "If there's any nobility, it's now."

"Stop it!" Rhiana implored him, her voice lost in the tumult around them.

Holland swept an arm across the gallery. "In his place they'd be long finished. All of them."

"I can't . . ." she said, and started to rise. But he held her by her arm.

"Anyone can quit," he said. "He won't give them that."

Another peon moved at the bull, his dagger ready to stab the occiput and sever the spinal cord. But the torero, one hand held aloft in a tawdry salute to himself now that his adversary was finished, waved him away from the fallen animal.

More hooting greeted him, but he was blind to it.

Then the beast, painted in his own colors, his tongue to the side, but serenely secure in his majesty, shuddered a last time.

Holland slumped.

"He's dead," Rhiana whispered.

"Amen," Max said.

Holland let go of her elbow.

"What did you expect he would do?" she said to him. "Invoke a miracle and get up to fight another day?"

Holland stared at the carcass. A tandem of mules were being chained to the bull.

"He beat the last *aviso,*" Holland said. "He shamed his tormentors."

"I'm not one of them," she said. "I'm not one of your executioners."

"Aren't you?" he said.

"Would you have me kill them for it?" she said. "Is that what you would do?"

But he was looking away, past her, to two men, Americans, one quite tall, who had walked down the steps and were standing in the aisle deliberately looking over the crowd.

Holland knew at once what they were about, knew the intent of their precaution, knew that their shirts were open at the waist in order to conceal firearms in their belts. The uniformity was unmistakable: stereotyped shepherds of some private sentry action.

The taller of the two moved his head imperceptibly. A man of middling stature and dense white hair came down the steps. He appeared to be preoccupied with the color of the sky overhead. One pace after him came a breasty, clean-waisted woman, a Victorian air about her in spite of the light print dress a bit too short for the current style. Behind her were two middle-aged banker types in somber vested suits, carrying closed umbrellas, in company with another pair of sentinels. Bringing up the rear was a slight angular man of olive complexion, Holland placing him as Italian-American. He also wore a loose shirt. They claimed empty seats in a row a dozen or so below Holland's vantage point.

Holland was keeping a practiced but inconspicuous eye on the group when Rhiana rose and brushed by him.

He went after her, saying quietly to Max, "Stay five minutes, then come to the car." Max pressed keys into his hand and resettled himself.

Rhiana was into the main corridor that circled the stadium before Holland caught up with her. Almost running, she had her hand over her mouth.

Most of the facilities were for men. The first they came to said "HOMBRE" on the door.

Holland stopped her there.

Inside, a lone man stood at a urinal. Holland took him by the arm and hustled him toward the door, apologizing in Spanish. The man cursed, resisting as well as he could under the circumstances, considering that his penis was loose and his bladder still emptying.

Holland pulled Rhiana in past the door at the same time he thrust the man out, then stood to prevent anyone entering.

The shocked victim of the exchange stood gaping at Holland while he fumbled with his pants, a neat trail printed up one pant leg. His size matched Holland's closely and he was obviously considering taking a swing. Holland put his hand on the man's shoulder to counter it, just in case.

"Please excuse me, my friend," Holland said in Spanish. "It was unforgivable, I know, but my wife is sick. This is the only place."

"Sick?" the man stuttered.

"You understand, I'm sure," he said, cupping the man's neck persuasively.

"Ah," the man said. "If your wife is sick, naturally I understand. You should have said so."

Holland motioned toward the ring, to where fresh waves of noise marked the beginning of another round in the program. "The match," he said. "You look like you know how women are about these things, right, my friend?"

"Seven kids," he said. "I should."

He looked sadly at his best Sunday pants.

"Let me at least buy you new ones," Holland said, tucking money under the strap of his suspender. The man plucked the bills free and counted them with hard calloused hands, showing satisfaction with a tilt of his head.

Another man scurried up to use the washroom. Before Holland could speak, the first man was anxiously explaining the problem. The new arrival stared stonily between the pair of perplexing obstructions and then hurried away.

Rhiana came out a few moments after, pale but collected, a tissue in her hand, her eyes still slightly moist in the corners. She avoided looking at the man.

"You alright?" Holland asked her.

She nodded.

Holland asked forgiveness of the man again, who saluted and quickly retook the washroom.

"I can't go back," Rhiana said, Holland barely able to decipher what she had uttered.

"We don't have to," he said, leading her toward the stairs. "Max is going to meet us at the car."

In the street they crossed the cobblestones and skirted the tired mariachi band and the clusters of vendors hawking dolls and tortillas and powdered bull horn. A harried policeman was ejecting another rowdy, chopping sharply at his shins with his truncheon, causing the rowdy to resort to an exaggerated flamenco step in his own defense.

At the car Holland left the doors ajar while they sat at either ends of the seat. Rhiana averted her face, crying without a sound, as though she didn't want him to know.

"Was it Moloch or the fight?" he said eventually.

Out of respect for her privacy, he didn't look at her.

"Him," she said, turning further away.

The clamor in the nearby arena was mounting again and could be heard distinctly.

"Oooh, I didn't want that to happen," she said, a tremor in her voice.

A wilted gnome on crutches hobbled up to Holland's open door. There was a distressed ladino set to his face, slits for eyes and an afro hairdo. Festooned on the shafts of his crutches were a multitude of STP decals.

"You wanna buy dope?" he said to Holland.

"Sir?" Holland said.

"Dope. You want any?" He was trying to get a better view of Rhiana.

"You got elephant?" Holland asked him, fending him off by raising a hand to the drip molding on the car's roof as an obstruction.

"Huh?" the gnome said, confused.

"You dig dirt?"

"What?"

"You know Mingtoydop?"

"You Yank?"

"Take a walk . . . or whatever," Holland said, making a move as though he were going to get out of the car.

The ladino stumped away in haste.

Putting his head back on the seat, Holland moistened his dry lips. An iced beer would have been pleasant, he reflected.

"What were you saying to him?" Rhiana wanted to know.

"Nothing," he said. "It's nothing."

But the byplay hadn't been for nothing. The double-talk was designed to find out who in hell the gnome really was. One thing for certain, Holland mused, the gnome was not what he pretended to be.

Things were beginning to become interesting, even lively in a way.

"I wish I knew what was going on," Rhiana said.

They waited for Max without talking further, each engrossed in separate speculations, he in anticipation, she in retrospect.

A few heavy raindrops pelted the windshield in a short flurry, then stopped.

There could be no mistaking that Max was acutely agitated as he stood behind the high wing chair and drummed his fingers on its leather surface.

The two of them were in his study. The room was panelled in oak and contained carved black walnut tables and groups of armchairs resting on a thick arbor green rug, the floor sunken two steps below the entrance.

Holland was inspecting some articles that obviously did not belong there: a dark plastic body-bag, some boxes of Remington handgun cartridges.

"You didn't have any trouble rounding any of it up?"

"No," Max said. "In the volumes I deal in, no one questions a couple of obscure entries hidden in a requisition taking forty pages."

"And none of this stuff could be traced to you personally?"

"Impossible," Max said. "The same for the car I rented you. Don't forget, my first consideration is Rhiana and Sarah. I won't see them compromised. But then, you thought of that before you enlisted them, did you not?"

"What about the gun?" Holland said.

"You were right, the importer didn't have one of that caliber in his inventory," Max said nervously, anxious to say his piece, "but he was able to locate one at a shop he supplies. It will be on my desk tomorrow, never fear."

"Good," Holland said, taking from his glass of beer. "You're a wizard, Max. These things aren't found just lying around."

"I have something I want to say," Max pressed.

"I can see that," Holland said.

"What you subjected Rhiana to this afternoon was terribly cruel," he said, his face flushed with indignation. "I'll never forgive it, and I want your word you won't do anything like that again."

"A bullfight shouldn't be so foreign to her—" Holland started to say.

"You're not a stupid man!" Max interrupted in a rising voice, provoked by Holland's immobility. "You know full well what I mean. She was in an arena just like that one when her father and her husband were butchered the same way they butcher livestock. Can you imagine what her fate would have been if the soldiers had gotten a good look at her? Can you imagine what she went through, knowing that? For day after day? And not knowing what had been done with her family? Did it occur to you what you were putting her through?"

"You're right," Holland said, extending the concession easily and without apparent reservation. "I'm sorry it had to happen that way."

"You'd do it over again," Max countered. "It was all so unnecessary. I could have identified Moloch for you."

"It wouldn't have been the same," Holland said evenly. "The traffic isn't there."

"Traffic?" Max said in disbelief. "Is that what you call the nightmare she's lived these past years? Traffic?"

"A figure of speech," Holland said.

"You see? You would do it again," Max accused. "I can't believe you didn't know what was happening. Even when she wanted to leave you wouldn't let her. If I hadn't been so worried by the trouble a scene might have caused us, I would have taken her out myself. You broke her heart keeping her in that place."

"Look," Holland said, "if a person has even the most modest powers of observation, you know the world will break their heart. I'm not the custodian of this woman's past, and I can do without the dramatics. She's supposed to be a stable adult. She'd better stick to the billing."

"You're an unholy son of a bitch, Holland," Max said. "Can you blame Rhiana for associating you with him?"

"Then she'll have the satisfaction of a consensus, won't she?" Holland said.

"I gave you credit you were unworthy of, no question of that," Max said. "I still say I could have pointed Moloch out without all of this being necessary."

"You know Moloch by being told who he is," Holland said. "Mistakes happen that way. Rhiana knows him because she's been there. It makes a difference."

"Good Lord," Max said. "Are you suggesting I could be mistaken about his identity? With what's at stake here? Why, that's preposterous. He's been here for years. I was born here. I know everyone. It's true I didn't know his profession before George informed me, but I could scarcely identify the wrong man to you now."

"You think not?" Holland said. "Sit down."

Max hesitated, but did as he was asked. Holland took a chair opposite.

"I'm going to explain something to you," he said, "then I want you to explain it to Rhiana, so I don't have to."

"Alright," said Max.

"Can I assume you've heard of 'The Jackal'?" Holland asked him.

"Of course I have," Max said. "Although the papers here refer to him more as 'Carlos' than as 'The Jackal.'"

"And you're familiar with the stories: The shooting of Sieff in London; the hand grenade in Le Drugstore in Paris, then the gunfight at his flat; the oil ministers' thing in Vienna, and like that?"

"Yes, some at least," Max said. "The first one I didn't—"

Holland cut him off. "That doesn't matter. The original 'Jackal's' name is Ilyich Ramirez Sanchez and the European press were the first to start calling him 'Carlos,' then switched it to 'The Jackal.' He was born in Caracas but now he operates out of either Bengasi or Algiers. His training as a terrorist came through the Russians."

"Go on," Max said expectantly.

"There are four different 'Jackals' that I know of, and one more I'm not sure of yet," Holland said. "One's a Lebanese, one's an Algerian, one a Dutchman, and one a Colombian. They're interchangeable. All use the same selection of passports and the same aliases, including Ramirez. They simply pass them back and forth as needed."

"What's interchangeable?" Max asked him. "The passports or the terrorists? You've lost me."

"All of it," Holland said. "Each was trained in the same institute about an hour outside of Moscow, and each assumes the tag of 'The Jackal' as it suits him or as he's directed. The same general description fits all round."

"I don't understand," Max said. "I thought there was only the one 'Jackal.'"

"Most on the outside do the same, and more than should on the inside. It was originally intended that way. The press are as predictable as the day is long. You should know that. This foolishness of them giving out romantic titles like 'The Jackal' and 'Carlos' is made to order for the terrorists. They suck it up and laugh all the way home."

"But, why? What's the purpose?"

"Headlines. Exposure. Manipulation. Dispatch. Brinksmanship," Holland said. "The public relations value is priceless. Think about it, but don't lose sight of the fact that the terrorists are ultimately financed by oil, and they're set up in the same manner as a multinational corporation: Personnel are transferable, and the gullibility of the public makes them the supreme pawns. One terrorist heads up a hijacking on Wednesday, the following Tuesday another masterminds a massacre halfway around the world. A 'Jackal' takes credit for both and becomes an infallible mystery man that the public lathers to read about. It becomes a highly imaginative adventure yarn, unless you know better. Catch one and the other hits you somewhere else an hour later. He not only seems unstoppable, but their cause does as well. The pattern is elementary and far from original, except to those who never tumbled to it."

"I never did," Max admitted, pondering the revelation. "These terrorists? Where does that leave you, or should I not ask that?"

Holland shrugged indifferently. "We're mutually exclusive of each other, if you want to know. Soul mates we're not. Throwing bombs and calling it a creative act is for whacko fanatics and hired cowboys like Ramirez. The point is, if you kill one of them you have to x-ray him and count his teeth and take his prints, and even then they can slip one by you if you're not careful. In this business you're seldom afforded the luxury of an autopsy."

"You'd hunt them, then?" Max ventured. "Or have?"

Holland said nothing.

"What you're getting at is that the man I know as Moloch may not be The Doctor at all," Max said. "Is that correct?"

"I'm explaining that the possibility is something I've had to take into account," Holland said, standing to retrieve what was left in the bottom of his glass. "And I've only done that because you've made it necessary."

Somewhere in the house a clock chimed seven.

Max slumped in his chair in dismay. "I see what you mean. What have you decided, then? Or are you not yet satisfied that he's The Doctor?"

"Moloch is The Doctor," Holland said, finishing his beer. "He's the one who's going down. If he gives me time, and an opening."

" 'Going down'?" Max said uncertainly. Then, "Oh, I see. Another 'figure of speech.' Yes, I suppose there isn't any way of knowing how much longer he'll stay. Not long,

I suspect. As I said, his appearance today was a rarity. He simply doesn't venture outside his estate more than once or twice while he's here. Often, not even that."

"You were mistaken about his visiting his sister in the mornings," Holland informed him. "The car comes to take her out to the estate, and then brings her back before lunch, every day for the past two weeks, maybe longer. He's never in it."

"That could be," Max said. "I've seen the car, that's all. Then you know she was the one accompanying him at the fight, not his wife?"

Holland nodded. "Do you know who the ones were in the Madison Avenue suits?"

"As far as I know, they work at the Embassy in some capacity, though I don't know what. It's likely I could find out if you think it's important."

"No," Holland said.

"Tell me," Max said, "this 'Jackal' named Ramirez, do you know him?"

"If I knew him it would follow that he knew me," Holland said, displaying an obvious lack of interest in the topic now. "And that wouldn't do, now would it?"

"No, I suppose not," Max reflected. "Nevertheless, the authorities can't seem to get close to him, which indicates to me that he must be pretty good."

"Not that he's so good," Holland said, starting to leave, "it's more a case of the rest being so bad; a universal standard we seemed to have adopted and come to worship. These days it's hard to get decent help. You could tell her that too, if you like."

He walked from the room, the body bag slung over one arm, the stray items in his hands.

Max shook his head.

A half-hour later Max and Rhiana stood at a bay window and watched Holland playing ball with Sarah on the patio behind the house. Rhiana's face was puffy from her abbreviated sleep. Max held a brandy.

The evening's light was beginning to withdraw, hurried to a degree by the dark clouds that had been hovering all day. Other than the brief sprinkling outside of the arena, the rain had held off until now.

Holland had two tennis balls, one of which he would release from each hand onto the bricks and up against the wall, catching them simultaneously again in each hand as they came back. When Sarah tried it, after learning to coordinate the tossing of the balls first, she was only able to concentrate on one ball at a time, invariably leaving the other to skitter by and be stopped by Holland. But she was determined to master the trick of it, performing the activity over and over, squealing exuberantly whenever she had a near miss.

"It's extraordinary the way he does that," Max marvelled. "I haven't seen it before."

"He's waiting for it to rain," Rhiana said.

"Sarah certainly gives the impression of liking him," Max said.

"The innocence of children is blessed," Rhiana said.

"And you don't?" Max said.

"He repels me," she said, staring from the window.

"That's graphic enough," Max said, raising his glass.

"He's the most insufferably irreverent person I've ever met, or ever care to," she said. Then she nodded toward the ball playing, "His attitude is just like that, as though it's a game he would rather not bother with. This morning he referred to Moloch's estate as the 'Enchanted Castle.' And after following the sister in the limousine to the estate and back, we spent the next couple of hours going from shop to shop looking for some antiquated American recordings he just had to have." She threw up her hands. "He wasn't able to find what he wanted so I have no doubt we'll do it all again. I'd be interested to know what bearing that could possibly have on what he's here for, and particularly when you say he's worried about running out of time."

"It is what tourists might do," Max suggested. "And it was for anyone to see."

"You should have been an attorney, Uncle Max," Rhiana said. "A public defender."

"Do you feel safe with him?" he asked her.

"Only if everything goes smoothly until we're gone," she said. "You should give that some consideration yourself. His kind look out for themselves and only themselves. If he cares about anything other than that, it escapes me."

"George doesn't think so, Rhiana, nor do Hector and Isabelle, and neither do I," he said. "But, what I meant was, do you feel threatened by him, being a woman?"

She shook her head surely. "No, don't worry yourself, Uncle Max. I won't pretend I didn't worry about it at first, but I think George's word was sound in that respect. In fact, he's considerate of our privacy, and especially Sarah's, I'll give him that. No, George may be deceived by Holland's vaunted prowess as an assassin, but he was right about his attitude with women."

"I'm relieved to hear that," Max said. "And, I must admit, I wasn't prepared for him to seem so passive. Were you?"

"Not at all," she said. "It throws me sometimes. That was Isabelle's reaction too, so we're not alone. Whether it's an act he puts on or not, he is convincing. George told me a story in confidence, one I'm sure he felt he was betraying his friend by telling, but the essence was that Holland was anything but a pacifist. The way I remember the phrase was: 'Cold-blooded, but with imagination,' whatever that was supposed to mean. Freud would have a wonderful time with our Mr. Holland."

"Or he would have with Freud," Max said wryly.

"He'd quite likely deal with Freud by shooting him," Rhiana said. "Don't be taken in by him. I'm afraid we'll find that his reach far exceeds his grasp."

"I won't make an issue of it," Max said. "But it's for certain I wouldn't want him after me. Your father told me one time, I think it was at your wedding, that you were relentless with the men in your life. I can see now that it was a keen observation, even for a father."

"My father said that?" Rhiana looked across at Max.

"He did," Max said. "Don't brood about this man and his place in the scheme of things, my dear, if I can presume to counsel. Let him do it any way he sees fit."

"He will anyway," Rhiana said. She sighed. "Alright, let's grant him the benefit of the doubt. Maybe he's just in a slump."

Max frowned at her. "Relentless. Did you say he was waiting for it to rain?"

"He wants me to drop him somewhere after the rain starts," she answered, "but he didn't say where. My guess would be the airport." Then, when Max appeared about to protest anew, "I know. Show him mercy."

Holland was standing now behind Sarah and throwing

the tennis balls against the wall in front of her one at a time, alternating so that she had to employ both hands. The tactic was working well, Sarah snatching the missiles with newfound dexterity.

She whirled to wave at her mother proudly. Rhiana applauded her and returned the wave.

"Do you think I look older than he does?" Rhiana asked.

"What?" Max scoffed. "I should say not. How old is he?"

"George said he thought about thirty-one or two," she said.

"Then he looks older," Max said, "and well he should. I had put him at more than that. Don't bother yourself, no one is about to think of you as anything but younger. But, honestly, Rhiana, it doesn't become you to slash at him with every opportunity."

At that moment the clouds finally burst and rain began to spot the glass. Holland and Sarah rushed toward the house.

Rhiana and Max moved away from the window, a tentative glance exchanged between them, Rhiana just then recalling Isabelle's caution about Holland's ability to read lips.

The rain was straight, steady, set for a long stay.

• 11 •

Where Holland wanted Rhiana to take him was an inhospitable dirt road that lay just short of a kilometer away from the flank of Moloch's estate, a proximity that Max had carefully related before he left the house, as well as providing the dark rubberized storm coat that he now cinched up tight at his neck. The squeezing of the garment barely helped stem the flow of water draining from his bare head and on down his neck.

He was cold and wet, hidden in the stand of trees surrounding the house.

The rain came down in a curtain that either burst into countless imperfect fountains or drilled deep into green.

The effect of the torrent caused most everything about to assume a vertical blend, even in the pitch of forest at night.

Before he had exited the car Rhiana had looked at the forbidding black forest by the side of the road and had shaken her head, skeptical of him finding his way anywhere near the estate. Sarah had offered the opinion that he might drown. Of the two, Sarah's observation was the more prophetic.

He sat crouched on his haunches and peered into the gloom at the dim outline of the walls. Hunkered down between the blade-like roots of a giant Ceiba tree, he had not moved more than his head since taking position in the natural cellar at ten minutes to ten. It was now past one A.M.

His place in the roots gave him view of the paved access to the estate, but the gate had gone unused tonight, not that he had anticipated it would be otherwise.

The closing in of mist was what he was waiting for.

When the mist grew to fog and billowed further from the trees he would be able to lurk with it, closer to the high stone walls and their garland of iron. Even now he thought he detected the lazy sweep of closed-circuit cameras atop the walls. Of that he would make certain before he left, although the cameras' existence did not really matter. In his own mind he had already ruled out any atetmpt at getting inside. Instead, he was doing what he had become accustomed to doing in Vietnam: watching, waiting for activity, seeking habits, hoping for the unexpected, feeling for the niche.

In part, there were similarities here to a piece of work he had done a year earlier in a sleepy village not far from Paris.

The man there had also occupied a house bristling with electronic devices, but he lived alone in splendid isolation, and therefore Holland did not have the added complication of bodyguards to contend with. By fixing a pressure gauge to the water pipe servicing the dwelling he was able to determine that the man took a long shower at the same time every afternoon, without variation. Once the pattern was confirmed it was a simple matter of watching the pressure gauge plummet momentarily on the chosen day, and then barging past the electronics and finishing the man in his shower stall. Leaving promptly, Holland had caught the Concorde to Washington and had seen the discovery of the body on the CBS evening news out of Miami. The job had afforded a certain intimate satisfaction from the standpoint of expediency.

But this was an animal of a different stripe entirely.

Actually, the soppy surroundings and oozing peat underfoot was not unlike Vietnam. The mist, the rain, the drooping foliage—force feeding itself. And the funk of shadows whose imagined movement could cut you with panic if you were not prepared to become one yourself.

On his first day over there he had christened it "Hobbit Country" and had called it that right up to the end, long after his CO had ordered him to stop using the reference because it supposedly undermined the morale of the team.

In Hobbit Country everyone hated the night. Everyone except the Viet Cong. In a Special Forces camp on the Cambodian border a well worn *Montagnard* scout had muttered a truth to Holland that rang with all the stainless fidelity that had somehow eluded the New Lamplighters and Philosopher Kings of the war and its legacy.

He said the V.C. would win because they wanted it more.

The *Montagnard* went on to distill the doctrine of the V.C. into the loveliest of pure elements: The V.C., clearly the largest and finest guerrilla army of modern times, recognized that the intolerance of the terrain was potentially as great an opposing force as was the combined Western military machine, and they made it their home.

The Americans and their fellows did just the opposite, predictably confronting the highlands and grottos and swilling jungle as another component of the enemy, fighting the land and making it their hell.

Any slick déjà vu of the Vietnam "conflict" was fermented in its bowels as far as Holland was concerned. When push came to shove the modified work ethic of the V.C. had prevailed in the muck and the bushes. Owners of The Truth employed in the cottage industry of baby rage blustered orations and scratched tomes of insights on the Great Conflict, sadly bankrupt though they were and though it failed to give them pause, old seers and new journalists who had trooped to "immerse" themselves like drumming ticket holders touching the glass in a snake-house, another war to fuck over after the fact, hype the ink with *brio* and pump the piece with zest, pop in a cherry on a plastic pick and wait for all to rise; the bravos will rain wild.

He spat, contributing to all the other teeming spit, and it was lost.

Shortly after his vignette to Holland, the *Montagnard* scout had had his brain bayoneted while on a night recon mission. Holland found him and lugged the body out. Thereafter he *loved* the jungle he had named Hobbit Country, and quickly learned to live in it. Through it all, and after, the love affair had kept him alive.

Now the fog was building and starting to swirl as it came out of the trees. A few more minutes.

Under his left arm the mass of revolver hung securely, the tip of the long barrel nudging his hipbone. When he got back to the hotel he would have to wipe the weapon thoroughly. But because the rubber lining of the coat did not allow his sweat to escape, oil would be necessary to take the saltiness from the metal. On Rhiana's side of the vanity he had seen a bottle of mineral oil which would suffice.

The dampness caused him to shiver, but he suspended the quaking by inducing relaxation into his limbs and shoulders, consciously willing it by keeping his tongue from pressing against the roof of his mouth. This last dodge always worked. An army doctor had instructed him that whenever he felt tension encroaching he was to pause and find if his tongue was glued to his palate. Inevitably it was. Keeping his tongue free lessened the tension, or maybe the purpose was served merely by the diversion of attention.

He rose slowly from his crouch. His knee cracked a lingering note as he straightened. Instead of conventional arm extensions the storm coat had only slashes that allowed the arms to stay concealed. Holland loosed the revolver and held it free under the garment.

He moved forward, each step taking minutes. He froze his eyes to the vague pan of the cameras, one on each end of the wall and another fixed in the center. Whenever on glass swept away, he moved, keeping a tree betwen himself and the other cameras. It was unlikely the cameras could separate him from his surroundings in any event, but there was no need to tempt them.

Closing the distance to the wall by five meters took a a full half hour until the gap was enough to suit him. The cameras could be distinguished now from his position behind another mature Ceiba. So could a chest-high erection of barbed wire a couple of meters out from the wall.

He had been standing in place for an estimated twenty minutes when he first heard the car approaching, and then saw the dim fingers of the headlights creep up the nearby road and stop at the gate.

A lone occupant emerged from the battered Fiat, leaving the engine running and the lights on, going deliberately in front of the headlights to face the gate, then hurrying back to the shelter of the car.

Holland slipped his arms from the confines of the storm coat and held the gun down and forward in front, ready to be raised and fired.

A full five minutes elapsed before the gate parted a few inches and the bulky form of the tall bodyguard came forward, clad in a raincoat and a wide-brimmed hat. The gate closed and the two men talked in the rain beside the Fiat.

Holland wondered that they didn't sit in the car out of the elements, then thought that it was perhaps a fortunate sign they did not. If brief, the conversation could indicate that the subject was of limited importance. On the other hand, a hurried meeting could carry the scent of urgency, considering that it was the early hours of the morning.

The man from the Fiat spread his hands noncommittally now and then, his listener standing impassively with his head lowered and his back to Holland. Only once did his breath rise in the air.

Rain was running into Holland's eyes and down his arms to rise in beads on the stark matte of the gun.

The verbal exchange was completed in short order.

The Fiat whined as the driver reversed the car from the gate and went off down the road. Only then did the bodyguard go back through the gate.

Holland eased the revolver under the storm coat and gently wiped it clean with his shirttail. When fifteen minutes had passed he began inching his way back.

The man in the Fiat had been the same one who had tried to pose as a dope dealer outside the plaza.

Slogging through the undergrowth, Holland considered it interesting that the imposter had moved so ably without benefit of crutches.

Rhiana was sitting up in bed, Sarah sleeping soundly beside her when Holland quietly entered the hotel room. Water continued to drip from the slick surface of his storm coat.

Rhiana reached for a bathrobe and got out of bed, taking care not to disturb Sarah. She looked at Holland in the darkness.

"You look as though you've been swimming," she whispered.

"Not quite," he said. "Where's the key to the other room? I don't want to wake Sarah."

Rhiana went to the bed table and returned with the key. "You're shivering," she said.

He nodded toward the door connecting the rooms. "I'll open the door on the other side. When you hear it, open this one."

Sarah raised her head, taking a moment to focus on Holland. "Did you walk in the woods?" she asked him.

"Uh-huh," he answered. "You were right, babe, it wasn't a good idea."

"I told you, Mr. Ace," she said sternly.

"Sarah . . ." Rhiana put a finger to her lips.

"Bring your bottle of mineral oil and my shaving stuff," Holland said to Rhiana before returning to the corridor.

"We're going into the other room to talk, dear," Rhiana told Sarah, "but I won't be long. If you're worried or can't sleep, just open the door and come in."

"I'm too tired, mummy," the child said, laying her head back.

In the adjoining room Holland tossed the storm coat onto the bathroom tiles and removed the shoulder holster and gun. His shoes squelched when he walked.

Rhiana entered with his robe and the oil. She looked at the gun. "Did you use that?"

"No," he said. "Were you sleeping?"

"You didn't really expect I would be, did you?"

He shrugged, and commenced drying the gun with a towel.

"Wouldn't it make more sense to dry yourself first?" she said. "Before you come down with pneumonia."

He supposed her concern more accurately reflected the question of his ability to continue, rather than the actual condition of his health. But he set the gun down.

"I'll draw you a bath while you get out of those wet clothes," she said, handing him the robe.

He stripped completely and donned the robe while she ran the bathwater. When she came out he was once again drying the revolver, the cylinder open, the cartridges on the bed.

"How did you get here?" she asked him.

"I hopped the back of a cattle truck when it turned a corner," he said.

"That explains the aroma," she said.

"Yeah, it's a bitch, ain't it?" he said, shivering again.

She intrigued him with a trace of a smile. Her smile, even in restraint, was a moment of perfect grace seen all too seldom. Sarah had it too.

"If I can make a suggestion," she said, "it would be that you get in the bath right away. You can close the curtain and tell me what you have to say while you're getting warm."

He indicated the bathroom, saying, "They're all connected by a common vent that works wonders as an amplifier. We'll talk here."

"Did something happen?" she said, glancing involuntarily to the wall beyond which Sarah was sleeping. "Is Sarah alright in there?"

"She's fine," he said.

"Then take your bath first," she said. "You should know you can't risk getting that cold and that wet your first few days in a foreign country." She put her hand out for the gun, "I'll finish that while I'm waiting."

"It has to be done right," he said. "I'll do it after."

"The gun is wet," she said, leaving her hand extended. "Cleaning and oiling a gun isn't unknown to me, Mr. Holland."

"How's that?" he said.

"My husband was a ranking trap shooter in our country," she said. "It was one of the things we did together."

He handed the gun over.

"And it's Holland," he reminded her.

"Holland," she said.

"Don't put the oil on with a towel—" he started to say.

"I know, it leaves lint," she said. "I'll use a tissue."

When he tried the brimming tub he found the water almost too hot to bear and had to ease himself down a bit at a time. Finally covered to his chin, his irritation dissipated, the chill with it. He came out of the bathroom feeling measurably improved.

"I want you to think about taking Sarah and going home this morning," he said, toweling his hair vigorously.

She turned from the window. "What happened?"

"You remember the ladino on crutches outside the plaza? The one trying to pass himself off as a dope dealer?"

She nodded.

"He turned up at Moloch's a few hours ago," he said.

"What does that mean?"

"I don't know," he said, going to the bed to inspect the revolver. He found it had been thoroughly oiled, wiped clean, and reloaded.

"What do you think it means, then?" she said.

"It means there are over a million people in this city and we've been here two days. I think it pretty well rules out a coincidence, don't you?"

"Why do you say he was pretending? How do you know?"

"He wasn't even close to being a doper," Holland said. "He should have been embarrassed."

"If you saw him there he must work for Moloch."

"Not necessarily. Maybe on a piecemeal basis."

"Stop fencing," she said. "You're not telling me anything."

"He's likely a part of the information apparatus, part of the street scene that keeps its eyes and ears open for anything that doesn't fit. If you really want to know, I figure him to be a narc with the D.E.A."

"I don't know what that is," she said.

"A narcotics agent with the Federal Drug Enforcement Administration."

"But that's American. How in the world can you connect him to that so readily. He was a ladino. I saw him."

"He was," Holland acknowledged, "but his English was perfect. So perfect he had to work at his own accent. And that denim shirt was made Stateside, not here, even though the same company has a factory here. Same for the jeans. What you don't understand is the DEA narcs are like . . . rectums; they're everywhere, and especially around the nearest toilet. This place is just the kind of toilet they thrive in."

"I still don't see what he would have to do with Moloch," she said, it being apparent the puzzle was assuming proportions she had not prepared for.

"If I'm right about the narc he's just a worm in the network Moloch can call on if there's something he wants to know, or vice versa if they think there's something he should know. The same applies to the resident CIA, naturally, and the police, militia, what have you."

"But there hasn't been anything for them to suspect," she said. "Has there?"

"Moloch saw you rush out of the arena."

Her hand shot to her mouth. She swung away from him to face the window.

"You're absolutely sure there's no way he would know you?" he asked her gently.

"It just isn't possible," she said, shaking her head. "I swear."

"In that case, Moloch may have thought you just couldn't handle the bullfight. He still wouldn't leave it to chance. The narc may have been standing around, which is what they usually do, and Moloch or one of his gunsels sent him outside to check on us. If so, there's nothing to get worked up about."

"Then why do you want us to leave?"

"I don't want you to do anything but decide for yourself. That's the way it is; you make your own decisions."

"You lip-read," she said. "Could you make out the conversation you saw?"

"A word or two," he said. "Nothing of consequence."

"It's possible the ladino took it upon himself to see who we were, isn't it?" she accused. "And when he found out he went straight to Moloch to warn him. That's what you're not saying, isn't it?"

"You're reaching," he said. "The shooting would have started if they knew anything like that. At the least they would have tried to follow us. They didn't. Nobody's been watching. What could they have found even if they'd looked?"

"You're the expert," she returned.

"Zip," he said. "The DEA is the same as the CIA and all the others, they're lucky to find their own assholes with both hands and a flashlight."

He was standing beside her at the window. The city before dawn was soot colored, pockets of leaded pigment determined not to succumb to day.

Holland anticipated that if she stayed at the window he would relish seeing her face in the breaking sun.

"Is Sarah in any danger?" she asked him without looking his way.

"No."

"Will it help if we stay?"

"That depends. I don't know."

"What are you going to do tomorrow . . . I mean, today," she said, correcting herself.

"Watch Moloch, or his dogs, or his sister, or whatever moves," he said. "One of these days, maybe today, maybe tomorrow, Moloch's going to leave again. People often break their patterns just before going away. He might."

"George said you would only do it here. If Moloch leaves before you have a chance, the whole thing's off?"

"Either that or I have to do something to prevent him leaving. It would go a long way if I knew when that was."

He left her, taking his shaving kit into the bathroom. She remained at the widow.

The blade in his safety razor was dull and he was annoyed with himself for forgetting to get replacements. The edge caught and left thickets of stubble untouched.

He glanced out at Rhiana. Her profile had a buttery gilt in the new sun. "You have any razor blades?"

"I don't use them," she said. But she entered the bathroom and took the razor from his hand. She extracted the blade and took a water glass from the fixture over the basin, then pressed the thin wafer of steel against the curved inner surface of the glass and began to turn one against the other.

Puzzled, he asked her what she was doing.

"The glass sharpens the blade enough to use," she said. "It's something my father taught me. I used to do this for him when he couldn't afford to buy new ones."

"When was that?" he said, absorbed at watching the improvised honing.

She finished and handed him the blade. "I can't remember."

In the razor the rejuvenated edge cut nearly as well as it had when new.

"Cleaning guns and sharpening razor blades," he said, catching her reflection in the mirror and giving her a droll squint. "You're a bloody marvel."

She went back to the window.

He splashed the remains of soap away and dried his face. "I could always shoot you along with Freud."

She reacted, glancing at him, then shaking her head.

Sarah came in from the other room, rubbing her eyes. She bumped into the bed.

Holland threw the towel over the gun before she saw it.

"I can't sleep, mummy," she said. "Can I stay up?"

"Yes, dear," Rhiana said. "Maybe we'll go for a walk before breakfast."

"Will Holland come?"

"Sure," Holland said.

"Will you tell me about the fish again?" she asked him, then she said to her mother, "He has a pet fish. Did you know that?"

Rhiana glanced at Holland doubtfully. "No, I didn't know that, but I'm beginning to think anything's possible."

"I'm glad we don't have this room," Sarah said, looking around critically. "It smells."

Rhiana turned to Holland. "We'll stay another day. Does that suit you?"

"Up to you," he said.

"I believe you made that point," she said.

"First thing I want to do this morning is follow the limousine," he said. "But we'll do it from the beginning, from Moloch's place to the sister's, and see if they're in the habit of making any stops on the way. After that we'll play the tourist for a while. Whatever you and Sarah want to do."

"Don't forget your recording," she said deliberately.

"That too," he said. "It isn't a recording, by the way, it's a cassette of Glenn Miller band music."

Rhiana walked from the room.

Sarah watched her go, then went to Holland.

He bent nearer.

She looked down and rested her hand where her stomach protruded against her nightgown, the swell normal for a child of her age. "I think I'm pregnant," she said gravely.

Holland was helpless to keep his face straight, but fought the urge to laugh. "I don't think that's possible, Sarah."

"You're not a doctor," she pointed out.

"No, I'm not. Shouldn't you tell your mother?"

"I'm afraid to. Mummy hadn't planned on this."

"What are you going to do?" he asked her, uncertain whether she actually thought the condition plausible or was simply having her fun. Of the latter he knew she was fully capable.

"I thought I'd wait to see if it gets worse," she said with perfect logic. "What do you think?"

"Good idea," Holland said. He lifted the gun, still concealed in the towel, and led her in to join Rhiana.

• 12 •

The brown Mercedes-Benz limousine moved sedately down the broad *Avenida* in the early morning traffic, slanted sunlight glinting imperiously from smooth paint and tinted glass.

In passing, the automobile exuded an ethereal aura that was compelling and at the same time veiled, the shaded windows of the sanctum within rebuffing inquisitive onlookers as surely as the panels of a hearse would. Those coming alongside to gape saw only their own reflections cast back.

Automobiles of such palpable opulence were seldom seen in Guatemala, a country where wealth was held tightly by a handful. But if one were to be seen at all it would be here, in the preserve of embassies. This was away from the beat of the city, set apart from the vast underbelly of teeming bodies, from those industrious in endurance, who wore brilliant colors to fool the ulcerous poverty; and children who seemed to spill from sluiceways . . . a boy of seven, if that, doing rope tricks in the street for food, all he knew, and the hordes passing without pause or a centavo for the dish . . . girl children as young who perform fellatio in doorways, for food, to live another day . . . all abandoned like bad luck puppy litters . . . deserted to the streets . . . sleeping there . . . more than two million in Latin America . . . every day a celebration of survival. Far from embassies.

At one of the foreign missions, appropriately the largest and most outwardly imposing, the limousine mounted the low curb to stop beside a sentry in a braided military uniform. The driver's window lowered only enough to allow the officer to look in at the occupants, then closed abruptly.

The limousine hummed softly on into the protective womb of the embassy compound, a world removed from the crass jangle of the street.

Seconds later a year-old Chevrolet with a rental sticker in the corner of the rear window went past without notice.

Inside the enclave two young men with college haircuts and doublebreasted blazers came forward to assume positions on either side of the limousine, even before it had come to rest. One of them opened the driver's door and nodded curtly. Brian Randolph unhinged his huge frame from behind the wheel to tower over the man of only average stature.

Randolph ignored the courtesy of the nod, and did the same when the operative on the other side offered a like greeting.

"Mr. Buggs is waiting in his office, sir," the first man said.

"Waterston?" Randolph asked, looking the grounds over carefully.

"Him too," the man answered. He tilted his head towards the passenger compartment of the limousine. "The gentleman can go right up. Everything is in order."

Randolph opened the driver's door, leaned in and said something, closed the door again, then walked alone into the building. The pair of operatives stayed where they were. So did the four indistinct outlines inside the limousine.

In an office on the second floor Deputy Station Chief Paul Buggs was thumbing through folders in a filing cabinet.

Buggs was an average looking covert action specialist in the Western Hemisphere Division of the Clandestine Services Latin American division. His red hair was in a Haldeman brushcut. Two of his fingers were stained a nicotine yellow. He was young to have a son in the Army Intelligence Corps and a grandson in the Panama zone. Every morning when he entered the office he habitually removed his jacket, loosened his tie, and rolled up his shirt sleeves, remaining that way until he undressed at night. Recently he had reconciled with his wife after the latest separation, and had purchased a three-bedroom rancher in the Tivoli suburb south of the city.

Boredom had overtaken him years before. Whenever it rubbed him raw his wife left for Utica. Last night she'd said she could no longer stand Guatemala. This time it was because the donkey shit made the car tires smell when she left the windows open.

He flipped a switch on the desk. An image of Brian Randolph materialized on a miniature screen built into the desk.

Randolph was clowning for the camera, his tongue projecting and a finger thrust up his nose.

Buggs pressed a button in the desk's top drawer. The door opened, accompanied by the whir of an electric motor.

Randolph sauntered in with a lopsided grin.

"This where I get my passport picked?"

"You've already done your nose," Buggs returned.

"Gettin' much these days?" Randolph asked.

"Randolph, what the fuck . . . ?" Buggs said irritably. "What's with this James Bond cartoon crap every time you come in here? You're expecting to find Ernie Lynch hiding in the closet of a fucking Section House?"

Randolph settled himself on the edge of the desk and unwrapped a fresh stick of gum, drawing it past his grinning teeth a short bite at a time. "Who the hell's Ernie Lynch?"

Buggs rolled his eyes. "Ernesto Che Guevara. Maybe you've heard of the man by his stage name?"

"Oh, yeah, that Ernie," Randolph said, assuming a scholarly stance. "Isn't that the cracker who invented the steam stapler and then got pissed when the capitalist pigs wouldn't finance production? That the dude? He's dead."

"No shit?" Buggs said, feigning astonishment. "I'd better get it on the wire so's the brass knows. Here they've been thinkin' they planted him years ago. You've been on the outside too long, Randolph. The way I hear it, The Company went right in the toilet as soon as you left."

"That's the way I hear it too," Randolph said, reaching for the switch and looking into the TV screen at the now empty outer office. "When you figure I took all my training by correspondence course, where does that leave you career turkeys?"

"Goddamn it, Randolph," Buggs said, a shower of spittle flying. "Why couldn't you just have told us what time he was comin' in? 'Sometime between nine and two o'clock, maybe,' doesn't cut it, you know. That means Waterston has to sit on his prat the whole morning, right through the goddamn lunch hour, waitin' for The Man. And why couldn't you just bring him straight on up? Jesus Christ, this security wrap can get outta hand sometimes. It's the end of the month; we've all got our grease to pay, and Waterston's got the big guys to look after. You used to do it. You know how it works."

"So they get their payoffs a day late," Randolph said, scanning the ceiling and walls. "What're they gonna do, start the revolution without you?" He pointed to a vault door in the corner, squeezed between an incongruous plastic plant and a substantial duplicating machine. "You sure Ernie isn't in there?"

"It's the commo room, for fuck sakes," Buggs said. He strode to the corner and pushed the duplicator out of the way, then yanked the heavy steel door open. "You've seen it before."

Randolph looked inside without bothering to enter. The walls were lined floor to ceiling with shelves swollen to a precarious state by files. There were no windows, only two fluorescent lamps. A young man sat in the center of the cramped space, surrounded by communications equipment, earphone and microphone harness on his head.

"Hi there, sports fans," Randolph said to him. "What's the score?"

The commo man gave him a stunned stare. "Who're you?"

"It's alright," Buggs said, slamming the door shut and pulling the duplicator back in place.

"Have you ever wondered what'd happen to your commo man if there's a fire in this hut?" Randolph said.

"He'd burn, baby," Buggs stated flatly. "Along with everything he knows and everything in the room. Neat and tidy."

"That wholesome attention to detail always thrilled me when I was on the payroll too," Randolph said. He crossed to the desk, lifted one of the phone receivers and handed it to Buggs. "Tell Waterston The Man is here, and tell him I want a look-see first."

"Randolph . . ." Buggs groused, tapping the receiver into his palm impatiently.

"Go ahead," Randolph said. "Humor me."

Buggs punched a button and spoke without the aid of the receiver. "Your morning appointment is here, Chuck."

"Excellent," came the response. "I'll be right out."

"Uh, hold on, Chuck," Buggs hurried to say. "He's still downstairs. Mr. Randolph would like to pop in and . . . uh . . . say 'hello' first."

"What . . . ?" Waterston said, a shifting pause, then, "Oh, well, certainly. By all means."

Buggs released the button and replaced the receiver, stepped from behind the desk and tendered Randolph toward Waterston's door with an exaggerated bow and flourish of his arm.

"What's he worried about?" Randolph said. "He got some morning rose with her legs spread all over the desk?"

"That's more what we expect from you and Crosetti," Buggs said, his face contorted for emphasis. "Those goddamn pestholes you guys hang out in, it'll drop off on you one of these days."

Randolph laughed as he went to the door of Waterston's office. "You never did have any class, Buggs."

He opened the door and leaned in.

Charles "Chuck" Seymour Waterston was sitting with his hands spread flat on his desk, waiting compliantly.

A tall man who had aged "gracefully," as Margaret Moloch had commented once, Waterston had wide set eyes, a strong nose, and a fine physique for a man of his age—an age that put him only six years from retirement. On the debit side was a yarmulke of bare skin on his head, vainly camouflaged by a thatch of hair swept up and over from a parting near his left ear. Various concussion prints of angry veins on his cheeks and nose testified to an established diet of Scotch whiskey.

In the trade he was one of those known as a "marker" —someone who was marking time until his retirement checks were poised for processing.

His desk top was a void except for the phone center. Behind him, propped against the flagstaff, was a golf bag and clubs.

"How are you this morning, sir?" Randolph asked him, smiling pleasantly.

"Terrific, Randolph." Waterston beamed. "How's yourself? You're looking well. Business as usual, I expect."

"And how's the family, sir?"

"Super. Kind of you to ask," Waterston said. "Off to parts south again, eh, son?"

"I wouldn't know that, sir," Randolph said.

"No, no, of course you wouldn't," Waterston said, scrambling as though he had let slip a weighty indiscretion. "Come in, Randolph, come in."

"Thank you, sir, that won't be necessary," Randolph said, his survey completed. "Everything seems in order."

"The gentleman shouldn't fret," Waterston said, arching an eyebrow as figment testimony to his Station's efficiency. "We run a tight ship here."

"Well, then, if you'll wait here I'll bring the gentleman up," Randolph said, backing out the door and closing it behind him.

As he swept past Buggs, now running copies on the duplicator, Randolph said, "Tight as the Titanic."

The smile both men traded was a glint of amusement between men who habitually used the same side of the street and knew they had the run of it.

Clement Moloch did not care for Chuck Waterston. The relationship, purely professional by nature, was tolerated by Moloch solely because Waterston had been appointed

Station Chief and there were sporadic occasions when he simply could not avoid contact with the man.

Moloch's dislike was compounded by the reality that he must depend—at least in small part—on Waterston and his gaggle of operatives for some aspects of his own security. He thanked his stars that those times were infrequent, as the man was incompetent. Worse, he didn't give a damn that he was, deluding himself that those around him were not cognizant of the fact.

Sitting across from him, Moloch had the satisfaction of knowing very nearly all there was to know about Chuck Waterston, which was immensely more than Waterston could presume to learn in return. A committed "paper pusher," Waterston had become part of enough major disasters to ensure his flaccid but steady advancement in The Company. An alumnus of the Bay of Pigs, the four abortive coup attempts in Argentina in 1962, and the attempted "destabilization" of half a dozen countries during his tenure, he had only survived the recent sacrificial purge of old-liners by the adroit blackmailing of certain of his superiors. Moloch possessed the ultimate power to veto Waterston's appointment to this Station but had bestowed his blessing out of sheer expediency, knowing that anyone else they would assign to the post would be from the same school, picked from the legions of bureaucrats who made endless mincing strides in the wastelands of mediocrity.

The truth was that Paul Buggs ran the Station anyway, and while he was somewhat short of inspired, he had been able to muddle through two decades of widely scattered Station postings without the roof having fallen in on any of them.

"I would have been happy to come to your house as usual," Waterston said to open the conversation.

"I was feeling cooped," Moloch said, sighting the framed and officious portraits in a place of prominence behind Waterston's chair: Richard Nixon, Henry Kissinger, Gerald Ford, all there against regulations. Jimmy Carter should have ruled the wall; but the small anarchy was Waterston's homage to the halcyon days when The Company had "really been able to cook"—as Waterston often told his golfing buddies.

Other than that the office was typical of links of others in the chain: One wall done in burlap or cork, the rest painted something imaginative like Saigon Sunset Saffron, and a set of leather chairs and sofa, a globe, a paper shredder disguised as part of the liquor cabinet. The ghost of a thousand insurance offices.

"Turner tells me the bullfights were not up to much of a standard," Waterston said, sipping his first Scotch of the day.

"It's the off season," Moloch said, "the time for amateurs." He had fully expected Waterston to be vexed at not being invited, especially as two of the embassy staff were taken along. Let the twit stew.

Moloch had come here knowing the time was ripe to foreclose on Waterston, and he was not about to dally with the niceties.

"Just as well I missed it then," Waterston said. "How is your lovely wife, Clement, if I might ask?"

The fool had been determined from the outset to use first names and Moloch had been equally determined they would not. Alas, Waterston had prevailed out of sheer perverse obstinacy, but Moloch was damned if he was going to stoop to the absurd corruption of "Chuck." Why Americans delighted so in fracturing their own given names, adopting a slovenly pidgin that an adult should have long since been weaned of, was beyond him, yet the same adults persisted in saddling their offspring with further lines of tasteless tinsel.

"You might," Moloch said. "Margaret is very good. She mentioned that she was thinking of inviting you round to tea while I'm gone. She asked if I objected."

"Very gracious of her," Waterston said, plucking a golf club—an iron—from the bag and holding the shaft to his mouth as he would a chicken leg. "Would you mind?"

"I encourage Margaret to have her own outlets," Moloch said, selecting the phrase with care.

Waterston's mental processing did a stutter step that was patently easy for Moloch to read.

"Every wife whose husband is afield as often as you should be so fortunate, Clement. Let me commend you. I'll tell Jude this evening at dinner. She'll look forward to it."

"Mrs. Waterston wasn't mentioned," Moloch said.

"Oh?" Waterston's mind backed up, feeling around for the trail.

Moloch thought him an awfully stupid man, even for a spook. What did he need, a barge pole?

Waterston, riddled with galloping uncertainty, knew there was a precarious, even dangerous geometry to what was being said, or not said.

The gulf of silent tacking went on.

"Nor was Mrs. Simon," Moloch said.

Waterston nearly dropped the golf club. The talk *was* taking a nasty turn. He stared wide-eyed at Moloch, but then his focus assumed a curious gravity and plummeted into some unseen chasm in the floor.

"Mrs. Simon?" Waterston said tentatively, but tossing his Scotch back with a swaggering virility.

"Mrs. Anita Simon, wife of one of the attaches with the Canadians," Moloch said patiently, truculence in repose. "I have always thought that lusting after the ladies at our age was unbecoming to all concerned. Chasing about in need of a coupling is for adolescents, not waning lotharios, Waterston. However, I suppose one must recognize that a certain colonization is inevitable when boys and girls find themselves in exotic saunas far from home."

Waterston hesitated, then thumped the carpet with the iron and guffawed loudly. "I only lust in my heart, Clement. I'm flattered you think I'm capable at my age, but I assure you I'm innocent."

Waterston's hearty laugh rolled around the room, the carefully coiffed hair beginning to slip to the stern. He stopped laughing when he settled on Moloch's poisoned demeanor, and sniffed the lucidity of contempt.

"You have me at a disadvantage, Clement. Is this a riddle or a battle of wits?"

"Whatever it is, you seem to have come unprepared," Moloch observed dryly.

"Now see here," Waterston said, slamming the iron back into the bag. "If you're insinuating there's anything improper between myself and the lady I'm going to be damned ticked off I can tell you."

"Be quiet, or you'll miss the point," Moloch said. "You've been bedding Mrs. Simon for months now. Four, to be exact. You grapple in the Hotel Florida every Tuesday and Friday at two thirty. Five weeks ago Mrs. Simon lost her wedding ring in the shower drain and the bloody hotel had to discreetly return it to her. This is the same lady you had an affair with in Bangkok in 1971, terminated by an abortion and your transfer. Tell me, did you arrange her husband's posting here?"

"It just happened," Waterston said, sulking. "Well, not exactly. Her husband's been poking one of the Italians; when she was moved here Simon put in for his own transfer."

"It's a rather sweaty circus, isn't it, this world of diplomacy and spooks," Moloch said, enjoying a flexing of the language when he knew the other could not reciprocate.

Waterston went to the bar and poured a Scotch.

"The Russians use the same hotel, did you know?" Moloch let drop. "For the same thing?"

Waterston paused with his drink half raised. Then, like a dog repelling water, he shook his head. "That can't be. I've never seen any Ruskies there."

"I suggest that keeping your eyes peeled was not foremost in your mind when visiting the Florida," Moloch said. "The Russians have been taking their sluts there for years. Did the clerk always give you the same room?"

"As a matter of fact . . ." Waterston started to say, ensnared by his own recollection.

"Use your loaf, dear boy."

"Eh?" Waterston muttered.

"Your loaf," Moloch repeated, tapping his temple with a squat finger. "Their Branch Chief has an accommodation. The rooms on that floor have a wire leading directly back to the Russian House. Every squeak of the springs, every slobber and grunt goes down on tape. They bugged the place so they would know what their ops were talking about. Then, to their great delight, in walks the leader of the opposition, his lady on his arm. Do you doubt the clerk received a fine bonus for steering you on the proper course, Waterston?"

Waterston stood where he was, mouth gaping, traumatized at hearing what every Station Chief does not ever wish to hear. "Does head office know about this?" he asked, his voice laced with dread.

Moloch put his elbows on the desk and bridged his

fingers. Adept with all manner of thumbscrew, he knew the power of knowledge was boundless when judiciously applied. "If they did, your blackmail of last year would be in danger of a turnabout, wouldn't you say?"

Ice rattled in Waterston's glass. He put the glass down. "I swear on my mother I didn't say anything in there . . . all we did . . . we didn't talk much . . . never about business. I'm a professional. She thinks I'm an officer with the AID program."

"I have heard the tapes," Moloch said quietly. "They were made available to me on my last trip."

A trembling wormed into Waterston's lower lip. He swept a hand over his head without thinking. His hair reared up and hung askew from the side of his head like an inverted crow flap. He didn't realize, and so left it. "You've heard them? But how . . . ?" Then, out of chaos, remembering what he should never have forgotten, "You work for the Ruskies too."

"Work for them?" Moloch said. "No more than I *work* for your people. If I work, it's for mankind, dear boy. There is an old Roman-law maxim that the security of the state is the highest law; the Romans knew well how to cover their backsides. My work, you see, rises above your petty differences—all imagined, I promise you. You despise them, do you?"

"Head office told me you've worked for them," Waterston said, attempting a feeble offensive. "They don't like it."

"Ignorance is the sister of lies, as they say. A Dostoevski could have flicked a dozen like you from the dirt under one fingernail. You should face his firing squad, Waterston."

"He's their Division Chief?"

"Dear God," Moloch exclaimed, throwing his hands in the air. Then, glaring, he said, "No, that's a gentleman named Tolstoy."

"If you heard the tapes you know I never talked business with her," Waterston said.

"Bully for you," Moloch said. "You happen to be quite right, your adventures seem to have been confined to acrobatics."

Waterston hung his head. Clutching though at this last snippet of solvency, he reached hazily for his glass, halted, withdrew the trembling hand. "Then you've got to tell them that. It's my only chance."

"I'm not a Russian grain buyer, I don't want it all," Moloch said. "What we're going to do, you and I, is strike a bargain."

Waterston hurried to the desk, intent on salvage. "What do you want?"

"Head office hasn't heard of this episode, doesn't even know the tapes exist. I'm prepared to keep it that way," Moloch granted. "But first things first. It's true you didn't spill any secrets while rutting around between your lady's legs. However, not long ago you played through—to turn a phrase—in a momentous scuttle. Rather disconcerting for the lass, you know, with her not being near finished, and you then tried to make amends by explaining your need to dash to the airport to confirm some important arrangements. If you'll recall, those arrangements were that The Company plane be ready to take me to Buenos Aires—for 'work' to be performed for you, not the Soviets. Needless to say, you piqued their curiosity. From there it was elementary for them to satisfy their itch. No harm done. This time."

Waterston sank to his chair, feeling furtively behind before he placed his buttocks.

Whereupon Moloch bolted upright in a fury and banged the desk with a tight fist, "Except that I bloody well won't have it! Do I have your attention, you bloody two-a-penny fool!"

Waterston rolled his chair in retreat, transfixed by the severity of his taunter.

"I won't have anyone knowing my movements," Moloch said. "I won't tolerate it. Fortunately, this time the ear belonged to those equally interested in my welfare, but if there were a next time it might not be. Don't concern yourself for me, Waterston. I'm destined for a natural death. It is for yourself you should be quaking. I would take enormous pleasure with you. It would be wise if you didn't tantalize me further."

Waterston's chair now lurched to the side, as if to blunt the threat, his features varnished a pale haunting misery. "I've heard," he said.

Moloch's mouth wrapped itself in scorn. "You've heard," he mimicked acidly. "You cross me up, Waterston, and

I'll put your parts in so many places it will take a year's rain to reach them all. From this day you'll leave all arrangements to Buggs. You'll know nothing."

"But I've already contacted our people in Uruguay," Waterston protested. "They're ready for you. The plane is waiting. The procedure was extremely tight."

"But that was to be two days from now. I've altered my plans," Moloch said. "I'll leave sometime between now and then. Maybe in an hour. Maybe in forty-eight. I'll go through Buggs and he won't know when until Randolph comes to tell him. You'll stay out of it. Is that clear?"

"I'll do anything you say," Waterston said eagerly.

"Secondly, you'll keep your randy bloody attention away from Claire," Moloch thundered, again assaulting the desk top. "She tells me you've phoned her a number of times since you met at my home, even after she made it plain your attentions were not welcome. Don't do it again. My sister has direct responsibilities to me which cannot be interfered with. If you were halfways equal to your position you'd know she's seeing Crosetti. If I were to drop one word he'd cut you off at the knees, and be immensely more partisan in doing it than I would be. Crosetti's a wild man. Even Randolph would be unable to hold him."

"I didn't know about Crosetti," Waterston said. "I didn't mean any harm. I didn't think."

"You know all you have to, and now it's not required of you to think. You will never again mention my name outside of these offices. I trust we have an understanding on the subject."

"Yes," Waterston said. "You have my word."

"I could have had your skin," Moloch reminded him. "You would do well to thank God you're able to continue filling out your days playing your foolish games of golf and passing out your money packets to the local officials."

Moloch turned on his heel and started for the door.

"Wait," Waterston said after him, anchored in his well of pulp. "What you said about Margaret . . . I'm not sure . . . I don't want to make a mistake . . ."

"I'll be bound," Moloch exclaimed in astonishment. "It will surely tax what sparse endowment you carry, Waterston, but give a mighty try at grasping this: When climbing mountains one occasionally finds it necessary to direct falling pedestrians. Now, as for you, if you cannot find your way the best course is to lie back and take in the points of passing interest. You'll eventually find your level."

The parable was too much for Waterston's comprehension. He stared back blankly.

Moloch appraised him for a long moment, then went swiftly from the room, tossing over his shoulder the single word: "Classic."

Waterston stayed where he was, a bloodless stalk seared of his vitals, his clay laid bare. Broken, at what he himself had been so good at. He would not have thought it possible.

He lurched to the bar and closed his hand on a loving glass.

He'd heard about Moloch. He'd listened to tales of what The Doctor was capable. Even in the gritty order of spooks there seemed a mania for one villain to be greater than all others, a crusader out of hell, a mystic monster. They had the one in Clement Moloch.

He took the glass and collapsed in the chair nearest him, the cushion still warm from Moloch. Some of the Scotch splashed on his polo shirt, blending with inlets of sweat already there.

The Doctor had strung him up in a slipknot, had shown him his own entrails, had destroyed him in a few minutes of talk.

And it was not yet ten in the morning in this godforsaken hole.

• 13 •

It was after one o'clock the next morning as Rhiana drove the rented Chevrolet through the pinched bottleneck streets of the worst barrio section of the city, threading the big car with only inches to spare past broken concrete kiosks and small adobe hovels. Almost all were darkened except for the saloons and whorehouses fronted by slab-sided prostitutes and bandy-legged pimps watching the car pass with sharp black eyes, and on a corner a group of children squatting around a fire of rolled papers and cooking bits of things held on the ends of bicycle spokes.

Sometimes the sides of the car would resonate with thumps as it went by the whores. Rhiana would look in the mirror and see a woman standing in the road with a breast bared for tender or a man holding his crotch and working his arm in the air like a piston.

Slouched in the seat beside her with his knees on the dash, Holland never bothered to look back.

The morning before, they had followed the limousine from the embassy to Claire Moloch's apartment building, where Crosetti entered and reappeared shortly after with her, the limousine then returning directly to the estate. Turning off, Holland and Rhiana had waited near the intersection of the road to the estate, Sarah sitting on the grass and assembling arrangements of dandelions. The day had been warm for the time of year and luminous with insects. At noon, when the limousine emerged to take the sister back, Rhiana and Sarah had followed, leaving Holland. He had taken to the trees then and made his way to the estate, to the spot he had been before, to watch without respite for the next twelve hours.

Rhiana had come for him at precisely the place she'd dropped him and exactly at the time specified.

She drove a different Chevrolet now, another color, switched by Max at Holland's insistence.

"You have the patience of Job or you're a total fraud," she said.

"You're sure they didn't know you were following them?" he asked her.

"I did as you said: stayed well back and turned off when I saw the limousine enter the estate road."

"What did you do after that?"

"Sarah wanted to see the model city again. She's seen it every time we've come here but never seems to tire of it. Then we went to the Archives and the Central Market, and had dinner with Max."

She jerked the wheel to avoid a motorized bicycle that was weaving crazily, its rider preoccupied with kicking at the balky motor. In the mirror, he paused to salute the car with a raised finger.

"Did you see anything at the estate?" she asked.

"Only what you saw. The limo leaves with the sister; the limo returns without her. Nothing the rest of the day or night. One of Moloch's gunsels drove out about an hour ago. Probably his night off."

"The one who's having the affair with the sister?"

"No. The large one."

"Is that why you're going to the bar?"

"I'm hungry is why."

She reached into her purse and put two cassette tapes on the seat. Holland brought them close so that he could make out the labels: original selections of Glenn Miller and Ella Fitzgerald.

Pleasantly surprised, he said, "Where did you find these?"

"They're compliments of Max," she said. "Oh, and this too."

She took out an automatic pistol, a Colt Commander in blue, chambered for .38 Super; the back-up gun he had requested from Max.

He pulled the slide back. A cartridge popped from the breech and fell to the carpet, its presence unexpected. The gun had been expertly loaded, with a cartridge ready to be fired by simply cocking the hammer.

"Who loaded this?" he asked her.

"I did," she said.

"You do know guns." He eased the hammer down on a live shell and scooped the other from the floor. Inspecting it, he discovered the round was a Remington 185-grain half-jacketed hollow point, again conforming perfectly with what he had asked for.

Next she handed him a lighter, one of the slim metal ones that operated on butane fuel. He flipped the top and thumbed the wheel against the flint, the flame flaring to the side instead of rising, intended for a pipe smoker.

"My contribution to the demise of the match," she said.

"They never last," he said. "I've tried them."

Offended, she said, "Neither do dogs that chase cars or men like you."

"I didn't know you'd tried one before," he said, ". . . like me."

She scrutinized him obliquely for a moment, looming a fender close to a wall, then brought her attention back to guiding the car.

"The gunsel who took the sister back to her apartment must have stayed a while," he said.

"About an hour."

"Long enough."

"What do you suppose Moloch was doing at the embassy?"

"Who knows?"

"I'd have expected they would be the ones to go see him."

"Uh-huh," he said, turning the radio on and searching the dial for a station giving the news. "You hear any baseball scores today?"

"Perish the thought," she said, "but I doubt they make a habit of reporting American baseball here."

"One of them does. I hit on it yesterday."

In due course he found the station. It was playing Spanish music.

"Is that why you changed plans and watched the house all day?" she said. "Because of the embassy?"

"It occurred to me he might've been setting up an itinerary. Like I said, people sometimes mess up when they're ready to leave. He hasn't, but I can't figure why he'd go to the embassy instead of having them come to him. So far he's given me nothing."

"He doesn't even leave the car," she said. "At least not where he can be seen."

"George did his homework. He said he wouldn't."

There was a short silence.

"Would it be possible to put explosives in his car?" Rhiana asked him.

"Possible," he said. "But dumb."

"Why?"

"Too much margin." He was trying to hear the radio now that the music was finished.

"That explains everything," she said, a pillar of skepticism only a foot or two from him, her smell a delicate contraband in the confines of the car.

"The same as the rifle business, and hemlock and magic phones that pierce the brain," he said. "Leave the folklore to books and movies and wet dreams. I didn't come here to romance the man."

"I just meant . . ." she started to say. But he held his hand up, listening to the radio. To her amazement the commentator was listing the baseball scores from last evening.

The New York Yankees had lost to Boston in their own ball park. Holland's brow knit slightly.

"Is that where you were loosed on the world?" she said. "New York?"

"Sssh," he said, leaning closer to the radio for the balance of the day's action. When it was completed he switched the radio off and sat back in the seat.

"Have you considered the sister?" Rhiana said.

"Down here," he said, pointing to a street on the right that was even closer and darker than the ones they had been on.

She negotiated the tight turn nimbly, impressing Holland with her precision.

"I don't like kidnappings," he said, once the car was straightened again, "on the matter of principle."

"Oh, principle suddenly rears its head."

"He doesn't keep anybody on her," he said, reflecting. "Either he considers her expendable or he's purposely trying to steer attention away from her. What do you think?"

Surprised that he would ask her, she was slow to answer. "To me it would be the former."

"Okay."

"Does that indicate agreement, or what?"

"I'd buy both."

"I should have known."

"Pull over," he directed.

She swung the car onto the worn cobblestone sidewalk, next to a garage and in front of an early fifties Volkswagen that had been stripped of wheels.

The street was empty. Low flat-faced buildings edged the cobble, whitewashed once but now smudged and defaced, undershot with decay, cracked and bowed by the humping of earthquakes. What cars there were would have better occupied a wrecking yard.

A cat went away in the headlights, eyes shining when it looked over its shoulder, incredibly frail, a useless front leg held clear of the ground.

The only light to be seen was that spilling from an open doorway on the left. They could hear music, voices and swollen laughter.

"Is that where you're going?" Rhiana said, looking.

Holland put the automatic in her purse.

"Go back and get Sarah and go to the hotel," he said. "Get some sleep."

"Can't we stay at Max's?" she said. "I hate to keep waking her like this."

"Take her to the hotel. I'll only be a couple of hours."

She took the keys from the ignition and swept her purse from the seat.

"Then I'll go with you."

"No," he said. "I don't need that."

"I'll volunteer. I'm a regular trooper."

"I'd as soon you didn't."

But she sat ready, matching him, whether out of some distorted siege of frustration or unshackling of artful defiance, he didn't know.

He allowed an interval to let her reconsider. She returned his look steadily, a sibylline witness in opaque shadows, superbly composed, lovely beyond any words he knew.

"Up to you," he said at last.

"I'll go with you."

"Then you'll keep your mouth shut and you'll live with whatever happens. If you see Moloch's gunsel in there you let me sit so I'm facing him. Don't screw up, understand?"

"Yes."

There was a maddening closeness between them, a short compulsive gripping without actually touching, made powerful by unknown treachery and the haunt of sinister surroundings.

Above the open doorway was a washed-out sign: THE JET BAR.

"You think they're ready for this?" he said, glancing back at her.

If there had been so much as the spark of a smile he would have left her.

She said nothing.

As they were getting from the car he added, "And don't ask for cognac."

The Jet Bar had a linoleum floor worn through the pitch in places, exposing boards beneath that twisted and squawked against shiny-headed nails when walked on. The boards had been walked on a lot, and fallen on and fought on and spit on and puked on and pissed on. They advertised years of it.

Cockroaches—clearly the mascots of the place—too intrepid to stoop to stealth, stumped across the open flats past their crushed brethren.

A row of undersized booths ran down one dimly lit wall and circled across the rear. On the right was a stand-up bar with a couple of listing stools held together by wire. The propeller fan on the ceiling had long since tired of stirring the stench of stale sweat and rented beer, its blades hanging paralyzed like the hands of a stopped clock. Behind the bar a mirror had yards of tape covering a maze of cracks and craters.

Entering, Rhiana caught her shoe on a turned piece of linoleum and would have gone down if Holland hadn't taken her arm. She glanced back at him, full of regret. Someone clapped his hands and whooped.

"Damn," she said under her breath.

Every eye in the place—all black save for one pair—had turned on them.

The din lessened somewhat, followed by a current of curiosity. A parroting of errant tourists. Hoarse laughter and elbow digs and the prospect of some sport, maybe bullying. A turn too improbable to believe and too promising to let pass.

Holland read the faces. An alignment wondering how in hell this gringo bastard had strayed so far from the bright lights. Even tourists and Bible Bangers didn't find their way this far down the gutter. And his woman. Not American but not a full Latin either, she was striking enough to be inspired by her own beauty, exquisitely formed in her white belted dress full of tiny expensive pleats. Her being with him made it worse. The mix rubbed their noses in it. This was not a place for that. They despised Americans here, convinced they had the right. Some Americans were crazy, trying to heat their women by taking them to barrio bars, idiots shopping for their manhood. This gringo had made a bad mistake.

One paradox of Latin hatred for anything American was evidenced in their feverish appetite for American pop music, most of which did not arrive until a year or two after the recordings had fallen from favor elsewhere. Purists, they insisted on the English language originals. On one end of the bar a primal Wurlitzer in a kaleidoscope of colors blared Fleetwood Mac at a ferocious level.

One booth was unoccupied, the second from the front. Holland steered Rhiana to it and sat her across from him so that he was facing the rear.

Littered with empty beer bottles and cigarette butts, the wood table was charcoaled, water rings and knife lesions and bits of food lending additional character. A colony of flies made their home along the border of grime on the perimeter.

Rhiana sat with her hands in her lap, would not elevate her vision beyond the booth.

When Holland looked at her she shook her head.

"You want to leave?" he said.

"This was a mistake."

"I thought I'd mentioned the possibility."

"My father warned me about these places." She tried to smile. It didn't take.

"From the name I thought the jet set watered here on their way to the south of France."

The narrowness of the booth had placed his knee between hers when they sat down. She shifted so they were no longer touching.

"I'll take you to the car if you want," he said.

"And come back?"

"I'm hungry."

"You're out of your mind if you eat here."

"Decide."

"I'll stay."

In the rear corner there was a door leading to a kitchen, judging by the grease smoke being discharged. Next to it was a plywood cubicle the size of a phone booth, rising to shoulder height and open at the bottom so that the base of the toilet was exposed. When someone stood at it their feet could be seen, when they sat on it their bunched clothing could be seen. Were it not for the noise and the music, their work would have been heard too.

Opposite the head, in a corner booth, Brian Randolph sat observing with bemused attentiveness. A Latin man was next to him, another across the table with a woman who looked over her shoulder at Rhiana. They were the only women in the room.

At the bar, every man was turned toward Holland and Rhiana. Although there was little likelihood of their being cane cutters, some had machetes on their belts. Cutters generally carried their blades strapped to their backs during toil, then shifted them to their waists after. Holland was unable to detect any scabbard outlines on the backs of these shirts.

"One of these hawkshaws figures to rain on our parade sooner or later," he said, grouping the empty bottles out of the way.

"I didn't see Moloch's bodyguard when we came in," Rhiana said.

"At the back."

Holland was stroking his lip with his thumbnail as he talked. Until now she had thought it only an idiosyncrasy.

"Has he said anything?"

"You've made an impression. He has carnal interest in your face, your breasts, your rear, and your legs. But he's not through yet."

There was no reaction from her. She took a tissue from her purse and began wiping the table.

"George Herman Ruth might have taken to this hogan," he said, scanning the onlookers, trying to decide which of them would be the first to sally forth.

"Who's that?"

"Babe Ruth."

"You're not the least uncomfortable, are you?"

"These places make life worth living. Do you want a drink?"

She turned her hand.

He got up, saying, "Keep my place," and crossed the few steps to the bar.

There he had to wedge himself between two unyielding dissidents who glared close enough to study his pores.

He excused himself, then motioned to the bartender.

"What you want?" the man behind the bar growled in English.

"Whiskey. Beer. One glass," Holland said. His unflawed Spanish got a reaction from those close.

"You American?" the bartender demanded, reverting to Spanish.

"You bet," Holland said.

"You crazy?" the bartender said after some consideration.

"I smoked marijuana once," Holland told him. "I've been crazy ever since."

The bartender threw his head back and howled past empty gums. The two on either side of Holland remained glum, not sharing the bartender's enthusiasm for whimsy. One was exerting a steady pressure, pushing Holland against his friend, the other pushing back.

Holland expected a hand to dip for his money at any second.

An unmarked bottle of whiskey, a bottle of beer and a water glass were slammed on the bar by the still chuckling bartender.

Holland took them and asked for a bowl of *pozole.*

The bartender said, "At the table. Then you pay."

One of Holland's flankers cleaned his passages with one long openmouthed hack and spit in the narrow space between Holland and the bar. Holland gave him a thin smile and went back to the table.

Rhiana fingered a chip on the rim of the glass when he gave it to her. "You want some of this?" he said of the whiskey.

She shrugged. He put a half-inch in the glass, which she raised and wet her lips with.

"Homemade," she said.

But he was busy studying the bottle of beer. The bartender had neglected to open it. He hooked the cap over the edge of the table and struck it sharply with the heel of his hand. The cap tumbled to the floor and rolled across the path of a marching bug.

"Lots of traffic down there," he observed.

"Did you have a somewhat unorthodox conversation with Sarah yesterday morning?" she asked him, possessed by a need to deny the menace.

His beer was warm.

"She thought she was pregnant," he said.

"Again," said Rhiana.

"I thought so."

The bartender brought his hominy stew and a plate of grizzled bread.

Holland paid him and said, "Another beer."

"At the bar."

Holland followed him and brought back another bottle, this time opened.

"If you have any sense at all you won't eat that," Rhiana said.

The steaming brown mush in the bowl was lumpy with meat and potato chunks and hominy, heavy on beans of varying colors.

Rhiana reached across and slowly drew off a black hair that, when finally extended, was seven or eight inches in length.

"Was that really necessary?" he said.

"Generally they use pork that's dried in the sun," she said.

"I know that," he said. "Maybe if it was accompanied by a Bourgogne red, say '76, one with the tenderness and rouge of a '72 and the force of a '61?"

Her eyes flashed the same way they had in the car. "Don't inflict those broad-stroked presumptions on me," she said. "I know what you've been thinking. Not that it matters, but you're wrong."

"Max takes a Highland malt after dinner and you sip a French cognac and listen to Mozart. All very proper and safely fashionable. Your style is faultless."

"Style and fashion have nothing whatever to do with it. It happens to be what we enjoy. Your insights are not very sound, Mr. . . . Holland. All of his life my father drank your treasured beer, because he enjoyed it. Every Saturday for years my mother had to keep dinner while he drank and listened to stories with the day shift from the mine. His employees got better conditions and more money from him than from any other owner, not because it was fashionable—it was anything but fashionable—and not because he had started like them, but because he still thought of himself as one of them and because he didn't want it all for himself, or for us. That didn't stop Allende from taking his mine from him. They didn't 'nationalize' it. They didn't pay for it. They just took it. The people had less then, much less; and Allende's Cabinet had more, much more. That also failed to prevent Pinochet from murdering my father. Now he has it all. One of his relatives even lives in our house."

"Is that why?" Holland said.

"You don't fool me. You're just saying words. George says you've seen more madness than all of us. Well, the maddest of all is Moloch. You swim with them. Tell me."

He had finished the first beer and started on the second. It too was warm. Surprisingly, he discovered the bread to be fresh.

She saw that he was not going to answer her.

"Don't worry, your kind always comes back in style . . ."

"Shut up," Holland said.

"George told me how you . . ."

"Shut up," he repeated.

Rhiana looked up at the man who had come to stand at their table.

The anger that had been in her face washed swiftly away. Her throat constricted. It appeared she might gag. She flicked her eyes away to Holland.

He was eating a piece of bread. "Don't heave," he said.

She didn't understand at first. Then she nodded.

Holland regarded the man with open conjecture.

A ladino, the man epitomized all that was rough and sneering. He wore a yellowed open-weave T-shirt exploiting a deep chest and arms that worked outside, a brawny neck with sinews rising into a short unkempt beard, above that an ear that was disfigured, the top half missing. A straight-line scar shot from his mouth into a nostril. He was without a machete.

The sketch, whatever it was to be, was the focal point of the establishment now, the house only dividing their attention with their drinks. Again, the human noise had lessened; a pall of anticipation. Yet the Wurlitzer continued to boom, Christine McVie of Fleetwood Mac singing *You Make Loving Fun,* the song recycling without cessation, Holland at first thinking there was a diabolic Pavlov in the emporium but then realizing the machine was stuck. And now that there were two pilgrims for entertainment, nobody cared.

The ladino sat down close enough to Rhiana to provoke either her or Holland. He was chewing coca leaf and breathing on her. Latins, when fortified with sufficient leaf, Holland knew, felt they could whip the universe and satisfy all the women in it.

His lurid inspection consumed Rhiana as though he were in the last moments before pushing himself inside her.

Randolph was smiling.

"What are you here for?" the ladino said to her in Spanish.

"He wanted to eat," she said in the same tongue.

"What are you with him for?" The ladino rested his arm behind her.

"He's my husband." Her voice was strung like a wire.

Three buttons at the top of her dress were undone, modestly conservative. But it prompted the ladino to try looking in, his face nearly touching hers. As well, he was ranging a finger in a horsy attempt to touch her breast. She kept moving her arm to deflect him.

Holland tore some more bread for himself, deciding that the ladino must not have heard him speak the language earlier and therefore thought him ignorant of what was being said.

"Only Mexican whores marry Americans," the ladino said.

"Keep away from me," Rhiana said. "Please."

"You don't need brassieres," the ladino said, fleetingly successful with his finger before it was once again turned away.

At the bar a man hefted his crotch and leered his tongue at the one next to him.

The cook, an enormously obese woman, emerged from the back room to take in the action.

Now the ladino discarded the ruse of touching. His hand dove beneath Rhiana's arm and took her breast, assuming possession. She twisted but he held firm. Using all of her strength she tried to close her arm to squeeze his out. Finally he let go and laughed. She tried to throw him off so that his body wasn't against hers but he stayed with an arm draped on her shoulders.

Roisterous laughter crashed about them from the bar and the booths along. Someone thumped a bottle on a table for encouragement.

"What's your name, friend?" Holland said, without looking up.

The ladino blinked at the clarity of Holland's Spanish.

"Cruz," he said. "You shit."

"We don't want any trouble, Cruz," Holland said, taking a spoonful of the stew.

The ladino swiveled toward the room with his features arranged piously. "Trouble?"

"This little number could heat Akron for a year," he said to Rhiana, meaning the stew.

She stared back, a limp mask of humiliation. He could make out beads of dampness where her hair met her temples. Around her neck was a slender gold chain, on it a single loop empty of a crucifix.

"What's your name, shit?" the ladino said.

"Orville Thudpucker," Holland said. "This is my wife, Emma Lou."

The ladino put his face close to Rhiana's again. There were soiled streaks across her dress where his fingers had been on her breast.

Holland gave him the syllables, "Thud-pu-cker."

"Thud-fuck-her," the ladino returned, snaking his tongue out on Rhiana's cheek. She leaned away.

"I saw a real bad talking picture like this once," Holland said to Rhiana.

"You should have left," she said.

"Easy," he cautioned her.

Her chest would rise against her dress every time there was some groping under the table. Her arms would jerk to get the ladino away. Her knees would clash against Holland's.

"This American shit is not enough for a woman like you," the ladino said to her. "He's not enough for a sheep."

Laughter rose once more, although Randolph was limiting himself to a smile. When the ladino laughed there was a collage of leaves.

The ladino took his arm away from Rhiana and dipped into his pocket to produce a long folded knife. Extended, the slim blade was long enough to reach through to a spine. Holland froze his attention to it, his eating unabated.

The ladino speared the two pieces of bread left on the plate and staked them to the table in front of Holland.

"I don't want any trouble," Holland said again.

"It's no trouble for me," the ladino said. "You came here. What were you looking for? Your mother?"

He hooked his arm around Rhiana once again. She

drew herself tightly together. Holland concluded that it was utterly impossible for her to appear graceless.

"Your face is beautiful. You're like a warm statue," the ladino said. "I always wanted to fuck a perfect warm statue like you."

Rhiana snapped her face away and kept it averted.

The only sound came from the Wurlitzer now, the gallery wholly absorbed with what the ladino was saying.

Stevie Nicks sang, "*. . . believe in the ways of magic . . .*"

"I'm going to take you into the kitchen and fuck your mouth like a Mexican whore's. Then I'm going to bend you over and push you around the room. We'll knock down the pots and pans. I'll suck on you. I'll make you sing. You'll know what a man is."

Rhiana's face was wet now. Holland had never known a woman who could weep so silently.

He pushed his bowl of stew away and began snatching flies from the table with croupier's hands. The ladino was too strung with coca juice to heed it. Randolph, though, was watching the quick blur of the fly stalking.

Looking from Rhiana to Holland, and studying him for a moment, the ladino concluded, "When I'm through I'll give her to my friends."

Holland's voice, when it came, was gentle. "You don't want to do that."

The ladino grabbed the knife and flicked the blade at Holland's hands.

"Don't tell me what I want, you gringo fuck," he said.

Holland showed his palms and put them under the table. "No trouble, Cruz. We'll leave."

"Then you leave without her," he said. "We're going to lock the door and have a party."

When Holland looked at Rhiana his expression was as empty as any she had ever seen. She experienced a burn of terror as unbridled as any in the Chile Stadium. There was only him.

Suddenly Holland leaned toward her, yet still not touching her.

"You feel your own mortality," he said. "That's hard to come by. Most people never experience it, and don't know what it is when it comes. Don't let it go."

"My God. One minute you're glib . . ." Rhiana said, her voice trailing off.

The ladino was watching diligently, his coherence in disarray. "Huh . . . ?" he muttered.

"This isn't something you do until you get it right," Holland said to Rhiana. "There's nothing vague in here. There's energy, clarity."

"Hey . . ." said the ladino.

Rhiana's eyes were brimming, but she couldn't pull her attention from Holland.

"This one, the one with the head like a bastard rat," Holland went on, ignoring the ladino as though he did not even exist, "doesn't live in a house on a hill."

"Who? Who's he?" the ladino said.

Rhiana's breath was catching.

"There's no divine right of Kings here. He doesn't pretend. He takes up front and lets you hit back if you can. That makes him better than they are. Then it isn't madness. Not the same."

The ladino's features were knotted by the effort to understand.

No one spoke for a long moment.

Christine McVie had started fresh, singing, "*. . . sweet wonderful you . . .*"

"What's it like? For you?" Rhiana said to Holland, losing the fight to control her tears.

"It's where I live," Holland said. "I'm alright."

He waited.

Then he said, "I don't need a bad luck piece."

"What's that?" said the ladino.

"I told you," Holland said to her.

"Shaddup!" the ladino shouted in exasperation, clubbing the table.

The knife quivered.

Holland slouched against the booth.

"No heart for it, eh, gringo fuck?" the ladino said to him, jerking his head toward the knife.

"No," Holland said.

The ladino spit on Holland's shirt. "Gringo's got no guts."

"Whatever's right," Holland said.

"Things change, eh, gringo fuck? You all lie down now. You won't fight anymore."

"Nothing changes, Cruz," Holland said, the same gentle tone returning. "Least of all that."

"Bullshit!" the ladino said. "You gringos couldn't even beat a bunch of rice pickers—"

Rhiana saw it first.

"Holland . . ." she started to say.

The ladino's mouth snapped open. He went bugeyed.

Holland was under the table to his shoulder.

The ladino pumped his mouth as though starving for air. He plunged one hand beneath the table, straining the other for the knife, but missing it and crashing to the floor beside the booth, Holland with him.

The spectators stumbled and got tangled trying to get out of the way. They saw that Holland had the ladino's scrotum in his closed right hand. The ladino writhed on his back, clawed at Holland's arm, tore his shirt and made furrows in the skin with his nails.

"Leave it alone!" Holland yelled back at Rhiana.

Only then did she think of her purse and grab for it.

The ladino bellowed from deep in his gut and hammered at Holland's arm with his fists.

Holland stood stiff-legged and bent at the waist, one shoe on the ladino's throat. The ladino wrenched from side to side to get free but Holland clung, twisting his hand to stress the pain.

Rhiana's first impulse was to run for the door. Instead she got clear of the booth and stood with her hand in her purse. The knife was gone.

Holland levered almost his full weight on the ladino's throat and lifted the lower body clear of the floor, repeatedly hefting the bulk against the scrotum.

The ladino's face was mottled shades of scarlet, his tongue distended and stiff.

One of the onlookers shifted as if to kick at Holland, but an arm came out and thrust him back. Some had climbed the bar for a better view. A cock-fighting circle had formed. A chair fell to the floor, the fat cook sent sprawling.

The fabric of the ladino's pants and the pouchy sac beneath were wrung through Holland's clamped fingers. A half-suppressed murmur ran through the crowd, corroborating the crush of the hand on treasured parts.

Rhiana slipped unnoticed through the press of bodies until she was near the door.

Holland leaned on the ladino's neck until his free foot

was only lightly touching the floor. The ladino's tongue seemed ready to disgorge, then his frame slackened and went limp. Stepping away, Holland flexed his hand for circulation, then, pushed a man behind him away so that he was backing alone into the empty booth.

He looked for Rhiana, then saw her near the door.

A man came out of the circle and looked down on the inert ladino.

"You've got strong hands," Randolph said, bringing his gaze up to Holland.

Holland dropped his attention to where rivulets of blood streamed down his arm. "He's got a glass bag, is all."

Randolph laughed, offering his hand to Holland.

Holland declined it, saying, "Pass."

"Brian Randolph," he said. "You were at the bullfights."

"You were a lot of help, Randolph. How come they don't hassle you?"

"I'm a regular," Randolph said. His smile vanished. He added, "Besides, they know better."

Holland looked again at Rhiana, then put his hand on the chest of a man standing too near and gently moved him back. There was little resistance. He suspected the cause might be Randolph.

"Where you from?" Randolph asked him.

"South Bronx."

"Hey, that right?" Randolph said with interest. "I'm from Bayonne, myself. Ever heard of Stagger Street?"

"You got any beer that's cold?" Holland asked the bartender, ignoring Randolph. "In cans maybe?"

This time the bartender moved without delay.

Randolph flicked his head toward Rhiana. "Your wife?"

Holland nodded. "The little woman."

The ladino stirred, groaning as he regained consciousness. One hand went immediately to his crotch, the other to his neck. He coughed dryly.

Holland slapped the ladino's hands away, unleashed his belt and pulled his pants to his knees. His scrotum and penis were swollen and discolored, displaying magenta-shaded welts where Holland's fingers had been.

"*That's* what you use?" Holland said.

A snigger coursed through the crowd.

"What do you do?" Randolph said to Holland.

"Neurologician," Holland said.

Randolph bobbed his head, not wanting to admit ignorance. He turned to the bar and took one of the cans of beer the bartender had lined up for Holland.

Holding it out, he said, "May you be in heaven half an hour before the Devil knows you're dead."

Then he compressed the can in his hand as hard as he could before turning it over to Holland.

Holland accepted the can and inspected it briefly. The sides were dimpled and the top bloated, but the seams had held. The feat was remarkable even for a man of Randolph's size.

Holland moved to put the can back on the bar. Then, just as his arm was fully extended, he squeezed, rupturing the container, showering beer in a wide spray and causing Randolph to jump quickly out of the way in order to avoid a pelt of suds.

"And all the ships at sea," said Holland.

The bartender swore.

Taking two fresh cans, and turning his back on Randolph, Holland tossed a bill into the slop on the bar and then made his way to Rhiana.

"You drive," he said to her.

She went out ahead of him.

When they got to the car they found the hubcaps and side mirror were missing.

•14•

Rhiana drifted between the nearer shores of wakefulness and the nether world of sleep, the natural sedation so necessary to quell the ordeal just past.

Sarah slept beside her, Holland on the floor.

The malevolence in the bar refused to leave her. *How long had they been in that baiting pit? Minutes? Hours? Days? The blink of an eye, the turn of a blade?*

And how long since they'd come from there? Not long, she thought. Seeing Sarah, drowsy, and happy to see her, had been a precious joy which made her heart burn. She had held tightly to her child all the way to the hotel, only granting Holland to carry her to the room, then held her again until Sarah was asleep.

Whether sleeping or merely edging toward it, Holland was inseparable from whatever chose to swoop through her mind—a dogged agent of disorder. He had treated the scrapes on his arm himself, declining her tepid offer of assistance and waiting patiently until she was through with the bathroom, curtly insisting that she finish first and then go to bed. She would have given anything to know what he was thinking.

In the bar she had been convinced he was going to desert her.

With that certainty upon her—facing her "mortality," as Holland had dubbed it—Clement Moloch had ceased to exist. So had her father, her husband, their memories. Everything but Sarah. There had been a limbo then, only Sarah and herself, and the animals who were sure to do unspeakable things to her. And all through it there had been Holland. She hated him, if it was possible to hate what she was incapable of identifying. How does one evaluate a genus nescience? There, that was a good name for him. She felt clever for it.

He had been so sure of himself in the bar. He had even tried to explain it to her, letting them listen. Without her there would not have been trouble. He would have done some little thing, she didn't know what, to let them know.

Before tonight there had been occasions when she had speculated that his serenity was based on insanity. Not that she believed, as some did, that all deliberate killers were psychotics. She knew better. And now she knew that Holland was not insane or anything near to it. His spirit could be as mean as any presented him, but he had control that was astonishing, and only allowed the capacity to flare after provocation that might well have derailed others. That much she had seen and understood, but what had his purpose been in going there? Had he failed? Had she failed it for him?

She had witnessed for herself that he could strike back, that he was threatened by very little, if anything. But the nagging uncertainty lingered. Even if he could kill, could he kill The Doctor? Viewing him as she had until now was no different than trying to peer into a clouded prism. Minute to minute the image altered, looming and then sketchy, darting and fading. Always a span between him and those around, indeterminate, unfathomable. Serene, then galling. Just as Isabelle had warned he would be.

She had shaken uncontrollably while driving to Max's house and had wanted to abandon the wheel, get out and get some air into her head that was not foul and surly and threatening. Holland had slumped in his usual posture for automobiles and had not looked at her once, a void between them. With him, she remained alone. Her emotions, when directed at him, were on a roller coaster. One instant she was desperate to get off the ride; another, she was desperate not to. One minute she wanted to smash his side of the car on an abutment and go on without him, race to Sarah and rush her away to Mexico; the next minute it was all she could do to prevent herself turning and asking him to forgive her.

Maybe she had. She couldn't be sure.

Blotting out all but herself and Sarah, as she had done in the bar, made her feel deeply ashamed of herself. Her father, and Agustin, would not have approved. Cringing in the corner, clamping her thighs tight while the ladino pig tried to force his hand between, praying that he would stop, not daring to fight back. All the while a gun in her purse. Was that truly the best she could expect of herself? And relying on Holland long after she knew that was folly. When he had moved it had not been because of her but because of a despicably immoral war, and because he was an American who was loath to live in his own country . . . but still an American who would not stand to be vilified. More than she had done.

She did not feel much of a "bloody marvel" for it. Yet, she had come through, knowing she should not have gone with him in the first place, and fearing the unknown even then. "Up to you," she heard, wishing he would leave her in peace now that she was sleeping.

But at least she had faced her fears to a degree, not in the way she had tried and failed at the bullfight. If she were honest, that was the real reason she had gone into the bar with Holland. It was the first facing up she had done since the Chile Stadium.

Her fears needed to be confronted, desperately, or her life might just as well have been spent along with her father's, and with Agustin's. Otherwise what earthly good would she be to Sarah. Presenting herself as no more than a durable companion was a travesty. She needed to be cleansed of her fears. Or she needed The Doctor dead. The first would bring her alive, but only the last would release her entirely.

Tonight was the first in years that she had gone to bed without the humbling contraption clamped between her teeth. Hector had prescribed the device shortly after she had come from Chile—a plastic socket that prevented her teeth from grinding together when she slept. Until then she had wakened in agony most every morning, and sometimes during the night, her jaw aching and knotted and often jolted by spasms that made her want to scream. The tension would take hours to ease. Holland had noticed it at once. She had wanted to smash the miserable thing then. but he had not bothered to comment and she guessed he knew what it was. Oh, how heady to be spared it, if only for one night.

Something wrenched her from sleep.

There was someone standing next to the bed, the room too dark and the shape too indistinct to be certain of whom.

It had to be Holland. Holland?

Had she said it, or only dreamt saying it?

"Holland?" she said aloud.

There was no response. The shape stood unmoved, looking down on her, on Sarah.

"What do you want?" she whispered.

Trackless silence came back to her. Damn him. She rose to one elbow—and knew it was not Holland.

Then there were two shapes in the murky shadows; half-tone images, like the back-lit puppet shows she used to see as a child.

The puppets came together and formed one, a jarring between them. There was a tremor of effort, then a grunt.

She watched mesmerized, straining into the darkness trying to decipher what was happening. One shape went rigid and seemed to grow taller. Then there was a chilling rattle as though air had been pinched from a balloon. Then a gurgling sound.

Something light and snake-like flew through the air to land on the bedclothes where her legs were. A sash, maybe a man's tie. She put her hand out to touch it.

The spot was wet. She recoiled. She grabbed for Sarah and threw her body over hers.

"Mummy?" was the first thing Sarah said. That was reflex. Then, startled, she cried, "What's the matter? Mummy?"

The struggling puppets were hurtling upright across the room, away from the bed.

One of them flung himself—*no, was propelled*—past the open door and into the bathroom. The other went after, as fast. There was the dull hollow thud of something substantial striking the porcelain bathtub, the shower curtain tearing, metal rings dancing along the rod, towels falling.

"Mummy? What's happening?" Sarah was saying.

Obscure sounds that were difficult to isolate came from the bathroom: a heaving, softer thumps on the porcelain. Something metallic clattered into the bathtub.

Then there was silence.

A faucet turned. Water started to run. A door slammed shut.

The room was still again. It had all been recorded at an incredible velocity.

Rhiana lifted herself from Sarah. They both sat up in the bed. Rhiana held the child to her. Her heart was thundering in her chest.

"I'm here, darling," she said. "I'm here."

"What's wrong?" Sarah said. "Where is Holland?"

"Don't worry. It's alright," she said.

She listened intently for anything from the bathroom but could only hear water running. Thinking belatedly of the corridor door, she whirled to see. It was closed. As near as she could tell nothing in the room had been disturbed.

"Lie down, Sarah," she said. "I'm going to see. Get under the covers and don't move until I come back."

The child did as she was told.

Rhiana slipped from the bed without disrupting the bedclothes. Where was her robe? Wait. Had she lost all reason. She went without it.

At the bathroom door she said in a low voice, "Holland? Are you alright?"

When there was still no answer she reached for the door knob, then paused, caught by a pulse of premonition. Should she get the gun from her purse? Was it still there?

What would she do with it? Was Holland dead on the other side of the door?

The door swung wide when she twisted the knob. Inside the bathroom was a shambles. Though dark, she was able to detect someone sitting on the edge of the bathtub.

"Holland?"

"It's alright." The voice was Holland's.

Relief engulfed her.

She reached for the light switch.

"Leave the lights," he said at almost the same instant.

But it was too late. Light flooded the bathroom. Rhiana reeled backwards, gasping.

"Oh, God!" she cried, partially muffling the sound with her hand.

"It's alright, Rhiana," said Holland.

A body was bent into the bathtub with legs jutting toward her and head lolling to one side. The neck was opened in a great gaping clown's mouth, painted full with crimson that brimmed and ran over. Eyes, unclosed and lifeless, were ciphers imprinted with a final incredulity. Blood was streaming into the tub in copious amounts, coursing over the knife that had belonged to the ladino, resting on the bottom. The blood spiraled down the drain.

Randolph's color matched the chalk white porcelain.

The shirt Holland wore in lieu of a pajama top was spattered with blood.

He stood to remove the shirt. He threw it into the tub. He flipped the light off.

Then he was coming toward her.

"Hang on," he said.

He took her by her arms. She dropped her shoulders, ready for him to shake her. Instead, he took a fist full of her hair at the side of her head and simply held it tightly without pulling. By some mysterious process the act compelled her to come alert.

"I want you to do what I say."

She nodded.

Sarah was sitting up, having heard Holland's voice. He crossed to her and pulled the top bedclothes off and balled them up. He sat beside her and took her hand.

Rhiana thought the child might draw away from him, but she did not.

"Everything is fine," he said to her. "Don't be frightened."

"Is mummy fine?" she said.

"Sure. You can see."

"What happened?"

"A man tried to steal something. He's not here anymore. Are you okay?"

"I didn't see him," she said.

"That's good. I'll have to get the police. You'd better go to Uncle Max's. Is that alright?"

She agreed readily. "Yes."

Holland got up and went to where his clothes were. "Rhiana, get dressed. Leave the lights off. Hurry."

He took his clothing into the bathroom along with his shoulder holster and revolver. The bed linen he stuffed into the toilet bowl until it was immersed.

Glancing out, he said, "Get dressed, Rhiana."

His tone, level and undistinguished, making entries in an audit of crisis, gave her confidence.

"Holland," she said. She had to look down, finding it impossible to escape the flat eyes in the bathroom.

"What?" He was opening the faucet more.

It was all she could say.

He regarded her a moment. Then closed the door.

On the window glass there was an angle of herself. The tracing was throwing off dislocated shock waves.

She got into a skirt and blouse, the first things that came to hand, forsaking stockings in her haste and hurrying Sarah with her dress. She instructed her not to go near the bathroom.

In her haste her skirt had twisted and was biting her hip. She was searching for her hairbrush when Holland stuck his head out.

"Can you hand me my baseball jacket?" he said. "In the closet?"

This would be the first time he had worn it since coming here. She passed it to him, necessitating a look into the bathroom and causing her to step back when she did.

Randolph's feet had been trussed together with strips of towel and then hoisted to the shower fixture so that he hung like a blooded carcass. The bathwater was still taking the waste and body fluids away, as well as the blood. The smell was unmistakable and she remembered being told that bodies released all functions at the point of death.

Holland had put his shoulder holster on, Sarah being the reason he had not emerged with the revolver uncovered. He did the jacket up to his neck but left his hand on the zipper pull in readiness.

Closing the bathroom door, he strode to the corridor door and opened it.

"The water . . ." Rhiana said weakly, ". . . shouldn't you . . . ?"

It was as though she had not spoken. The corridor was as dark as the room, Randolph having unscrewed the bulbs before stealing into the room. Holland stepped out and looked around.

"Let's go," he said.

His hand remained on the zipper pull all the way to the car.

Outside the hotel Holland cruised the rental until he found where Randolph had left his own vehicle. A Chrysler, it sat in a dimly lit area close to the rear of the building. He pulled the Chevrolet to the curb a short distance ahead.

"Get out for a minute," he said to Rhiana.

Then, to Sarah he said, "I'll see you at Uncle Max's. Okay, babe?"

"Okay," she said sleepily.

He got out with Rhiana and closed the door. From where they stood they appeared to be the only ones on the street at the early hour, the night air cool and damp and refreshing on the skin.

"You and Sarah are going home," he said to her. "Drive straight to Max's. Make certain you're not followed. Take a few turns until you're satisfied. Tell Max to get you on the earliest plane. As soon as you know when that is, you call the room. I'll pick up the phone and say 'Quasimodo,' If you hear anything else, hang up and head for the airport. Otherwise just give me the time the plane leaves. Nothing more. Not a word."

She nodded. struggling to get her thoughts in order. The embroidered "Y" over "N" on his jacket front provided her point of focus.

"I'll pack your things and bring them to Max's when I know the time."

His emotional valence in the aftermath of what had transpired in the scant hours past was numbing to her. Still his sound had only the inflection of order.

"But what if we are followed?" she said. "And I can't get away from them?"

"It won't be like that. Randolph went fishing on his own or they'd have been on us like a blanket. But okay, if you're followed, they'll just want to see where you go. In that case, come back here."

"If I can't manage that?"

"Let's not cover every 'what if.' You've got the automatic?"

"Yes."

He went to the back of the car and opened the trunk, taking from it a large burlap sack containing something bulky and obscure.

"What's all that?" she asked him, observing the other sacks on the floor of the trunk.

He closed the lid.

"Forget it," he said. "Don't point the gun unless you're prepared to use it. Never. You know that, right?"

"I know that," she said.

"No. No, you don't, Rhiana. Now it's you who's just saying words. Knowing it and saying it are different disciplines. There can't be any reservations about it."

"He won't get his hands on Sarah, or me. I'd use the gun first."

For a short time he looked at her, not certain if he had heard right.

"It won't come to that. In a few hours you'll be home. I want you to get in the car and lock the doors, then wait and keep your eyes open. Watch for me to come out the back door of the hotel. I'll have Randolph with me, so don't let Sarah look. If you've seen anything suspicious flash the headlights as soon as you spot me coming out."

He turned with the sack under his arm.

"Holland," she said. "Wait. Tell me what happened."

"It's started," he said. "I got lucky."

"Lucky . . . ?" she said, stunned.

Ten minutes went by before she saw, through the rear window of the car, the fire door to the hotel swing wide and Holland appear. He had a large black bag slung over his shoulder. From his stance it was apparent that the bag concealed a considerable weight.

There had not been anything to indicate a need to warn him, so she let her hand rest on the light switch without pulling it.

He waited in the shadows before coming forward, then went directly to Randolph's car and dumped the body in the trunk.

Rhiana started the Chevrolet. She entered the empty street. Sarah was already asleep, her head on her mother's lap.

Back in the room, Holland hung the "Do Not Disturb" sign out and locked the door behind him, then put the lights on and gave the room a meticulous examination.

The blood had not had time to seep through the top bedclothes before he had torn them off. But there was a crescent shaped flare on the bronze carpet, more blood on a round wicker table, a few widely spaced blotches on the way to the bathroom, and a streak down the metal door frame. Inside the bathroom there were pools on the tiles of the floor, some smears above the bathtub, and a swirl of designs in the tub itself.

He considered that he had been most fortunate.

Removing blood could be a demanding task. This time the largest part could simply be wiped clean with a wet cloth, the rest having been limited to manageable spillings on a carpet that was compatibly shaded. Randolph, being of good size, had emptied impressive measures of blood into the drains of Sheraton's finest. Holland turned off the faucet. He started with the carpet. First he wet down the immediate area with liberal amounts of cold water, being mindful not to rub the blood into the fibers before the water was given time to disperse some of the substance. While the water soaked in he washed the tiles and bathtub using hand soap and facecloths. On the caulking between the tiles and around the tub he scrubbed with a toothbrush until satisfied that there would not even be microscopic traces left. He did the same around the drain, the fixtures, and the toilet. The wicker table got the same treatment.

In Rhiana's belongings he found a bottle of bubble bath.

With it he made a heavy concentrate of suds in the ice bucket and then moved to the carpet and scrubbed it. This he sponged away with damp towels, and repeated the application again and again for the next hour. Once more resorting to Rhiana's things, he used her hair dryer to restore the patches of carpet to their prior state of synthetic frizz.

Finally, he wrung the toilet water from the bedclothes and looked them over, finding, as he knew he would, that the blood had been prevented from setting. They could be taken to a launderette later in the day.

He packed clothing, took a shower and then reclined on the bed to take stock of events.

The sun had risen clear of the hills outside the window when he dozed off.

The telephone wakened him not long into sleep.

He said "Quasimodo" and Rhiana said "Eleven thirty-five" and then the phone went dead.

He replaced the receiver and went to the window and looked out onto the city, his mind on her. The bullfight and the bar and the thing with Randolph had given her a battering, as they would have anyone. But it had also brought forth strength, more than he had credited her with at the outset. That was a side due a measure of admiration. From his inured haven of reference it was difficult to know which episode had been the worst trial for her. Randolph had not been a pretty sight with the grey mucus of his windpipe exposed.

In the corridor he heard the maid making her rounds.

He put his tweed jacket on and went out to speak to her.

She was Indian and had long coils dangling from her ears.

"We were out late last night," he said to her. "My wife and daughter are sleeping. There's no need to do the room, señora."

She smiled, straightened her glasses, and accepted the bill he gave her.

At the desk he told the clerk that they would be making excursions into the country in the next few days, their plans uncertain. He paid the bill and another week in advance. The clerk betrayed nothing irregular and the hotel seemed to be functioning as it should.

A party of Japanese tourists was gathering to board a tour bus, fidgeting with cameras, and dipping at everyone who passed.

Returning to the room, he gathered the luggage and went down to the street by way of the stairs, leaving the "Do Not Disturb" flag in place on the door. A survey of the street and the people moving about led him to Randolph's car without further concern. The automobile was still in the shade. It would have to be kept out of the sun as much as possible, and moved to where it would not be easily spotted.

Putting the bags on the seat negated the necessity of opening the trunk.

He started the car and took Randolph's gun from his pocket, an older Walther PPK in .380—standard fare for spooks who did not really need to depend on firearms. The pistol gave every indication of having never been fired. He ruminated whether the diminutive piece provided him proof of Moloch's preparedness or merely underlined Randolph's inclination to bull his way through whatever confronted him. More likely the latter. Randolph had not impressed him as a man for guns.

He wiped the Walther and placed it in the glove box, locking it.

From the breast pocket next to his own revolver he fished out a folder compiling the Yankees summer schedule. Dropping a finger down the list, he rested at the current date: Boston, again, in The House That Ruth Built.

He tapped the folder on the car's two-way radio.

A shoeshine kid searching for early commerce came to his window and tried to see in at his shoes. He had a jackknife on a rope around his neck. When he saw that Holland was wearing tennis sneakers he looked dejected and started away, scraping his box of fixings behind him. Holland lowered the window and called him back, giving him a couple of quetzals, only enough that the incident would not stick in the boy's memory.

On the way to Max's he stopped to purchase a pair of supple, tight fitting gloves, and called the Thomas Cook office to see if George had left any word. The girl there informed him that she did not have anything for Mr. Tyler.

* * *

The door to the garage was open and a space empty when he arrived at Max's house. He put Randolph's car inside and closed the door. Max met him and ushered him into the study with harassed attendance. "Is there anything else wrong?"

"I didn't know there was anything wrong," Holland said over his shoulder.

Rhiana was waiting for him.

There was a single amber-colored drink on one of the tables, the sun slanting on it and making the liquid inviting.

She stepped up and struck him in the mouth with her closed hand.

Max scurried between them. "Now, wait," he said.

Holland moved away, feeling where the inside of his lip had been split. The illogical assault had allowed her small fist to catch him, before he could even think to react.

Max was watching nervously. He seemed prepared for anything from either of them, although Holland could see that his own astonishment was shared.

"What is going on here?" Max said.

"I don't know," Holland said. He could taste salt creeping over his teeth.

Rhiana's cold stare sized him with open contempt. "You know," she said to him. "The difference is that now I know."

"It's late for this."

"You're depraved. You don't have any principles whatever."

"I didn't know that."

"Then lie to yourself."

"Where's the automatic?" he said to Max.

"I have it," Max said. "I don't know what this is about. Should I stay?"

"No," said Holland.

"Rhiana," Max said. "No more of this, please. It doesn't help."

"Oh, but it does, Uncle," she said. "I feel wonderful for hitting him. Isn't he here so we can all feel that way? Isn't that what he was bought and paid for?"

She turned her back on them.

Holland went to the fireplace and spit. "Someone should have told my mouth how wonderful it was going to be."

Max was helpless to know what he should do. He offered Holland his anxious sympathy, thought better of it and went back to Rhiana.

"Rhiana," he said, "no more hitting."

Both men watched her expectantly.

She nodded.

Max went to the door. Before leaving he said, "I'll be just outside."

Neither of them moved after Max left.

Finally Holland lifted the glass, assuming it to be liquor. Instead he found he had a mouthful of Coca-Cola. The acidity scorched his lip before he could spit it into the fireplace.

Rhiana faced him. She had not calmed much.

He went to Max's desk and sat behind it, deliberately putting the furnishing between them.

"Where's Sarah?" he asked her.

"Your sudden interest in her welfare is touching," she said.

"She didn't get hurt. She didn't even set eyes on him."

"By whose grace?" she said, staying where she was. "Don't you dare take credit for that."

"Come closer," he said.

Her step to the side was uncertain, fearful. Then she glanced at the closed door and knew what he meant. She closed the distance by half, taking refuge behind one of the wing chairs.

"It doesn't matter," she said. "He knows."

"He shouldn't. The more he knows the more danger he's in."

"Isn't it rather late for that too? After you've had him collecting guns and bags to put bodies in and renting cars in fictitious names?"

"He volunteered, remember? He's a regular trooper."

Day after day they had scanned each other's faces. For the first while it had been done while the other was looking away, but no more. Now they went head to head.

"He didn't volunteer to be a sacrifice, any more than I volunteered Sarah. You knew that man was coming; you set it up that way. You were waiting for him and you wouldn't warn me. The second latch on the door was left open. So was the chain. You used us for bait."

"No more than I used myself," he said. "You've been in

a lather to have something happen. In the rush I'm afraid your endorsement was overlooked."

For an instant he thought she might try to hit him again.

"And after lunch he rested," she said.

"Sarah's as good as new. So are you. You're going home. That's the promise I made to George and the Lomolins."

"What did it do to kill that man? In the same room with us. Did you promise them that?"

"Moloch won't leave now, not without one of his top dogs. Not until he's sure of what went down and who's responsible."

"So he'll back further into hiding and you'll never see him. If that's a sample of your brilliance, George should know he's a fool to rely on you."

Holland packed his pipe and lit the tobacco with the lighter she had given him, taking his time. She watched him solemnly.

The smoke curled and hung blue over the desk.

"When you get home you won't relate any of what's happened here to either George or the Lomolins. Tell them those are my instructions. Tell them it's going to work out. That's all."

"I don't believe you," she said, turning away. "Why should they? You're not any closer than when we came."

"I'm an impossible dreamer. A hidden virtue."

"You're just impossible. Impossible to believe, anyway."

"Listen, a successful assassination is only a carefully constructed play in which every member of the cast except the victim knows his part perfectly. That may sound like an odd analogy but if you think about it you'll find it makes sense. Especially when it's over."

"It sounds more like the little red book. I had you all wrong. Here you are in show business and all the time I thought—"

"Did you know that Mao's wife once decided she didn't care for the sound of a tuba," he said, interrupting her, "and had the instrument removed from every orchestra in China? Did you know that when Mao died they found he had a fabulous fortune? In the grand classless society—"

"Stop it," she said, her turn to cut him off. "Stop doing that."

"Leave it, Rhiana," he said. "Go home. It'll get done."

"In your own inimitable fashion. No, you'll be like the others who tried. I don't even care what happens to you."

"Alright, I'm operating on instinct and past transgressions. There aren't any scripts out here in the weeds, okay? Randolph missing will keep Moloch here and get his attention. That's more than I had before. Now I'm going to rattle his goddamn cage. By this time tomorrow he's going to know someone's out here and he's going to want to know why. Eventually he'll crawl out of his hole and screw up. They all do. All I've got to find is which string to pull."

What he had said kept her occupied through a short silence.

There was a stand of tapers in a candle holder on the table. He got up from the desk and started one with the lighter, then applied the taper to his pipe. He blew out the flame and straightened the slim wax sticks.

"You hurt your hand?" he said.

The question confused her. She shook her head, then changed direction and said, "A little."

"I've always wondered why people insist on hitting with parts of their own bodies. Rapping someone in the mouth is the same as hitting your hand."

"I suppose I'm not as sophisticated at hurting as you are," she said wearily. The fight in her had banked somewhat.

Nearer to her, he said, "You were right. I figured Randolph to come. When you're home and you've considered how it happened, you might also consider forgiving the circumstances. It would've been different if you hadn't gone into the bar."

She took so long to acknowledge him that he assumed she wasn't going to. He started for the door.

"I'll forgive you when he's dead," she said.

He stopped, studying her across the room.

"Deal," he said.

While Rhiana went to get Sarah, Holland accompanied Max to the garage and switched their luggage to Max's car for the trip to the airport. He kept the gloves on until he was finished with Randolph's vehicle.

"There's a body in the trunk," he said to Max. "It's sealed in one of the bags. I'd prefer to leave the car here until tonight and use the rental in the meantime, but if you object I'll take it away now."

Max obviously did not relish the prospect, but said, "If you think it's safe you can leave it."

"The car's been wiped clean, so don't touch it. Can you get me a shotgun today? A pump, 12 gauge. Any brand. The barrel length doesn't matter because I'm going to cut it off. And a box of SSG shells?"

"A shotgun is easy. You'll have it by tonight."

"Have you any tools? A hacksaw and a round file?"

"They haven't been used in years, but there are new blades."

"That'll do. I'll call you this afternoon to see if the plane left and again tonight before I come back. If there's a problem, just say 'no.' If not, say 'yes.' "

"I understand," he said.

Rhiana and Sarah entered the garage from the house, ready to leave for home.

Sarah came to Holland. He fastened his jacket so she wouldn't see the revolver. He knelt to her and took her hands.

"I don't want to leave yet," Sarah said. "Mummy says we have to. Do we?"

"You'll be glad once you're home."

"Can't you come too?"

He was thankful she refrained from addressing him as "Uncle."

"I have work to do."

"Will you come to our house after?"

"No, I can't. But I'm happy I've met you, Sarah." He kissed her cheek. "You're a pearl. A perfect pearl. Your mother's fortunate to have you."

"I want to see baseball and I want to see your fish. Ker . . . Ker . . . si . . ."

"Quasimodo," he said, helping her. When he formed the name his swollen lip caught on his teeth.

Rhiana had a distinctive way of pursing her lips when she connected something past and present. He saw it when she heard Quasimodo.

"We'll go to a baseball game, dear," she said. "I promise."

"What's the matter with your mouth," Sarah wanted to know of him.

He glanced once at Rhiana. "Uncle George will take

you to see baseball if you ask him," he said to Sarah. "And don't forget the helicopter ride."

The suggestion failed to raise the desired enthusiasm. Dejected, she let them know she really did want to stay. It distressed Holland to know why and he half wished she had allowed them to go without seeing her. The child had drawn as close to him as her mother had not, having been as well behaved through the three days as any child could be hoped to, never once wanting her way or getting cranky in the long trying interludes of waiting.

He resisted an urge to hug her.

Standing, he looked last at Rhiana.

"You've helped."

Her demeanor softened unexpectedly.

"You'll need luck," was all she said.

"Tell George to pencil him out."

"Is that true? Is it?"

Their space was as divided by massed partitions as it had been when they first landed at the lake, Moloch the sole linkage between them. A metaphoric failure. Or preview.

"Listen to him, Rhiana," Max said.

But Holland left them and walked out to the rental without answering.

•15•

"Tea time."

The high, feline voice trickled through the ground floor of the house, chafing at Clement Moloch's concentration, prompting him to glower at the paper beneath his pen.

To him, Margaret's sound was a wherret that fairly sang of tight skin. That was increasingly the way he had come to envision her, and Claire: The Tight Skin Twins, slavishly obsessed with the obliteration of wrinkles and folds that would otherwise be reviewed as the draftings of maturity and character. Margaret's . . . well . . . her batteries had always been suspect. But from Claire he had expected far more than to have her embrace the same insipid narcissism. If both women had been conceived on the wrong side of the blanket he could grant some redemption for their doxy faddishness, but each had been coddled in God-fearing Christian homes with ample opportunities to acquire more penetrating insights.

Even the pen he used was a source of irritation. He favored a metal instrument with some heft to it, a gold nib employing real ink that left stains on the cuff to attest to its mettle, not the plasticized expresso scribblers that trailed some disgusting petroleum goo. What in heaven's name was the matter with ink wells? Was there nothing of substance left in the world? The Super Soft Superior Stylus Scribe he held poised in his hand was one such miracle of the modern age. Fat and ungainly and poorly suited to his short feelers, the felt-tipped thing nevertheless swept across a page and dropped its imprint without violating so much as a single fiber of the paper it mated with. Sort of like artificial insemination between a bat and a dove in flight.

"Tea time."

This time the announcement escaped him entirely.

He was sitting in an alcove at the front of the house, at bay windows facing onto a courtyard of tarmac stretching unbroken to the walls enclosing the estate. The solid barrier marking the entrance was directly in his field of vision. Morning dew was pretty much evaporated from the asphalt and birds were pecking at whatever delicate morsels the night had left.

While he wrestled with the process of transferring thought to paper he stared stonily at the gate, anticipating Randolph's eleventh-hour appearance. The lad should have been back at his duties no later than four in the morning. Not only was it an unpardonable violation of responsibilities, but profoundly uncharacteristic of him. Randolph had never been cavalier with the schedule, not once. His intention had been to send Randolph to the embassy first thing this morning so that they could be in the air by midday. That was shot all to bits now.

Randolph would have some wholesale explaining to do.

In fact, if Randolph were not such an asset, Moloch would banish him from this trip to Uruguay, leave him at home to make penance. Besides, Randolph was dear to him, a likable rascal who seldom strayed from his obligations. Not a jewel, was Randolph, but at least a shiny penny. In his mind Moloch was quoting his father.

He went back to his paper.

The theme of the passage he was struggling with was that man had become a race of hunters who no longer hunted, thus leaving dregs of takers and cheaters and largely accounting for the dearth of backbone that had become so prevalent in today's leaders. As illustrations of those who had scaled the Everest between appeasement and aggression, he was using Alfred Nobel, Andrew Carnegie, and General Hughes de l'Estoile. Dynamic geniuses all, yet mortal centurions who had transcended their detractors and were now recorded in the tomes of history as devout pacifists. They he knighted as "Trojan Horses." In the contemporary ranks he was confined to the lesser lights of Rommel, Nasser, de Gaulle, and Kissinger. He would have rejoiced to include Mengele, but events had been so distorted and recent publicity so unflattering. However, time and a proper perspective would restore—

"Tea time."

The summons reached him. She knocked on the door softly.

Margaret always enclosed her knuckles in a handkerchief before applying them to wood.

The door was locked.

At the door he said, through it, "Be still, woman. For pity's sake, don't pester me. I'm trying to make the best of this waiting."

"The tea is piping. Thy will, dearest."

"I have work," he said.

"Take a reprieve, then. You haven't even bothered to dress yet."

He glanced down at his robe and his bare feet, then squirmed his toes into the pile of the Persian carpet, enjoying the sensation.

"Very well," he said, resigned. "I shall be right there."

Now she lowered her voice. "Shall I have Raymond and the others join us? I've made enough."

Moloch considered the proposal.

"No," he said.

Back at the alcove he plopped the pen into the ormolu cup, and gathered his papers. The papers he took to one of the bookcases, a section of which swung aside to expose a wall safe. He placed the six sheets of notes in the safe and secured the door, then donned his slippers and left the room after a final sidelong squint at the gate.

Still no sign of Randolph.

In the chamber reserved for Moloch's aides, Ray Crosetti sat on a stool next to a billiard table and pondered a stack of girly magazines before him on the rich green surface. All had been looked through at least once and a new batch was called for.

The large room was bristling with equipment. Besides the billiard table there was an improvised badminton court, a table-tennis table, card and chess tables, dart boards, a putting carpet, a treadmill, a boxing bag, a speed bag, a press bench and complete weight-lifting apparatus, pulleys and cables and skipping ropes, climbing racks, a rowing platform and trio of cycle exercisers, home games, televisions and sound systems, a cassette and album collection, a projector and screen and a video-cassette combination, a jumbled library of trashy stuff, even shower and whirlpool and change room. A soundproofed firing range for weapons was relegated to the basement.

Crosetti was alone in the room.

"Tea time," he heard.

Margaret was skulking about the menage again, but he knew her bidding would be limited to the patriarch of the place this morning. Moloch was too pissed at Randolph's absence to have the hired help join them. When it came to those two he had learned that anything under the sun was possible. Therefore he decided that he had better take a drop while the opportunity was favorable.

From the pocket of his cardigan he drew a prophylactic bound with an elastic band. He squeezed off three capsules from the stash and popped them in his mouth, swallowing in a single coordinated action. Pill boxes were prone to rattling noises and for that reason he used the membrane as a depository.

Last night it had been Quaaludes; this morning Dexedrine. He estimated the number of capsules remaining. Were it not for being leery of Margaret or Clement coming in, he would have spilled the contents onto the nap and taken an accurate figure. Moloch would go apeshit if he knew the help was scoffing pills. Christ, he'd have a shit hemorrhage if he went further and found that Claire was his source of supply. What fucking crap, he thought. Moloch would pump folks full of fucking chemicals until they jellied and their eyes fell out but he forbade his own employees from taking drugstore beans. This in a country where the fucking farmers grew marijuana for windbreaks and you could buy lids of heroin from traffic cops at aspirin mark ups.

He had just snapped the elastic and deposited the stash back in his pocket when Moloch strode in, slippers flapping, robe dragging.

Crosetti's employer dressed in such ill-fitting clothes that Crosetti could hardly believe it. Of course, Margaret selected the man's wardrobe for him and bought it without benefit of fittings, so that partially explained his perpetually disheveled appearance. Still, after all these years, you'd think she could at least remember the fucking sizes. Actually, Crosetti suspected that she dressed him too.

Moloch seized Crosetti by the forearm.

"Has there been a peep from Brian?"

"Jack's been tryin' to raise him on the radio all morning. Can't get nothin'."

"This is a bloody dreadful performance, Raymond," Moloch said. "Really shoddy."

"Yes, sir," Crosetti agreed, awaiting the amphetamine.

"Such a radical departure for Brian, I can't help thinking he's gotten himself into a mess. I'm not pleased at all."

"More probable he got himself into one of those tamales at that grungy lonely hearts club he goes to," Crosetti said. "More probable he's still balls deep."

Moloch appeared repulsed. "Rubbish. Brian wouldn't allow a woman to come before his work. Any more than you would. Would he?"

"Hey, some of those tamales know tricks that go back to the Incas," Crosetti said, inspired.

"Alright, Raymond, alright," Moloch said, a flurry of desisting arm waving. "And it's Mayans, not Incas."

"Whatever. He's out dippin' his wick is what he's doin'."

Moloch scrutinized him closely. "You're exceptionally coarse this morning, Raymond."

"Sorry 'bout that. I'd just like to get movin', same's

you. Sittin' around all this time can make a guy go ratso."

"I quite agree with you on that point, I must say," Moloch said. He was absently fanning the girly magazines without really absorbing what he was seeing. "We're being counted on by very important people. They would not be impressed if they knew why we are not on our way."

"Yes, sir. Why don't I go out and see if I can turn him up."

Moloch cast about with a harried look.

"I'd much prefer to send one of the other chaps. You know I don't like both of you away at once."

"But I know the places he goes and the crack he usually humps."

After some difficulty, Moloch said, "Very well then. You go. But keep in contact with Jack so that he's able to keep me abreast. If you're not successful at his usual haunts, pop in and see Paul Buggs. Not a word to Waterston. It might be useful to see if Buggs still has the flair he was once known for."

"Yeah, I can put Buggs on to the locals if I have to."

"Not likely that would be of help, I'm afraid. They're notoriously slack."

"Yeah, but they might be able to find his car. Find his car and we'll find him."

Margaret was waiting for him in the glassed rotunda at the rear of the sprawling house, the bulletproof glass commanding a view of her garden dotted with Japanese bonsai trees. A canopy of ivy above contributed a haze of green below.

On the lawn a community of squirrels crisscrossed with vain tails arched over their backs.

The mirrored table gave a double image of the sterling tea service and vase of freshly cut lilacs from her greenhouse. Ringing these were china plates piled high with gingersnaps and English rolled wafers and Scotch shortbreads. Alongside Clement's setting was a bundle of newspapers from far flung places.

He bustled in and snatched a lace napkin from its ring.

This he spread over one knee, a convenience allowing him to sit sideways to the table so that he could read his papers unencumbered by furniture. He snorted.

"This is a truly beastly turn of events," he said. "I can't imagine what could have possessed Brian to act so irresponsibly."

"I'm certain there is a perfectly innocent explanation for Brian's truancy, dearest," Margaret soothed.

He unfolded the first newspaper and shook it out.

Margaret commenced to pouring the tea.

Over the wall, high up, a jet airliner soared in a banked climb, sifting down its faded boom and sparkling in the sun before diminishing from sight.

In the same afternoon, in Mexico City, George Hidalgo was the picture of distraction as he wandered through his house to emerge eventually on the balcony.

He unfurled an outsized chart and began tracing the graphics thereon with the point of a divider. The chart, a complex illustration of the earth's crust on which Mexico City was situated, gave prominence to soil and rock and subterranean water formations by means of sectioning, and would hopefully enlarge on the subject of the article he was writing.

"Did you find what you were looking for?" Mariana asked him, twisting in her chair.

"Maybe," he answered. "It's difficult to know when you're dealing with theories and phenomena."

She lounged next to him, resplendent in halter top and shorts, reading English. Strapped around her head was an eye-shade. She returned to her book.

The object of George's distraction was his ignorance of the state of affairs in Guatemala. Whether to take solace in the fact that there had been no news—and therefore no adverse notices—and construe that as promise, or become alarmed because no news might be sign of grief, was becoming more arduous to endure with each passing hour. For that reason the article being composed was a forced labor, resorted to in order to keep from turning himself inside out.

Mariana as well was far from engrossed in her choice of distraction. Occasionally she would sweep him with a furtive look. As much as she craved broaching the question, she had kept her distance, respecting his undeclared wish for discreet support. Whatever was responsible for the listless floundering was, she sensed, a dilemma best left to his own devices. Now that they were together again there seemed every reason for optimism; she was resolved that they would survive regardless.

The past two nights she had stayed without returning to her own villa, for which George was quietly grateful, although the tenuous time of waiting had even then infringed on their lovemaking so that, on the second night, no overtures had been made. Oh, she knew he was waiting on something, she just didn't know what it was. Last evening they had declined a dinner date with friends she would have liked to see. Earlier, George had demurred when his father invited them to look at some prospective properties. The excuse offered had been that he was anticipating an important telephone call.

At intervals during the day he telephoned the Thomas Cook office to inquire after messages. Each time the reply was the same: *Nada.*

The helicopter sat at the ready, a slumbering mantis perched on an airfield minutes from the city.

Mariana linked her hands behind her head. She was watching him again.

"Is it true the city is sinking a third of a meter every year?"

"At least that," he said. "That's all they will admit to."

She laughed, trying to be light. "You're no fun anymore. You've become a doomsayer."

"I don't mean to be," he said, reaching for her hand. "It's only speculation that they knew at the time, but the city should not have been built on this site."

"What's causing it to sink?"

"It has to do with the water table and with underground rivers that erode—"

The shrill note of the telephone made them both start. He threw the chart aside, tripping on the rush mat in his headlong dive inside the house, and had lifted the receiver before the third ring.

"George?"

"Yes, Isabelle. Have you news?"

"Rhiana and Sarah are here. You had better come quickly."

•III•

HUMAN WRONGS . . .

On 18 April 1972, I was attacked by several people on the street. My eyes were covered by a special black band and I was forced into a minibus. The vehicle did not move for a few minutes. During this time I noticed that the people around me were addressing each other with expressions like 'my colonel,' 'my major.' They started asking me questions from the first moment they put me in the minibus. When I did not answer, they started threatening me in the following manner. 'You do not talk now,' they would say, 'in a few minutes, when our hands will start roaming in between your legs, you will be singing like a nightingale.'

The vehicle travelled for quite a long time before it stopped before a building I could not recognize. When I got off the minibus, I realized that I was in a relatively high, open space. I was then taken into the basement of the building, and then into a rather spacious room. I was surrounded by people whom I guessed to be military officers from the ways they addressed each other. They asked me questions and kept on saying that unless I spoke it would be quite bad for me and that we would have to do 'collective training' together.

After a short while they forced me to take off my skirt and stockings and laid me down on the ground and tied my hands and feet to pegs. A person by the name of Umit Erdal beat the soles of my feet for about half an hour. As he beat my soles he kept on saying—We made everybody talk here, you think we shall not succeed with you?'—and insulting me. Later, they attached wires to my fingers and toes and passed electrical current through my body. At the same time they kept beating my naked thighs with truncheons. Many people were assisting Umit Erdal in this. One was a rather large man, tall, with curly hair and a relatively dark skin. A second was a small man with relatively dark skin, black hair and a moustache. The third was rather elderly, of middle stature, and of a dark complexion. He constantly wore dark glasses. The fourth was rather old, fat, of middle stature and with blue eyes and grey hair. At the same time, during the tortures, a grey-haired, stout and elderly colonel, and a grey-haired, blue-eyed, tall and well-built officer would frequently come in and give directives. After a while, they disconnected the wire from my finger and connected it to my ear. They immediately gave a high dose of electricity. My whole body and head shook in a terrible way. My front teeth started breaking. At the same time my torturers would hold a mirror to my face and say: 'Look what is happening to your lovely green eyes. Soon you will not be able to see at all. You will lose your mind. You see, you have already started bleeding in your mouth.'

When they finished with electric shocks, they lifted me up to my feet and several of those I mentioned above started beating me with truncheons. After a while I felt dizzy and could not see very well. Then I fainted.

When I came to myself, I found out I was lying half-naked in a pool of dirty water. They tried to force me to stand up and run. At the same time they kept beating me with truncheons, kicking me and pushing me against the walls. They then held my hand and hit me with truncheons in my palms and on my hands, each one taking turns. After all this my whole body was swollen and red and I could not stand on my feet.

As if all this was not enough, Umit Erdal attacked me and forced me to the ground. I fell on my face. He stood on my back and with the assistance of someone else forced a truncheon into my anus. As he struggled to stand he kept on saying, 'You whore! See what else we will do to you. First tell us how many people did you go to bed with? You won't be able to do it any more. We shall next destroy your womanhood.'

They next made me lie on my back and tied my arms and legs to pegs. They attached an electric wire to the small toe of my right foot and the other to the end of a truncheon. As I resisted they hit my body and legs with a large axe handle. They soon succeeded in penetrating my sexual organ with the truncheon with the electric wire on, and passed current. I fainted.

A little later, the soldiers outside brought in a machine used for pumping air into people and said they would kill me. Then they untied me, brought me to my feet and took me out of the room. With a leather strap, they hanged me from my wrists on to a pipe in the corridor. As I hung half-naked, several people beat me with truncheons. I fainted again.

When I woke, I found myself in the same room on a bed. They brought in a doctor to examine me. They tried to force me to take medicines and eat. I was bleeding a dark, thick blood. Some time later they brought in Ismail Muhsin, who was in the same building as myself, to put more pressure on me. They wanted to show me into what state they had put him. I saw that the nails of his right hand were covered with pus. I realized that they had burned him with cigarette butts. They themselves later confirmed this. The sole of one of his feet was completely black and badly broken. The same night we were transferred to Istanbul, together with Ismail Muhsin.*

The next morning, the colonel I have already described came into my cell (I do not know where the cell was). He beat me and threatened me, 'Tonight I shall take you where your dead are. I shall have the corpses of all of you burnt. I will have you hanging from the ceiling and apply salt to your cut soles.'

When he did not like the answers I gave him, he beat me again; then he had my eyes tied and sent me to another building. I was brought into a small room with my eyes tied. I was tied on the ground to pegs from my arms and ankles and electricity was passed through my right foot and hand. They then administered falanga.

During the whole time I was in Istanbul, my hands were tied to chains. Because of this and because my tongue had split, I could not eat. A doctor would occasionally come to look at me and suggest first aid.

One night I heard the sound of a gun and the sound of a man fall and die on the ground very close to me. I cried out: 'Who have you killed?' They answered, 'It is none of your business. We kill whomever we want and bury him in a hole in the ground. Who would know if we did the same to you?' As I knew already, there was no security for my life.

During the ten days I stayed at MIT (the Turkish Secret Service) the same torture, insults, threats, and

*Fictitious names have been substituted to prevent possible reprisals against the individuals, their families and acquaintances.

pressure continued. On 28 April I was sent to the house of detention. Despite the fact that I went to the doctor at the house of detention and explained that I was badly tortured, that my right hand did not hold and that I had other physical complaints, including the fact that I had no menstruation for four months in the following period, I was given no treatment. Some of my physical complaints still continue.

6 February 1973 *Signed here and at every page,*
Alexandria.

—One of 20 affidavits from female political prisoners in the Ankara, Turkey newspaper, *Yeni Halkci,* in November of 1973.

Miss Alcxandria Sulma Emoud,* a Turkish-born citizen, was 23 years of age at the time of her arrest.

Because of increasing pressure from the Council of Europe and Amnesty International, the acting Prime Minister, Naim Talu, announced an internal government investigation into long-standing allegations of torture in his country.

In January of 1974, every government agency was cleared of all charges, and all allegations of torture denounced as groundless.

·16·

Night had fallen as Holland stood at the entrance to Claire Moloch's apartment.

The double doors were symmetrically panelled in rough pine, faithful to the building's Spanish motif of dimpled stucco, coach lamps dispersing yellow light, and arched doorways. Even the doors of the single elevator were arched, though Holland had avoided its convenience.

Instead he had used the stairs, entering by the rear door to avoid the attendant in the lobby. Not long before he

*Fictitious names have been substituted to prevent possible reprisals against the individuals, their families and acquaintances.

had followed Claire Moloch to a dining room about five minutes away. There the maitre d' had showered her with attention and seated her alone at a choice table. As soon as her drink was brought her, and a menu, Holland had hurried away and returned to pick his way past the security door with little more bother than if he'd used a key.

The sixth floor of the plush structure encompassed only two suites. At the second suite he was unable to detect any sounds from within, and, seeing a letter still stuck in the mail slot, presumed there was no one home.

From his pocket he produced a fountain pen which he disassembled as he had done downstairs, this time choosing a different pick from the hollow tubes, a slimmer one with less spur on the end. He mated this with a tension bar and inserted both in the keyhole. The pick cancelled the lock's pins one at a time, Holland holding each aloft with the tension bar until the final pin was tripped and elevated to the right proximity. A slight compensation with the tension bar snapped the spring-operated latch bolt back and Holland was inside, relocking the door behind.

Some of the lights had been left on, so that he would not have to use more than his pocket light. Leaving the lights burning could merely be her habit, or could warn that she was planning to be back relatively soon. If he knew more about her a judgment would be possible.

He noted that the drapes were drawn; an auspicious token.

Facing the threshold was a combined living and dining room, to the right a kitchen, and on the left a hallway glassed on one side and looking out on a balcony. The drapes were drawn there as well. Two rooms and a separate storage space opened onto the hallway, one room locked, the other empty. He guessed both were intended to be bedrooms. The woman's own sleeping quarters were at the end of the hallway, large enough to enclose the full corner of the suite.

The floor plan, with the exception of the sealed room, was covered by Holland in one contracted sweep.

His initial impression matched the one when he had first sighted Hector Lomolin's office in the clinic: spare, temporary, grudgingly inhabited by a transient.

The kitchen held enough utensils to get by on. In the

dining room were a breakfast table and four folding chairs. A free form sofa ensemble was positioned around a low accent table in the living room, on it a portable television of Japanese origin and a piece of Canadian Eskimo sculpture.

The management's interpretation of vogue broke up the white walls here and there with Toulouse-Lautrec prints in chrome-plated frames. Were it not for wall-to-wall carpeting, the place would provoke pangs of loneliness.

Of all the rooms only the woman's bedroom and adjoining bathroom showed positive signs of habitation. The mammoth bed, unfettered by headboard or framed boundaries, was covered by the pelts of some animal he didn't care to identify. That too was white, blending with the carpeting and walls. Her wardrobe did justice to the walk-in closet, leaning decidedly toward slit skirts and the tight fitting things he had seen her in previously. All had local labels. The bathroom was a riot of cosmetics and creams, fragrant preparations for toenail to hair and every niche between.

Holland gaped at a pair of open crotch bikini panties that had been hung to dry in the shower.

How old had Max said she was? Watching her enter the limousine every morning had confirmed her figure to be up to the standards of Max's description, and the bra cups in the drawer were certainly ample, but crotchless lingerie on a woman in her late forties was a new experience for him.

Equally puzzling was the almost total lack of reading material. Other than a copy of the New Testament on the bedside table and a few copies of National Geographic, there was absolutely nothing to read. Max had estimated her stay at a year. By all accounts she did not go out much, when she did it was to her brother's estate or on limited sojourns to eat or shop, and even that apparently most often confined to the company of the gunsel she was romancing. Holland supposed that the companion could at least account for the sexy underwear. After all, the gunsel Max had pointed out was at least fifteen years her junior, and for her to keep that fire going had to require something more imaginative than the convenience of association. For a moment he considered scouting after whips.

But what did the woman do with the rest of her time? Particularly when Moloch and his gunsels had been absent a good portion of the past year?

He went through the closet and rifled the drawers of her bureau, leaving the contents as they had been and turning up nothing of consequence other than garter belts and negligees. The search of the balance of the rooms was as fruitless. No passport. No address book. No diary. No calendars with dates checked off.

In the storage room there was a set of custom luggage crafted by Madler's of Offenbach; stripped of claim tags. Her musical tastes ran to regimental marches by the Grenadier Guards and Her Majesty's Royal Marines. A provision of frozen sole lay forlornly in the refrigerator.

The balcony too was barren except for a rather large hibachi, a refuse container beside it. All that seemed to have been burned in the hibachi was paper, not unusual for apartment dwellers, the consumed wisps of pulp crumbling instantly in his gloved fingers. There wasn't a trace of coals. He thought that virgin coals might be in the refuse container but found only a charred grime in the bottom.

That left the locked room.

He deluded the simple mechanism without so much as resorting to the tension bar. The room was windowless, enabling him to switch on the light. Before him was a black-lacquered rolltop desk and a stenographer's chair. Over the desk was a blank bulletin board with some push-pins in the cork.

The slatted cover of the desk was locked, as well as the drawers. That gave him some basis for optimism, though he suspected the black lacquer was originally designed to retain fingerprints. Because he had closed the door to the hallway he would be unable to hear if she were to return before he was through, so he listened for a moment, then bent to the lock.

When he slid the top back he was disappointed. There was a stack of untouched bond paper, a selection of soft-tipped pens, and an electric typewriter with a fresh ribbon in place. He had anticipated there might be a cache of letters in one of the small compartments, but even the cubbyholes were desolate. Voiding the locks on the drawers uncovered a similar state. There should have been writing paper, instead there was only the office-sized stuff.

Why then have everything locked up, including the room itself?

He applied a detailed search, probing under and behind the drawers, the desk, the chair, and the typewriter, combed the carpet, wallboard, and walls for eavesdropping equipment, took to the carpet on hands and knees looking for paint chips that would show the walls had once been tampered with. The room ultimately divulged no more than domestic bliss. Claire Moloch had a fetish for cleanliness or he was contemplating her brother's fabled attention to detail, it had to be one or the other.

Putting everything back as it was, he relocked the door and went over the rest of the suite, taking more time than he had planned but experiencing a mounting frustration that he could not find evidence to justify her presence in the country.

Beside the bed, next to the Bible and a clock, was a telephone. He unscrewed the speaking cap of the receiver and scrutinized the relay puck beneath. It proved to be standard phone company issue. He then used a kitchen knife to remove the baseplate on the phone and peered inside with the aid of his pocket light, looking for a foreign transmitter. Every component the light touched on was as temperate as the day it had been assembled.

He stole a look at the clock as he replaced the screws. Forty minutes inside. Too long. He would get out as soon as the phone was reassembled.

A faint rumbling was felt in the floor. He paused, reading oscillations rather than listening for sounds. The elevator was moving, nearing his level. He quickened his pace with the phone. Still two screws to turn home.

The elevator shuddered to a stop. The sound of the doors reached him.

Damnation. The last screw spun off its placement and fell into the fur of the bedspread. He felt around for it.

A current of voices carried on the air, more than one. Let it be her neighbors, he thought, doubting she would have eaten a formal dinner in the time that had elapsed.

But a key entered the lock. The door opened on a man speaking.

Holland found the screw and hurried it into the threaded receptacle, running the fastener down with his fingers and abandoning it without a final twist with the knife.

A woman's voice answered the man.

He was on the wrong side of the bed to make the closet, and the drapes in back of him were too sheer. Leaving the room was out of the question. He cursed himself for staying until he was trapped.

The voices were turning into the hallway.

He drew the revolver.

Claire Moloch was saying, in a British accent, "Where could he be, then? Randolph couldn't have disappeared into thin air. Not in a place like this."

"Fucked if I know," the man said. "He's shacked up, you can take odds on that, but where and with who is anybody's guess. Randolph's ugly enough to go ape hunting with a stick, but every once in a while he comes up like a rose. I looked in every beer joint and turned over every rock and all I got was tired."

Holland knew that as well as the man did, having followed the man who was talking for most of the day until, in the late afternoon, it had become apparent the gunsel was wandering aimlessly.

"Clement must be livid," Claire said.

In desperation, Holland dropped to the floor and squeezed under the bed.

"You got it. He's about ready to call out the Marines."

They entered the room, Claire crossing to the closet. The man's feet were small, the woman's large. Her ankles were slim through the socket but thick fore and aft. She wore a leather skirt.

"He wouldn't take kindly to your using time to come here," she said.

She kicked her shoes off.

Holland placed the useless kitchen knife on the floor and, with difficulty because of the bed's proximity, swiveled his head to sight around the confined space. The only object in evidence was a hardbound book against the wall near the head of the bed, a single sheet of paper projecting from between its pages, too large for a bookmark.

"Hey, now that I got a chance for a last rack to tide me over, I ain't about to pass it up," the man said, his voice thickening. "Once Randolph shows, we'll be gone three-four weeks, maybe more."

"Ray . . ." Claire said, her tone receptive.

Their feet came together near the closet.

Beneath the bed struck Holland as a strange location for a book.

"Have you tried the police yet?" Claire said.

"Soon's I leave," Ray answered. "Clement said to hold off on that until I ran out of leads."

There was the fluid sound of garments, of bodies moving against each other.

Holy Christ, not now, Holland said to himself.

"Did you find any leads?" Claire wanted to know.

"Naw. The barkeep at that hole he goes to says he was there 'til after midnight. Supposedly he got all steamed up over some woman tourist who came in with her husband. There was some kind'a hassle but Randolph wasn't in on it. From the description it could'a been those two we saw at the bullfights. Those fucking greasebags lie like rugs though."

Fabric tore and two small cream-colored buttons bounced on the carpet, one travelling under the bed close to Holland. He eyed it anxiously, expecting a hand to come after.

"Ray . . ." Claire said in reproach.

A buckle was undone. The fur bedspread sloughed onto the floor.

Holland strained to read the title on the binding of the book, thwarted by the lack of light.

Ray moved her up against the wall.

Holland couldn't quite make out the imprint.

Ray bent at the knees, pushing off from the carpet, the rest of him raked upwards between her splayed legs.

Holland reached a hand out gingerly, intending to turn the book more fully toward him.

"Ray . . . wait . . ."

There was an adjusting of feet. Claire bent to slip her pantyhose off.

Holland had just turned the book. He snatched his hand away in the event she might see it.

She limited herself in her haste to the removal of only one leg, letting the nylon dangle loose.

Ray hiked her dress to her waist and slid her feet apart on the carpet.

"Let me see, goddamn it," Ray said. "Let's have 'em . . ."

Her blouse tumbled down, then her brassiere.

The book was Milton's *Paradise Lost*.

Her legs were wide and locked, touching only with the balls of her heels. Then they buckled and surrendered the function of support, relinquishing that to the man's limbs, clamping for purchase, riding, the frantic launch making her leg muscles swell and come hard.

"Hold on . . ." Ray said.

Holland lurked a hand toward the book, unable to stem his curiosity, the piece of paper too inviting.

"Ray . . ." Claire was saying again and again, with less distinction each time, blurred by the work of copulating to total abandon.

Ray had her pinioned on his fulcrum and was jacking her against the wall—hoisting her up the wall—with short explosive exertions that burst his breath and thumped the partition loudly.

"Jesus . . ." Ray grunted.

As Holland slowly pulled the paper from between the book's pages he reflected that these two really did mean to move the earth. It wasn't love they were making, more like the labor of trucks on a mountain grade. And Claire, not merely yielding, was giving as good as she got.

He brought the paper close and tried to make out what was on it. Other than determining it to be lines of typing, he could not see well enough to actually read the presentation.

"Ray . . . !" Claire hollered.

The two, remaining locked together, crashed onto the bed in a great writhing heap that nearly collapsed the moorings. A wooden frame-member was driven down into the rise of Holland's cheekbone, parting the skin, the wire netting under the mattress digging in where strands crossed. He was literally trapped.

The hammering pair above gave little indication of slackening. If anything, Ray had escalated his travel.

Every time the man plunged, the bed frame creased Holland's flesh. He pressed his head as far into the yield of carpet as he could but the wood still reached him. Already his head was turned as much to the side as was allowed. Never before had he been witness to a couple making love and he was surprised at just how audible and strenuous a haul it could be made. This was an encounter the very word "fuck" had been coined for, surely, its bedrock lucidity matched admirably to the ugly airing above.

He could smell the woman, hear the man pummeling the source, listen to the flat, tight bellies slapping, feel the legs jerking and clasping and beating the bed.

Claire heightened her vocals until the suite was made party to the act. Holland shut them out and pictured his beach.

When they were finished and finally rolled apart gasping, and the bed frame cleared his cheek, Holland estimated that they had been coupled in excess of three-quarters of an hour. He almost shared their sated relief when the wood stopped assaulting him, though their cracked breathing continued to flutter it near.

While Crosetti straightened his clothing and prepared to leave, Holland considered the implication of the cloistered book and tried to tie it to something productive, anything. His fear was that the book had simply been dropped or placed there as a convenience for her bedtime reading. But then, why not with the Bible? Why *under* the bed? Why under *anything?* Being one of only two books in the place must have made it exclusive for more than that. The paper would provide an insight.

Crosetti went to the door, saying he was going to check with the police next, and if Randolph was found soon she would not hear from him until they returned from the trip south.

Claire returned to the bedroom and discarded the balance of her clothes to the floor, stretching languidly and emitting a noise not unlike a cat's purr.

She poured a sherry and sipped it while filling the bath, then went to the stereo and put on an album filled with marching feet, horses' hooves, shouted commands and brass bands.

Quick step, march! Hu-two . . . Hu-two . . . Hu-two! Ratta-ta-tat . . . Ratta-ta-tat . . . Ratta-ta-tat . . .

Holland waited.

Although leaving the door to the bathroom open, she could not see out once she was in the bath. When he heard her step into the water he eased out from under the bed and immediately studied the paper.

Matching the typing to the book, he couldn't imagine why she would want to transcribe Milton's epic into manuscript form. And this transcription was of a page that was two-thirds through the book. Where was the rest of it?

He moved to smell the paper. And then he knew. The odor that had wafted from the desk when he had first rolled the top back. He should have known then.

In the kitchen he rapidly found the corroborating evidence: three huge jugs of copper sulphate and an equally large tin of sodium bicarbonate on a shelf hidden below the sink. Still, he had time to confirm and he decided that he had better do so.

He ran four ounces of water into a glass and added a teaspoon of sodium bicarbonate—more commonly known as "baking soda"—to it.

Seconds later he was examining the results when he felt the familiar tremor of the elevator. He hurried across the living room to the edge of the hallway, certain this time it would be her neighbors.

But the lock snapped open.

Ray Crosetti stood inside the door. He looked around, calling, "Claire? It's me. I forgot to mention . . ."

The militia on the stereo drowned him out. He frowned in its direction and went to lean into the kitchen, raising his voice, "Claire . . . ?"

Holland had to move quickly and elect even faster. Crosetti had perhaps only had time enough to reach the street and turn around again, but the interval had been enough to change everything. Holland had found the string to pull. There would be no stopping him.

If the talisman were kind today, he would have left Crosetti in the street. Instead the gunsel would materialize in the hallway in a second or two.

"Claire? Where are you," Crosetti called. There was a subtle alteration in tone. Holland concluded that Crosetti had seen the paper in the kitchen.

He took the lighter that Rhiana had given him from his pocket. He opened the top but did not ignite the gas. The butane made a low but distinct hissing sound as it escaped its confines.

He set the lighter down on the ledge behind the curtains flanking the hallway, then slipped into the storage room opposite.

"For fuck's sake, Claire. What the hell's this?" Crosetti was in the hall.

He stopped.

"Claire . . . ?" There was a clear note of suspicion.

Holland, separated from him by only a couple of yards and a door that was slightly ajar, knew the call was not loud enough for her to hear.

Crosetti came forward warily, a step at a time, a Walther in one hand, the paper in the other, intent on the crack of the door. Just as he was abreast the opening he became aware of the hissing sound behind the curtain. It unnerved him; he turned on the imagined threat and stepped away, back toward Holland.

Holland shouldered the door aside and clubbed the back of Crosetti's head solidly, once, with the heavy barreled revolver. In the same motion he clamped his hand over Crosetti's where it held the Walther, preventing the automatic from being fired by reflex. Crosetti crumpled to the floor.

Stripping him of the Walther, Holland stepped over the inert body and went into the bedroom.

From her bath Claire called out, "Ray? Is that you?"

"Yeah, it's me," Holland said, faking Crosetti rather poorly.

He picked up her discarded pantyhose and tore them leg from leg.

The impersonation seemed to have been superior to his own critique. Claire said, "Did you forget something?"

Water lapped the tub, dripping as she rose. She was going to come out.

He tucked the Walther into his belt along with one-half of her pantyhose, pulling the other half over his head until it was taut across his features.

The woman met him in the doorway, naked except for a towel in her hand. She dropped it when she saw him coming at her. He covered her mouth with his hand and drove her back into the bathroom, circling behind and slamming her to him with his free arm.

She squirmed, slippery with beads of moisture and bath oil, and almost broke away. He took a firmer hold and raised the revolver between her breasts, jamming the tip of the barrel into the soft triangle under her chin.

"You can go dead two ways," he said. "Do it yourself."

She ceased her struggle and went limp in his grip. She had wet the front of him through to his skin.

"I won't hurt you, so don't be foolish. Don't fight me and don't make a sound. *Comprende?*"

She moved her head in compliance.

"I'm going to gag you and tie your hands. Do it easy."

She nodded again.

He took his hand away.

She stood quietly, not bothering to cover herself.

From the cosmetic selection on the vanity he chose a medium-sized plastic cap and unscrewed it.

"Put it in your mouth," he said, offering the cap.

She did not move.

Keeping the barrel pointed at the floor, he brought its length gently between her legs. The chill of the steel jerked her straight and brought her hands there.

"Play dead," he said. "It's better."

She bared her teeth as he nudged the barrel deeper into the crook of hair.

"Please," she said.

"Your mouth. Open your mouth."

She accepted the cap in her teeth, but he pressed it past until the whole of it was enclosed. He dipped a hand towel in the bath water and bound it over her mouth, then sat her on the toilet and secured her hands with the spare leg of her hose. Another towel encircled her midsection to bind her arms.

In the hallway he took Crosetti by the arms and dragged him into the bedroom and onto the bed. There was a large damp imprint where they had lain.

From a receptacle under his right armpit, opposite his shoulder holster but on the same rigging, he extracted the silencer and screwed it into the revolver's barrel with a solid click.

He put the extension six inches from Crosetti's chest and fired three rounds into his heart.

Crosetti's body bucked free of the bed, flaying its limbs with each entry, Holland having to await a settling before delivering the next. Even so, there was a rhythm to it, an almost lyrical precision. One of the effects of a bullet's entry into the chest cavity of a human form is that the cheeks puff inordinately, the result of air displaced from the lungs by the enormous crush of ballistics. Another is the dispersion of energy throughout the anatomy, even in to the minor extremities, whipping the fingers and flaring the nostrils and flowing ripples under the skin. Crosetti's flesh did all of these.

The sound of the revolver might have been as pronounced as a gum bubble breaking.

Leaving the dead Crosetti, he dumped the woman's purse and picked out the keys he wanted. These he used to open the sealed room and the desk, taking with him the stack of blank bond paper he had passed over before.

Claire was sitting smartly with her knees clamped together when he went into the bathroom. She had not seen Crosetti's fate.

He fanned the papers for her.

"I'll sell them back," he said. "A whole lot of money."

She shook her head to imply futility. She transmitted dull noises through her gag.

"Enemy of Mankind, and like that," he said. "Fitting choice, Milton."

She rolled her eyes to show the paper was worthless.

He framed the single sheet from the book for her. This time her eyes went wide.

"It's not Milton, but it'll have its price," he said. "We'll talk."

Behind the door there was a robe. He used the sash to bind her legs to the base of the toilet, then left her, saying, "It won't be long."

In the hallway the lighter was still obediently releasing its essence. Holland snapped the top shut and placed the implement in the top drawer of the bedside table, alongside his tobacco pouch. The keys to Randolph's car he concealed in a jewelry box on the dressing table.

After stripping the stocking from his head he wrapped Crosetti in the fur bedspread and carried the body to the door of the apartment, setting it on the floor and making sure the corridor was empty before retrieving the elevator.

When the elevator arrived he put it on "Hold" and hurriedly deposited Crosetti in a corner. Above the floor selection buttons was a small, locked access panel. He opened the lock easily and examined the switches beneath.

He pressed the button for the floor below, and as soon as the car moved he threw the "Emergency Hold" switch, aborting its descent at his estimation of eye-level. Flipping another toggle released the doors and proved his calculation to be correct.

He crawled back onto Claire's floor without difficulty.

He stood away and contemplated the cables now exposed above the car, replacing the three spent cartridges in the revolver while he did so, dropping the empties into his pocket.

The initial round parted all but one strand of the primary cable, leaving it to strain and chatter under the massed weight. He was bent at the knees with the revolver held straight out on locked elbows, one hand cupping the other. He sliced the last strand with the next round. The car pitched crazily and slid a few feet further, grinding its protest, but brought to bay by the remaining auxiliary cable. The broken winding lashed the shaft violently on its way down.

He lined the revolver on the other cable. This time the elevator's last umbilical cord was severed cleanly, sending the car rocketing down the shaft while at the same time Holland scooped up the papers and the book and raced the crash to the stairwell.

Crosetti's vagrant coffin struck the depths of the building with a thunderous crack that shattered windows and rained plaster. A storm of dust and debris assaulted Holland on the stairs, the doors flung wide, fragments of glass and painted concrete showered down. The lights went out, then flickered, came back on. Someone in a room next to the stairs began to scream.

He took the stairs in wild bounding passes, leaping handrails and dropping cat-like in mid flight. On the bottom floor he stopped to detach the silencer and put both it and the revolver in their places.

He walked out as though for a stroll, the building quivering behind until he was lost from sight.

• 17 •

Clement Moloch received the first telephone call at 11:51 that evening. The hours before had been trying, loading his mind with implacable imagery. He knew trepidation after a long absence.

Margaret held the telephone out to him.

"Charles Waterston," she said.

He took the receiver and held it until she had left the room.

"What is it?" he demanded.

"Chuck here, Clement. I'm calling from Claire's apartment. There's been—"

"Claire's apartment?" Moloch interrupted. "What would you be doing ringing me from Claire's apartment?

"There's been a bad piece of business here, Clement. Claire hasn't been harmed, mind you. Upset, of course, but she's calmed considerably."

He listened for a response but none was forthcoming.

"Clement?"

"Go on."

On his end, Waterston had the receiver pressed between ear and shoulder, the phone out at arms length while he walked dislocated circles beside the bed. On his face he wore what he thought to be a furrowed depiction of grit, a practice he made of suiting his expressions to his telephone conversations, something he assumed everyone did.

"A maniac broke in and tied Claire up and shot Ray Crosetti. Then the creep put Ray in the elevator and—"

"Raymond was shot?" Moloch interrupted again. He held the receiver away and looked at it a moment. "By whom?"

"We don't have that information yet, Clement. But I promise you we'll have him tracked down in a matter of hours. Claire was not assaulted. . . ."

Moloch looked at the phone a second time.

". . . I have everything well in hand. The locals had enough sense to call immediately."

"What the devil was he doing there?"

"Who? Oh, you mean Ray. Well, you said he and Claire . . . just a second . . . let me ask her . . ."

Moloch placed his forehead in his palm. "Don't do that. Is there any sign of Brian?"

"Brian Randolph? Why, no. Should he be here?"

Unnoticed by Waterston, a small screw fell from the base of the phone to disappear in the carpeting. In his other hand he held one half of Claire's hose, the half he had lifted from the side of the bed. A neat line of blood near the knee had also eluded his attention.

"Is Paul Buggs with you, Waterston?"

Waterston shot a distressed glance around a suite milling with uniformed and plainclothed policemen. One uniformed policeman was cleaning his ear with a rifle cartridge. Two others sat on the floor trying to lace their boots a new way, having spotted another officer's done in a pattern that had caught their fancy. A plainclothes policeman smoked a long cheroot of quality tobacco, half ash.

Paul Buggs was picking through a jewelry box on the dressing table.

Waterston lowered his voice so as to not be overheard. "As a matter of fact, I had Paul meet me here. But he's been drinking, Clement. Yesterday the poor bastard's wife left him and went home again. He won't be much good for a few days. I can handle this. We'll have this unravelled faster than it takes to play nine holes."

As much as Waterston's face was animated in telephone communications, Moloch's was not, often given over to periods with his eyes closed. He did so now.

"Put him on," he said tersely.

"Clement, can't we forget this unpleasantness—"

"Put him on, Waterston. And get the locals out of there, you with them. Make them understand that this is an internal matter, and none of their concern. They are to wipe it from their reports and stay away. Are we hearing each other?"

Waterston sighed heavily. "I think I can do that, yes."

"My dear fellow, remove yourself from the premises and put Buggs in charge. The office and all its resources are to be put at his disposal. Full cooperation. Clamp a wall of secrecy on this, Waterston, your future may depend on it."

A suspension followed, during which Moloch paced and looked at the ceiling. A fly was dive-bombing the room repeatedly.

"This is Buggs, sir. I'm sorry about what happened."

"Is it true you've been drinking, Paul?"

There was a short silence. Moloch thought he heard him swear.

"I've had a few. I'm alright."

"Should I come there?"

"I wouldn't advise that, sir, not until we know what we've got here. It wouldn't be wise, in my opinion."

"Good lad," Moloch said expansively. "I like to hear a man with his wits about him."

"The place is crawling with vaquero cops. They wave these goddamn machine guns around and stink up the place." He took his mouth from the receiver and said to a policeman undoing his pants and about to enter the bathroom, "Hey, amigo. Fuck off, you know?"

The policeman sulked away.

"I thought Waterston was shooing them out," Moloch said.

"Yes, sir, he's doing that now. But they're idiots. Most of them never used those machine guns and they're just itching for something to open up on. They've got it all worked out that some crazy Indian busted in here and they've got the hots to wipe out some Indians."

"I've requested of Waterston that you assume control. You'll have all the assistance you need. Tell me what you see."

Buggs looked down on the sanguineous spoor on the bed.

"A mess," he said. "Chunks of Ray's heart are spread all over the bed, half of his back with it. I guess your sister went hysterical when she saw it. She was tied up in the can . . . in the bathroom. She's better now. The guy threw Ray in the elevator and cut the cables. Hell, we'll have to pick him up with a shovel."

"Waterston said a maniac broke in."

"Not true, sir," Buggs refuted firmly. "There's no sign of forced entry and, as much as I can make out, nothing was stolen. There was a locked room, but your sister opened it and I went in to look with her. She said nothing was lifted there either. As far as the guy being a whacko, I'd have to argue that. This was a killing by somebody who knows how, and in my opinion that was what he came for."

"That would seem to be indicated," Moloch agreed, "considering Claire was passed over. Did she see him? Is she certain there was only one of them?"

"She saw him and she talked to him, although he had a stocking over his head." He bent to pick up the single hose that Waterston had discarded. "He was alone, at least while he was here. She says he could be Italian.

"Put Claire on the line, would you?"

Claire's voice was swollen with the backwash of shock.

"Yes, Clement?"

"Is it gone?"

"Yes."

"Give me Buggs."

"Did she provide you a description?" he asked of Buggs.

"As complete as she could: Five-ten, maybe eleven, but I'd say six feet because people look shorter when they're masked; not too big; but strong and athletic. He had a gun she'd never seen before, although that could have been because he used a silencer. Other than that she wants to wait until she talks to you. Should I have some of our men bring her out?"

"At once. I must speak to her. Send four men, so that she's well protected, and then have them stay here. Brief them yourself if you feel it necessary. Waterston is excluded from this. I have Jack with me and three of my other lads, but until we get to the bottom of this I cannot make snap assumptions. Next to Brian, Raymond was my best man."

"Too good to get blown away the way he did. All his clothes were on, sir. I can't figure it. And it eats my ass the guy would break him up in the elevator like that. There was nothing to cover up. No reason that I can see."

Moloch experienced a twinge of disappointment in Paul Buggs.

"What about Brian? Has there been anything promising?"

"Not a trace. Ray had already run down the hospitals,

the trains, the airlines, the whole bag. Have you considered this could be connected?"

"That would be an obvious deduction, but we must ask ourselves why the killers would make such a spectacle of Raymond while, if we assume Brian has come a cropper, they've hidden him away so well. That is what they've done, you know. They've used Raymond as an oracle."

"What for?"

"Ah, now that's the teaser, is it not?"

The fly was casing him as it cut the air in chopped loops. Strange, he observed, flies were seldom attracted to him. He swatted and missed by several aerobatic maneuvers, his pudgy hand a jigging cleaver in the air. Flies were supposed to be awfully stupid. So then, they surely couldn't laugh. Or could they?

"You keep saying 'they.' Your sister saw one man."

"We can be dead certain it's a group, Paul. An individual wouldn't dare try it alone. I don't have the faintest notion what group it could be, there are dozens of candidates: The Mossad, The Montoneros, The Kurds, The Basques. You know them as well as I; the world is rife with seditionaries. It may be they'll be satisfied with Brian and Raymond. Or they may be holding Brian for some sort of ransom. What transpires next will tell us."

"If it is a group, their front man has to be reckoned with. Ray was no slouch. I wouldn't have liked to go up against him myself. He must have gotten some licks in though. There's some blood on the stocking the guy wore. But the rest of the apartment's as slick as a whistle."

"You were a fine hand when you were in the field, Paul. I'm counting on you. I'll need a replacement for Raymond."

"I'd like that," Buggs said. "I've had it up to here sitting behind a desk and signing grease vouchers."

"I'm confident a position can be arranged. Address yourself to this patch and we shall see what we shall see. Come to the house the minute you're through there. We'll put our heads together. I caution you, Paul. Don't take these people for granted."

"I never do."

"Good lad."

Buggs put the phone down and picked up his paper cup

of coffee. The liquid was cold and streaky, like melted chocolate ice cream. The way he liked it.

·18·

She constructed a modest fire which gave her uncommon comfort. She sat beside it with her legs tucked under her. She stayed close even when the flames made her jeans hot against her skin and caused her face to burn. She pulled her sweater tight and hugged her middle. She had relished the time spent staring into fires ever since she was a child.

The room was not the least chilly. Just dark.

Her eyes ached, abrasive when she closed them. Tired, she still could not sleep. A shotgun stood beside the fireplace. Somewhere in the room a clock ticked, though she could not see it.

She knew she should eat something, but that was another of the things she couldn't do.

After a while an incantation of Valkyrie came to her. She really was tired.

The door banged open.

She uncurled and stretched for the shotgun, then stopped before reaching it when she saw the Yankees jacket.

He walked slowly toward her, the revolver at his side. Under his other arm he had a book and a sheaf of papers.

"Swell," he said to her.

All her painfully reasoned preludes fled. Her mouth went dry as she forced her attention from the revolver.

Max came behind him, switching on the lights.

"This afternoon you told me you'd watched the plane leave," Holland said to him.

"It did. It did," Max said. "She took Sarah to the clinic and came back on the next flight. I would have gone with her if I'd known."

"Go now. Both of you."

"I won't," Rhiana said.

"Run that by me again," Holland said.

Rhiana huddled closer to the fire, returning his stare.

"You're not surprised," she said. "It hasn't been long, but I know you that well."

"I don't know whether to get off the floor or off the ceiling. I'm totalled, wiped out. I may go berserk and shoot you both full of holes. Sell my clothes, mother, I'm going to heaven."

Max stepped away from him.

"Uncle, he's not even angry," Rhiana said. "He's clever, he won't allow it. He says things instead."

"They're not funny," Max said soberly.

"No, they're not," Rhiana agreed, standing.

Her jeans had a crease in each leg, enclosing her low shoes to just the correct height. They were tight and sleek and Holland concluded that they were tailored.

"Do you use drugs?" Max asked him tentatively.

"He doesn't," Rhiana said.

Holland placed the book on a table, the revolver on top, then arranged the paper in a neat pile beside them.

The cut on his cheek was a red horizontal edge, ringed fuscous by bruising. He turned back to her.

"You don't know what you've done," he said. "You don't know what you're doing."

"I think I do."

"Give me a reason."

"I had to get my daughter away from predators like you."

"That's her. What about you? Give me a reason."

"I have to see him dead. I have to know. Waiting and not knowing, or waiting and knowing, is worse than running . . . is worse than being dead myself. It's hell—"

He said, "Shut up."

"You don't understand."

He said, "Shut the fuck up."

Max said, "Holland, please—"

Holland turned on him.

"What I don't need is a bitch-goddess trailing after me. This thing is already touch and go. With her in between now it could go right in the toilet. Personal vendettas are a poor man's form of suicide."

Max could only look miserable.

"I'll stay with Max," she said. "We'll hide if we have to."

"Too late," Holland said.

An ominous uncertainty took over.

"What did you do?" Rhiana said to him.

"Max?" Holland said.

He was confused and didn't seem to hear his name. His clean scalp beamed under a hanging lamp.

"Max?" Holland repeated.

"What? Yes?"

"I need some baking soda and some water. Not much. A few cotton balls."

Max nodded, eager to leave them.

When they were alone Rhiana moved closer.

"Did they find the body? Is that it?"

"That one's still in the garage," he said. "I gave them another."

The impact of the revelation was indiscernible on her, though he picked out the effort it took.

"His?"

"No. One of the gunsels, named Ray. I think it's safe to say I got our friend's attention."

He began separating the sheets of paper on the table.

"Is that how you were cut?"

"I'm glad you asked that."

She waited.

"Well?" she said.

"There's a humorous side. You wouldn't care for it."

She turned his head sharply and inspected the cut.

With their faces close, he said, "There's a conflict raging about the origins of the word 'Fuck.' Some attribute its creation to the Scottish poet William Dunbar, while on the other hand some say it first saw the light of day in the late fifteenth century in a British quarterly publication called—"

"Fascinating," Rhiana said. "Given a choice, I'd rather not hear it. I don't like the word."

He couldn't be sure if she was frowning at him or the state of his injury. The lee of her eyes were reddened from lack of sleep. She pressed on the bruise more than was necessary, causing his eye to water. But he would not flinch for her. She looked full into his face for a moment.

"Then again, maybe it's the generation gap," he said.

The comment annoyed her but she refused to rise to it.

"I'd be interested in knowing what a 'bitch-goddess' is."

"A woman who wouldn't admit to ever having needed

a bathroom," he said without deliberation. "How's that?"

"Silly."

"Is it? When you're here and you should be there? Tell me, then, for the record, have you ever in your whole fucking life had to go to the bathroom?"

His smile was furious and ladled with mockery.

She walked away from him. "I said you wouldn't understand."

"Maybe I understand too damned well," he said, going after her. "You've hung yourself around my neck and I don't want you there. Your rationale gets people killed."

She drew up in front of the fire. Cedar was smacking there, tossing bits of glowing shrapnel against the screen to burst into butterflies of flame.

"When I came here I was frightened to death, even worse than I was in Santiago. I thought I'd never stop shaking. When I left I wasn't frightened the same way. I've drawn from you, I'll admit that, but I'm not asking for your protection. I just need to know he's finished."

"Bless your heart. That'll be a comfort to Sarah when Hector and Isabelle tell her she no longer has a mother. Either."

Rhiana whirled on him but he caught her hands.

"What's the matter with you?" she cried. "That's *all* I've thought about. That's *why*."

"Then it's insane. Any minute now they'll connect me to the bullfight. They'll connect us both to the bullfight. They'll look for two. I was only one. I could run at them or away from them and they wouldn't know which I was doing. What am I supposed to do with you now? They'll be watching the airlines and the trains and the buses. The border points will be playing ticktacktoe. He'll get you. He'll get you sure as hell."

He continued to hold her hands.

"Then he'll get Max too," she said. "He was at the fight."

"I don't see they'll make the connection that way, if at all. Max didn't even stand up, there was no reason for them to suspect we were with anyone. But there's that ladino narc. They'll tap into him somewhere down the line. We were sitting in Max's car. If the narc happened to take down the plate, and kept it, then the cows will never come home."

Bewildered, she looked down at her hands. "You're hurting me."

He released her.

She asked him, "What do we do?"

He took the shotgun.

He said, "Welcome to the edge of the earth."

When Max returned Holland was leaning over the papers, his arms stiffened to the table. He was saying, in a flat monotone, "Fucking fuck, fucking fuck, fucking fuck . . ."

Max gaped at him.

"I lack the social graces," Holland declared. "Rhiana's coaching me."

He accepted the provisions Max brought, then pumped out the loaded shotgun and handed it to him.

"Can yon cut the barrel for me?" He showed the older man where.

"I think so," Max said.

"Don't file the burrs, I'll do that. I don't have much time, Max. I've got to move. I've got to take her with me, or he'll get her."

Max looked at Rhiana.

"I'll do as he says, Uncle," she said. "I'll be alright."

"George must have been thrilled," Holland said to her. "And the Lomolins."

"What could they do? Force me to stay with them?" she said, though not without sympathy. "George said to stick to you."

"Wonderful," Holland said. "You want to adopt me?"

They had arrived at another standoff.

"Will you take the body away?" Max asked him. He was apologetic and it amazed Holland that he could be at a time like this.

"Uh-huh."

Max was relieved.

"It's a longshot, but Moloch may come after you," Holland warned him. "Find a safe place. Get your housekeeper out. And the ones at the lake."

"He is not the only one with friends in high places."

"It's not the same, Max," Holland said. "They're the landlords. They can do whatever they want."

"Then worry for yourselves, not me," Max said, touching Holland's arm. "Don't let him have Rhiana."

"Don't be brave, Uncle," Rhiana said.

"I'm not, my dear. I'm not at all. Holland is the one."

"Him, and the folks he moves with, scare me shitless," Holland said to Max.

Rhiana and Max looked at him.

Then Max left with the shotgun.

Holland went to work on the papers, taking a sheet from the bottom of the pile and segregating it from the rest. Mixing the same portions of baking soda and water as he had in the apartment, he moistened one of the cotton balls.

Rhiana came to watch. She read the title on the book.

"What are you doing?" she asked him.

He handed her the sheet of paper he had treated earlier.

She read while he swabbed the blank page lightly with the damp cotton.

Halfway down the page, she whispered, "My God."

Before him, lines of handwriting were raised onto the paper as the swab passed over.

Rhiana leaned over his shoulder. "The writing was invisible. How is that done?"

"Dozens of methods, both wet and dry. This is wet. The paper is saturated in copper sulphate to conceal the writing, which is done with a soft pen to prevent the texture from being messed with. It's brought out again just the way you've seen. He could have used microdots, commission-codes, negatives, whatever; but this is simple and effective and doesn't require equipment."

"But this page has typing on top. And the script is fine, I'd even say feminine."

"He has his sister rewrite and edit, as far as I can tell, then she burns the originals in a hibachi and soaks the ashes before throwing them out. The book is typed in after, using a ribbon that doesn't react with the sulphate. I assume that's what the morning visits were all about. She'd collect the day's work and do her thing. The typing is just to alleviate suspicion and make the stuff safe to move around."

"Is that where—?"

"She didn't get in the way. She didn't get hurt."

"But it's incredible that he would do this," she said. "He's written his memoirs. There must be three hundred pages here."

"It isn't complete, but that's what he's doing. Names, dates, places, modus', philosophy, and like that."

Shaking her head at the implausibility of the exhibit, she said, "It's beyond reason."

"So were Nixon's tapes. While he fucked over the entire free world he couldn't resist getting it down for posterity. Most have done it and most will keep on doing it. Plenty of time for editing later. Call it vanity, perversity, weakness, theatrics. Contempt. Mental deficiency. Who's to say? They'd see it as vindication. They'd see it as deserving of immortality. Who cares? More semantics for the cafe intellectuals and the philosopher junkies. He did it. I've got it. He knows it."

"George would love to see this," she marveled. "Everyone would."

"In good time. So would various other inscrutables. Listen carefully: Moloch wasn't writing this for pure pleasure. Look at the insurance angle. Say some of the characters he's worked with were to decide his knowledge was a liability to them. It's had to have happened more than once, right? What better way to keep them in line than by letting them know it's all been recorded, and that if something unfortunate were to happen to him it would all hit the fan anyway."

She nodded. "His welfare becomes their welfare. It's politics, isn't it?"

"Take it one step further. What would these characters be likely to do if they knew the material had already fallen into the wrong hands?"

"Try to get it themselves," she reasoned.

"Only after they'd removed the corroborating evidence —Moloch."

"They'd try to kill him themselves," she said.

"And us. Unless Moloch could get to us first and show them he'd put the lid on."

Her color lightened.

"But he'd have to come out of hiding," she said. "He couldn't entrust that to someone else. They'd have to know."

"Now you've got the handle," he said, satisfied. "Take your bra off."

It took a moment for his words to register.

He was busy arranging the papers to wrap in oilskin.

"Take it off."

"Why? Tell me what you're doing."

"From here on in we won't have time for formalities and explanations. You've got to do what I say first time. If we hesitate and they don't, they'll be better than we are. They're not, so do it."

She reached behind and undid the snap, then pulled each shoulder strap down the sleeve of her sweater, over her hands, and then back up the sleeve. She produced her brassiere without having lifted her sweater.

He had not seen it done that way before.

"Well, at least you don't wear sunglasses in your hair," he said, shaking his head. "You know what an 'apodesmos' is?"

"It was a binding used to flatten breasts when that was the fashion. You want me to look like a man, is that it?"

"The least we can do is give them a little subterfuge. Like I said, they'll be thinking a man and a woman. Every hour we can keep them off balance is one hour closer to getting Moloch in the open."

He raised her sweater and gave her breasts a fleeting, critical appraisal.

"This may not work worth a damn," he said. "You're not small."

"I'm not large, either," she countered.

"I know, you're every man's dream," he said, slighting her again. She pulled the sweater down. This time her nipples were marked eruptions in the wool.

"If we use strips of linen," he said, considering her clinically, "and get one of those satin-finish jackets that don't drape much. I imagine it'll hurt some . . ."

"Gauze," she said. "Max will have some. You'll have to help me."

He swept her hair back from her face and tight against her head, another appraisal.

"No," she said, tossing her head violently and knocking his hands away. "Not that."

"All of it. Short. We'll do it quick now and finish later."

A sweet spark of desperation closed on her eyes as she followed his.

"Please, not my hair. We'll do something else . . ."

"Your neck will be too white. Make-up can cover that . . ."

"I don't use cosmetics, just lip color. Holland, please . . ."

He was circling her.

". . . Trim your eyelashes and cut your nails back . . . give you some razor nicks and some dark stuff for a five o'clock shadow . . . rough your skin up with detergent or something . . . put a match in your mouth. You have any jeans that aren't tailored? Some sneakers?"

She kept shaking her head.

"We'll get some," he said.

He stepped in front and put his fingers to the delicate flat between her stomach and thigh.

"We'll stick some tissue paper down here," he said. "Which side do you want to dress on?"

"What?"

"Never mind." He pressed the brassiere into her hands, taking her elbow and hurrying her from the room. "Get what you'll need. I'll introduce you to the boys in the band."

She stopped at the door, resisting him.

"Holland . . ."

He pushed her through the door ahead of him.

"Look, I know," he said. "I've seen you do your hair. But you ran me clear out of options. If we live right, it'll grow back. If we don't, we won't live. Let's find out."

• 19 •

After administering a sedative to his sister and seeing her safely under guard in one of the guest rooms, Clement Moloch hurried grimly through the house.

Nothing like this had ever happened before. There was no coherence. It was all so wildly lacking in form.

Perhaps Waterston had been right for once in his life, perhaps this bunch really were maniacs. Claire had said they wanted money. For papers that were unparalleled, inestimable, for papers that could wreak untold repercussions in far corners, they wanted mere money. Mighty bloody preposterous.

Terrorists. They had to be.

He strode under an octagonal domed ceiling, past velvets and walnut, a Canova sculpture, a reliquary bust of Saint-Cyr, a desk lamp with a shade depicting a fox hunt in sixteenth-century Wales, a Flemish tapestry of battle, a gardenia that Margaret had worn earlier and which she had thrown to the floor when he instructed she not leave the estate until further notice.

He entered the room that served as a communications center, taking a moment to draw his breath.

Jack was supervising a bank of television monitors, each presenting a view from one of the estate's closed-circuit cameras. Jack was not the man's true name and from whence the anglicized adoption had come from, Moloch had no idea. His real name was Truong Thi Hung and he was Thai.

Moloch put a hand on the man's shoulder and studied the screen focused on the front gate.

"No evidence of Buggs yet?"

"No sir," the Thai said.

The gate, awash in multi-angled spotlights, showed that a warm, dry wind was up, waltzing pockets of dust across the pavement and into the darkness beyond.

"Tired, son?" Moloch asked.

"Not so much," the Thai said.

"I'll have you spelled soon. But first I'd like you to chase someone up for me. Do you remember the young ladino chap who came to the gate a few nights ago? Brian went out to speak with him."

"Yes, sir. He's with the Americans."

"Correct. Can we locate him on short notice?"

The Thai swiveled his chair and reached for a three-ring notebook. "He is in our book. There are some numbers."

"Call at once. Tell him it's urgent. Tell him to come here without delay."

Three phone lines reached into the room. The Thai took one of the telephones and placed it in his lap. He smoked cigarettes, a habit Moloch had been unable to break him of. Smoke hung in grey bands over their heads.

"You've been trying to raise Brian on the radio, have you?" Moloch asked him.

"All day and night, sir. I have not had any success."

"Keep trying, Jack. Keep trying. I'll be in the sitting room. Summon me the minute Buggs arrives."

Moloch left him and took a more leisurely pace to the sitting room. There he poured himself a bitters and sat, stretching his legs to an ottoman.

He chewed the side of a finger and labored to collect his thoughts, riding a compulsion to get ahead of events instead of being dragged behind.

If they were terrorists plumbing for funds to buy arms and finance their doomed delusions, how had they known to take his papers? How had they perceived what they were? Did they know now? He ruled the proposition out; it would call for more cunning than the general run of terrorists could lay claim to. And there was Raymond. He must have come on them while they were in the act. Claire said he happened by merely on chance, probably just part of his parcel search for Brian. Still and all, that did not account for them painting the cellar with him.

Revolutionaries. Perhaps local guerrillas. It was true the government had not yet brought some of the agitators in the mountains to heel, but that rabble seldom if ever ventured into this echelon for their kidnappings. Why, they still had public executions by firing squad for them, he had seen for himself in Mazatenango in 1975, a crowd of thousands watching, though that sort of dispatch scarcely deterred those bent on subverting the order of the State. Besides, Claire had been theirs for the taking, when in effect all they had done was truss her up and go straight for the papers.

That was what truly troubled him. Was he to believe that they somehow knew the relative value to him of either commodity? And had therefore taken the papers instead of Claire. Looming was the sinister portent of them having a more intimate knowledge of him than he thought possible. Only Brian and Raymond knew him that well. Perhaps Claire herself, but that was reaching. If true, there was a sophistry here that blew all unfiltered conjecture into a cocked hat.

Maybe the Mossad, or someone like them who were sworn to his destruction, although that was reaching too. The Mossad were more prone to the spectaculars of the military mind, in league with the politics of fund raising. Not likely them. They had been waved off long ago anyway, and if they were to steal his papers they would certainly take them back to the Institute for a detailed evaluation, not try to strike a bargain on the spot as these had done.

And then connecting the man and woman at The Jet Bar to the two seen at the bullfights . . .

The in-house telephone made a soft buzzing. He lifted it and heard Jack say that Paul Buggs was at the gate. Instructing that two of his aides were to bring him in, Moloch then went to wait at the door.

Buggs required a shave twice a day and now had not shaved in as many days. He refused an offering of liquor, but accepted a glass of ginger ale which he gulped down.

"What have you got, Paul?" Moloch asked him.

"A goddamn puzzle, that's what," Buggs said, going through his pockets as though he were drawing lots.

He eventually held aloft a mangled lump of lead about the size of a thumbnail. The head of the bullet had been spread in a uniform pattern resembling a mushroom, pulled back in ragged disarray over the gilded metal jacket.

"I dug this out of the bed," Buggs explained. "It's a semi-jacketed hollow point, not real big like a .44 mag' but I can tell you it was damned fast. One of these could kill a 747. He used three. Could be a hot loaded .38 or .357. I'll have to get it checked out."

"Professional, then," Moloch said, examining the projectile. "Is that what you're telling me?"

"Very," Buggs said. "Europeans like itty-bitty guns; Latins go in for the bigger-the-better; Americans like the hot, fast stuff."

"That's a somewhat broad generalization, isn't it?"

"Yes, sir, it is," Buggs allowed. "This isn't."

He took a set of car keys, a tobacco pouch and a lighter from his pockets and placed them on the table.

Both men regarded the articles for a moment. Moloch closed his eyes and lowered his head. A harbinger of suspicion began to percolate through his powers of deduction.

"You found these in Claire's apartment?" he asked.

"The lighter and the pouch in a drawer beside the bed, the keys in a jewelry box. They were wiped. No prints."

"Claire doesn't smoke anything, much less a pipe. The keys are for a Chrysler, the type of car Brian drove."

Next Buggs produced a pill box and opened it for Moloch. "Uppers and downers. A whole lot of them."

"Claire doesn't use those either," Moloch said gravely. "What are you suggesting?"

Buggs spread his hands noncommittally. "I don't know what he . . . they . . . were after any more than you do. If it's you, it's a damn weird way of going about it, I'd say."

Moloch retreated into thought.

After a while Buggs broached the obvious. "Just a shot, sir, but could Brian be implicated in this? I mean, he is conspicuously absent. Ray isn't."

Moloch said, "I'm tired, I'm terribly tired."

"You've talked to your sister?" Buggs said cautiously.

"I have. I think we can dismiss the Italian idea. He only used one word of it and she couldn't sound out an accent. However, before they were surprised Raymond told her that Brian had been at a place he frequents regularly, a barrio drinking place called The Jet Bar."

"I know it."

"He was there the night before. In any event, there was some sort of skirmish to do with a woman tourist who was with her husband. Brian can be oddly brutal when he sets eyes on a woman he wants. It's happened a time or two, I'm afraid."

"Excuse me, sir," Buggs said. "But that dump isn't a place I'd expect to come across tourists. Talk about taking your life in your hands . . ."

"That occurred to me," Moloch said. "But it also occurred to Raymond that the couple fit the description of a pair we happened to see at the bullfights a few days back. From what Claire related I'd say Raymond might have been on to something. You see, we got no more than a glimpse of them because the woman hurried out just as we arrived. It caught my attention and although I didn't think anything much of the incident, Raymond recruited one of those narcotics chaps who are always standing around and had him go outside as a precaution. When he came back he said they were Americans and that the woman just seemed to be upset by the bulls. As a result, I promptly dismissed it from mind."

"Was Brian with you?"

"Yes, but he didn't appear to have noticed them. Anyway, I have this chap on his way here now. He'll be able to give us a complete description and tell us more of his impressions."

"Shouldn't we call in the locals for some of the leg work?" Buggs said. "They could put out a bulletin for Brian's car and could probably produce those tourists if they're still here. Let's face it, this isn't Acapulco. We're not overrun with American tourists at any time, but sure as hell not this time of year."

"I'd much prefer to avoid that eventuality if we can," Moloch said. "They can really bung things up if they're not closely supervised."

"Pretty hard to cover that much ground without them," Buggs said reluctantly, looking around for more ginger ale. "But, whatever you say."

"We'll see what this narcotics lad has to offer," Moloch said. "In the meantime I'll get you more ginger beer and you can reconstruct this man's movements for me. I'm a bit foggy as to how they were able to get a man in the apartment at the same time Raymond was present. Claire says . . ."

On the road leading to the estate a young ladino shifted his aging Fiat into top gear and watched his wake of blue oil smoke.

The pigmy motor had seen a host of better days and was unaccustomed to being operated in the upper reaches of its already overtaxed capacity. The lobes of its camshaft were worn down to pitiful lumps that barely urged the valves to open, while the pistons—two of which were cracked on both of their skirts—slapped and clattered against the cylinder walls, protesting their dilapidated condition by allowing generous amounts of oil to slip past the sealing rings and enter the combustion chambers, there to be partially consumed in the sooty furnace and eventually expelled into the night air via the holed exhaust pipe.

Behind the wheel the ladino kept the gas pedal pressed to the metal floor, the rubber mat having long since succumbed to the ravages of constant use. He steered the car with extravagant sweeps of almost prayerful control, the mechanism altering the car's direction reluctantly.

The curves of the winding road came up fast and often

blind, hidden by close trees and the last of night, not to mention the single headlight that shook and darted in its socket.

Another sharp bend came up fast, one whose camber went the wrong way, not unusual in a country where roadbuilding was considered more a lottery than a prescribed service.

The ladino thanked Christ that the road was paved, sawed at the shine-spotted wheel, jammed the balky transmission down a gear, let the clutch out, and felt it chatter before taking hold.

He slowed only enough to keep the tires from rolling on their rims. The lonely headlight panned across the trees banking the curve, jouncing like an early silent film.

As he hit the apex and straightened the wheel to exit, he saw something white on the roadway . . . too close to halt for . . . too large to go over.

He stood up on the brake pedal, literally, lifting himself off the seat as he held firm to the wheel.

The thing thudded the front of the skidding Fiat and went under, lifting the car and causing it to slip soundlessly a few more feet until it stopped, the motor dead.

The ladino banged the door with his shoulder and tumbled out. He went to his hands and knees beside the car and looked.

The naked body of Brian Randolph was caught full under the Fiat, grotesquely entangled in the front suspension. Where the bones showed and the flesh opened was red. But there was no bleeding.

"Motherfuck—" he started to say.

"You."

The notice came from behind.

He spun, rising, putting a hand to the car for support.

He froze, staring into the barrel of a revolver trained on his breastplate.

Holland, in a military crouch in the grass at the side of the road, the massive revolver held out between them, steadied it with his other arm.

"You got a gun?" Holland asked.

"Could be," the ladino said.

"Leave it. You're not fast enough."

"Yo," the ladino conceded.

He wore a serape with a pattern of lightning over each

shoulder, glitter chains and a stud medallion around his neck.

"Put your hands flat on the car. Behind you. Out to the side."

The ladino followed instruction well.

"You're the one," he said to Holland.

"Which one is that?"

"The bullfight. Who are you, man? Who you with?"

"I'm part of a conspiracy to murder the Easter bunny."

"Oh, yeah?" the ladino said, displaying a smile at the promise he perceived in Holland's fancy.

The ladino stayed quiet. The first light of day was coming over the trees at his back.

"I'll bet you've got a name like Link or Troy or Lance," Holland said.

The ladino looked down at his chains with discomfort. "It's a scene, man. I ain't like this."

"He send for you?" Holland asked, flicking his head up the road toward the estate.

The ladino nodded. "You don't know what you're into here. You don't know, man."

"Should I lose sleep?"

The ladino rolled his eyes, blew breath past tight lips to show reckless passion. "Wow," he said. "Oh, wow."

Holland said, "You got delusions of dog, or what?"

"Hey, man, I'm with a regulatory agency of the United States government. You shouldn't oughtta fuck with me."

"Again. Should I care?"

"I don't mean you no grief, man," the ladino said.

He was edging his hands along the sheet metal of the car.

"That's what you're doing here, huh?" Holland said. "Looking out for my interests?"

"Uh, don't put me in the wrong on this—"

"You're not coming off a position of strength, amigo. You guys are like sycophantic maggots. Wherever there's carrion."

"Not me," the ladino disputed, enforcing his ignorance of Holland's accusation. "I'll take a walk. I'll take a vacation in the north country. Just give the word. You process me and you'll be in a world of hurt, man. The full force of the United States government will be down on your head."

"I'm going to wet myself."

The warm breeze tossed Holland's hair. It felt good. He was glad the sun was coming up to bury a long night.

"What did you tell him?" Holland said.

The ladino's hands were still moving.

"Hey, man, I just took the call at home. I ain't had time to tell them a thing. I ain't *never* talked to that man in my entire life, I swear."

The ladino was suddenly all movement, twisting, shifting, a hand going for the small of his back.

Holland's first slug truck him to the left of his chest and slammed him against the Fiat, straightening him and rocking the car on its springs. While he was still stretched out, Holland hit him twice more in the center of the chest, parting the chains and tossing them in the air, the revolver staying settled with each discharge, twin flutes of flame spurting upwards from the unique gas ports in the tip of the barrel.

The ladino pitched forward, leaving spider webs of shattered glass where he had been.

Holland found a snub-nosed revolver in the ladino's belt at the back, threw it into the trees, and then went through the pockets.

Finished, he ran up the road in the direction the Fiat had come from, cutting into the trees, throwing aside brush that had been used for cover.

Rhiana had her forehead on the steering wheel when he opened the door of Randolph's car. Great whacks of hair were now gone from her head.

The interior lights had not come on with the opening of the door, their activating buttons on the door jambs having been taped over by Holland. The license plates had been changed for those from one of the rented Chevrolets.

"You should have had the car moving," he said. "You've got to do better."

The way she looked at him was not a pleasant sight to see.

"Did you have to do that?" she said.

He pushed her aside and joined two bared wires hanging beneath the dash panel. The car started then idled quietly in the grove of trees next to the road.

He handed her a bit of paper he had taken from the ladino. "What's this?"

"I can't see," Rhiana said, trying to catch light.

Holland put the car in gear and eased it over the rough ground. As he got close to the pavement he accelerated hard in order to clear a low relief, the tires spinning on the pine needles, shifting the rear of the car so that it clipped a tree on its way past. They skidded out onto the pavement, moving it an easy rate, lights out.

"Stay loose," Holland said. "The road's probably clear but if it isn't be ready to use the guns and run. Shoot for the chest, forget the head and anything else. A skull can be a half-inch thick except at the temples, there it's only a few hundredths. The head's for when they wear vests. You'll know."

Rhiana had the shotgun across her knees and the automatic on the seat. She was trying to read the piece of paper by the haphazard light blinking through the trees.

"It's a phone number," she said finally.

Holland said, "Bingo."

"Did you find any identification?"

He confronted her with an echo of disbelief.

"Not hardly," he said.

"Where are we going now?"

"To find a phone."

He put the radio on to search for the ball scores.

The second telephone call came at 7:24 that morning.

Buggs, suspecting that the ladino would not keep his promise, had been too impatient to wait. He left with instructions to contact the authorities in Uruguay and inform them that Moloch would be delayed an indeterminate time.

Moloch accepted the call in the sitting room.

"Very well," he said to the Thai. "I'll talk to him. Don't listen in, Jack, you hear?"

"Yes, sir," the Thai answered.

When the line opened Moloch said, "Who's speaking, please?"

"I've got your tome here."

"Whatever are you talking about?" Moloch tested indignantly.

"Let's try to keep this exchange tasteful, eh, cocksucker?"

Moloch altered his position when he heard the address.

"The fact remains that I don't have the faintest notion what you mean."

"Do the names Verri and Beccaria do anything for you? How about Manzoni? Bentham?"

Moloch refused to acknowledge the barb.

"C'mon," the voice said, "keep those cards and letters coming in."

"As I recall, they were writers and theorists who lived in the 1700's," Moloch allowed.

"They theorized about the use of torture, about what motivates you folks. There's always a market for complicating clarity."

Moloch was captivated, his weariness flying off like old clothes. He decided to pursue it, saying, "Which is?"

"You believe that the many are there for the divine right of a few, and by their grace," the voice said. "I saw the movie. How am I doing?"

Moloch opted to lead him a bit. "These merchants of theory never appear to see the ends of their own sentences, refusing to accept that the truth is an inherently conspicuous strain coursing throughout the chronicles of our brief history. You are an existentialist, then?"

"I'm not a participant. I'm just passing through."

"Ah, such a narcosis you enjoy. But someone must rule, now mustn't they?"

"It wouldn't hurt so bad if it wasn't so good, right?" the voice said. "Put your hand on the radio and be saved, brother. Be born again."

"Don't be flippant with me," Moloch said, clenching his stunted hand into a fist.

"Gosh. You wicked old thing."

"You undoubtedly have a way with words, young man," Moloch said, stilling his paroxysm willfully. "What is it you think you have that would interest me?"

He was listening intently for intonations that would aid the hunt. The insertion of "young man" was the first hook he would throw.

The voice, spitting the hook, said, "Not *that* young, old man. Never was."

A short silence of respect followed, Moloch granting that there could be irreducible tides running in this voice.

"I could always put these papers in the marketplace," the voice said quietly. "I'm confident that gentle people like

Qaddafi or Stroessner or Pinochet would find the writing enlightened reading. There could even be massive social consequences."

"That could also be a tricky proposition for the broker," Moloch pointed out.

"Never could resist a good magic show. I'm modest and unassuming. I'll make out. Don't worry about me."

With that Moloch realized his worst fears. His adversary was either exceptionally crafty or entirely baseless, and was not about to betray which.

"What is it you want?" he said.

"I don't want you, understand that," was the qualifier. "It's money I'm here after, and not in the hereafter. I'd as soon not have any more shooting if it's all the same to you."

"And the sum you had in mind?"

"Five hundred thousand in large American currency. No hondel. No slap and tickle. Such a deal I give you."

"How many pages are presently exposed, may I ask?"

"Four. One at each end and two at random."

"How will I know you haven't duplicated the material in question?"

"The material in question will remain in question. You'll get the papers back blank. I'm sure you can recognize the handwriting to be authentic. The four pages are useless without the rest."

"That will necessitate an examination before the exchange," Moloch returned.

"We'll do it in stages. Keep the home fires burning. I'll get back to you."

"Wait," Moloch said quickly. "Tell me what group you are with. Perhaps we could explore other avenues."

"No group. I'm a free lance. I presume you'll wish to keep this transaction strictly between ourselves? No cops and no spooks?"

"Very astute of you. Interesting, I must say." Then Moloch came down on it hard: "Who are you?"

The voice said, "Think of me as an accountant. Think of me kindly."

"You live dangerously, my boy."

"Everything happens in the fast lane. Catch me if you can."

Moloch deliberated whether or not the statement was a challenge.

"There is no sadder spectacle than a person who fails to recognize his own limits," he said.

"You took the words right out of my mouth."

Then the voice was gone.

Moloch slumped in his chair, drained by the few minutes of viperous dueling.

His canonical brooding was mercilessly short lived as the Thai burst into the room, pointing with a frenzy.

Buggs, out of breath, had a gun in his hand. His toughened features were seared by fury. He waved his arms.

Claire had materialized from somewhere behind, confused by what was happening.

"Buggs is at the gate again," he gasped. "There's something wrong. They're bringing him in."

Moloch, forgetting himself, rushed to meet Buggs in the asphalt courtyard.

"Son of a bitch! Down the road!" he shouted in the early morning tranquility.

Moloch steadied him. "Calm yourself, man. What is it?"

"Brian and the narc. Plastered all over the road. The same gun. Son of a bitch."

"Brian?" Moloch whispered, awed.

Buggs took in the anxious faces of Moloch and his aides, and Claire standing behind in the doorway. He smacked his gun hand into his palm, and swore, "I don't know what the hell he wants, but from now on that son of a bitch is gonna get all of our business."

Moloch, stunned, stood isolated in the mellow wind of the coming day.

•IV•
HOLLAND'S LAW

The wholesale killing of campesinos (peasant farmers) and their "disappearance" after detention is probably the most serious aspect of human rights violations in Nicaragua. The populations of entire peasant villages have been reported exterminated or taken away as prisoners by the Nicaraguan National Guard troops. The few who are released allege severe torture. The "disappeared," who are never acknowledged to be in custody and who never reappear, must, in many cases, be presumed to have died in custody.

In a pastoral letter of 8 January 1977, signed by the Archbishop and all six bishops of the Roman Catholic Church in Nicaragua, the bishops state that as a consequence, "The accumulation of land and riches in the hands of the few increases . . . humble campesinos have their lands seized and are threatened by those taking advantage of the situation . . . the state of terror obliges many of our campesinos to flee in desperation from their homes . . . investigations continue against suspects using humiliation and inhuman methods: from tortures and rapes to executions without civil or military trial . . . many villages have been practically abandoned, houses and personal belongings are burnt . . ."

In a letter to Nicaraguan President Somoza of 13 June 1976, 31 Capuchin missionaries, all United States citizens, documented torture, illegal detentions, and disappearances of campesinos at the hands of the National Guard. Included was an account of incidents in Zelaya province between November 1975 and May 1976 in which some 92 persons were seized by the National Guard and had since "disappeared." They also reported the discovery of numerous hidden grave sites. Two bodies were found in the area of Irlan in April 1976, one of a farmer who had disappeared, the other an eight-year-old boy who had been hanged and then decapitated.

Missionaries provided the names of 44 peasants cap-

tured and executed by the "Hilario" patrol of the National Guard at the end of January 1977, a patrol accompanied by seven local judges. The list included 29 children, 11 adult women and four adult men. All of the women were raped before being executed.

In an open letter of 1 January 1977, signed by the Franciscan Fathers of Matagalpa diocese and delivered to the National Guard Commander of the Northern Zone, the Fathers included these accounts:

—on 9 December, the Mincho-Chavelo patrol, without warning, destroyed the home of Gloria Chavarria in Bilampi and killed her, her three grown daughters and two children. All were completely defenseless. Four small children were left and are being cared for by relatives. Afterwards another patrol arrived. The soldiers continued the massacre in the surrounding area.

—the Santos Martinez house in the Ronda de Cuscawas near Bilampi was set on fire and all the members of the family, that is, the mother and father and two youths (reserve members of the National Guard) were beheaded. Two small children fled.

—Marcelino Lopez was killed by the National Guard a few months ago. Then the so-called "Patrulla Negra" (Black Patrol) came and set fire to the house and murdered his wife and four members of the family (two were reserve members of the National Guard). Two small children escaped.

—the same "Patrulla Negra" went to the house of Santiago Aruaz and killed the eldest children, Arnoldo and Antonio. The rest of the family fled, leaving behind everything they possessed, including their cattle and their land.

—near Ermita de San Antonio, still in Cuscawas, the "Patrulla Negra" destroyed practically the whole colony of 18 houses, murdering several peasants. A large number of the colony fled.

A Roman Catholic priest made a submission in June 1976 to the United States Congressional Subcommittee on International Organizations of the House of Representatives Committee on Foreign Relations, during hearings on human rights in Nicaragua, stating that among advisers at the Rio Blanco camp (in Matagalpa province in central Nicaragua, the largest of several rural detention and in-

terrogation camps, and notorious for reported tortures and atrocities) was a former United States AID police training adviser and a former South Vietnamese army officer, both working under contract to the National Guard. The Father also provided the names of these advisers.

During the same hearings, held in the United States Congress, a spokesman for the United States Department of State confirmed that the American adviser in question was, until 1974, the head of the Public Safety Advisory Program of AID, but that, since October of 1974, the man had been working in his private capacity as consultant to the Nicaraguan National Guard, and added that the "Vietnamese" adviser referred to by the priest did not exist.

In October of 1976, the Minister of Defense of Nicaragua reported that the American adviser in question was in fact an adviser to the National Guard and the Managua police, and that the "Vietnamese" adviser cited by the priest was in fact a Korean "professor of judo at the Nicaraguan Military Academy, and not a torturer."

•20•

"What would 'Holland's Law' be?" Rhiana wanted to know.

It was early afternoon. They had hardly spoken a dozen words the whole day. Rhiana was tired and had tried to sleep without success, her senses and limbs numbed. The sensation was similar to a tranquilizer's onset, although she had none to take.

"Nothing of use to you," Holland said.

He had slept two hours before Rhiana made them lunch in Max's retreat at the lake, having arrived in the morning to find the place empty, going over it and the grounds carefully, gun in hand before deciding it would provide a reasonably secure lair while they waited for night.

Rhiana had stood watch while he slept.

"Is it a joke?" she said.

They were drinking coffee in the large room at the

front of the house, seated across from each other in frumpy old armchairs that had been relegated from quarters in the city.

Holland smoked his pipe, listening to Ella Fitzgerald sing *A Sunday Kind of Love* on the cassette player with his revolver beside him.

"That's as good a description as any," he said. "George must have told you."

"Only to ask you."

In the morning they had bought provisions and some clothes for her. Now she wore loose work pants, a man's cotton shirt, dirtied tennis shoes, and a vest. At present the bindings were not necessary and she had discarded them. After lunch he had finished cutting her hair with a proper pair of clippers until it looked acceptably masculine. She had been quiet ever since.

"Do I have to pry that out too?" she said.

"Don't credit me with the designation," he said. "That was George's contribution. The law, if you will, is that man is too stupid to recognize how stupid he is."

She flinched, raising her hand and moving to shake out her hair the way she used to. The espial was awful to watch.

"George said it when he was taking me back to the airport."

"Not meaning you," Holland said. "I know George. He's incapable of saying something like that to a woman."

"Is that the premise you operate with when you're doing this sort of thing? That we're all too crushed by limits to save ourselves?"

"When doing all things," he said. "It's a premise that's compelling, therefore constant. A child with infinite fathers."

He was watching the birds on the windowsills, starlings who had come in flocks for the loaves of bread crumbs he had sowed the lawn with, enlisting the unsuspecting birds as surrogate sentinels.

"But you include yourself," she alleged.

"Certainly. If I didn't, I'd be at a worse disadvantage." The tobacco in his pipe he tamped down with an empty cartridge case. "George must've said it in context with something else, not just out of the blue."

"He said if I was determined to come back here I should stay as close to you as I can, that you'd keep me alive. That was when he said to ask you about Holland's Law."

"You sure as hell did some steady grinding on me in the beginning," he scrutinized. "How safe do you feel now?"

"Safe," she said. "It makes my skin crawl sometimes, but I feel safe with you. I didn't on the plane. I thought about the 'Stockholm Syndrome' then. Are you familiar with it?"

"Not firsthand. As I understand it it's a sort of emotional transference that occurs between hostages and their captors. They begin to share the same threat. They become 'we.' I think it's more accurately explained as a shared identification to survive, growing out of a mutual will to live that imposes a supernatural bond. Just as often the captors feel empathy with their hostages, and while identification isn't voluntary, it is practically inevitable. I've read that the syndrome isn't at all a phenomenon with animals, but is very common even among different species—"

"Alright," she protested defensively. "You know about it. I just thought that certain aspects obviously—"

But Holland proceeded undeterred. "People who were perfect strangers only hours before become intensely involved out of all proportion to conventional standards. Some fall in love. Most have sex. In the strangest places and the most unlikely circumstances. Bank vaults, prison offices, airplane washrooms. Often in front of others and in plain sight of rescuers. Sometimes, when it's over, the victims visit the hijackers in prison . . ."

Exasperated that he was doing it purposely, and relentlessly, Rhiana got up and left the room.

Holland watched her go, then put a match to his inactive pipe.

Past the windows the lake was sufficiently flat to mirror higher ground. Clouds were high and streaked.

She surprised him by returning with fresh coffee.

She put a cup beside him. "Did the lighter fail or did you just throw it away?"

"Now that you mention it, the lighter served exceptionally well," he said. "But I had to leave without the little devil when it became necessary to improvise. I'm grateful you gave it to me. Thank you."

She removed her sneakers and curled her legs under her in the chair, gazed at him with something more than curiosity. Water could be heard lapping at the quay when a rowboat went out for fish. The fisherman would be superstitious and would believe in a god.

"I wasn't suggesting that the Stockholm thing applied to us, other than the obvious conditions of wanting the same outcome and running from the same people."

"We're not running," he clarified. "Not yet."

"I don't have any idea what we're doing." She smiled, though it required an effort, and added, "You said 'we.' There's my point."

"Well taken," he said. "But you're not my hostage and unfortunately we don't have the wisdom of animals. You did come back when you should have known better, that does defy reason."

"We're also of different species, don't forget that."

"I won't buy it either. And remember that you're supposed to be male. Male isn't my personal persuasion, I assure you."

"I had never supposed it was."

There was a silence. Ella Fitzgerald was finished. Holland shut off the player.

"That song would be marvelous in Spanish," he said, more to himself.

He went to the window, crossing through perimeters of light. The birds on the sill left for the grass. He held the revolver in his hand, as he did almost constantly now. The way he moved with it implied an extension of his flesh.

"Isn't it somewhat incongruous that you and George know each other so well?" she said. "That he would know what you do?"

"It is," he agreed. "George's greatest strength as well as greatest failing is his curiosity. At the time he didn't give me much of a choice."

"You mean kill him?" she said. "He must have realized that."

Holland nodded without looking at her. "He didn't know what I was into, he just suspected. George is that rarest of individuals: He's trustworthy and he's seen enough to know that we no longer enjoy the luxury of making those kind of judgments. You see, George doesn't share your conflicts about what I do."

She examined his face in profile, taking pains to separate what she saw from the gun.

"How did it happen? I'd like to know."

Now he turned to her. "I'm sure you would. I'm equally sure Moloch would if he got his hands on you."

She lowered her head. Again he had anticipated what she had not.

"Just keep thinking," he said, going back to the window.

He stared out on hedges and oaks and a band of white nun orchids, a few short palms of a hardy variety, and a squirrel who was raiding the bread.

"I can be trusted too," she said quietly. "George said he first met you in Vietnam."

"That's interesting. What else did he say?"

"Don't condemn him. He knew I was frightened of coming here at first and I suspect he just wanted me to feel more secure."

"You're neglecting to mention you asked him."

"Yes. I asked," she admitted. "Wouldn't you?"

"What did he tell you?"

"That you were sent to Vietnam as a weapons expert, which accounts for the way you use guns and things. He said if anything went wrong to expect that. He said you didn't like being an adviser and became a . . . I can't remember what term he used . . ."

"I led a scout team," Holland said. "He might have said a 'Lurp.' "

"So that you could fight."

"The first time I was dropped out in the Beyond with some grunts I saw one of them crying when the chopper went away. He was a grown man. The grunts always watched the choppers leave, and waited like abandoned orphans until the sound was gone. You should have seen those faces when that quiet came crashing down. It was sort of a war, if you'll remember," he went on, speaking rhetorically, his tone flat and even, that of a contemplative monk. "They christened it a 'controlled conflict.' If you were there you saw it as something they didn't have words for. You fought or you played house or you made money off the war. I was apolitical, so I fought."

"George said he was assigned to write a series of articles about soldiers who had fought at close quarters, because that was relatively rare. He interviewed the ones the authorities sent him to but he kept hearing stories. How you had made a specialty of fighting them face on. How you went out at night and when you found them you'd yell that you were an American. That was all," Rhiana said. "I think that was what he wanted to say. Tell me."

She was certain he would not. And for a long time he stayed silent and gave no indication that he would tell her. She waited and listened to the claver of feeding birds.

Inside the house the only sound was the low hum of the refrigerator.

Finally he left the window and took his chair, sat forward, facing her, his elbows on his knees, his fingers forming a bridge in front of his face.

"Once you've made the decision about what you can live with and can't live with, it comes down to applying yourself," he said. "In 'Nam my scout team was twelve men. Every one was black. Their leader would have been black too except that I asked for the action. That was mostly where the 'control' came into 'controlled conflict': sending blacks out on the assembly line. It's been said that soldiers are dreamers. They neglected to mention that in 'Nam they were mostly black."

He stopped. She thought he might be struggling, then saw she was mistaken.

"We worked at night because we had to and because those guys were as good as any there were. In thirteen months we only lost five men, which, when you were doing what we were, was a damn high batting average. That's where the 'new' phenomenons like your Stockholm Syndrome really got to working. You're right about George though. He came in on a chopper one day in the spring, wanting to do a story. Trouble was, Army Intelligence was showing an interest in me as a killer person, right about the same time, so they went through channels to make sure George didn't write anything."

"Why was that?"

"You've got to understand that the Intelligence folks

used the war as a recruiting campus whenever they needed people to do their killing for them. I mean, ostensibly we were there for that anyway, so doing it by directive was only a difference of degree if an aptitude was indicated. They figured I did and gave me the full treatment, waving the flag and flogging the patriotic line and like that. Nobody bought that crap but you've also got to understand that 'Nam was as corrupt as anything ever conceived, and at the time I was slow enough to think the CIA was interested in cleaning out some of it."

"Is that who you worked for, then?"

"Sometimes. We were passed back and forth between whoever needed 'a selective piece of work' done. My original training was arranged by the CIA and done in Thailand, the rest I picked up as I went along. We were pretty well expendable as far as they were concerned. Nobody lasted long. Sometimes the new recruits were sent out to finish off our own people because some asshole had decided they knew too much about his shell game. A lot like a revolving door."

He waited.

"For myself, I only did two jobs before I went over the wall. That was how long it took to tumble to the fact I'd sent down two heroin brokers because they'd started to move in on the trade of some ARVN generals. That was enough."

"But where did George come in?" Rhiana wanted to know.

"Like I said, JUSPAO—the public affairs office told him to get lost when he came to see me, mainly because my cover was already in the works. That started George to wondering. You see, the way they made you invisible was by 'arranging' to have you killed in action: passing some grunt's body off as yours and all of a sudden you took on whatever identity they gave you. It helps if you don't have any family, which I didn't. When I quit them I did the same thing, except I did it well enough that even the spooks were convinced. By finessing my own death in Cambodia I ceased to exist, and I still don't to this day. Trouble was, George read the casualty roster when I was 'killed' the first time and, by pure chance, recognized me on the street in Mexico City a couple of years later. Knowing how these things worked, he put them together and came up with four. Patrick helped him some. Did you know his brother?"

"Of course," Rhiana said. "I dated Patrick when the family came to Santiago in the summer, when we were teenagers. He was killed in Vietnam. To this day I don't even know what he was doing there. What do you mean, 'he helped'?"

Holland tried his coffee but found it cold.

He paused, listening, then continued.

"If you knew Patrick you must have known he had a flair for wine, women, and song."—Rhiana nodded—"Well, he also had a compulsion for spy thrillers and an adolescent idea that being a spook was glamorous. George took him over there so he could help with errands and stringing and stuff, and the first thing he knew Patrick was running errands for the CIA, just hanging around looking for the flash and glitter. He ended up working for a CIA front known as Aeschylus PetroChemie, moving information for them and doing go'fer jobs, nothing serious. When George tried to add up what I was all about, he naturally asked Patrick's assistance. Patrick got as far as finding why my first death was phony, but was killed before he could turn up anything further. George told me the sequence later."

"How was he killed?" Rhiana asked. "George said it was in a freak bombing. An accident."

Holland nodded. "It was made to look that way and George may or may not believe it, I don't really know. But Patrick was grenaded at four in the morning on Dong Khoi Street by two ARVN's who'd been hired by a French diplomat. Patrick had been having an affair with the man's wife. There was a lot of that over there. Something for everyone. Glamorous, huh?"

Rhiana shook her head. "I suppose it was quite a lovely war, as wars go."

"You could see that the countryside had once been very pleasing to the eye. Do you remember when the Cambodians took the *Mayaguez* in 1975, just after Saigon fell? Do you remember the picture the wire services carried of Kissinger and Ford in the Oval Office when the Marines got her back?"

"I remember," Rhiana said.

"Two mental degenerates laughing and scratching and clapping each other on the back as if they'd won a bet on the World Series. Fifteen on our side dead, another twenty-three went down with a chopper, and we get two slugs who couldn't operate a one-hole outhouse posing for pictures and celebrating a 'moral victory.' Outrageous. Fucking outrageous. *That's* where we live. That's what floats to the top."

He stopped short, his attention locked on the door leading to the kitchen, behind her. He had heard something. He reached for the revolver, pointed to the shotgun at the foot of her chair, then held the flat of his palm to her.

With the shotgun in her hands, but remaining seated, she scanned the windows. She could still hear the birds.

Holland got up and went past her. On floors that creaked when she walked on them, he could not be heard.

She sat still and watched the doors and the windows, straining to hear a menace she could not define.

After several intolerably prolonged minutes Holland appeared. "Field mice in the walls."

She eased her mind as much as she could.

He took the shotgun from her and replaced it on the floor.

"Why don't you get some sleep?" he said. "It may be another long night full of bumps."

"You didn't finish," she said. "You didn't tell me why you yelled at the Viet Cong. Someone should know. Can that be true?"

"It was folklore that got blown all out of proportion," he said, standing again at the window. "Trying to catch sappers was like trying to catch fish piss, and nobody knew it better than they did. At night we'd go out in the Beyond and I'd break off on my own. Every once in a while I'd come across a VC or two by themselves, mainly because they did more lone wolf stuff than we did. They knew they had us in their own living room and it was only a matter of time, but they still carried around that freaked-out phobia about the mythically invincible Yankee fighting machine. If you were sneaking through the jungle and all of a sudden a round-eyed Lurp came screaming out of the lily pads, yelling 'American! American!' as he came on, you'd likely take a second or two to get your gear together, wouldn't you say?"

She looked away from him, unable to prevent herself. She chewed the inside of her mouth. "I wouldn't be expecting that. Not psychology. Is that what you mean by applying yourself?"

"Something like that." He sat back. "Get some sleep."

"I can't."

A dowager piano, another cast-off from the city house, occupied the room. He took a pillow from a chair and went to the piano, closed the keyboard and placed the pillow there.

He put Ella Fitzgerald on again, and indicated to Rhiana that he wanted her to sit on the bench.

This time she did not question him but got up and crossed in bare feet, sitting facing the piano and allowing him to lean her forward so that her head rested on the pillow, letting him place her hands comfortably on the tops of her thighs.

He began with a firm upward stroke on her spine, using the flat of his hand on each side, then flaring out over the shoulders and upper arms, returning down the sides of her body to the shoals of her hips and starting again.

"It's called *effleurage*," he said.

"Oh, I know," she said. She closed her eyes and felt him drawing tension off. "Where did you learn?"

"I'm a voracious reader," he said.

His hands were gliding over her back.

A church bell began ringing in the village, for which he could not think of a reason.

"Why do you do it?" she said.

He gave her a pronounced sigh. "Another miner. Even when drowning in the swamp everyone needs to know why. You wonder why Moloch rips the wings off of people?"

"No, I don't need to ask that. But you're a maze. Talking to you is like doing a striptease with my soul. You frighten me and then you make me ashamed that I am."

"No extra charge," he said.

"Is what happened in Vietnam the reason?"

"That would be convenient," he said quietly, "but 'Nam was just a time and a place. It was what I always intended to do, I just had to learn how."

She opened her eyes, sharply defined, then closed them again.

"Why would you always have a wish to kill people?"

"Because some people need killing and there isn't so much as a judgment to it. Because I knew I could. Because we're all born with someone's hands in our pockets and someone's cock up our ass, and we smile and we bend over farther because we want our fleeting little space and we don't know how to hit back. I don't like it. I hit back. The ones I go after have the same option I have, to stop me they have to stop me. Except that they made the rules to suit and they own the board. I'd rather have a choice, but I don't . . . My apologies for being indelicate."

His fingers plied the outlines of her shoulder blades, thumbs working along the edges, then held the muscles flowing from the neck to the back and pressed progressively with the other hand, going left hand-right hand-left-right. Now even her breathing was at the behest of his hands.

"Speaking of money," she said. "You do take money."

"You're grinding on me again," he said, "and your assumption is false. There are few times I take money because there are few times I work for anyone but myself. George and the Lomolins aren't paying. George knows that. Besides, I made enough money in the beginning to last the duration. And where I live doesn't require much in the way of material sustenance. Money is only necessary to go after the next one. Any fool can make money."

After massaging the base of her skull and the nape of her neck, he drew her head back easily and stroked her temples with small eddies of his fingers. Her head swept back, face rising.

"Where do you live?" she asked him.

"Where I live . . . is peaceful," he said, considering his choices carefully. "I have friends there. An old couple and a fish. I can read by natural light until nine or ten o'clock, have a sunset every night. I use an oil lamp maybe three times a month. I listen to music. I can be left alone and I can still watch the parade."

"It sounds blessed."

"I can't change anything there, and wouldn't. I can't change anything here, and would. But by making a few of them accountable I can at least go back."

"Should I believe you?"

"You can believe whatever you like," he said. "The truth is, I'd prefer to live in Camelot. But we don't, we live here, so for me it's better to be a good assassin than a bad priest."

"Why don't I hear hard edges? Or obsession? Why do I feel I should?"

"Obsession feeds on illusions of change. It's enough that they know there's someone out here who won't bend over."

"Now it sounds bleak."

"Don't light candles for me."

Now he had frightened her. She knew the reason and she did not feel ashamed at knowing.

"Yes," she said.

"You should sleep now."

He lifted her and carried her from the piano.

"In the chair," she said. She was ready to sleep.

She curled up when he set her down.

He got himself fresh coffee from the kitchen and returned to sit across from her.

She opened her eyes and looked at him past softened barriers, watching him watching her. Then she went to sleep.

•21•

As Rhiana slept, Clement Moloch and his sister were strolling in the garden at the rear of his estate.

The Thai walked far enough behind to allow them a prescribed privacy. He carried a machine pistol on a sling and watched the walls with a diligence that had never been as compelling as now.

Claire's gait seemed curiously stilted, her steps reluctant. She held a hand to her throat, an elbow buttressed on the arm crossing her waist. She wore peach colored slacks and a chain mail belt borrowed from Margaret. Her wrist clinked with bangle bracelets.

They stopped under a green codling tree.

The Thai hung back, out of hearing.

Claire was saying, "Surely you're not entertaining the suspicion that I'm somehow an accomplice to what's happened? Clement, how could you? It's a travesty that you would stoop to such questions."

"Claire," Moloch said, "let me remind you that we are not speaking here about tales told out of school. These mystery aliens homed in on my papers without putting so much as a pencil out of place. Paul Buggs tells me that not a single item was missing. Only you and I and the thieves knew—and still know—what they were seeking, and where to get it. They didn't even find it necessary to force their way in—"

"Clement, this is ludicrous—" Claire protested.

"Be quiet!" Moloch rasped at her.

She glanced at the Thai anxiously. He appeared appropriately inscrutable while looking busily away. He chewed gum with his front teeth.

Moloch forged on. "Am I to believe that a burglar, entirely without aid, stole into the apartment while you were present, overpowered you without disturbing a hair on your head, went for my papers straightaway—without guidance of any kind—and did away with Raymond with equal dispatch when discovered? All miraculously transpiring in a scant matter of seconds? Is that what you would have me believe?"

She cowered under the relentless onslaught, turning away to clutch at her throat.

"It's the truth, Clement," she said solemnly. "I swear on Mother's name, it's true. If I knew how it was done, don't you think I would—"

Moloch shook his head mulishly and pulled her sharply by the arm. Like Margaret, she was taller than he, and it was necessary to direct his malevolence at her higher elevation.

"The facts speak ably enough for themselves. Paul Buggs, like Brian and Raymond, is a very able fellow in the art of detection, my dear. According to his estimate this bounder could not have been in the apartment longer than five minutes, that is if we are to accept your version of the tale. How is it that this single mortal could dispense with someone as finely trained and as formidable as Raymond, and so quietly that you weren't even aware of it?"

She skirted the tree, trying to put the trunk between them. But he stuck to her relentlessly. A warm breeze stirred the leaves overhead.

"I don't know," she said. "I just don't know. I told you I didn't see how it happened. I was in the bath."

"How do you propose to explain the keys to Brian's automobile, then? The tobacco pouch? A lighter intended only for a pipe?"

"I can't," she cried. "I've never seen them before. Can't you accept that they were placed there deliberately to lead you astray?"

"And the barbiturates?" he demanded. "Pray tell what they were designed to impart."

"The pills belonged to Raymond," she said. "I don't know where he got them . . . but he asked me to keep the balance because he knew you wouldn't approve. He didn't use many. He said he shared them with Brian. It was all quite innocent."

"Obviously enough that you didn't feel it prudent to inform me he was defying my rules," Moloch accused bitterly. "You know I have rigorous codes of conduct for my aides."

"I should have told you," she said.

Her capitulation served to moderate Moloch's ire, if only for a brief lull. His thoughts were ripe with free associations, yet all with elements he was unable to hang her with.

"It's to your favor that the lighter and the keys did not have fingerprints," he said evenly. "That can almost be chalked off as deliberate. And Raymond did have a few capsules on him, lending some credence to your version."

She gave him another gravely injured look.

Claire's ideology was as compatible with his own as Siamese twins were in sharing blood types. From the earliest days she had recognized the virtues as well as the urgency of his calling and had supported him without qualification, observing with him the denigration of authority by festering student agitators—tomorrow's anarchist ringleaders—and the desecration of the ruling class by low-caste worker malcontents—tomorrow's rank and file conspirators—everywhere the dupes of destruction being cast on winds of defiance.

When their father died and the socialist kites had picked his fortune clean, it had been Claire who had worked to keep him in school so that one day he could be instrumental in the restoration of discipline and order. Oh, he had been that beyond his wildest aspirations; standing alongside some of the masterful figures of power, until ultimately his own power had eclipsed theirs.

Claire had not wavered throughout, though it was true she lived her own life well within herself and had only come to have intimate knowledge of his activities after he had asked her assistance with the compilation of his papers. He had gifted her with money until she had refused to accept more. She had freedom of movement and time, certainly more than he enjoyed, and she had her paramours.

If there was a fault it would be her mania for staying young, her girlish infatuation with affairs of the heart. Gad, Raymond had hardly been that. Even so, either penchant could account for heretical departures.

"Have you been seeing anyone but Raymond?" he asked her sharply.

The hand at her throat pulled on a ridge of loose skin. Incredibly, he saw the flash as she became aware of the sagging. One more time.

"Don't be silly," she said. "You'd know if I were."

"Tell me, then, how is it that Raymond was with you when he had specific instructions to search for Brian? Could he have been lured there? Have we missed something, Claire?"

She looked miserable under his surgical dissection.

"If you must know, he came to make love. I told him he shouldn't . . . but . . ."

Moloch stepped back and fixed her with a look of withering condemnation, then snatched a codling from a low limb and squashed it between his sideshow hands.

"Sluts for fast bedding are two a penny. At least, Margaret . . ." He stopped, mortified with himself. There, he had done it again—confused them.

"It was only a half hour before he left . . . What could I do? . . . Leave me, Clement. Please."

Moloch grabbed her and swung her to face him.

"You said he left. How could he leave when he was killed on the bed? On *your* bed?"

She held her head to collect her thoughts. The garden was reeling.

The Thai was watching now.

"He did leave," she said haltingly. "But he must have forgotten something and come back . . . I had gotten into the bath . . . I thought I heard him and went to see . . . the next I knew this man with a stocking over his head was there . . . I don't know where he came from . . . He may have been hiding while we . . ."

She grew quiet, shaking, checked by her brother's fresh show of scorn.

"Did you scream?" he said.

"I couldn't. He had a gun . . . he was strong . . ."

"Why do you say that?" Moloch demanded. "He didn't hurt you."

"His hands . . ."

She offered a bruise on her wrist as evidence.

"His hands?" Moloch echoed.

He looked down at his own.

The short paws Moloch displayed were wet with soft apple meat, void of strength and dexterity.

He stared at them for a while, an impoverished cast to his eyes. Then, from some wintry parish of the mind, he said. "The one in the bar had strong hands." He was still mired in private ponderings, still looking at his hands. "Buggs said the tourist in the bar had strong hands."

"How does he know?"

"He went there this morning. The description of the man and woman sounds close to the pair we saw at the bullfights. Apparently the woman is rather extraordinary. Buggs has some of his people out trying to locate them but hasn't had any luck."

"Why don't you ask Mr. Ortiz?" she said.

Moloch broke out of his reverie, suddenly alert.

"Who did you say?"

"Mr. Ortiz. I met him here, at one of Margaret's dinner parties. He's a wealthy businessman living in the city."

"But what has he to do with the tourists?" Moloch asked impatiently.

"They were with him at the bullfights. Mr. Ortiz was

sitting beside them. The man spoke to him when he was leaving."

"Are you sure?" Moloch asked her, heavy with anticipation. "Perhaps he was just excusing himself for passing."

Claire looked uncertain, but said, "I had the impression they were together."

Moloch sped away abruptly, hurrying toward the house at an awkward lope.

Passing Jack, he snapped, "Bring her inside just the same."

Paul Buggs was sitting at his desk in his office at the embassy, picking through a late lunch with enthusiasm considerably less than convincing.

Pressured, he had sent an operative out to McDonald's.

Charles Waterston was with him, after a leisurely lunch of garlic guinea hen and bananas flambé at one of the city's more exotic watering holes. Despite the knit turtleneck under his blazer, Waterston exhibited none of the effects of the relatively warm day outside.

Buggs suspected the flurries of scented powder he used were responsible for his perpetually arid condition.

A telephone number with an area code was scribbled on a note pad. Buggs tore the page off, balled it up and dropped it in the "Destroy" basket. He had been trying to reach Utica, but either his wife refused to answer or his in-laws wouldn't allow her to. He had counted twenty-three rings before some sharp-assed operator had pointed out that no one was answering. What would he do with the fucking house? He realized that that was the way he had always thought of it—the "fucking" house—and that was even the way he had always put it to her.

Waterston went into his office and returned with a glass of ice and a bottle of Chivas Regal, circling the bottle over Buggs' plastic cup of soda fountain cola.

Buggs accepted through a mouthful of Big Mac and fixings, watching his cup fill.

Waterston dispensed his own drink and scooped some of the french fries from the desk.

"You know how to tell good fries?" he asked Buggs.

"Yeah, if I like to eat 'em," Buggs said, using what he considered to be exemplary logic.

"Naw," Waterston said, taking more. "If the salt doesn't stick, they're good. That's how you tell."

"That right?" Buggs said optimistically, thinking what a Gucci prick he was, thinking that Waterston was one of those who sucked up incoherence while believing it to be an avant-garde aesthetic.

"Take my word," Waterston said, flicking at his Yale pin. "Any new developments?"

"Hell, I don't know whether to shit or wind my watch," Buggs groused. "Moloch won't let me use the locals to look for those tourists, or for Randolph's car, even though the paint scrapings on the tree match the color of what he was driving. He finally agreed I should put a clamp on the airport and border crossings, so at least they're on the lookout for anything looking suspicious."

"What about the tourists?"

"Them too. I got a man out checking the hotels and stuff, but as far as I'm concerned this thing about a man and a woman is a real shot in the dark. That narc happened to be going down the right road at the wrong time, that's all there was to it. Moloch's got it all worked out that the guy couldn't have been calling him and wasting the narc at the same time. But the nearest phone's only three kilometers away, so what's the problem? Moloch's got it in his head there's a whole horde of 'em out there, that's what the problem is."

Waterston hiked his knee-high socks. He wore white shoes.

"And you don't think so, Paul?"

Buggs paused to wash some fries down with the Chivas, then squeezed more catsup from the plastic envelope onto those left.

"Tell the truth, Chuck, I got my doubts. Look, we've had a lot of postings, you and me. You ever see a night's work like that?"

Waterston raised his glass in a salute.

"That why you asked for Floyd Cannell and some more assets?" he said.

Floyd Cannell was a journeyman working out of the Miami station, an expert on the Latin American underground scene and one of the most accomplished manhunters in any of the clandestine services, as well as possessing some prior experience with Clement Moloch. He would be arriving by private plane later in the day, at Buggs' request. And "assets," the traditional trade sobriquet for operatives, had been requested. Cannell was bringing three additional assets with him.

"Aw, Christ, Chuck, that was none of my doing and you know it," Buggs said. "You and Moloch got a personality conflict, what am I gonna do? Cannell knows his way around this kind of thing and if it's gonna be a war he'll come in handy. That's Cannell's bag. I'm rusty and I can use his kind of craft. I'm not proud when I've already been embarrassed three times, I can tell you."

Waterston produced a pocket atomizer and sprayed his yawning mouth, revealing rows of nickel fillings.

"Anything happens to Moloch and heads will roll from here to head office," he said. "The man's got a lot of friends on either side. Did Cannell run a check on the files?"

"He said he'd plug into the computer and see if there were any loose ones that might be involved or couldn't be accounted for," Buggs replied. "He'll bring the readout with him."

Waterston emphasized his words with a wagging finger.

"Those are real blunt instruments you've got out there," he said. "Last night was about as bad as it can get. I'm out of it, but I side with Moloch; there's no way you're dealing with one potential here."

"You want to know what I think, I think we're dealing with the sister too. I think she's dirty, and whoever she's hooked up with ain't no primitive. From where I sit he's three moves ahead of us and I haven't got a fucking clue where he's going or who he's gonna take with him."

The mention of Claire Moloch renewed Waterston's interest. He took his feet from the desk, put his glass down. He leaned forward.

"Claire," he said. "That's why he squeezed me out. Because of Claire."

Buggs humored him, feeling foolish. "Could be. Could be."

"Is," Waterston exclaimed, slapping the desk with the flat of his hand. He looked satisfied, even pleased. He tried to shoot his cuffs before realizing he didn't have any.

"We've got a political thing here," Buggs said. "I think we're looking at a political assassin after Moloch."

Waterston was peering up the sleeves of his blazer.

"Did you present that to him?" he asked.

"Not in so many words. Moloch's convinced they're radicals out for funding. That's why he insists on paying for those papers he claims were stolen, and for not having any shooting until we've got them back. He wants the perpetrators alive. He wants them in the worst way."

"I could just imagine." Waterston refilled his own glass but not Buggs'. "What did he say was on the papers?"

"Technical stuff: cause and effects, dosages, techniques, research. He claims it's only important to him. The writing's covered, so there's no way of knowing exactly. That's the way he wants it returned, too." Buggs banged a desk drawer open to make his point. "Hell, he's already given me three bags of fifty thou each in case we've gotta move fast and little money's needed."

He lit an unfiltered cigarette with the lighter found in Claire Moloch's apartment. His own had been forgotten in the rush from home. Using an item of evidence was against regulations bu he couldn't have cared less.

Waterston was about to question the odd flame travel of the lighter when the telephone rang.

Buggs lifted it, listened for a while, nodding, then finished by saying, "I'll get on it. You'll hear from me."

With the phone down, he arched his chair and contemplated the brief exchange.

"Moloch says the tourists were seen with Max Ortiz a few days ago," he informed Waterston. "You've met Ortiz. He's big in business circles. Old line money."

Waterston exaggerated his recollection. "Oh, yes, of course. A decent fellow. Is Moloch sure?"

Buggs shrugged. "Says so."

"What are his politics?"

"Nothing dangerous. He's a straight-arrow, always riding the fence. It was before your time, but the '74 election was ours, right out of the manual. We could deliver anybody and anything. Boy, was it a sweetheart. But Ortiz refused to take sides, just wanted to stay clear, and from our information I understand that's been his way no matter who's dealing the cards."

"What're you going to do?" Waterston said.

"What can I do? The man speaks," Buggs said, pointing to the phone as he stood, knocking Big Mac crumbs to the floor. "I'll have him brought over here for a little confab, and if that doesn't work I'll give him to Moloch. Ortiz'll either be at home or his office this time of day."

"Don't forget his place at Lake Amititlan," Waterston said as Buggs started for the door.

Buggs halted. "Lake Amititlan?"

"Yeah, Jude was thinking of renting for weekends and the broker happened to point out where Ortiz was, trying to hype the neighborhood. Big old place with a green roof."

"Okay, that too," Buggs said, striding from the room.

Waterston reached for the last of the fries, avoiding the catsup.

•22•

Holland sat cross-legged on the slope of the roof, dividing his attention between sky and lake.

Stringy clouds had given way to more ample congregations, although still granting expansive azure straightaways for the sun's march on the Pacific. On the lake the flat bottom, high prow boats of Indian fishermen lay deliberately clear of the deep, mindful of *el chocomil*—the capricious wind that frequently poured off the mountains in late afternoon.

Diagonally across the water could be made out the high apollo spires of the Posado Centro America Hotel. Past the river and on the way to the village, the spires appeared almost oriental in the distance, behind them bristling pine ridges streamed down the mountains.

Near where the river spilled into the lake were several thermal bath emporia laying claim to medicinal properties in their waters. He would have liked to try them. He would have liked Rhiana to try them too.

Maybe that was still possible. Maybe at dusk, if all remained quiet.

He shifted his scrutiny down the shore to his left, to rock arbors and huts with thatched roofs situated between the dirt road and the beach. No one was around.

From the village the singsong of church bells came again.

On either side of him rows of large private homes facing the water all seemed shut, waiting to come alive on the weekend. Some were splendid, opulently landscaped, yet overwhelmed by the magnificent Agua and Pacaya volcanoes in the distance.

He wondered if the owners had ever considered that.

A plume of dust was rising from the road near the lily pond, coming fast. He waited, watching the grey ghost swirl.

Between the trees the drab formal shade of the car set off alarms in his head. Hubcaps. Blackwalls. Sedan. Side mirrors on both sides. Tinted glass.

He tucked then rolled sideways down the roof to the edge, then dropped to the grass, the barrel of the heavy revolver in its holster thumping his knee as he landed.

Inside, Rhiana was curled in her chair.

He kneeled in front of her and took her hands gently. She came awake without being startled.

"Sarah. I was dreaming."

"She's fine," he said.

She touched the cut on his cheek unexpectedly. The skin around it had yellowed.

She said, "You're healing."

He covered her mouth without touching her.

"Uh, we'll have guests in a minute. We'd better take a walk."

She jerked her head and moved all at once, reaching for her sneakers. He grabbed them first.

"We don't have time. Take the shotgun and one of the knapsacks."

"He must have Max," she said.

He didn't answer but tied her sneakers together with the laces and hung them around his neck. He swept her bindings from the table into the other knapsack and slung it over his shoulder, loosing the revolver and clutching a pair of Dade speedloaders.

Holland had a sack full of the plastic facsimiles of a revolver's cylinder, which held the same number of cartridges and allowed the fastest possible reloading of the gun. Once the spent shells were ejected, the speedloader dropped fresh cartridges into the chambers with one lightning motion instead of requiring individual insertion.

Rhiana was getting into her windbreaker.

"Do that up," he said. "Where's the automatic?"

She showed him the knapsack.

He motioned her behind him and went through the kitchen to the back door, taking an oatmeal cookie from the counter and pulling the plug on the coffee pot. Before going outside he examined the terrain, taking his time. Rhiana was close enough to bump him.

He locked the door, staying close to the house until they reached the lake, then following the water's edge in the direction of the village, back from where the car had come. They would probably cut in a couple of houses down from Max's, sending a man or two to cover the front while the rest arrived from other sides, depending on their number. Whatever they did, Holland calculated that he and Rhiana had stolen enough of a lead to be past them.

He walked briskly but not fast enough to draw attention, keeping to hedges or fences when he could. The revolver he held to the side of his leg. Rhiana followed his example with the shotgun, and did not look back.

Holland waved to a fisherman offshore, had the greeting returned.

He pointed to the sparse strip of sand along the water's edge and said over his shoulder, "Don't step in anything like that or they'll know you're a woman."

Having anticipated him, she said, "I know."

He said, "At'a boy."

A day-glo Frisbee bobbed in the shallows, reflecting against a volcano's cone. Holland waded into the water to examine it, leaving Rhiana to wonder how he could take time to forage when their pursuers were only minutes away. Then she saw him snatch a look behind.

At the rock huts they went inland and crossed the road, Rhiana like a fakir, showing no visible discomfort at the sharp gravel under her bare feet. He would be willing to debate whether she feared more for herself or for Max.

The rented Chevrolet had been left in the campground

back of the lily pond, concealed by dappled foliage. Holland stood at the driver's door and felt the pockets of his Yankees jacket.

Across the car he said to Rhiana, "Did I give you the keys?"

She shook her head, a note of urgency. "Hurry. They'll see us."

He tossed her sneakers across. "I want them to. I want a chase."

"Why?" she said. "No more killing, Holland, please. There's been enough. Just him."

He found the keys.

"Up to them," he said, getting in the car and starting the engine. "They'll have orders not to fire, you'll see."

She came around to his side. "If there's going to be a chase, I'll drive. You drive terribly."

"Nice thing to say. I'm not that bad."

"Yes, you are. I won't go with you."

When he saw her determination, he slid over.

He said, "If you crash I'm going to write you out of the will."

As soon as she put the car in gear he reached over and slipped the shift lever into neutral.

"Wait until they show," he advised her patiently.

He watched behind while she sat gripping the wheel tightly.

It took ten minutes before the car, a Plymouth, appeared. Four men were inside. They would be wondering about the warm coffee pot, the warm chair, the smell of his pipe in the house. If they were good.

"Go," he said.

Rhiana smashed the accelerator, sending clots of dirt out behind, the car fishtailing violently across the campground. Before they reached the road he saw that she was setting the car up to head away from the Plymouth. He pushed the wheel, nearly causing them to collide with a portable toilet.

"Past them," he said. "Go past them."

She spun the wheel and slued the car onto the road, raising a gusher of gravel as she fought to keep control. The spinning tires slid toward the ditch. She directed the front tires there too, easing the accelerator to retrieve traction, catching the mass in time to hold the surface.

"Jesus," Holland said, feeling for something to hold on to, amazed that she had somehow completed the maneuver.

As they rocketed past the stunned occupants of the Plymouth, he reached out and lobbed the oatmeal cookie across the roof, then watched the Plymouth slide to a stop with its wheels locked, the four inside covering their heads and diving for the floor.

The cookie bounced across the roof, rolled off into the dirt.

"Give them time," he instructed Rhiana.

She slowed the car.

Making certain the shotgun had a round in the chamber, he wedged the weapon in the crack between the seats, pointing toward the rear.

The Plymouth was mobile again, doing a bootleg U and coming furiously after them.

"Okay, driver," he said to Rhiana. "Turn it around."

Even that did not bring her eyes from the narrow road.

She said, "I can't."

He said, "They can."

"Alright," she said angrily. "Show me where."

He remembered something from the reconnaissance made before going to Max's. He pointed.

"Up ahead," he said. "There's a house with a circular driveway. On the right. A red tile place. Here . . . here! . . ."

They were on it already. Rhiana stabbed the brakes intermittently to prevent the car sliding, just able to complete the turn without striking the brickwork at the entrance. She guided the car in a relativey tidy drift around the semicircle and back onto the road, consuming their own dust where it still hung.

The Plymouth, with less anticipation, was not so fortunate and glanced off the portal, powdering bricks and creasing the side of the car and deflecting its course through an echelon of plaster lawn figures.

Rhiana said, "They're still coming."

"That's the plan," he said, watching the rear window. "Keep them there."

The warm afternoon air was rushing dust in the open windows, requiring that they shout over the noise.

"You'll have to tell me earlier," Rhiana complained.

"When I can," he said. "Just keep the rubber side down."

She held the car well on the long sweeping curve following the lake, past dormant sightseeing boats and paper-strewn refreshment stands, then to the right where the road left the lake and went toward the village. A man on horseback rode up a bank out of their way, the horse dancing and throwing its head at the clatter of gravel under the car.

They passed the exit to the old colonial bridge and wash buildings and the main access to the village. At the next junction he directed her left, toward Escuintla and the slope to the Pacific, away from Guatemala City.

The Plymouth had gained, enough so that Holland could observe a door jerk open and a man emerge running, carried by momentum a few jive steps before sprawling near the gas station.

"They dumped a man to phone Moloch," he informed Rhiana. "That's fine."

"Or to notify the police ahead," she said.

"No chance," he said. "He wants this kept in the family. The Nationals will be the last to know."

He made himself comfortable with his back to the door and an arm braced to the dash, settling in to keep log of the Plymouth.

The drop through the mountains did not take long, particularly at the rate Rhiana was holding. Stuck to steep mountainsides, the road rose and fell constantly, rife with switchbacks. Often they rounded a blind bend only to scatter pedestrians and donkeys. One donkey, braying at the Chevrolet already past, kicked out when the Plymouth followed closely after.

"Lot of character, that ass," Holland observed.

Seldom did they encounter other vehicles, but when they did it inevitably imposed a frantic accommodation on the treacherous margin. They slowed to an acceptable speed through the only village on the route, it choked with children just out of school; the Plymouth followed suit and matched their acceleration coming out.

For a short while they ran with the Maria Linda River, catching glare from the late afternoon sun. Rhiana was forced to shade her eyes with one hand. The air got warmer and stickier as they went lower. A fresco of insects covered the windshield to mark the river run.

In the flat, rambling town of Escuintla the Plymouth loomed close enough for Holland to make out the faces within. Scowling, enigmatic spooks stared back, genuine buffs. Rabbits thinking they were foxes, Holland mused.

Back to speed, they flashed over gradually deflating hills checkered with impossibly slight *fincas* growing corn and wheat and fodder for owners' tables. Each gaunt patch had its own residence. Most were one- or two-room adobe with a corrugated tin roof. Some were huts of sticks with a thatch roof.

Holland, sounding like a tour guide gone adrift, said, "Two percent own seventy percent of the land in this fucking roost they call a country. A peasant farmer disappears every eight hours. You figure maybe the gentility's winning?"

If Rhiana heard him over the thunder of the road she gave no indication.

The land grew flatter as they went. The Plymouth came on.

Rhiana's face was streaked with grime and perspiration. The strain of racing the heavy car through the primordial grid was showing. Her precision used more of the road. Her hands crept higher on the wheel. She tried to unzip her windbreaker for air. He did it for her.

He said, "How're you doin'?"

She said, "We can't drive into the ocean."

"How far is that?"

"I don't know. Thirty kilometers. I'm guessing."

He leaned over to read the gas gauge.

The speedometer was reading past seventy miles per hour on a stretch that would have been dicey at fifty.

"Their car is faster," she said.

"I know that," he said. "You're up to it. You're good."

"I'm afraid."

"That's why."

"We have to do something."

"Uh-huh."

She looked across at him for the first time since the lake.

He was searching one of the knapsacks, tossing speedloaders out on the seat.

"What are you going to do?"

"Make the next turn," he instructed her. "Don't be picky. A goat track will do."

"What are you going to do?" she demanded again.

"Wreck his head some more."

He took spent cartridge cases from his pocket and shifted closer to her, pressing the closed end of each into her ear cavities. He did the same to his own.

She did not need elaboration. The makeshift earplugs were to dampen a gun's concussion within the confines of the car.

Without notice she skated the car, executing a hard turn onto a path that was not far removed from his description. Scrub limbs encroached, slapping the windshield. Branches exploded against the sheet metal, shot twigs in the side windows. A pair of ruts, too close for the big car's track, straddled a rock-strewn spine that scraped and hammered the undercarriage. Depressions engulfed the wheels and slammed the suspension solid.

Inside, they were tossed like corks in a gale. Somehow Rhiana clung tenaciously to a thin thread of control.

Holland was swearing, emptying speedloaders onto the seat. From there they bounced and rolled about on the floor.

The Plymouth still came, hounding the scent of destruction.

"What are you looking for?" Rhiana wanted to know.

"I've got some teflon shells in here. They'll go through an engine block and stop it where it stands."

A tight switchback allowed him to see the Plymouth through the side windows.

The path began to traverse a series of humped ridges. On the first crest the Chevrolet cleared all four wheels and came down grinding dirt. Holland's teeth jarred.

Speedloaders were everywhere, most on the floor. One had caught under the accelerator pedal. Rhiana yelled. He dropped to his hands and knees, his head rebounding on the underbelly of the dashpanel. Rhiana had the pedal flat to the floor the instant he cleared his fingers. A red light glowed in the instrument cluster.

Holland dumped the knapsack out on the seat, Moloch's oilskin wrapped papers flopping into view with the rest.

"I thought I was better organized," he hollered at himself.

On the seat the speedloaders resembled jumping jacks. He spotted one holding the elusive green teflon-covered bullets. Emptying the revolver with a quick plunge of the ejector rod, he dropped the cartridges from the speedloader into the cylinder, indexing the chambers into latch in a fluid motion as he swung to the rear window.

Before he was fully around, Rhiana yelled, "Look. *Look!*"

They were hurtling down a steep incline to a table of land carved from a gully, a cradle nestling a single farm. Ahead lay a small adobe shack with a chicken yard in front and stands of mature corn flanking it on either side. The rutted path terminated at the front door. When he looked, the stoop was no more than twenty meters away.

Holland said, "Goddamn."

"I can't stop in time," Rhiana said.

He said, "Take to the corn."

The chickens were already in awkward flight.

He leaned out the window and looked back at the Plymouth. The first of the corn stalks clipped him before he ducked inside.

"Just keep it moving," he told Rhiana. "Round and round."

Under them the soil was scorched hardscrabble that proved more accommodating than the road, and were it not for corn stalks higher than the car's roof, they would have had little difficulty sustaining respectable velocity. As it was they were slowed considerably by the broad hood cleaving the stubborn growth. Ears of corn windmilled across the hood, piled up in the trough at the base of the windshield. There were loud tearing sounds.

Still the Plymouth came on, closing now, threading the swath already cut.

Holland blew a jagged hole in the rear window glass of the Chevrolet with the shotgun, filling the car with a deafening roar that caused Rhiana to wince.

The landlord ran from his shack, spitting his dinner and holding a knife. When he heard the first gunfire he ran back.

Trying to level the revolver on the pitching radiator of

the Plymouth was risky, despite the close proximity. The pair of impromptu harvesters completed three circuits of the field that way, cutting new corridors each time.

Finally Holland, kneeling backwards, gripped the seat and told Rhiana to "Hit the brakes hard and then stand on the gas quick."

She did it perfectly. The rear of the Chevrolet heaved seductively. The Plymouth whacked its iron full on, rat-shaking both. With a final spasm the mating behemoths broke free, the Chevrolet moving away again.

Holland squeezed off three rounds, placing two through the radiator and on into the engine's innards, shattering the timing gear and the water jacket of one cylinder head. The third he put square in the outline on the driver's side of the windshield. The Plymouth stayed where it was.

As they moved away he opened the door and held it ajar with his foot, ejecting the teflon ammo into the knapsack and reloading conventional cartridges, then grabbing a couple of extra speedloaders.

Steam was beginning to billow from under the hood of the Chevrolet.

"Go to the end of the field and keep it moving as long as you can," he said to Rhiana. "Make noise. Give me some time."

He couldn't tell if she was nodding or being shaken by the car.

He tumbled out, rolling on the sharp projections of broken corn scrub, stumbled headlong for the cover of untouched crop. Once hidden, he stood a moment to get his bearings and place a fix on the Plymouth. The sound of the Chevrolet was withdrawing. Voices could be heard, two of them, not far from where he was.

He cut deeper, starting down between tailored rows, hunkered on his haunches to pass under the dense network of husks and tassles that would betray his presence.

The talking ceased. One of them was running. Holland aborted his tack, listening.

One of them was running after the Chevrolet. Heavy thrashing of broken stubble in the corridor next to him was pronounced.

Stupid, Holland thought. Or provoked to an irrational sortie.

He could see the man now, an awkward halfback in a business suit and a field of corn in Hobbit Country. A black handgun was held in his pumping arm. The man fired two wild, snarling shots at the Chevrolet as he ran.

The first of Holland's rounds caught him high in the chest, lifting him to the side in a lazy arc that deposited him a couple of yards from where he was. As soon as he touched, Holland hit him twice more with heart placements.

The horn of the Plymouth blared.

Holland replaced the three empty cartridges from the loose change in his pocket and sprinted into the open, racing fast down the scythe toward the Plymouth.

Three of the car's four doors were open. The third man, also in a suit, stood beside the driver's open door watching Holland's assault as though his eyes were betraying him. He spun, throwing an arm back to snap away a shot that plowed dirt well away from Holland. He ran first for the shack, then altered his course for the wall of corn.

Holland went after him, crashing into stands of coarse dried fiber, guided by the moving swell of corn ahead. They went twenty meters that way, Holland able to gain because of his sneakers, the chased being hindered by stiff leather street shoes and an open suit jacket that snagged on knotted husks.

At the edge of the field a low embankment erupted with a gauntlet of thorn bushes and loose tumbleweed. Upon reaching it the man whirled and fired, the bullet skipping through the stalks near Holland's face. Holland tossed himself to the side, rolled for a meager opening.

His initial round took out the side of a knee, the following the hip above, twisting the man against the embankment and into the thorn bushes. The final two rounds stitched under the outstretched gun arm to pound the chest cavity.

When Holland got to his feet the gully was quiet except for the wail of the horn and the muted threshing of the Chevrolet in the far corner.

He walked to the Plymouth and pulled the driver away from the horn button. The teflon-coated bullet had punched a neat hole in the cheek and exited cleanly at the back of the skull. All three men appeared to be in their thirties.

Clouds of steam hissed from the corn-encrusted grille of the Chevrolet. The rear glass was shattered.

He pulled Rhiana from the car.

"You get hit?"

She shook her head.

"What happened?" she said.

"They're done. There were three of them."

She looked at the small satchel he carried. "What's that?"

"Money. It was in the spooks' car." He handed it to her along with the shotgun and one of the knapsacks. "Make a count on your way to the house. Don't let the farmer shoot you and don't let him talk to you. Watch the road. I won't be long."

He zipped her jacket up and let her go. She walked away in an unsteady daze.

Repacking the other knapsack and wiping their fingerprints from the car took but a few minutes. Fresh earth put a pleasant taste in his mouth as he hurried the house-cleaning.

He caught up to her before she was out of the field. She had slowed near the body in the dirt and was now staring at the Plymouth as she passed.

He pushed her ahead of him, causing her to stumble.

"That's six," she said, an accusation.

"I wasn't counting."

"You've killed six men in three days. Even you can't do it that easily."

He pushed her again.

"The bitch is back," he said.

She faced him and raised the shotgun.

"I told you to never point a gun unless . . ."

She said, "I remember."

He glanced at the Plymouth. "Show me the choice. Show me the reason."

"It was you who said they wouldn't fire at us."

"They meant us harm. They mean everyone harm. You'd have preferred they deliver us to Moloch?"

She looked helplessly at the shotgun.

He brushed by the gun and put his hand gently on the back of her neck, moving her with him.

The farmer wanted no part of them when they approached the shack, emphasized by the stem of a .22 rifle poked past a crack in the door. An early 'fifties flatbed farm truck sat beside the shack, its staked platform serving as a temporary pen for two enormous sows who looked mean, grunting their displeasure through the slats.

So were the chickens bold, having reclaimed their turf in front of the shack. Holland left Rhiana behind and went to stand near the chickens.

"I don't want any trouble, friend," he said in Spanish to the door. "I wish to pay for the damage."

A wait ensued. After a while Holland realized that the revolver was still in his hand. He put it under his jacket.

The crack in the door slowly widened, the farmer showing himself a measure at a time.

Holland held his hands away from his sides. "What we did to your farm is unforgivable."

The farmer gradually emerged onto the stoop, the rifle leveled on Holland.

"You are bad or good?" he solicited.

He was wide and brawny through a short frame, his arms thick, feet big and brown. Binder twine held up his pants.

"What year is your truck?" Holland asked him, ignoring the inquiry on his status.

The farmer shrugged at a reference that was trivial to him. His eyes were incredibly clear. Holland guessed him to be in his thirties, like the others, but found it difficult to determine age on a man who had worked all his life to put something in his belly.

"Ten acres of corn and your truck. Decide on a price that suits you." Then, remembering the pigs, he added, "The truck does run?"

The farmer nodded. "But you can't take it. I need my truck."

Holland walked back to Rhiana. She was counting the pads of bills in the satchel.

"How much?" he asked her.

"I've counted twenty-five thousand. I think there's twice that."

He said, "Give me the twenty-five."

The farmer covered him with the rifle as he returned. Through the open doorway he could distinguish a woman with several small children gathered around her skirt. He thought she was holding a baby but couldn't be sure.

He said to the farmer, "How much would you have to pay to replace your truck? To buy the one you want?"

"I know one, up Siquinala," the farmer said. "Seven hundred quetzals."

"I'll give you a thousand American dollars for the truck," Holland said. "Equal to a thousand quetzals."

The farmer accepted without hesitation, just as Holland knew he would. "Yes. You want the pigs too?"

"Not today," Holland said. "And I'll offer twenty-four thousand American dollars for the corn we ruined."

Dreams welled in the farmer's face. He couldn't help himself, and looked back at his wife. She must have heard, for she came to the door, nursing a baby.

"The corn isn't worth half my truck," the farmer stammered. "Less than that."

"We violated your space and offended your dignity," Holland explained. "I'm sorry."

The farmer, Holland decided, had never heard that before.

"I have to go," Holland said, holding the stack of currency out. "You don't need the gun. You have my word, we don't want trouble."

The farmer looked across at the Plymouth and made a statement concerning generations of enforced deception. The rifle remained on Holland.

Holland then offered the money to the wife as a solution. She came forward, the baby losing the nipple as she stepped from the stoop. The woman's color was darker than Rhiana's, but just as luminous. Reluctantly she returned Holland's smile.

While the wife held the gun, Holland and the farmer put a ramp to the truck and herded the sows into the shack, the farmer explaining that he would build an enclosure before nightfall. Holland looked around for wood he might use, saw none. The slatted sideboards on the truck lifted free with little trouble, so Holland left them for the purpose.

The decrepit engine started with a belch of oil smoke and a chorus of wear in the valve assembly. Only when Holland had ground the floorshift into first gear did the farmer inform him that reverse had mysteriously ceased functioning some years earlier. He was vague about the exact date, looking at Holland strangely when asked how he managed without the services of a reverse gear.

Indicating the field, Holland told him to leave the bodies and the cars as they were, to touch nothing. The farmer nodded readily.

"How far is San Jose?" Holland asked him.

"Twenty kilometers," was the answer.

"Some men will come and ask you questions. Don't lie, except about the money. Take the money and bury it well. Use it slowly, after you've changed it for quetzals in the black market. You'll get more for it there. Do you know how?"

"The priest. He knows how."

"Can you trust him?"

The farmer shrugged. "The church always needs money."

"They try to take your farm yet?"

"Yes," the farmer said. "They get them all some day. Coffee growers with friends."

Holland stopped for Rhiana, wondering if the truck would make it up the first grade.

Rhiana looked back at the carnage until the *finca* was lost from sight.

Once the engine was up to operating temperature it refrained from backfiring and smoothed surprisingly by the time they reached the main road.

Holland drove toward a sun hanging low in the sky.

Rhiana sat forward as soon as she saw their direction, stiffened by lethal premonitions. She turned in the seat.

"This goes to San Jose. I heard you ask him. He'll tell them whether he wants to or not."

The sun laid a flaxen hue over the long seaward slope ahead.

"I told him to," Holland said. "They won't hurt him. I'll bet this old bucket is known by every peasant for twenty miles around."

"Then they'll know where to follow us. I've been to San Jose before; this is the only road out. We'll be trapped."

"You're confusing the cavalry with the desperados," he said. "Relax and enjoy the sights. We're chasing the sun into the ocean. How often have you done that? People pay enormous sums of money to . . ."

"Why are you doing this?" she demanded. "Tell me."

"The ocean. I need it. A fix. A spike. I have to have it."

She was incensed by what she construed to be frivolity. "Don't do that. I asked you not to do that."

Several moot stirrings finally brought the transmission into third gear. He looked across at her.

"I don't know if I can drive a truck," he said.

His look was softer than she had seen it since they had met.

"Rhiana, all I want is to see the ocean before the sun's gone. You're coasting now. If you don't get more sleep, you'll be completely wiped. That means I'll have to take the watch. I'd rather do it by the ocean, that's all."

When she wouldn't look his way he went back to driving.

A distance on, he spotted the farmer's cache of coca leaves atop the heater box.

Over the next summit an electric glint of ocean rose.

She studied him for a long time then.

•23•

Fifteen minutes in light early evening traffic was sufficient for Paul Buggs to review events to date for his companion. They occupied the back seat of a car driven by one of Buggs' operatives, another car herding closely behind with the three "assets" Floyd Cannell had brought with him.

The transit from Guatemala City's La Aurora airport to Clement Moloch's estate would take less than half an hour. In the jargon of the trade, Cannell's flight had been "black," a flight unlogged by either friendly or unfriendly authority before, during, or after—an untraceable passage.

"What you're laying on me is that you've got a bag of snakes and every time you stick your hand in you get bit," Cannell said with a faint manic smile. "But you don't know how many snakes you got or what their stripes are."

He also looked disgusted, but then, as Buggs recalled, Floyd Cannell seemed confined to a permanent snarl of disgust, a projection not always endearing him to those he worked with. Someone had once remarked that Cannell had probably cut himself from the womb looking that way, although it had been so long ago now that Buggs was unable to remember who had said it.

Under Cannell's acrid scrutiny Buggs felt compelled to shore up his own sway.

"We don't know where Ortiz fits in yet, but we will," he stated flatly. "The same with this tourist and his old lady. If they're involved, we'll find out soon enough, but I think that angle's just a waste of time. The hotel where they stayed said they even had their kid with them. Fact is, as soon as I heard that, I took my man off the detail. I'm running too short of manpower to be beatin' the bushes for sightseers."

"And you haven't heard back from your asset out in the boonies?" Cannell said, dabbing at his trim moustache, then adjusting his lemon-tint aviator glasses. The glasses were a fixture worn day and night. Buggs realized that he could not envisage Floyd Cannell without yellow eyes.

"Not yet. Like I told you, I sent four ops out to Ortiz' weekend place and they supposedly scared up two guys in a car. They dropped a man at a phone and then went after them. Hell, let's face it, they could be chasing a pair of low-lifers who were just breaking into cottages. Anyway, I told my op to get hold of a car and find out what the story was and report back to me. That was . . . I don't know . . . three o'clock maybe. I still haven't heard."

Cannell swiveled around to make sure the second in the convoy remained in attendance. Tall and bird-thin, Cannell wore new denim jeans and a jacket that made stiff, rustling noises when he moved. On his feet were low-heeled riding boots. He ate breath candy compulsively.

"You informed The Doctor?" he asked Buggs pointedly.

"Sure I did," Buggs said. "He says 'Bring them to me.' You know what he's like."

The faint manic smile drifted back. "Do you?"

Buggs cleared his throat, knowing he had to simulate serious reverence, aware that Cannell's veil of disgust was in reality intense devotion to all things enforced. Cannell was a perfect company man. Buggs would have relished telling him that when all of this was over he would himself be in the employ of Moloch, but thought it would be far more satisfying if Cannell heard it a few weeks hence, after it had been filtered through the ranks. Cannell's envy would be a bonus.

"Enough," was the reply Buggs selected.

Cannell's smile vanished as he met Buggs' eyes cynically. "You know 'enough' about The Doctor? That what you're telling me?"

Now it was Buggs' turn to smile. "Floyd, don't put words in my mouth. I've been at this station for years. Moloch lives in my precinct. It's required knowledge, for Christ's sake."

"Who asked for me?" Cannell returned without pause. "Him or you?"

"I did," Buggs said. "Naturally I put it to Moloch first to see if he'd object. He knows you're a specialist and he thinks highly of your qualifications. He thinks you might be just what we need."

"Just what The Doctor ordered," Cannell grinned. "Except that you wrote the prescription."

"C'mon, Floyd," Buggs said.

"The Doctor dumped it in your lap, Paul. *You* need my help. Don't be shy."

"Yeah, I need it," Buggs admitted reluctantly, annoyed by Cannell's mongrel machinations. "I've been riding a desk too long. What do you want from me? A valentine?"

Cannell laughed and proclaimed his camaraderie by punching Buggs' arm, leading Buggs to reflect that he had not been punched in the arm that way since leaving his college fraternity.

"Don't get tight, old buddy," Cannell soothed. "We've seen some action together. We'll mop this up and make some dog meat and I'll be back in Little Havana before the week's out."

Cannell's vocabulary was peculiar to himself and incorporated a sprinkling of his own inventions, in which he took a flagrant pleasure in applying. Miami, from where he operated, was "Little Havana." What was known to everyone else in the company as "Head Office," became "the sponsor." Any enemy assumed the designation of "squash." There was a certain Zen calypso to conversation with Floyd Cannell. People talked eerily about him when he was gone. The effect was carefully contrived.

"Did you get anything useful from the wires?" Buggs asked him.

"Hey, I know every hired gun and rinky-dink bandit working this hemisphere; all present and accounted for," Cannell advised. "Before I left the shop I plugged into Mossad, SIS, SDECE, Bundesnachrichtendienst, the whole bowl. They said they haven't heard any static about your cozy little sandbox here. No plans, no possibles, no suspects, no nothing. The CRO in Tokyo says they're onto some Red Army activity in Venezuela, but they've been monitoring that scene for months and it's got no connection with this area. Whatever you've got here is either a new model, a one-off, or a resurrection of some shitface guerrilla outfit. Lookit, Paul, you fucking well haven't given me much to go on. I thought you had a nice quiet bakery operation over here."

He rested the sole of his riding boot against the seatback, leaving a dark streak on the plastic material.

"We do. We service what we sell," Buggs defended. "What about political assassins?"

"Same thing. We've pinpointed every known squash in that line of work." His face went stony with contempt. "Ah, the SDECE have an empty file on some killer squash they're not even sure exists. The fucking French, well, you know, you ask them something simple like the difference between sheep shit and cherry stones and they got to make a production. There's always a few killings hard to account for. So, instead of getting their frog crap together, what do they do? Open a goddamn file and start a romance, that's what they do. The worst screw-ups I ever saw. No contest."

"The country's run by the military," Buggs commiserated.

"Wait," Cannell exclaimed, zealously fueling his hatred of what he construed as unworthy of trust. "Wait'll I slip you the bottom line. You know what name they gave this empty file? You ready for another one of their candy-assed names? You'll love this. Them and their fucking names."

Buggs had to grin despite himself. "C'mon, Floyd, the punch line."

"The Fennec. I'm giving it straight, so help me. They call him The Fennec."

Roaring with self-induced delight, Cannell kicked the seatback like a jackhammer.

"What the hell's a fennec?" Buggs wanted to know.

"I looked it up," Cannell said with an air of authority. "It's the smallest fox there is, about the size of a poodle, I guess. They live in the Sahara, hunt at night and crawl under the sand during the day. Camel-jockeys make pets of them so they'll keep snakes away, for shit's sake. Dead heavy name for an assassin they can't even put a country to, eh?"

His throaty laugh soared again.

"SDECE must've had something in the file," Buggs suggested. "It couldn't have been empty."

Cannell's revelry spent itself in a fit of coughing. He removed his glasses and wiped his eyes with a red polka dot handkerchief.

"They had a killing in a chalet south of Paris about a year ago. One of the Black September boys was hiding out and the frogs were looking down their pants like usual. The place was wired to the rafters but some dude waltzed in and opened the asshole in the shower. Then a couple of killings up in Canada. That's a decent place to hang loose if no other country'll take you and you grease a few of the right people. Some of the Viet generals who were balls deep in the heroin thing are up there, and a couple of them have been blown away recently. Same with those Hong Kong cops who were on the take back home—I think the Chinese used to call them the Five Dragons. But there was a lot more than five and most of them ended up in Canada in '70. One of them was murdered back in '76. Now, the sponsor has them down as internal hassles over money, but the French won't go for it. They claim that this squash they call The Fennec was responsible for those and about four other unaccounted killings."

Buggs watched the cavalcade of humanity walking the side of the road on their way from field work, some of the squat rural women wearing wildly colorful rebozos. "Have they got him down as a political assassin?"

"Nope," Cannell said, clapping his hands. "They couldn't even give me motivation or MO. They don't have a description, nationality, known contacts, who hired him, present suspected whereabouts, zip. The only connection I picked up on was that two of the Canadian jobs were done with a .41 magnum."

Buggs' interest escalated sharply. "Ray Crosetti and the narc were both shot with that caliber gun."

"I know, you told me," Cannell said patiently. "Paul, you peg this thing as a political assassination attempt on The Doctor and the sponsor will give you your separation order in the next batch of cables. Let me tell you something: Don't let The Doctor's addled professor act fool you. The man's been around a long time and knows all the tricks, knows where all the bodies are buried. If he tells you we're after more than one squash and they have these papers of his, then that's exactly what we're looking for."

Buggs held his hands up, shaking them shaman fashion. "He won't budge, you're right about that. He's convinced they want money for the papers."

"Alright." Cannell leaned earnestly toward Buggs. "I'm gonna let you in on the ground floor. If you want the real reason I figure he wants the locals kept out—"

His surreptitious disclosure was interrupted by a buzzing in the front of the car. The driver lifted a telephone receiver coupled to a radio, passed it back to Buggs.

Buggs listened for a moment, then said, "When?"

Listening again, he waved the driver to the shoulder of the road.

"Give me that again," he said into the receiver. He took a pad and pen from his suit jacket and began writing.

Cannell looked behind to be certain the second car had pulled over in file. A family of peasants was looking blankly in the windows. Cannell proffered them a finger. They scurried away.

Holding the receiver away, Buggs said, "I've got three dead in a cornfield about seventy kilometers from here."

From Cannell's reception he might as well have been listening to a favorable weather report.

"Yours?" he said.

Buggs nodded furiously.

"Let's get on down there," Cannell said. "It's time we gave this some personal attention. These fucking squashes are gonna know what it is to hurt."

Buggs went back to the receiver. "Call him back and tell him we're on our way. Tell him to keep that farmer from wandering away. Shoot the sucker's feet off if he has to."

Then, he concluded, "Patch me through to Moloch."

•V•

THE HAND-TOOLED BIBLES ARE SELLING NICELY, THANK YOU

"He was not wearing a shirt and was covered with wounds. On his whole body there was not one inch of skin without injury. He was sweating profusely and saying 'water, water.' "

This was the description of Marco Sandro, an Argentine citizen, as he lay motionless on a mattress in a Buenos Aires detention center. The description was given by his wife, Etelvina.**

Marco Sandro was a pediatrician who provided his services to children of the poor, trade unionists, political prisoners and their families, as well as his usual patients. These activities were responsible for his abduction and imprisonment.

Sandro and his wife were removed by force from their home in Buenos Aires by four armed men on 25 November, 1976, and driven in separate cars to the detention center about twenty minutes away. A three-year-old son was taken by relatives to his grandmother's house in the country. Etelvina was placed in handcuffs, with chains and padlocks on her feet. She was hooded and given the number 103. While she was being questioned about her husband's activities he was being tortured in the next room. She heard him screaming "Murderers!" and heard the continuing sound of great rushes of water. Loud music was played without respite.

Etelvina listened as her husband was tortured several times that first day, as well as others. When in the same room, she twice became aware of her husband having difficulty breathing. The music would cease and a doctor would be called: "I could hear someone running and then the doctor saying that my husband couldn't take any more if they wanted him alive."

She heard the water and the cries of torment every time someone was brought into the room. Someone in a

*Fictitious names have been substituted to prevent possible reprisals against the individuals, their families, and acquaintances.

position of authority came in on one occasion and requested a progress report. When informed that two men and one woman had died he told them to take more care because "That was a lot for one day."

About 50 prisoners were kept there, as near as she could tell, among them a lawyer and a schoolteacher, a veterinary surgeon and his brother. In December about 40 of the prisoners were removed. A guard said they would be "food for fish."

Etelvina was released without explanation on Christmas Eve of 1976 and warned not to communicate with her in-laws and to stay away from Buenos Aires. She found her way to Europe.

Her husband's fate is unknown and writs of habeas corpus *have been ignored.*

•24•

At the train station in San Jose, Holland inquired after the schedule and then used the telephone in an attempt to reach Max. After an interminable wait while the primitive relays lumbered into service, he waited through an extended series of unanswered rings, then returned to the truck.

On the way to the Native Market, Rhiana said, "I want to know what you think."

"I think you know Max a whole lot better than I do," he said. "Would he have had enough sense to leave?"

"Enough sense, yes, but maybe too much pride to run. This country's his home. Everything he lives for is here."

In the marketplace an Indian medicine man was burning copal incense in a pot swung on a rope. As he walked past the native merchants the smoke mingled with the free scent of salt from the sea. Holland left Rhiana in the truck while he bought a bottle of water and another of strained fruit juice, some hot *tortillas* and bread, and a sack of fresh fruit and vegetables.

One of the women squatting behind the produce baskets wore an English bowler hat with a stars and stripes band and a long, graceful quetzal plume rising from the crown. She was old and bent and smiled with startling white teeth that were as perfectly formed as any Holland had seen.

They drove east on a paved road toward the village of Iztapa, but turned inland just before the smaller pocket of Likin, finding a bush trail that snaked through heavy jungle and appeared to follow an arm of the sprawling Chiquimulilla lagoon.

"You have any idea where the main canal goes?" he asked Rhiana.

"I think it leads all the way to the border with El Salvador," she said. "They rent boats at Iztapa."

On a high bluff he eased the truck from the trail and coasted through the dense cover until they emerged on the edge of the lagoon. The ocean lay below, close enough to see and smell. The solitude of the place was what he sought.

He walked back and hid their tracks as far as the trail, laying dead branches to deceive anyone's tracking, then scouted the immediate area in a rapid intersect pattern.

Rhiana was sitting on the end of the truck bed, picking reluctantly at the food. She put the shotgun down when he came out of the shadows. He sat beside her and took one of the still warm *tortillas*.

The sun touched the curvature of the sea, then sank from sight, sea reaching for sky, sky reaching for sea, never-ending facets of gold-colored mercury hung in time in the house of the sun.

Rhiana watched him stare at the sunset.

"You have a look as though you'd drink all of it," she said. "That's why you were hurrying."

She thought he was too engrossed to have heard her. "You do live by the ocean, don't you?"

"Would I lie to you?" he said finally.

"This one?"

"The other. How far away is it?"

"The Atlantic? From here, I suppose four hundred kilometers, more or less."

"We could make a raft and sail off the edge," he said. "If we were flat-earthers, and if we had courage."

"What would we be looking for?"

"Whatever's there. Somewhere there has to be intelligent life."

He offered her the jar of fruit juice. They sat and watched in silence. The shadows grew longer and deeper dark as the sun went away. The ocean slowly softened from blood to blue to black, the lagoon from green to vine-filled tar.

He got up, taking the cassette player from his knapsack and setting it on top of the truck cab. He tripped the switch, the tape producing Glenn Miller. He turned it low. He looked at the jungle.

Rhiana stared at him. "Someone could hear."

"Only the crocs," he said, sitting again. "They won't mind."

Behind them a wall of mountains rose, the spine of two continents, below them a desert of restless, teeming ocean. Theirs was a vertebra where Mayans had erected temples a thousand years before Columbus. The air was fair and tropically warm. Holland liked it here.

"Why did you need to see the ocean," she asked him. "Do you think we're going to die?"

For an instant he seemed annoyed. "Should I assume you feel a need to talk?"

She pulled her knees up and put her forehead on them. "I can't do this. I'll break. I know it."

He said, "Alright."

She turned her head in the cradle made by her knees. "This isn't . . . it's a war . . . I can't accept that it's happening even when I see it and smell it and taste it . . . I can't trust my senses any more . . ."

He said, "Alright."

". . . today, in the field, in the car, I thought I'd lose my mind . . . if the car had stopped before you came I would have gone crazy . . . I couldn't think . . ."

He said, "Is that as good as you get?"

She looked at him and he saw panic.

"Please. I can't."

"You came back," he reminded her once again.

She put her head back on her knees. She was crying.

He stood and, taking her under the arms, lifted her to her feet, then took her wrists so she had to face him.

"What are you doing?" she said. She would not look at him.

"Dance with me," he said. "Can you do that?"

Now she looked at him with disbelief, her face wet, dirty. Her hair was matted in front.

There were secret shifts in the brush, in the water. Creatures. He was ready for a sudden change. But it never came.

She let him bring her slowly to him.

They danced to *Moonlight Serenade,* then to *Take the "A" Train.*

Holland didn't give a damn that the brass might carry in the jungle. Let them come.

At first Rhiana's tension trembled against him, then gradually the brittleness ebbed and she became an ethereal warmth that moved with him. She had stopped crying.

"We're not doing this," she said, sounding convinced.

"Oh, I don't know," he speculated. "Dancing on the back of a pig truck mired in the jungle takes a certain style, I'd say. It becomes you."

They went from dancing to holding each other. Neither knew precisely when that happened. She clung to him tightly.

"Some of the natives come along, they'll have cause to suspect we're a mite fey," he said softly.

"What did he sound like?" she said.

"You mean Moloch?"

She nodded against his chest.

"Classically Machiavellian," he said. "A zealot in the best traditions of old-time religion, or new, for that matter. If you expected the stereotyped Nazi schweinhund, you'd be terribly disillusioned. There's always less to them than meets the eye. Nothing happens in isolation, least of all the Molochs."

The way she moved her head implied acceptance.

After a while, she asked, "Does he really scare you as much as you said?"

"Sure he does. Until he's dead he's as dangerous as anything that lives. But when his time comes he'll shuffle off as quietly as the rest of us. I hold to the theory that at some time everyone confronts the truth of what they are. It could be when we die, which would account for not leaving any change."

They grew silent. She did not slacken her grip on him. He stroked her hair.

"You're remarkable; a revelation," he said. "I don't know how to deal with you."

"Neither do I," she said.

"In a different place and time you'd have to run into the ocean to get away."

"From you?"

"I'm the one," he said.

"The fated sex of the syndrome," she said, looking at him. "You want to make love to me."

He smiled. "Why would I want to do that?"

She said, "I can't smile like that. I want to make love with you, but I won't. Not now. Maybe a long time from now, if that's possible. Maybe never."

"No, you're right. Not now. That's what I was thinking."

"And if all I feel when I'm with you is a gun?"

"Is that meant to be profoundly symbolic?"

"No, I feel the gun under your jacket. It's difficult to separate from you. I've tried. Sometimes I can."

"It's what I do. It's what I'll always do, until they stop me."

She said, "Yes."

"You'd spoil all other women for me. You'd alter my days."

She looked away.

He kissed her hair then went to sit on the end of the truck.

He searched his pockets. "I must have lost my pipe."

"You probably left it in the house," she said, standing beside him.

He found his second pipe in the knapsack.

She looked at the forbidding pool of swampy water. "It's not very inviting, but I have to wash. I can't stay dirty like this."

"I'd rather you did," he said. "You're supposed to be a man. The dirtier the better."

"I won't wash my face, but I have to get clean."

"Not here, then. There's a pair of alligators across the way."

She stiffened. "I didn't see them."

"Momma and poppa. They saw us."

"What else did you see?" she said, apprehensively scanning the carpet of ferns.

"There's a stream that empties further down. You can use it. They don't take to moving water."

She gathered the food while he wiped the truck clean, then followed his lead through the pitch dark undergrowth. They cut along the grade and came out where the stream formed a basin in the bank of the lagoon.

Holland stepped on an aluminum film container as he scouted the periphery, and rolled over a pickle jar that, from the smell, had recently held a homemade brew. Nearby was a discarded sock and a man's undershirt.

Rhiana stripped her clothing and waded to her thighs while he stood watch. Soaping herself thoroughly, she would then dip under the water to rinse. Holland watched as the stream's current carried suds out into the lagoon's placid pools. If there was a moon it was sealed behind the mountains. Her movements in the water were enchanting to watch.

When she came out she sat on the grass and washed the bottom mud from her feet with water from the pickle jar. She waited where she was for the warm night air to dry her.

"Have you ever been in the Danieli Hotel in Venice?" he asked her, standing in trees.

"No, why?"

"It doesn't matter."

He passed her clothing a piece at a time.

She took the end of her bindings from his hands and turned so that he could help her put them on. Angry red welts still crisscrossed her breasts and lined her back where the bindings had been.

"You won't need that until morning," he told her.

She stood watch while he washed. For the first time she saw the wealth of scars on him.

Making a broom of ferns, he beat out their footprints until the mud obscured them. The staccato passage of an outboard motor drifted up from the main lagoon. An owl made its presence heard higher on the bluff, pleasing Holland. He was satisfied, as much as he ever was, that all was well with creatures he could identify.

By keeping to the lush tropical concealment and away from the scattered fields of sugar cane, they backtracked until he estimated they were a mile or so from where the railway crossed the road used earlier. Along the way he reminded Rhiana to step wide over fallen logs, to prevent coming down on snakes in one of their favorite cellars.

"Snakes can't hear," he whispered. "They smell, feel for vibrations in the air and in the ground."

Once, he stopped to let something cross ahead of them, something she was unable to detect regardless of how she strained into the darkness. It occurred to her that the lowlands might closely resemble Vietnam.

In time he selected a suitable rock outcropping with a mat of dried moss and an unobstructed view of approaches from the road and the settlement beyond. Around it he placed a wide circle of dead twigs.

Placing the revolver and the shotgun within easy reach, and making sure Rhiana had the automatic, he sat back against the rock shelf. He made himself comfortable for the night, knowing he would not move more than a few inches until morning.

Rhiana put on his spare shirt plus her own under her jacket. She lay on the moss at his feet, utilizing one of the knapsacks for a pillow.

"Wake me when you have to sleep. I'll watch."

"Okay," he said, having no intention of doing either.

"How long are we going to do this . . . hit and run?" she asked him.

"Not long. I figure we're getting close."

"How do you mean?"

"Every time we take down one of Moloch's gunsels, that's one less between him and us and one more to convince him we're after the money, not him. Soon he'll have to come out to see for himself. He's been waiting for a fast ball and we've been throwing him garbage. Tomorrow is probably a good day for a change-up, but I want to think about it."

"You don't want me to know."

"No, I don't want you to know."

"We passed a military base earlier. It's not more than five miles from here."

"I know."

"Surely he could have brought in the police or the army. They'd scour the country and find us in a few hours."

"He won't," Holland said with certainty. "Anybody seeing the papers we've got would have a damn healthy curiosity about what they are, blank or no. Men like Moloch can't afford to trust a soul. I was amazed he even trusted his sister as much as he did. No, he's been taking a chance sending his gunsels out, and he knows it. By now we must've removed most of those who were close enough for him to gamble on. That's why I took down his gunsels first. He'll have to move soon."

"When you phone him?"

"I want it so one call will open the palace gates."

"But in his own mind he still wouldn't let us get away."

"No, in his mind he couldn't allow that."

She became silent.

Holland chewed some coca leaf to stem his fatigue and insulate the chill he knew would come off the ocean in the early hours. The familiar spot in his upper arm began to throb.

A half hour passed. He could see Rhiana's eyes catch glints of light when she studied him. Dew was already beginning to pearl on the leaves.

"Come and sleep here," he said to her. "It'll get damp in the morning."

She came beside him, curling under his arm, her face in the crevice between his face and shoulder.

"A female at rest produces little more than half the heat calories a male at rest does," he said. "Statistics are one of the greatest causes of hypochondria and mental anguish."

"Be quiet," she said. "Or do you feel a need to talk?"

He bent to kiss her mouth gently, an epoch of fidelity that might have been conceived in her desperation.

"You're a ghost," she said softly, burrowing closer to him. But she grasped a fistful of his jacket and held on.

She slept that way until first light.

•25•

Battery-powered lanterns winked in the shambles that had been a corn field, ranging wide and lapping tongues of light over every inch of ground and every stain that told of what had happened there. Other than the coterie of fitful beams, the field and the countryside was sealed in the vault of night.

Three cars were parked in front of the shack. From inside the dwelling there suddenly rose a high-pitched squalling, followed by the hurried clump of shoes in flight.

Paul Buggs lurched into the open and, in his haste to slam the door behind, dropped his lantern to the stoop, shattering the glass.

"Son of a bitch!" he said between short bursts of breath.

A man ran around from the rear of the shack, his lantern bobbing erratically.

"What happened?" he said urgently.

Buggs was incensed. "There's nothing but pigs in there. Great big motherfuckers. They bite like a bastard, you know that?"

"They get you?" was all the man could think to say.

Buggs called him an asshole.

A gruff voice carried from where the Plymouth was. *"Something wrong over there?"*

Several of the lanterns shone toward the shack.

"It's okay," Buggs shouted back. "Goddamn son of a bitch."

He snatched the lantern away and directed the beam in the man's face. The man tried to squint beyond the light.

"What the hell's wrong with you?" Buggs accused. "There's no fucking farmer here. I told you to keep him nailed down."

"What was I supposed to do? Pile him and his old lady and all his kids in the car while I went looking for a phone? I warned him to stick around. I told him it was official business. I showed him the fake tin."

"Lot of good it did. You could've put one of his kids in the trunk. That would've kept him here."

Buggs kicked at broken glass in the illumination thrown by the headlights.

"He said there were two of them? That's all?" He waved an arm toward the field. "For this?"

"Two were all he saw," the man said. "They swiped his truck and wanted to know the way to San Jose. Hey, that used to be a song. He said they were Latins. He was positive about that."

Buggs looked at him contemptuously. "You'd better not eat that, it's bullshit. You fucking college preps."

The gruff voice sounded again in the dark hollow. *"Buggs. C'mon over here."*

Paul Buggs strode across the field, snaring his shoes repeatedly on the broken stubble. Men were talking in various sectors of the plot, using their lights like worm pickers on a golfing green. Floyd Cannell stood beside the Plymouth, a lantern placed on the fender enabling him to examine something in his hands.

Three bodies were lined up in the dirt next to the car, the skin alabaster where it showed, or was pulpy red meal.

Cannell looked up as Buggs approached.

"Farmer gone by-by, right?"

"Yeah, the fucking little creep vacated," Buggs admitted. He'll get his when I find time to look him up."

"Your asset didn't do good."

"Tell me about it," Buggs said irritably.

"This country's a fucking pest-hole, you know it?" Cannell observed.

Buggs lit a cigarette with the lighter that had belonged to Holland.

Cannell, noting its unique function, said, "What you got there?"

"For a pipe," he said, demonstrating. "I found it in the sister's apartment, where Crosetti was killed. So far I can't tie it to anything solid."

Cannell handed him a straight-stemmed pipe that still had some damp soil encrusted on the scalloped bowl.

"Tie it to this, maybe?"

"Hey," Buggs said. "Where'd you get this?"

Cannell gave a vague nod toward the open field.

"The sister's dirty," Buggs declared. "I fucking well knew it." He beamed.

"Leave the internal screws to Moloch," Cannell advised. "Who she's coupled to is what we've got to handle, and fast."

"I know it," Buggs said. He looked down at the bodies, then scanned the field disconsolately. "Looks to me like they had a goddamn wreck-em race."

Cannell indicated where lanterns played over the Chevrolet at the far end of the field. "Your asset confirm that was the car they started chasing?"

"Confirmed. There were two guys in it and that's what the farmer said were here. He shit my op about them being

Latins. Believe what a greasebag tells you and you might just as well believe they were Martians on skateboards."

"Maybe so, but they did take his truck. The grass is all yellow where the tires were sitting. The car's a renter, but the sticker in the window doesn't match the plate. We won't get anything from it either."

"Okay," Buggs said. "They asked about San Jose. Let's go."

"Hold on," Cannell said, catching his arm. "Where's that?"

Buggs pointed south. "It's a port on the coast, one of those sleepy little *mañana* places."

"Forget it," Cannell decided punctually. "They didn't go there."

He opened his pants and commenced to urinate against the side of the Plymouth. Urine cascaded to the ground, forming rivulets that meandered under the bank of bodies. Neither man appeared to notice.

"Look, Floyd," Buggs said. "I know you're a specialist in this craft, but even I know they could've said San Jose so we'd think it was too obvious, then go there anyway."

Cannell finished urinating.

"You're right, this is my craft and your logic isn't bad. As far as it goes. What you're not allowing for is the evidence they keep hittin' you with. These guys know how to touch the tiger, you know? They're not thrill killings you got here, not with heart shots every one. Goddamn. We're looking at excellent form. These guys aren't stunting, Paul. And there ain't no way they're gonna put their backs to the ocean. Never happen."

Buggs frowned. "Let's not start to worship, huh?"

"No such," Cannell allowed. "But if they said San Jose, they're just messin' with our heads."

"Then we'll have to look up-country," Buggs reasoned, prepared to accept Cannell's expertise. "They can't move around without being seen. Not in a big old truck."

"Were there any spent shells in that apartment or on the road where the other killings went down?" Cannell asked him.

"None. Any here?"

"Only this." He tossed something through the air at Buggs.

The object bounded from Buggs' chest and fell to the ground. Buggs retrieved it, examining without recognition. He held an empty speedloader.

Cannell explained how it worked, finishing by nudging one of the bodies and saying, "Two of your playmates were opened up like flower pots. The speedloader holds six rounds. That could be your .41 magnum."

"Except for the driver," Buggs disputed. "He's got a hole could've been made by a drill."

Jerking a thumb toward the gaping hood of the Plymouth, Cannell assumed a gloating smirk of satisfaction. "Teflon-coat bullets. Killed the motor too. Ain't no use wearing vests if they've got those."

Buggs shook his head. "I must've been out in the sun too long. Where we at?"

Cannell took the speedloader from Buggs' hand, holding it up for display.

"There's maybe a half-dozen makes of speedloaders, this one happens to be the fastest of the lot. Only thing is, it doesn't lend itself to rough use, so it's limited almost exclusively to competition matches. Guy's gotta know what he's doin' using these in the field. Next, a .41 magnum has as much muzzle velocity as a .357 mag but almost a third more energy after a hundred yards. Compare it to a .44 mag and the .41 will match it for muzzle velocity and energy, and still shoot a whole lot flatter and not kick you half as much, particularly when it's hotted up. Put the .41 in a good piece with a decent barrel and it'll be damn near as accurate as an open-sight rifle, besides knock down redwoods for fun."

Buggs was getting impatient with the pedantry. "Say it. One of them's a gun mechanic. Maybe both."

"Par excellence," Cannell elaborated. "But only one of them. If there's anything I've learned it's that you never get two dudes who're that slick working together. One of them always has too much vanity. You've got a marksman who can do a number on six of your assets—slittin' the throat of one—and keep coming back for more. That takes experience, my friend."

Buggs flipped his cigarette away, the glow a darting firefly in the darkness.

"Experience such as a political assassin would have," he said tentatively.

Cannell threw his hands in mock acceptance. "You've convinced me. They want The Doctor."

Buggs presented him a sour countenance. "Okay. How do we handle it?"

"We'll send two of your assets down to that San Jose place, just to make you feel better. The rest of 'em, my assets included, we'll spread out to beat the bushes and the towns around here. Like you said, somebody's had to see them. Once we get a fix on their location, we'll go in and snuff them ourselves. No mistake."

Buggs started for the parked car, Cannell following.

"I've gotta get a phone and fill in Moloch," he said.

Cannell caught him while they were still far enough away to prevent the others hearing.

"Tell him about the pipe only," Cannell specified. "Nothing about our conclusions here."

"The hell," Buggs protested. "I look stupid to you? The smartest thing is to get him out of the country on a black flight, right now."

"No," Cannell declared firmly. "I'm gonna finish what I started to tell you in the city. You listening?"

Buggs managed to look both expectant and agitated. "What's going on, for Christ's sake?"

Cannell lowered himself into a crouch and pulled Buggs with him. He scraped a yellow slug from the toe of his riding boot. A trail of slime was left where it had lain.

"There's been a rumor hangin' for years about The Doctor writing everything down. I'll bet my whole bag that those're the papers were lifted."

Buggs' face blanched in the residue from the headlights. "Head Office tell you that?" he said.

"Didn't have to," Cannell countered. "The outfits he's worked for . . . the stuff he's done . . . the names . . . the operations he knows about; that man lives between the biggest rock and the hardest place. If it was me, I'd sure write it down and put the word out about what'd happen if the shit hit the fan. Why'd you figure he's got his ass in such a knot over some empty papers? Why'd you figure he wouldn't use the locals? Why didn't he just take off and leave the driving to you? Ask yourself."

Buggs took a clump of hard soil and threw it to the ground.

"Waterston should have told me. He should have known."

"Waterston doesn't know shit," Cannell said vehemently. "They wouldn't trust him with a copy of the Constitution. I tell you one thing, old buddy, if we don't get to those papers first, both our bags are gonna be in the wringer."

"Yeah, I can see that," Buggs said, taking out another cigarette. "But we're ahead of these guys now."

Cannell put his arm around Buggs' shoulder, smiled close into his face.

"You imagine we'll smell like a rose if we produce those papers for the sponsor?" he proposed softly.

The unlighted cigarette hung slack from Buggs' mouth. He said, "Holy shit."

Cannell looked fiercely at the black wall of corn. "Laugh, clowns, laugh while you can, cause I'm gonna have you."

•26•

In the early hours of the morning, before the sun was up and the moon down, Clement Moloch sat in a room deep in the bowels of his house, fingering a coil of ordinary household extension wire, absently caressing the slippery rubber coating between his short fingers, staring fixedly at a point only imagined in the mind.

Dank and cold as a cave, with slab concrete floor and bare block walls, the room had been empty since the time of the estate's assembly. Others like it took up this section of the cellar, all intended for storage except for this one last corner, which had simply not been needed. Until now.

The air was clammy and dead like that in a tomb, mirroring Moloch's mood. His face serene, he was contemplating evil.

All that occupied the space within the close confines was the steel chair on which he sat, a naked lightbulb dangling above his unruly white hair, and a single electrical outlet tacked to a piece of lathing on the wall.

That he was alone did not prevent him from talking aloud.

He said, "Nearer the moth to the flame . . ."

He spread his hand and held it against the light in such a way that it cast a giant shadow against the opposite wall. That pleased him. His expression grew even more euphoric.

She had visited him with treachery.

He felt old, tired, vulnerable—the last a new sensation to him. He should have known. This clever demon—the voice on the phone—was killing those around him, rendering him as impotent as a yearling.

He struggled to revive the words of a verse from home . . . a Welsh idyll . . . a warrior's chant. The lilt came but the words eluded him

When he had first gone to school in England—*How he had hated it there*—there had been an endless procession of Sunday afternoons when he had walked to the crossroads to wait for his father to visit him, waiting for hours while the afternoon waned and the carloads of proper English parents—even nannys—passed by on their way to the school, staring blankly at him from behind glass. Like a castaway, he waited until dark, until after he had missed the evening meal, a foolish child on a bench, going there in the first place because he could not bear to have his mates know his father had not come, and staying there for the same dreaded reason.

Then he had been good at waiting; now he was not. On the few occasions his father had appeared, Clement would ask that he recite the warrior's chant. Oh, how he loved its cadence.

"*. . . splendid in battle . . .*" he said pensively.

No, that wasn't it.

Suddenly the metal of the chair disturbed him. He eased slowly to his feet, then turned to regard it. The chair was a common type, spare office furniture suitable for the communications room, made of thin square tubing, four legs and two arms, the arms covered in rounded flutes of metal.

A realization struck him as he stood. Going to one knee, he unscrewed the rubber bumpers from under each of the chair's legs.

Standing again, he tilted his head speculatively and said, "*. . . I am a flash against a host, my attack . . .*"

No, that wasn't it either.

What manner of warrior was flashing against him, he wondered. Who had she betrayed him to? The trouble with warriors was that there was always one more gifted, more deadly, more favored. Was he still the one?

He gathered the short length of wire and severed the female plug from one end with a specialty tool from his pocket, a pliers with a selection of apertures and edges within its extended jaws. Then he pulled the siamesed wires apart for about a foot along from the cut ends, and again using the pliers, stripped the insulation away from each. The bared lengths he twisted into a single long braid, stretching the cord out in a trial to be certain it reached comfortably from the outlet to the chair.

It was maddening to be without proper implements, having to improvise like a dock worker. But, of course, this was his home and he did not do this sort of thing here.

Slumping, exhausted by his meager labors, he reached furtively for the light, plunging the room into abject darkness, feeling for a corner and sitting there on the ruthless concrete. He closed his knees and wrapped his arms around them, lowering his head, his back in the cleavage of cement blocks.

The menacing stillness of the sanctum was soothing, removed from ruin and lifted of load. If only he could remember the chant.

His breathing came easier in the dark.

Why didn't the voice phone with the terms as he had promised? The money was ready. In fact, the voice already had a tenth of the agreed sum. Or so Buggs alleged. Perhaps Buggs had filched it himself. Or Cannell. Cannell was as wicked as any made, but an excellent headhunter nonetheless.

Moloch had tried to contact Mengele earlier, to talk as confidants, to commune as partisans; though nothing would be mentioned of this calamity. The lines had failed. How outrageous for the man to be confined to a country where even the telephones were unfit.

There were intervals when Mengele was truly isolated,

and, until now, he had never understood how it was Mengele endured. Now he himself knew what it was to be isolated. Now he was himself alone. How long had it been? How many days? He thought: I'm having trouble assimilating, probably because of weariness. What rest he had snatched had merely been dozing in a chair, waiting for instructions to come. This . . . voice . . . was deliberately eroding his reserves, deadening his senses, taking his sweet time. He knew it, and was powerless.

He slammed his hand on the concrete. Waiting while being manipulated! Emasculated by the cursed papers! Surgically slit from his spheres of influence by shadow cabals he could not so much as flush into light!

Claire wanted . . . he didn't know what.

When he got the others he would incinerate them on a slow spit of what he *did* know.

There should be an altar in this chamber of containment where he imposed discipline and ruled with order.

He pictured graffiti on the walls. That excited him for a moment. Graffiti had an incandescent life to it that he would not tolerate, could not tolerate; it led to anarchy. Did it not birth disorder? Decadence? Look at New York.

Once, he had used the washroom in a church and there had been graffiti everywhere, rude bleatings of unwashed squatters.

The garde-manger was cool and impregnable. He would stay here if he could.

Had he locked the door? No, of course not, he reasoned.

He imagined grotesquely bloated things crawling on the floor in a wet, sticky paste. The things knew to avoid him, keeping their distance from the avenger, the fixer.

Later he would take an axe to them, then turn the blade and powder the graffiti from the walls. He was a Collector of Justice.

The ceiling was a blanket of stars, though he was not looking there. His mind was playing tricks, but that was just exercise and did not distress him.

Something—not a person—screamed *Human Wrongs!*

What had possessed her to turn on him when he had given her everything?

The noise from the things crawling in the paste on the

floor was deafening. He held his head, feeling the skin moving like a loose coat.

The crawling things were mouthing graffiti. Where was the axe? Was that its whisper on the air?

Light violated his space when the door opened.

Claire was thrust into the room, her arms held from behind by the Thai. Her nightgown was a rich forest green.

Moloch sighed, then got slowly to his feet.

He went to the light and switched it on, standing directly beneath its halo as he confronted his sister.

"Women make the best terrorists, Claire, did you know?" he asked quietly, looping the electrical cord, the bared ends scraping across the concrete.

Her face was a garish wreath of horror. Her eyes seized on the wire.

The Thai had a collection of leather belts thrown over his shoulder, his jaw rolling with gum.

"It's true," Moloch continued. "There have been studies on the subject. One of the few sectors where women have achieved equality."

A cord in her throat trembled as he approached.

"You'll be first, Claire. Please, it would be easier for both of us if you were to disrobe yourself. . . ."

• 27 •

Holland and Rhiana were on the move well before sunrise, striking out for the train station at San Jose. A bank of fog had surged in from the ocean during the night, cutting visibility to a dozen yards in sheltered pockets near the woods and around the sugar cane, shrouding livestock in closets of mist where they grazed.

Nearly a quarter-mile of walking was required before the ache left Holland's right side, the side not favored by Rhiana's warmth. He chewed some leaf to aid the rehabilitation. The dew quickly wet through their sneakers and crept up the bottoms of their trousers.

When they reached the cinder bed of the railway they

saw Indians walking the crossties with baskets of produce and wares, going south to the market in San Jose or waiting for the train into the city.

Figures materialized from the fog and passed by, fading into the curtain like apparitions in a dream; men carrying staggering loads on their backs, supported by straps reaching across broad foreheads, some with as much as two hundred pounds of clay pottery on wood frames resembling antlers; women balancing baskets on their heads, dressed in vividly striped skirts and magenta shawls and bright turquoise hair ribbons, blazes of color in a grey swarm. Some of the men wore skirts as well.

A day of commerce ahead, they paid scant attention to Holland and Rhiana.

Holland found a tattered burlap bag between ties. He used it to wrap the shotgun.

"Don't look anyone in the eye," he coached Rhiana. "Look past them with as little interest as you can."

"They have to be searching for us," she said, peering along the steel pincers.

"More likely down at the pier or along the road, probably watching for the truck. If it happens, follow my lead and stick close, unless they point a gun. If they do, move and start shooting. Can you do that?"

She said, "I don't know."

"Sure you can. You'd be surprised."

"You might be too," she said wryly.

The way he looked at her now was different than it had ever been. She no longer saw reason to be frightened of him.

"Today seems a good day," he said. "Let's go for it."

Something in her constricted.

"Are you asking me? You can't ask me, Holland."

He waited while an Indian with firewood passed, then he asked her what time it was.

She took the Cartier watch from her pocket and showed it to him. The delicate wafer of gold metal seemed absurdly alien in the surroundings.

Further along the tracks they came up on a woman carrying a fish net stuffed with floppy straw hats. Holland bought one for himself and one for Rhiana and asked the woman where she was going. She told him the Native Market in San Jose. When the woman was gone he drubbed the hats on the cinders until they were frayed and soiled. Rhiana, following his example, scrubbed her hands with moist dirt from the track-side runoff and packed black grime under her fingernails.

At the train station the Indians had just begun to congregate, squatting near the platform, forty-five minutes or so before the train would come up from the pier for its arduous climb over the mountains to the city. An enterprising vendor had already fired his stove and was hawking an array of early morning fare from flat clay pans.

Armed with hot biscuits and coffee, Rhiana trailed Holland to the telephone and stood by while he again tried unsuccessfully to raise Max. Due to the hour the phones were working with surprising dispatch.

He brushed away horseflies and placed his second call as planned.

Upon hearing George Hidalgo's voice, he used the reference designated as a means of identification: "Ebbets Field calling."

The relief on the other end was obvious.

"Yes, Mr. Field," George said. "How is it?"

"Not wrapped yet, but the hand-tooled Bibles are selling nicely, thank you." He looked at Rhiana. "The refugee's with me."

"We didn't know," George said. "That's good. That's good to know."

"I can't say the same about our associate. You know anything about that?"

In a tone designed to assure, George said, "He's here. In fact, we've been talking most of the night. The others are here too. He had business to conduct and decided to come before there were restrictions on travel. I understand those restrictions have now been put in place."

Holland covered the receiver, said to Rhiana, "Max got out. He's there."

She almost smiled.

George said, "Can I offer assistance?"

"Send out the Bibles," Holland declared, implementing the only other instruction that had been predetermined. "How soon will they fall?"

"Noon, or shortly after," George replied. "You'll hear them."

"Okay," Holland said. "Have a nice day."

He hung up.

The numbers waiting for the train were swelling now, some close enough that Rhiana knew it would not be wise for her to speak. Holland looked over the same assembly, seeing nothing to concern him. If there were gunsels around they were not here yet.

Going ahead of Rhiana, he crossed the tracks and went diagonally away until well cloaked in the fog, then turned north and slowly closed the angle, once more following the tracks.

They assumed a steady gait away from San Jose, and the ocean, Rhiana walking the ties while Holland kept to a rail as though it were a foot wide. He constantly examined the brush and the banks of shale alongside. An unfriendly dog shadowed them long enough to coax a biscuit from Rhiana, snapping it out of the air and loping away, hackles raised.

After a while they noticed that the Indians were not passing them, but were now going in the same direction.

"Must be a place ahead to catch the train," Holland reasoned.

"Where are we going?" Rhiana wanted to know.

"Into the mountains," he said. "I think I know where."

A pale light began to filter through, burning the fog into haze. Then with a rush the sun flared in fingers through the mountain gaps, painting the peaks brown on top and purple below.

Elated by the light, Rhiana said, "I'm glad Max got out. I feel better."

Presently they reached the first steep grade and, just short of the crest, a straggling line of Indians waiting by the side. Holland and Rhiana respected protocol, taking the last positions. Rhiana took oranges from her knapsack. Eating the sections, they looked down on the retreating mist, sometimes seeing evasive glints of ocean.

After ten minutes, Holland could make out the soot-black breath of a diesel locomotive on full choke, struggling up the incline after the all too brief spurt from the pier. The closer it came the more it strained and slowed. At the metallic braying of the horn the Indians hefted their loads and prepared for the boarding.

Boxcars, some sealed but most with doors slid back,

made up the bulk of the short string, a single first-class carriage bringing up the rear.

Trotting alongside, the Indians pushed their diverse goods into the boxcars and then hopped nimbly aboard, quickly clearing the door to make room for the following. The man next to Holland had too many chicken crates to hoist at once, and no one to help him, so Holland did so.

Rhiana caught the handrail and swung herself up as convincingly as the others before her.

A guard with a cowboy hat and a World War I British revolver in his belt stood inside collecting fares from the latecomers. Holland paid for himself and Rhiana. The guard looked him over, and, seeing he was not native, substituted Mexican coin in his change. Holland picked out the queer pieces and handed them back, objecting in polite but firm Spanish that the man had made a mistake. The man pushed his hat back on his head and twirled the lanyard attached to the butt of his revolver, watching while Holland took leaf from his jacket pocket and began chewing. Finally, the guard shrugged indifferently and dropped valid coin in Holland's outstretched hand.

Holland tipped his hat in acknowledgment and went to the ladder at the far end of the car, climbing up and out the square hole in the roof. Rhiana followed.

Regular riders occupied the roofs, favoring the privacy, a privacy that for some reason seemed reserved for males. The roof was ringed by a pipe railing about three inches high, a board running the length of the center providing a place to sit.

Rhiana settled there while Holland stretched out on his back beside, placing his hat under his head. Near them, two young boys were playing checkers on a board employing pegs. One of the boys had long gleaming braids, reminding Holland of Sarah.

"What if they come looking for us up here?" Rhiana said, careful not to be overheard.

"I doubt they've got anybody on this thing," he said, his voice sounding tired. He got to one elbow and spit the leaf over the side. "If anything, they would've cased everyone getting on back at the station and then forgotten about it."

The train topped the grade and now had a reasonably

flat, open run to the mountains, the black diesel smoke laying back. Swarms of bugs, seeking the warming sun, were beginning to wash back over the tops of the cars.

The day would be hot in the lowland, cooler in the highlands.

"They could have notified the guards," Rhiana persisted.

"I didn't see any evidence down below. The guard or conductor or whatever he is will usually make one pass up here. If you see more than one of them coming, let me know. Otherwise, wake me up once we get into the foothills."

Rhiana pulled the wrapped shotgun close and held tightly to the board against the swaying of the car.

He wakened once when the train stopped at Masagua and again when it paused outside of Escuintla, then dozed again each time the couplings clashed and the train lurched forward. The sun seeping through his jeans and the breeze tugging at his jacket were a perfect opiate.

Sometime later Rhiana put her hand to his shoulder. He sat up to observe rolling hills inching by and to find their progress again reverting to a crawl.

Moving next to Rhiana, he inhaled the sharp scent of pine and stretched his arms overhead, feeling more solvent than he had an hour earlier.

Rhiana said, "The guard was alone when he went by."

"I know," he said. "Anyone look at you like a woman?"

She shook her head, a trace of irony in the way she pressed her lips together.

"I guess if the guard didn't tumble to you when you went up the ladder, no one's going to," he decided.

He glanced around at those sharing the roof. The number riding on top had increased with each stop.

"What were you thinking just then?" he asked her. "When you woke me up?"

Her visage was no less alluring when she said, "I was thinking that we're not going to make it. Not even with Holland's Law. I was also thinking about Sarah. Mothers do that. And I was wondering what 'send out the Bibles' signified, and when you'd get around to telling me."

"You have any idea where Corduran is?" he asked her.

The name registered immediately but he was unable to determine the extent she reduced it.

"Near here," she said. "We may have passed . . . no . . . it would still be ahead. To the left somewhere. Corduran can't be seen from here though, and the road comes in from the other direction."

"But a spur line must come out," he said. "They wouldn't bother tearing it up."

Now he could see her beginning to comprehend, to remember.

She said, "No, they wouldn't have torn it up."

"Get your gear together. We'll jump when we come across it."

He shifted to the left side of the car and hung his legs over.

The foothills had given way to knife-edged ridges and plunging canyons clad with conifers. Further ahead were the looming massif pickets of the Sierra Madre range. White slashes still denoted shifts from earthquakes past.

When he spotted the rusted rails sweeping out from the overgrowth he turned to Rhiana and pointed down.

On the platform, he took the shotgun and her knapsack and told her to pick her spot.

"Land on both feet and roll like a doll," he said. "The train's hardly moving anyway."

She nodded, stepping to the foothold at the corner of the car. She jumped and was lost from sight. He threw the knapsacks and shotgun, then bailed out himself, needing only one roll before he sat up akimbo and watched the last car move lethargically away. No one appeared to take any particular notice from the windows; in a region where foot travel could be extended by hours simply by waiting a few extra turns of the train, jumping from the lumbering conveyance was not at all uncommon.

Rhiana was already up and dusting herself off. He retrieved the knapsacks and shotgun while she searched for their hats, then inspected a cinder burn on the heel of her hand. Blue jays announced their arrival in the pines. Other than that, and the fading beat of the locomotive, the woods were quiet.

They followed the rails lower. "Max owns the mine at the end of the spur line," Rhiana said. "You knew that, of course."

"Uh-huh," he acknowledged. He removed the burlap from the shotgun, discarding it on the ties.

The mine she spoke of had been exhausted years before and then boarded up, but when in operation, had been one of Max's greatest prides, and therefore a place George had known about. Another consideration had been that Rhiana possessed a rudimentary knowledge of the mine, having been there at least once that George knew of. The long-established bond between Rhiana's father and Max Ortiz had been, of course, inspired by their mutual vocations, although in Max's case his mining interests had been but a single facet.

"This is the detour we took when we flew in," Rhiana said. "I wondered what George was doing. He's supposed to pick us up at the mine, isn't he?"

"It's the best we could come up with," Holland confirmed. "If something happens to me, if we get separated or I go down, find a phone and call George. Give him the rendezvous time by counting the alphabet down from midnight: 'A' for one A.M., 'B' for two, and like that. It'll be enough. Don't mention the mine. He'll know it's you and he'll come for you."

They reached the decaying spur line and followed it away from the main set of tracks. The spur was notched into the side of the highest elevation since the coast, the sort of subaltern highland promising veins of silver and iron and nickel and gold.

At length a turn afforded a vista through the tops of the pines. Down the thousand feet or so to the valley floor, the whitewashed village of Corduran queued up along narrow ribbon streets fanning out from the village square and belfry of the church.

Across a deep fold in the slope, higher up, was the mine. Faded blue paint still clung to a portion of the tall shafthouse, a cavernous place more closely resembling a prairie grain elevator. It had a lonely, forlorn air about it.

Holland selected two ties that were more thoroughly dried of creosote; they sat and looked into the windless valley. Rhiana peeled the last two oranges.

"Why are we going to the mine now?" she asked him.

"We're not," he said. "We'll go to the village first."

She waited for elaboration that never came.

Instead, he pointed out a scorpion scaling a boulder.

"They're supposed to be extremely shy, and reluctant to sting."

"I don't know," said Rhiana.

The countryside was much to his liking, a green mosaic of forest and meadow, one corner of one tile salted to mark the village. Beneath the trees the surface was bald rock or brown carpet of pine needles.

He removed his hat, dropping it between his feet.

He said, "I really screwed up."

Rhiana turned to look at him. "What do you mean?"

"We're not all that far from the farm. I should've given you a different direction away from the lake yesterday. Last night I was thinking about it."

"There was no way of knowing what was going to happen," she said. "Besides, the farm has to be at least ten kilometers from here."

"South. They'll probably be working their way north, asking everyone in sight. Question is, have they been here yet? If we're lucky, we'll get in and out of the village before they do. If not, you'll have to live with my mistakes. I'm sorry. Jesus, I should've been anticipating better than that."

"Is that as good as you get?" she asked.

He hung his head and laughed.

They listened to the forest for a while. Ravens cruised in the warming updrafts overhead.

Staring plaintively in the direction of the village, Rhiana said without warning, "I have feelings for you that have nothing to do with this. I want you to know. You should."

"It works for me," he said. "You should know."

After another silence he said, "Give me the automatic."

She took the Colt from her knapsack and passed it to him. From his pocket he produced a number of elastic bands which he wrapped around the gun's grip just back of the trigger guard.

He handed the gun to her. "Put it in your waistband, under your shirt. The elastics keep it from slipping."

They picked their way down the steep incline until meeting a footpath leading toward the village. Holland left her there and walked up the path, almost out of sight, before returning.

Water as clear as fine crystal came out of a granite face next to the trail, affording them a drink. Lower, the path crossed soft ground where tree roots, their pelt worn away, formed a natural stairs eventually terminating at a dirt road showing signs of recent use.

"This can't be the road to the mine," he said doubtfully.

"No, we're too far over the ridge," Rhiana confirmed.

He looked up but could no longer see the blue shaft-house. From the position of the sun he judged it to be about eleven o'clock. Coming near.

Near the web between the uplands and the valley floor there was a deep cut in the rock with fast-moving water at the bottom, a drop of forty feet. Across it a bridge of round wood beams continued the road. It was not a structure on which Holland would have taken a vehicle with any enthusiasm.

Standing beside the railing, they watched water slip-stream through the gorge.

"Someone's coming," he said abruptly. "A man and a boy."

Rhiana could make them out through gaps in the trees. When they emerged into the open she knew from their skin and dress that they were Indians. Unmistakably father and son; the boy might have been twelve.

They stopped short at seeing Holland and Rhiana, knowing at first sight that these two were intruders from outside their valley. Then they hurried forward.

Holland reached under his jacket, resting his hand on the revolver.

The pair were strangely dressed even for Indians, in riotously colored blouses and pants, the pants dropping only to the knee, and woven headdresses as multi-hued as a peacock. The boy carried an empty chicken cage that spilled feathers as he ran.

"There must be a festival," Rhiana whispered. "The colors identify their village. They've been on the mountain sacrificing a chicken."

"Just so they don't sacrifice us," Holland said.

As they jogged up, the father pointed to the road and said with some urgency in forced English, "Two men are coming, *señores*. Looking for you. We could see them from above."

"Who are you?" Holland returned uneasily.

"Hurry," the father said. "They have guns. DeJesus said to help you."

He reached for Rhiana's arm. She deflected his hand with the barrel of the shotgun, prompting the boy to step back.

"DeJesus?" Holland said.

"It was his farm where you had your trouble," the father explained, glancing nervously toward the bend in the road. "We will wait until they're gone and then tell you. Do not worry."

Holland looked around for refuge. The trees were at least thirty paces away and did not hug the ground close enough for adequate cover. The sides of the gorge were too steep.

"Under the bridge," the boy said.

Holland went to his knees to see. The boy was right: A busy network of beams made a substructure as tall as a man. Taking the shotgun and locking his grip on Rhiana's wrist, he swung her beneath the railing and over the side, then went after her.

There were sufficient supports to run their hands along for balance, although the footing was on round poles made slippery by age and pocks of moss. Holland took out the revolver and fastened his attention to the underside of the bridge. Rhiana stared starkly into the depth of thundering rock and water.

Barely three minutes elapsed before voices carried from above, near the railing. An American who sounded young asked the Indians if they had seen anyone they didn't know. The father said he had not. The Americans said that if they did they were to come and tell them. He mentioned the name of a village other than Corduran and promised money. The father pledged cooperation in convincing rote.

Silence settled once the boots left the bridge.

While waiting, Holland put his hand to Rhiana's face and caressed it with the gentle diligence of a blind man. The gesture was pure impulse and she looked at him with a blend of requital and fascination, a child receiving gifts, a woman dispensing them. She ducked her head to catch his hand at her neck when he was about to withdraw.

A wren swooped in, saw them, skidded in the open air, then fluttered away with its composure in tatters.

From above, the father said, "Okay, *señores*."

Holland left her with them and went silently through the trees until he was able to spot the two Americans higher on the road. They were in their mid-twenties, clad in safari suits that probably came from an L. L. Bean catalogue. One had a shotgun, the other carried a lever-action deer rifle.

Back at the bridge the elder's face showed traces of impatience as he looked from Rhiana to Holland.

"He can't speak," Holland said, indicating Rhiana and making a motion with his fingers in front of his mouth.

The father bowed in deference to Rhiana's imagined impairment, "Forgive me, *señor.*"

Holland asked him how he knew who they were. The father said DeJesus had told some of the native people to watch for them, to help if they could, even hide them. He had known Holland by the cut on his face and the baseball jacket; the smaller one because he carried a shotgun with a pig barrel. He labeled the Americans *perverso,* assuring him that the natives would tell them nothing. His name was Leonel Valasquez, his son Louis.

"You killed three of them?" the boy asked Holland, his eyes struck favorably with the sensation of events close at hand.

His father cuffed him lightly on the back of the head.

Holland pointed gravely at Rhiana, who just looked surprised.

As though to anticipate Holland, the father offered, "Those are the only ones we see. They are going to the next valley."

"We're grateful to you," Holland said. "Where are you going, *Señor* Valasquez?"

"To our village. I have a cafe where you can eat. It is safe because everyone is busy with the saint's festival. I know DeJesus well; you and your friend are welcome in my cafe."

"Do you have a phone there?" Holland asked him.

"Yes, come." He started across the bridge.

Holland called him back in a low voice, explaining, "If you saw them from above, they'll see us as easily. We should wait a few more minutes."

Realizing his mistake, the father broke into a wide grin and shut his eyes. His son wagged his finger at him.

While they waited, Holland and Rhiana went aside.

"So far so good," he said softly. "The valley's probably been cleared. The natives are simpatico."

Rhiana's nod did not reflect the degree of certainty he would have liked to see.

He gazed up at a sun now higher in the heavens.

• 28 •

Clement Moloch was not enduring the wait with the aplomb that had characterized him throughout his career, a career which required fathomless depths of patience by its very essence.

Outwardly he was calm, collected, even contemplative. Inwardly he was impaled on the most debilitating of destinies: a foe who matched his patience, his detachment, his poise, even surpassing them in some respects, and was therefore made worthy. After a lifetime, a worthy opponent. Or plural: *opponents*. He could still not—even after Claire—make that distinction.

The voice had promised new contact, but how definite had the assertion been? He sifted the conversation once more, as he had so often that now his mind had worn thin in that place. Had the voice finally been frightened away by the sheer weight of killings, had he taken the papers where he perceived the climate to be less lethal? Six killings in so brief a span could spook even those most hardened to the rules of havoc. Thus far Buggs had been a dismal failure in his handling of the situation. Perhaps Floyd Cannell would be the one to deliver.

Most of his morning had been taken in the garden because he could no longer tolerate confinement. And because of Margaret, chafing at his continued refusal to allow her to leave the house, and then outraged when told Claire had left for the airport—and home—before breakfast and without the courtesy of a civilized farewell. She would not accept Claire's being distraught over Raymond. She and Claire were as close as blood sisters, the best of friends; but after this breach of faith it would be a frosty morn before she spoke to Claire again.

That was true.

Margaret had never been one to hold views, only the due process of appearances.

In a flare of impatience rubbed raw by the waiting, he had locked her in her room. He put his head back on the chair and soaked up the sun.

Bursts of shimmering light soaked through his eyelids, fiery comets making the cavern in his head glow, illuminating flapping images with empty eye sockets—charred, they were—who strained mightily to yell through lips sutured shut. They were not new. They were known to him. One was Dostoevski's suffering man. What they were determined to rant about did not interest him in the slightest. However, their condition did help to neutralize the outrage.

He was dozing when one of his aides came to tell him that Charles Waterston was at the gate, demanding to be seen at once, extremely agitated about something which he refused to define.

Moloch's reaction was to turn his face back to the sun for a moment.

Very well, he would see him in the courtyard.

Moloch swung his legs over the lawn-chair and sat for another short interval, imparting a certain resigned inevitability to every step nearer news he did not wish to hear. He sighed heavily as he got to his feet, reminded of the extent his reserves had been depleted.

Waterston was pacing relentlessly beside his car when Moloch made his appearance. For once he was not wearing his golfing togs.

"Good God Almighty, Clement."

"What is it?" Moloch said quietly, thinking the scene was strangely like that when Buggs announced the discovery of Brian Randolph and the narcotics agent. He wondered how his enemies could be so precise with the timing of their pressure points.

"The commo room is going crazy," Waterston sputtered. "First it, then the embassy switchboard lights up like the Fourth of July. Head Office practically burned the lines down. Then the INR boys in the State Department—they're not supposed to do that, you know—they never do that. Even some jerk from the Defense Department. Jesus Christ. Then the wire services, the newspapers, the magazines. Even the Europeans. The Palace was calling when I went out the door. Head Office wants an explanation. I want an explanation. Where in Christ's name did they get this shit?"

Moloch seemed merely curious in the face of the diatribe.

"You'll have to tell me what shit you mean, Chuck."

Waterston hesitated, puzzled by Moloch's seeming passivity, stunned by what could even be construed as indifference.

"Stories about you, about torture. Somebody's feeding the wire services." He jerked a notebook from his pocket and ran down some hurried scrawls: "First-hand accounts . . . sworn statements . . . transcripts from trials . . . depositions . . . who hires you . . . where you live . . . your real name . . . they've got you down as The Doctor: The Overlord of The International Torture Cartel. Head Office says there are dozens of stories, accounts that sound convincing. Naturally the wire services are trying to check them out, but they say they've already got enough verifications to go with. In a few hours this stuff'll be splashed all over the place. We'll be crawling with goddamned journalists. Apparently the material's coming from a half-dozen different sources, not one of them connected to us, not one of them so much as sympathetic. Now what the devil's going on?"

Moloch was actually smiling. Waterston mistakenly interpreted it as amusement at his boldness.

"Clement, I warn you, there will have to be explanations. Not only to us. Your other friends will be climbing the walls as soon as they get wind of this. You'll be flooded with some pretty disturbed people wanting some sound answers."

"Rubbish," Moloch said in the same sedate way. "The people you speak of are more sophisticated than you give them credit for. Can't you see? It's a conspiracy, pure and simple. This material is nothing but old, stale trap that's been lying around for years. Willful distortions surface periodically to stir things up for a few days and then sink again without a trace. Nothing comes of it."

"That may be so," Waterston returned, "but there's tons

of it this time. This time you're specifically identified, where you live, accurate descriptions, all of that. It's not a mistake. They know."

"A ton of feathers does not equate to a ton of iron, dear man." His smile contained a thin, chilling edge as he stared at the asphalt. "You're well versed in how to conduct these denials. Issue the standard statement of outrage at malicious assertions, ridicule the allegations as trumped-up hearsay. I'm a businessman, an advisor on matters of economics to various governments. I'm currently out of the country and you don't know my whereabouts. Come now, you know how it's done."

"Sure I do," Waterston said, pulling lappets of damp shirt from where they stuck to his skin. "But what about Head Office? They're sending a man down from Operations. He'll want to talk to you. How do we explain the murders of Randolph and Crosetti? And the narc? How do we explain Floyd Cannell being down here?"

"Chuck, leave that to me," Moloch soothed, taking Waterston by the arm, steering him toward the car, the contact signifying the first time he had actually touched Charles Waterston. "I have the situation well in hand, I assure you. Buggs and Cannell are in the countryside at this very moment. We're closing in. I have a feeling we'll have the answers we require very shortly."

Waterston detected the tiniest whiff of body odor from Moloch. That was strange too. If Moloch's dress left something to be desired, then at least he was fastidious in his personal cleanliness. Every bit of it was strange: the bland reaction; the moderation in attitude; the wistful aura; the Cheshire smile. In fact, his spirits appeared to have escalated, if anything.

Waterston stubbornly shook off Moloch's hand.

"Clement, whoever these conspirators of yours are, they say there'll be developments to substantiate everything they maintain is factual. They say they'll give hard, conslusive evidence within the next few days."

"Yes?" Moloch said. "I know about that. It's an empty threat by a conspiracy of lepers. Nothing will come of it, never fear."

Startled, Waterston said, "Lepers?"

"Speaking figuratively," Moloch assured him.

He went to the car and opened the door graciously.

"Return to your office, Chuck. Tell your people not to worry, I'm taking care of this in the same manner I've taken care of all the others. They needn't have concerns of being compromised. Nor does The Palace. I'll need room to maneuver. That's important. I'm counting on you."

Waterston got behind the wheel reluctantly, far from convinced that Moloch was being candid with him, and equally uncertain of which course would best insulate him from the scourge bound to come. Only a few years from pension, Waterston was determined not to get squeezed in the gears again.

His final words were: "I'll do what I can, but no guarantees. If it pukes, my ratings with Head Office are shot to hell, then it's every man for himself. They're already going to wonder why Buggs and Cannell are running the show instead of me. The only choice I've got is to inform them that the decision was yours. I cover your ass and you cover mine, that's the way it's got to be, Clement."

Moloch put his hand through the open window and clasped Waterston's shoulder, smiling reassurance.

"Trust me," he said.

The gate opened and Waterston backed his car out. In the few empty seconds before the gate closed he looked back at the enigma that was Clement Moloch, a man infinitely less accessible than any he had met in his lifetime, yet now standing on the tarmac inside the open gate, white hair in the sun, clothes rumpled, hands thrust in his pockets, exposed to the outside world. That too, he had never done before.

One of Moloch's aides, the one at the gate, seemed dumbfounded by his employer's deliberate incaution.

Moloch even waved. Good lord.

Waterston returned the wave awkwardly then drove away slowly, a stone resting cold in the pit of his belly.

When the gate closed Moloch looked at the sky, then turned toward the house, bowing his head in thought.

So. Every time he closed for a pawn he found himself placed in check; his king in mortal peril. Another incision made. The execution was superb, done wisely and well by a chessman in mufti. He could but admire.

He made a rapid tally, concluding that Waterston had purposely not been informed of the three killed yesterday.

Therefore Buggs and Cannell knew of the papers—and the nature of their contents. Probably Cannell's doing. Cannell had the rapacious instinct for the jugular, no matter whose.

But Buggs and Cannell would not have the papers. The chessman had too much wizardry for them. This ploy with the press was simply to close the time frame and strip his prey of options.

Moloch entered his silent home.

Now the call would come.

His smile was indulgent and precarious at once.

Now it would happen with blinding speed.

• 29 •

"We're keeping you from the festival," Holland apologized to their Indian host.

From behind the counter where he was making them sandwiches and coffee, Leonel Valasquez said, "Ah, *señor*, we have many festivals. This is only one, for the children more than us. Louis will go soon."

His cafe consisted of a single small room at the front of his living quarters, a tight kitchen off to the side, open across the counter, and five round tables. Locked when they arrived, Valasquez had opened the door only long enough to let them slip inside, then locked it again and drawn the curtains.

Rhiana sat at the table farthest from the door, sipping a cup of cold water, eating a piece of German bread. Holland stood at the window and looked out on the festival through a part in the curtain.

According to Louis the procession just passing the cafe was not the climax to the festival, but instead an assemblage that petered out from time to time during the afternoon while the participants took shade or refreshment, and, whether revived in body or resurrected in spirit —or both—once again went to weaving through the streets while holding pictures of saints over their hearts or crosses aloft, some of the crosses emblazoned with sunbursts at their junction. The throng walked a carpet of colored sawdust and bits of chopped paper rained down from the roofs along the way. Arches of palm leaves and bright flowers had been erected at strategic locations, usually where clouds of incense rose, and there was the constant shrill note of horns competing with the clack of wooden noisemakers.

Faces were almost exclusively Indian. Like Louis and his father, they boasted the magnificent bone and towering strength of Mayan heritage.

Louis said the fireworks would begin soon.

Holland smiled to see his anticipation, and ruffled his gleaming hair.

The boy's father brought sandwiches to the table and asked his son to pour coffee. Holland joined Rhiana and asked Valasquez about the barricaded road passed on the way into the village.

"It was for a mine that is empty now," Valasquez said. "No one goes there. If you need a place to hide, you can stay here."

"That's kind of you, *señor,* but we'll move on as soon as we eat and use your phone. We'll go to Honduras."

Valasquez deferred to Holland's wish with a shrug. He returned with his son to the kitchen. While walking to the village Holland had asked him about his family. Louis was his only child, the boy's mother having died three years before. Valasquez did not know of what. No one had thought to tell him.

When Rhiana tried the sandwich she found it to be salted beef with peppercorns and lettuce. The coffee was locally grown, a delight to savor, smelling as rich as most other brews actually tasted.

On the wall was a poster of a Mexican actress in the role of Mary, alongside it a metal placard in the shape of an Orange Crush bottle, the old-style bottle that was deep brown and shaped like a rolled cylinder. In the bottle's center was a thermometer with a broken bulb.

Rhiana turned in her chair to look around. Behind them was a closed door.

"Anything wrong?" Holland asked her.

She shook her head, went back to her sandwich.

"There a washroom back there?" Holland then asked Valasquez.

"*Sí,*" Valasquez said. "Please."

Rhiana shook her head again. She avoided looking at them, only at Holland, indicating silently she wished to finish and get out of here. Holland placed his leg under hers under the table.

Louis asked his papa with elaborate courtesy: Could he join the festival? Obtaining permission, he took his picture of the saint and pulled the headdress down over his hair. He told Holland and Rhiana he would return soon, and, snapping the bolt back, opened the door on a brief swirl of noise before closing it behind.

Holland, still hungry after the sandwich, buttered a piece of the German bread.

"Will you join us, my friend?" he asked Valasquez.

The Indian was pleased. "I will have coffee with you."

Approaching the table, he noticed the unbolted door. He raised a hand to the heavens to deplore the absent minds of children, set his metal cup down and started for the door, lamenting, "Louis, Louis."

Holland glanced at Rhiana and grinned.

The door opened before Valasquez could reach it.

A man entered, looking back over his shoulder, preoccupied with what he was saying to the man behind. Therefore it was his companion who saw Holland and Rhiana first, and from his stunned expression the one in front knew to look.

Rhiana scraped her chair back a couple of inches before Holland stopped her.

"Easy," he said under his breath.

The two stood rooted.

Valasquez, badly frightened, said, "We are closed, *señores.* You cannot come in."

The taller one in front stared at Holland through aviator glasses.

"You don't look closed," he said in a flat voice. Both men were older than those Holland had seen a half-hour earlier. Neither had rifles or visible sidearms, although it was the absence of rifles that surprised him more than the dusty business suit on the one drawing up the rear.

Valasquez showed more courage than was warranted. He persisted. He indicated Holland and Rhiana. "These are old friends. We are having coffee. I am closed for the festival."

The one in front moved him aside with the flat of his hand.

He said, "Then your friends won't object if we have a beer."

Valasquez looked helplessly at Holland.

Holland said to him in Spanish, "Let them drink."

Rhiana stole a glance at Holland. In contrast to Valasquez, he seemed profoundly disgusted. She began to slide her hands from atop the table. He nudged her with his elbow. She left them where they were, making fists.

The Americans sat at the table nearest the door, facing them, the eyes of the one in denim never leaving Holland.

Valasquz took two beers to the table, then scurried back to his kitchen, his eyes apprehensive over the counter.

The shotgun was propped against the table leg between Holland and Rhiana, partly shrouded by the tablecloth. Holland would have dearly loved to know if it could be seen.

"Finish eating," Holland said softly, his finger running across his upper lip.

She dropped her sight, drank her coffee.

"This beer's warm," Cannell complained to Valasquez, without wavering his gaze from Holland.

"All I have," Valasquez said, shrinking lower.

"I said it's warm," Cannell pursued.

Holland said, "You're in my friend's house. Drink or get the fuck out."

His overt flourish of anger established an intimacy between himself and Cannell. What Cannell registered was negligible, a slight tugging at the corners of his mouth. Buggs, on the other hand, went for the bait with mouth agape.

He said, "That attitude could lead to certain hostilities."

Holland said, "Then you'd better make your first move the best one you've got."

Rhiana cringed, her legs stiffening under the table.

Valasquez went down behind the counter.

Buggs broke sweat beneath his rage; even his brushcut matted.

Cannell brought forth a sickly smile, letting four or five seconds go by, then whispered something to Buggs, words Holland and Rhiana could not hear, but which Holland could read. Cannell said: *Don't be stupid.*

Holland judged that Buggs would have a handgun in a holster at the small of his back, probably a small automatic; Cannell, the professional, being right-handed, would have something larger under his left armpit. A .357 magnum or a .45 automatic, Holland thought. But going for guns—even the shotgun—was suicidal. There was too little margin, too intense a concentration, too shallow an arena. The survivors, at best, would get holed.

Cannell removed his aviator glasses. "Who are you?"

"I work the midway. I watch the freaks watching the freaks."

Buggs sneered. "Yeah? What about your buddy? He a freak?"

"He's hell on wheels. If I don't get you, he will."

Something extraneous was needed. If Valasquez only had the presence of mind to throw something over the counter.

"My name's Floyd Cannell."

Holland said, "I could give a shit."

Buggs bared his teeth.

Cannell said, "No need to get ugly."

In the background was the festival.

"I have it on good authority that you guys give the best head this side of Hollywood," Holland said. "That a fact?"

Through clenched teeth, Buggs said, "Don't lose your . . . head."

Cannell said, "You ever hear tell of a fennec?"

"It's a desert fox. I could arrange easy time payments on the Brooklyn Bridge too."

Cannell laughed. "Let's talk about it. Money's the least of our problems."

"Yeah, I've never known a government to have cash flow problems. There's a bug, you know, black with two yellow stripes. Every time it comes across something dead it eats the guts and buries what's left, no matter how long it's been laying there. The little booger's called a sexton beetle, the undertaker of the insect world."

Buggs said, "So?"

"So you stink up the place. So I wouldn't piss on you if you were on fire."

Buggs moved slightly in his chair.

Cannell continued to smile. "That won't work."

Holland knew it to be true. Each wondered who the other was and how long the laissez-faire would hold. Rhiana was forcing her leg against his but he could not decide the reason for it. Both men had their hands open on the table. All it would take was the one fast move that had not yet come.

Then he realized that Rhiana was thinking of Louis returning.

Cannell said, "You've got the papers. We'll pay you and let bygones be bygones. All that interests us are the papers."

"That's you. What about him?"

Buggs said, "Fuck him. The papers are more valuable to us. What do you care?"

Holland turned his hand on the table. "Sure thing. What do we care?"

Buggs said, "Do we have your word on that?"

Astonishment blinked in Cannell's eyes.

Holland smiled. He was making some progress after all. "You can believe almost every word I say."

Outside, the fireworks got underway with a clatter, causing Buggs to start.

Rhiana leaned to Holland, whispered in his ear. Then, waiting for his reaction, she added, "It will work. I want to try."

Still watching Cannell, he whispered to her in return, "Up to you."

To Cannell he explained, "My friend has to use the facility. You've made him nervous and it goes straight to his kidneys."

Buggs said, "That why he asked your permission?"

Holland said, "Think of it as a courtesy. We simply want to keep things copacetic."

Cannell directed his voice toward the empty counter. "Hey, *amigo,* there any other way out of the toilet? Any windows?"

From somewhere near the floor, Valasquez said, "No, no."

Smiling at Holland, Cannell said, "Your friend should keep his hands empty except for his prick. We simply want to keep things copacetic. You understand."

"Hard for him to do otherwise."

Rhiana rose slowly from her chair and went into the washroom. Buggs watched her. Holland concluded they had not seen the shotgun beneath the table.

He said, "You guys are great. Really great. You should be on the silver screen. I mean it."

Cannell now adjusted his posture, opening the gap under his arm to better facilitate his move when it came.

He said, "I told you that wouldn't work."

"But you haven't looked at your friend lately. He's really steamed. I'd wager he practices in front of a mirror. Am I right?"

Cannell's smile diluted somewhat. He said, "I'm looking at you."

Buggs asked, "How much for the papers?"

The staccato rattle of the fireworks escalated in the street. Holland hoped they would keep Louis occupied a while longer, until the charade broke of its own weight.

He said, "I've got my heart set on a Mercedes for each day of the week, a place in Bel Air and another at the beach, an intimate twelve-room chalet in Gstaad, some shares in I.T. and T., and like that. Those things are important to me, you know? Chapter and verse."

Buggs said, "We're sympathetic. We'll match the half million."

Holland looked offended. "You want me to rent? Hell, an empty lot at Malibu costs that much. You're talking robbery here."

Before Buggs could react, the door to the washroom swung wide. He looked there, and his face went slack. Then Cannell looked.

In the instant Cannell glanced away from Holland he realized he had been committed to his own demise. The discharge from the shotgun blew him back over his chair, smashing him against the wall, then swept on to Buggs who had lost his balance while grabbing for his gun and had tumbled sideways from his chair. The pellets raked his side. As he struck the floor another round sprayed him so quickly that all three shots sounded a continuation.

Cannell should not have been moving but was, scrambling in a weird sequence of attitudes. Rhiana raised the automatic and fired at him. Holland yelled, dropping the shotgun and scooping the knife from the table. Cannell already had his hand under his arm, sprawled on the floor in the corner next to the door. Holland reached him in three strides, in time to come in under the rising gun so that it fired into the ceiling. He levered Cannell's gun hand to the floor, pinning it there with his knee on the forearm, freeing his own hands. One hand went to Cannell's face, pushing his head back, the other plunged the butter knife hard into the fold at his throat, directing the blade up for the skull cavity.

Cannell had found enough movement to swivel the gun toward Holland. It went off, Holland feeling the heat slam his ribs. Rhiana screamed somewhere behind him. He brought the heel of his hand down on the handle of the knife, driving it deeper, until only an inch was left protruding. Cannell shook his legs in a solitary convulsion. Holland tore the gun from his fingers and sent it spinning across the floor. Cannell's tongue projected through a crimson screen of foam, fluttering. Air seeping from his lungs made pregnant bubbles, one breaking to form the next.

Holland rolled onto his back, looking for Rhiana.

She was staring at him as though in shock, still with the automatic half-raised, still bare breasted. Her shirt and jacket could be seen on the floor in the washroom.

"You're shot."

Feeling his chest at the side, he said, "No."

She said, "It's red. You are."

"Powder burns," he said, going to inspect Buggs. Satisfied that he was dead, he closed the bolt on the door and then took the automatic from Rhiana, let the hammer down safe and handed it back, telling her to get dressed.

Crossing to Cannell, he yanked the shirt away from his chest to expose the lightweight Kevlar vest under, pockmarked black where the pellets had struck but not penetrated. It seemed odd to him that Cannell would have the protective vest while his partner did not, although the anomaly scarcely mattered now.

Valasquez was crouched in a cavity beneath the counter, his hands clasped tightly over his ears.

Holland helped him to his feet.

"I'm sorry this had to happen in your place. We wouldn't have come if we'd known, *señor.*"

Valasquez looked numbly at the bodies spread on the floor.

Holland said, "We have to go. Are you still willing to help us?"

The Indian's slow nod came without choice.

From under the counter Holland took handfuls of rags and stuffed them against Cannell's neck and alongside Buggs' chest to stem the blood before more streamed to the floor. Rhiana, dressed now, came to help him.

Holland told Valasquez he would have to stay in the washroom while he used the phone, that he shouldn't hear what was said. The Indian went at once, closing the door without a sound.

Streamers of smoke hung heavy near the floor. Holland inhaled the corrosive smell of cordite while waiting for the operator to complete the circuit with Clement Moloch.

Rhiana had placed her knapsack on the remaining upright table and was reloading the shotgun.

"I want to know if you're alright," he said to her.

She nodded without looking up, her mouth moving soundlessly, once.

Holland said, "Leave him the rest of the money. We won't need it."

The voice of the Thai came on and Holland told him to get Moloch and get him fast.

Covering the mouthpiece, he then asked Rhiana, "How about outside? Anything wrong out there?"

She went to the window, parting the curtain slightly, waiting a few seconds, turning back. She shook her head.

The fireworks continued to roll noise through the narrow streets, lessening now.

Moloch said, "Who is this?"

"You know a man named Cannell? Another with a brushcut?"

"You've killed them."

Rhiana wondered what precipitated Holland's pause.

"It's time to wrap this transaction, ready or not."

"I'm ready, young man."

"I thought you might be. It'll take you an hour and fifty minutes to get here if you go out the door right now. I'll allow two hours. If you don't show, we'll be gone and the papers will be put to market. One time and it's got to be right. Any trickery and it all goes down the dirt-chute. Let's have a consensus."

"You must meet the conditions we agreed upon. I have

to confirm that the papers are genuine and not tampered with. I'll not come alone."

"There's two of us. That means you can bring one. If I see more—and I'll see you before you see me—you'll never know. We just want the money. Enough is enough."

"You'll have the money. Where am I to come?"

"South and west of you is a village called Corduran, it ends the road from Santo Cadiz."

"Yes, I know the one."

"Before the village there's an old mining road off to the left that's overgrown and barricaded. You can move the barrier aside and then drive on up. We'll meet you somewhere on the road, or at the mine, or not at all. That depends entirely on your discretion."

"Discretion tells me my position is untenable, but you don't seem to have given me any recourse but to comply."

"You'll be as safe as in a church. Two hours. Leave now."

Holland hung up.

Rhiana looked at him expectantly.

He said, "Who knows?" He thought a moment, added skeptically, "Maybe he believes in money."

Valasquez had recouped much of his composure when Holland brought him from the washroom.

Showing him the money, Holland asked if he would hide the bodies once it grew dark, adding that the pair had probably come in a car that would have to be hidden as well.

"Sí," said Valasquez. "I'll send Louis to bring DeJesus. He's a few kilometers from here. He will help."

Holland thanked him, then went through the living quarters to the door in back, removing his revolver and holding it down at his side. Checking that Rhiana was close behind, he stepped into the sun.

A narrow, rising passage of steps joined the rear of low adobe buildings on either side behind Valasquez's cafe, an uninterrupted crust of whitewash molding steps and walls together as though they had once been molten in a furnace. The only relief was the odd doorway or window, or intersecting passage so narrow it was difficult to separate from a doorway. Tile roofs projected overhead. Walked for centuries, the steps were worn to scooped troughs exposing stonework in the lowest parts.

Holland accustomed his eyes to the glare from the whitewash, then saw Louis running toward them. Other than the boy, the passage was deserted.

As Louis neared he caught his sandal on a step and flew forward, Holland catching him under the arms before he went down.

Louis, gasping, said, "Hide, *señores.* Three Americans are in the village. Someone saw them before."

Holland said, *"Three?"*

Valasquez must have heard his son from inside. He opened the door.

A shotgun roared in the passage, the charge cleaving the air between Holland and Rhiana, hitting solid further down. Holland looked higher to see the gunman dart for cover. Rhiana grabbed for the boy and pushed him into the doorway, slipping as she did on smooth stone, falling to her knees.

The second report sounded before Holland could get the revolver on track, the pellets skipping across the flat of a step, then slapping into Rhiana.

Holland jerked a random shot he knew would miss, puffing limestone opposite the gunman's position. He could not look back at Rhiana. Instead he crouched, open, locking his arms and bearing down, blanking everything except himself, the gun, the target.

The gunman had concealed all but one leg, from the knee down. Holland squeezed, blowing the shin away and pirouetting the gunman into the open, out onto the whitewashed incline. Holland advanced steadily on the steps, emptying the revolver, tossing his target like an unstrung marionette, the gunman dead well before he got to him.

He looked back at Rhiana while he dropped the contents of a speedloader into the warm revolver.

She sat within an edge of sunlight, her legs folded under her, looking back at him. He thought she shook her head, but couldn't be sure.

He took the gunman's arm, dragging the body behind him down the fall of steps. This part of the village was quiet now. The festival, still alive, went on in another corner.

Rhiana said "Damn" when he bent to her, her eyes wet, her face lined with perspiration. The wound was on the outer portion of her thigh midway between hip and knee, a red eruption soaking through the pant leg.

"Stand up," he said, lifting her.

The door opened on Valasquez, Louis in the background. They hesitated an instant, came forward to support Rhiana.

Holland said, "No. Pull the body inside, please."

He glanced up and down the empty passage. Rhiana, unsteady, leaned against him. He said, "Put weight on the leg. Let it bleed."

He knelt to probe the wound with his thumbs. Rhiana made a slight noise, standing free except for the handful of his hair she held. Two or three pellets squeezed out with the blood and fell to the white steps. She caught her lip in her teeth, then raised her face into the sun.

The body out of sight, Valasquez and his son emerged again. The boy stood away, staring at the spoiled print of the pellets on Rhiana.

"Come inside," Valasquez said. "I have things. I'll fix you."

Holland declined, wrapping his arm around Rhiana. With his other hand he urged Louis toward the door.

"Go in and wait five minutes," he said to Valasquez. "We'll be gone then. Wash the blood from the steps, then do as I asked when it becomes dark."

Valasquez commenced to protest, "But, *señor*. It's better you stay—"

"It's better we go. We'll be alright." He put his hand alongside Louis's head. "You're both good men. We're grateful for all you've done for us. Please, my friend."

Valasquez turned reluctantly.

Louis kept his eyes on Rhiana until the door closed.

• 30 •

Once away from the village and into a glade in the woods he had Rhiana unfasten her trousers and lower them. The twill fabric, matted with blood, peeled slowly away from her thigh.

As near as he could tell, the shot used had been 1 Buck, of which Rhiana had caught about a dozen of the pellets.

Most of those had worked themselves out by movement of her leg in getting this far; the rest he pricked from under the skin with the point of a folding knife held in the flame of a match.

"Hurt the step more than you," he told her. "It's a good thing the pellets hit there first."

She looked down at herself.

"It's easier when I move than when I stop."

"It burns, right? More than it hurts?"

"Yes," she said. Of course he would know.

He flushed the wound with the last of the bottled water, then sponged that away with a piece of the gauze she had been using to bind her breasts. Leaving the skin uncovered, he gently raised the trousers so she could zip them.

"I'll dress it later. You'll bleed some more but that'll keep the leg from tightening up. Just walk it out. Put your mind on something else."

She nodded, reaching for the shotgun.

He shouldered the pair of knapsacks, held the revolver in one hand.

"Tell you what, if you have trouble, if you get pain, find something to say to yourself. Repeat it, aloud. Your mind won't know it from a spike of morphine."

She leaned full weight on the leg, took a few firm steps.

"I'll walk. That's silly, someone would hear me."

"Let me worry about that. You'll *climb,* and you won't hold us up. If you know a better way to keep your mind off it, okay."

He waved her ahead, detecting only a slight flinching bias to one side.

For over an hour they climbed, cutting first for the road and then walking higher, skirting the switchbacks to save time. Holland roamed wide from the road, disappearing into the trees for minutes at a time. Sometimes she would see him flitting through the breaks in the pines, hurdling fallen timber on a dead run. She tried to hear him but could not. At first it was frightening but then she decided there must be some method to what he was doing, having learned that there inevitably was. Small birds followed him in the treetops, as curious as she.

The afternoon had warmed pleasantly, an afternoon offering itself to who would take it.

On one of the occasions when he rejoined her, she said, "What should I say? I can't think of anything to say."

He inspected the blood on her trouser leg, a stain now spreading lower than the knee. "Feet, don't fail me now. Try that. It has a rhythm."

She initiated a monotonous repetition of the phrase as she slogged up the forgotten road. He retreated into the trees once more.

Finally, when she was not far below the mine site and the roadbed could be seen right up to the shafthouse, as she was struggling to keep her leg working and the pain distant, he took her arm and partly carried her.

"What were you doing?" she said, her breath shallow and hot in her lungs.

"We'll have the high ground, so we'll be able to make out the car almost as soon as it turns onto the road. I just want to be sure of what we're looking at."

They gained the slight plateau that was the mine site. The majority of buildings had been dismantled and taken elsewhere, leaving foundations smothered with weeds and thistles, the blue shafthouse and an open-ended Quonset hut all that remained in the way of surviving structures. Hard against the rock shelf carved near the summit the shafthouse rose three or four stories, commanding an unobstructed view into the basin and to the ridges enclosing the canyon. Locks had long since been broken. Even two of the doors had been vandalized from their hinges.

Inside, the shafthouse was a tall empty box open to the roof, stripped of everything but its skin and supporting skeleton. The shaft itself had been sealed with tons of uncrushed rock lifted from the depths, then covered with beams and cables anchored in poured concrete pilings.

Rhiana sat on the boards inside the doorway while she caught her breath. Holland scouted the site quickly. Clear water still trickled from a sluice where the cook house had been. He tasted it, filled the bottle, took it back to her.

"Did I shoot that man back there?" she asked him. Water dripped from the bottle, spotting her jacket.

"You missed him. It hardly matters though, does it?"

"No. I tried to hit him."

He was taking speedloaders and shotgun shells from the knapsacks, lining them up on a ledge near the doorway. The rest he stuffed in his pockets.

"You're probably the reason we're alive," he told her. "That idea was magic. The one's face damn near fell into his pants."

He went from door to window to door, sizing angles, taking sightings. He measured time and distance by number of paces.

This time she found his deadly preparations to be a source of dread, enough that she was threatened by bile creeping into her throat. She covered her mouth, resisting. She decided the urge to sickness was because Moloch was coming and it would be over soon.

"What if he brings ten soldiers with him?" she said. "What if he brings a hundred?"

"He won't do that," Holland said, jamming shotgun shells into her jacket pockets. "He's been backed into a corner, with both feet in a hole. This is his only way out, one foot at a time. We can count on him trying something flashy, like bringing in extra gunsels, but not in those numbers."

"But he is coming to kill us."

"He's coming to see if he can get the papers, then kill us. And not necessarily here. He's obsessed with knowing who we are, just like those two in the cafe. Once he knows that—and has the papers—he'll be content to walk away and let the military play cat-and-mouse with us. Maybe. The key is the money."

Rhiana's look was incredible. "The money?"

He stooped to sponge some of the blood from her trouser leg.

"How he relates to it, and how he thinks we might relate to it. If he relates poorly, and thinks we're something like rabid revolutionaries or whacko mercenaries, then he might accept that we'd waste that many people just to get at a half-million dollars. The figure's purposely marginal, one that bandits would kill a small army for, while a professional would kill only one. The result, if I'm right, is that he's still guessing."

Rhiana shook her head as though to clear it. He took her under the arms and lifted her. She leaned against the building.

"What's the leg doing now?"

"Throbbing."

He put his face close to hers so that she was unable to

avoid him. "That's good. The throbbing's as bad as it gets. In three or four hours it'll ease and from there it's downhill. I'll look after you when this is finished, alright?"

She stood away from the wall. "Yes."

He pointed to the ladder that hugged the wall clear to the roof. Halfway up was a catwalk encircling three sides of the structure, another just below the roof. At each were openings to the front and sides. He asked her if she could climb it.

Staring into the lofty reaches, she made up her mind that she could.

One last time, he asked her, "You're sure you want to do it this way?"

She nodded firmly, and hobbled to the ladder.

Going ahead, she climbed with difficulty and a mounting respect for the height, but faster than he anticipated. He stayed close to her, providing his shoulder for the two occasions she paused. They passed the first catwalk and went to the second. From there the serpentine road could be seen its full length, connecting to the one leading to the village. The village proper was hidden by a flanking ridge.

He passed her the shotgun and placed a neat row of speedloaders on the catwalk, two of them holding the teflon-coated bullets. He showed her a dense thicket of trees next to the road, about halfway down the slope.

"I'll try to make it there before they show. If there's only two in the car when it passes, I'll cut across the hill and be here before they are. I want you to watch them all the way, make sure they don't stop or let anyone out. If they do, just remember where and how many and tell me when I get back. What they might do is leave an interval and then have other cars follow. If they do, fire the shotgun in the air so I'll know, then go down the ladder and start hiking across the spur line as fast as you can. I'll catch up."

"Couldn't they come in from behind?" she said. "Over the top?"

"That'd take them a day. There aren't any roads back there. I saw to that when we came in with George. And don't worry about them doing the same. Using a helicopter would mean bringing in men he can't afford to have around."

Rhiana watched him swing over the side and down the

ladder so fast that for a moment she thought he might be falling. On the descent he shouted, "Any time now. Think about what you have to do."

He sprinted across the apron and then down the embankment under the pines. The blue of his Yankees jacket turned to purple in the sun, casting a silky sheen where it rippled. He ran light, only the revolver suggesting otherwise. Blue as well, its matte finish trapped the sun instead of reflecting.

He was at last swallowed in the trees. When she could no longer see him, she felt utterly alone and defenseless. Losing him, even from sight, was a garotte at her throat that quickened her breath and caused her heart to pound in her head. She slumped to her knees. She held tightly to the bottom ledge of the opening.

Straining to pick him out of the trees only caused red dots to dance behind her eyes. He remained all there was between her and Moloch, as he had all along. Without him she was straw waiting for the scythe to snick on its way.

She peered down into the shrinking folds of the shafthouse, to the floor that seemed no larger than the flap at the end of a carton, and experienced vertigo. To steady herself she stared intently at the weathered wood where her hands gripped. Her knuckles were white.

She searched again for Holland, could not see him. Pigeons on the roof overhead droned in an unruffled way. Once or twice she heard their slender feet slipping on the metal as the commune shifted position.

From her pocket she took a damp patch of gauze which she placed against her face. The coolness gave comfort. Then she decided to wipe her face as clean as possible. If this was the day she would die, or whenever Moloch was finished and allowed her to die, she would do that as a woman.

She began to say, quietly, ". . . Don't fail me now . . ."

The rhythm was missing and it just made her empty.

Dust trailed a car turning onto the road, the sun finding it to send brilliant shafts of light back at her. She groped for the shotgun at her knees, then left it, feeling foolish for the reaction.

Arriving at the barricade, the driver got out, lifted the

poles away, drove through, went back and completed the barrier once more. He returned to the car and came ahead at a speed greater than she had expected. She knew the brown car to be Moloch's. Holland had said it was armor plated and that the glass was impenetrable. Even the tires were designed to stay erect after taking shots. She wondered if that included his unique ammunition.

The car passed the thicket where Holland said he would make his decision. The quiet in the canyon was terrifying, the only sound that of the tires on the road and the faint hum of the engine on the steeper grades. She concluded that the pigeons were gone too.

Holland did not appear. As the Mercedes approached, her apprehension mounted to panic. There was no sign of him, not a rustle or flicker of movement. She searched each place where she thought he might come out. She scrambled from her knees and stood to the side of the opening, the throbbing in her leg forgotten.

The Mercedes was close enough to disclose a man in the front seat beside the driver. He had white hair, his face close to the windshield as he scanned the terrain.

She said "Holland" distinctly, the unwanted sound of her own voice echoing in the chamber only frightening her more.

Holland was not coming. She was cornered.

The crested grille of the Mercedes reared up over the edge of the apron and slowed to a crawl, the car a bloated brown thing casting about for whatever was lame and easy to seize. Its form struck Rhiana as being massively threatening even from this height.

She grew frantic to know what to do.

"Rhiana." The voice floated softly up from below.

She forced herself to look down.

Holland was standing next to the ladder.

"One car. Right?"

"Yes," she said.

"Come down."

He went to the side of the doorway. Outside, the Mercedes sat idling, aloof and splendid about thirty yards away, a heavy layer of dust all that soiled its appearance. Angled so that the passenger side was closest to the building, it allowed Holland to observe Moloch clearly through the window. He was watching the building closely, saying something to the driver. The driver's features were oriental.

Holland watched Rhiana as she came down the steps of the final section, the shotgun slung over her back. He saw that her face was cleansed somewhat, that the blood had drawn a thin line to her trouser cuff.

"How many are there?" she asked him.

"Two."

She regarded him as though the answer was the worst possible one he could have given.

"What does it mean?"

"It means things aren't the way they seem. More than that I don't know."

She removed her jacket.

"Will we still try it that way?"

"Up to you," he said, watching her carefully. Now that she was not wearing the bindings, with the worst of the grime from her face gone, it was impossible not to know her as a woman—and not necessary to ask her why she needed Moloch to know.

She said, "Yes."

He discarded his own jacket, the shoulder holster with it.

A man's voice swept across the apron.

"You can see us. Let's see you."

The Thai had lowered the window on his side slightly, shouting through the aperture.

Holland chose not to hesitate. He laid the revolver on the ledge and stepped into the doorway, exposing himself fully.

"They'll shoot you," Rhiana said, moving away.

He said, "Not from in there they won't."

He could feel Moloch's eyes devour him. The Doctor sat forward in the seat, staring eagerly, talking incessantly.

"Where are the others?"

It was the Thai.

"You want to stand here?" Holland asked Rhiana.

Leaning the shotgun against the wall, she took his place. Holland retreated into the shadows. It was a rare pleasure to watch Moloch's head jerk as he saw Rhiana. The men glanced at one another in disbelief.

He pulled her away from the opening.

"How many more?"

The Thai again.

"Like I said, there's two of us," Holland shouted back. "If you don't believe us or don't like it, you can kiss the papers goodbye and go back the way you came. Otherwise, let's make the exchange and be on our way."

He asked Rhiana for the papers. She ripped open one end of the oilskin wrapping and handed him the package. He held it in plain sight.

Moloch lowered his window under power a couple of inches.

"Come to the car so I can examine the papers. One of you can stay there."

His voice was hoarse.

"One of us is a woman, for Christ's sake," Holland returned. "You count that?"

His attention fixed on the car, he walked twelve paces, placed the package on the ground, then backed up to the doorway. He turned once so that they would know he was not armed.

"You can do the check right there," he said. "Bring the money. The other remains in the car. We'll stand where we can be seen, hands empty. Stop fussing like an old man."

Behind the glass, Moloch's face hardened. He said something to the Thai.

Holland had tied a noose-like loop in the cord fastened to the shotgun. Rhiana put the loop around her neck so that the firearm hung free in front of her, then stood at Holland's back until they were touching, the gun concealed between, her hands on his shoulders for display. They remained in the shadows inside the doorway for three or four minutes. Holland could feel her trembling against him.

"What's he going to do?" she said.

Before Holland could respond, Moloch's door opened. He emerged with a leather satchel in one hand, in the other a small glass container. He wore a white shirt open at the neck and rumpled trousers that might never have had a crease. Like Holland, he had not shaved in days.

On the other side, the Thai stood in the open door, watching across the roof of the car. Holland could not see his hands.

"Keep an eye on Moloch," Holland said to Rhiana. "I'll watch the driver."

They moved into the doorway where they could be seen clearly.

Moloch walked boldly forward then, until he was standing over the package of papers. He lowered the satchel, looked past Holland to Rhiana. He smiled tightly.

At the same time, the Thai placed a molded leather gun rest on the car roof. From the front seat he extracted a bolt-action rifle with a telescope and a bull barrel, nestling the forward portion of the stock in the V ot the rest, then making himself comfortable as he sighted on Holland.

Observing calmly, Holland asked Moloch, "What's that all about?"

"He's no more a fool than you are, young man," Moloch said. "If you should attempt anything inappropriate he'll shoot you on the spot. But of course he can only shoot one of you at a time, leaving your companion to get inside at the firearms I'm certain are there. I'm unarmed, you see, and as lovely as the lady may be, I don't accept for an instant that she's as harmless as you'd have me believe."

Holland was tempted to ask how the sniper would know to fire at precisely the instant his target moved, considering the essential delay in reaction, but then decided against it. Besides, the real complication was in the angle the sniper had on them. If he were to feint out of the way, whether down or to the side, Rhiana might receive the shot sent for him. Judging the angle, he thought she would be missed, but not by much, and even that depended on how well she remembered his instructions.

"Quite right," said Moloch, bemused. "Only one of you could get out of the way in time. Let me assure you that he's rather proficient with that rifle."

"I'll take your word," Holland said, bringing his eyes from the Thai.

"You are the couple I saw at the bullfights, aren't you?" He studied them in unison, fascinated by Holland's hands, wanting to see more of Rhiana than was afforded behind Holland. "You're not terrorists at all, or anything of the sort."

"I've never been able to distinguish the line between subversion and righteous rebellion," Holland said. "I guess I'm defective that way."

He looked back at the Thai. Were it not for the bull

barrel trained on him and the glint of glass over it, he would have moved by now. The more he plotted the trajectory the more certain he was of Rhiana being outside the bullet's path—and the more uncertain he was of her doing it correctly.

"Ask rather what you can do for your country," said Moloch.

At that Rhiana spoke. Flaring, she said, "I guess that's the way in which you're defective."

But she also used the opportunity to begin sliding her hands from Holland's shoulders, the motion imperceptible.

Moloch smiled at her sadly. To Holland he said, "It was me you wanted all along. Not the papers, or the money. You're a very unorthodox young man. Until the last few hours you had me convinced that Claire was in league with you."

Holland knew the talk was going on too long. In his instruction to Rhiana earlier he had said there would be as brief a prelude as was possible, only as much as was needed to set the sequence. That opening had been provided them. Except for the sniper.

He reverted his attention to Moloch. "How's that again?"

"Come now," Moloch chided. "You left those articles in Claire's apartment deliberately, as you did the pipe in the field. Are you saying your purpose was other than to implicate her?"

"The stuff in the apartment was just to muddy things up for a day or two, and could've pointed a finger at your two gunsels just as easily. The pipe was lost, not planted."

Rhiana was pressing the length of the shotgun against his back, telling him she was ready, urging him to *do it now!* Talking to Moloch across twelve paces of Guatemalan dirt—when there was nothing to be gained—was the height of folly and ran counter to all he knew. Except for the sniper.

"Yes, in the end she did convince me, just as you've done," said Moloch, taking a deep breath.

Surveying his face, Holland perceived resignation, perhaps even a terminal frustration. Holland thought he might be beginning to understand.

"On life's great stage," Moloch went on, "torture is equally effective in establishing innocence as it is guilt.

Are you certain I'm the one you want? Are you truly so raw that you believe my death would alter—"

Holland said, *"Move back when I do."*

Moloch said, "What?"

Holland snapped forward at the waist as Rhiana took a step back and lowered the shotgun, firing across him at Moloch, the roar of the shotgun matched by that of the rifle, the pellets and the bullet crossing paths where Holland had been the split second before. He twisted, falling back and to the side, skinning the doorway as he rolled past, reaching for the revolver on the ledge above him. In that suspended link in time he heard Moloch thump to the earth, the metallic pump of the shotgun on its travel, the bolt of the rifle snapping like dog's teeth.

The rifle splintered wood between him and the doorway. Rhiana backed up, firing furiously through the opening as she went, jerking the pump back and forth and sending pellets at Moloch until the gun was empty.

He scooped her jacket from the floor and flung it at her, the shells in the pockets helping to carry the flimsy cloth through the air. She caught it and turned to run the few steps to a concrete piling beside the sealed shaft, crouching behind. Another round from the rifle punched through the wood, lower and closer, whining through the hollow confines.

He crouched, starting for the side doorway that would afford him a position. But before he got more than a few feet the air was filled with the monstrous din of machine gun fire. It surprised him and he stopped where he was in the middle of the floor. The boards at the front of the building were coming apart, raked by an onslaught that threw spikes of wood and raised banks of dust as the bullets came through in wild sweeping patterns. The compact clatter told him all he needed to know: The building was being sprayed at better than a thousand rounds a minute by an Ingram machine pistol.

Finished with their destruction around the doorway, the .380 rounds began to cross at hip level, closing on him. He leaped for the ladder and scrambled upward, barely clearing his legs as the barrage crossed below. Thrusting the revolver in his trousers, he scaled the ladder as a man possessed with his mortality in time of war.

On the first level he could look down on the Mercedes and the Thai kneeling inside its door, the absurdly short Ingram firing across the hood toward the base of the shafthouse, spent brass streaming steadily out the ejector onto the windshield. The Thai emptied the clip, popped it out and reversed for the one taped to its end.

From the opening Holland could see enough of his subject's head and shoulders to satisfy. He assumed the position, steadied his forearms on the base of the opening. The Thai's hair whipped with the impact, the bullet entering his skull just back of the hairline, seeming to swell the head grotesquely from the inside and spraying matter the way a stone does when dropped into still water. The Thai's body was driven into the dirt where some of his parts already were. Cartwheeling in the air, the machine pistol fell on his chest and rocked there, settling finally. Holland finished with two rounds beneath where the machine pistol lay.

Then, leaning over the catwalk, he called Rhiana's name.

She came slowly out from behind the piling.

"You didn't get hit with any of that?" he said.

"No," she said, barely loud enough for him to hear. "Are they dead?"

"Moloch isn't. He's not moving but he's not dead."

She limped through the doorway.

He dropped down the ladder, expecting to hear the report of the shotgun before reaching the floor. The sound never came. He reloaded the revolver as he walked outside.

Rhiana stood looking down at Moloch. He lay on his back, eyes open and staring without focus, waiting on death when it had once been seen. Rhiana held the shotgun at her side.

She said, "I can't."

Holland stepped forward and leaned over Moloch, put his face in the blank path of vision. He waited. Slowly, with protracted will, Moloch's eyes took hold, but remained void of expression or acknowledgment. Holland stayed in his space, violating his space to the end, even as he placed the three rounds in his chest.

Rhiana turned away.

She sat next to the ravaged doorway and covered her

face with her hands. Holland went to kneel beside her. But there was nothing to say, so he went to the car and shut off the engine.

He opened the trunk cautiously, revolver ready, the heavy lid rising lazily to jounce against its hinges. All that occupied the cavity was a tire, a body-bag, and the acrid smell of burnt, decaying flesh when he zipped the bag back. Deep black lines encompassed Claire Moloch's naked torso where the electrical cord had done its work.

Taking the bag but leaving the body, he put the Thai in with her and closed the trunk. He rolled back the high door at the side of the shafthouse and drove the Mercedes inside. He hung Moloch by the feet from a beam and bled him, then washed out the body bag at the sluice. Rhiana watched him. When he was finished he sat beside her.

"Would they have heard the shooting in the village?" she asked. Her face was pale and deflated from the days past. She just seemed tired now.

"Only the rifle would carry that far, and in these canyons there's no way of telling where it came from. Besides, Louis said the festival would go on into the evening."

He inspected the side of her trousers. The blood had dried. He put his hand there. He looked in her face and thought she could have been grieving.

"What do we do now?" she asked him.

"Wait. When it gets dark I'll go down to the cafe and phone George. He'll be here at first light."

She turned to him, as uncertain of what he would do as she had been the day it began.

"Will you come back? I mean, come back here?"

He put his hand to the nape of her neck for a moment, then bent to untie the laces of her sneakers. He said, "I'll be gone only as long as it takes. We'll need some food, and Valasquez may even have some tolerable wine."

She looked through the doorway to where Moloch's body hung, then shivered.

"What was he doing?"

Holland looked with her for a while. Finally, he shrugged.

"I don't know. If whole countries have wanted you dead all your life, I suppose you could get worn down until you're too tired to keep making the moves. He was old for his trade and even someone like him had to wonder how old he could get. Even his gunsel was fooled. I don't know, and now that it's done I don't really care why he did it that way."

Rhiana said, "I do."

"Make your own conclusions, then. I'm not interested."

He removed her sneakers and tugged gently at her trouser leg.

"I'll dress your leg," he said. "Undo."

In the evening they sat against a pine on an outcropping above the spur line, within sight of the shafthouse and able to see anyone who might approach, though Holland was certain that any danger of that kind was past.

At valley level and in the deep clefts of the hills, dappled shadows were changing to night, the depths rising up the canyon as the sun sank lower and eased its light away.

Rhiana sat against Holland as she had the night before, enclosed by his arm. She had washed earlier, under the icy spring coming from the sluice, and now felt immensely better for at last being a woman again. While washing she had been unable to look away from the shafthouse, the macabre spectre of Moloch's hanging body imprinted in her mind as though he were watching her. The vision had repelled her and caused her to hurry. She had asked Holland to cut him down but he refused, saying something vague about Indians—American Indians—having hung their victims by the feet as a last token of contempt. He said he wanted Moloch to hang like meat now that he was.

While waiting for darkness, Holland asked her about her husband. She spoke of him for more than an hour, talking with a compulsive release she had not allowed since . . .

She stopped, drew away from him and wrapped her arms around her knees.

They remained silent for a long time. Holland listened to small animals in the woods. He zipped his jacket to the neck, wishing he had tobacco left for his pipe.

"How're you doing?" he asked Rhiana.

"I'm alright," she said quietly. "I'm sorry, although I suppose it was natural enough."

"I think so."

She came back to him. "No, you don't understand. Suddenly I felt I should be ashamed for talking about

Agustin and our life, and I wasn't and that made me want to feel ashamed too. But I didn't then either, and it all just made me confused."

"Me too."

His words provoked a smile from her.

He said, "I was beginning to think you'd never do that again."

Of course her smile went away then. She lowered her head to his chest, slipped her hand into his.

She said, "I want to see Sarah so badly."

"In the morning," he said.

The silence that followed caused him to think she might have fallen asleep. But then she stirred ad raised her hand to his face the way he had to hers under the bridge, then withdrew it again.

"If I asked, would you let me take Sarah to a baseball game?"

"Yes," she said.

"If I asked, would you come with me to the Danieli Hotel in Venice?"

"Yes," she said.

He kissed her hair. "When I was a kid in New York there used to be an ice cream parlor called Puritan Maid, with the best ice cream anyone had a right to ask for. They closed eventually, I don't know why and I've never seen another one, but there's a place in Venice that comes close. Not the same, but close. You'll see."

"Sarah would like to see your fish. I don't think she believes you. And I'd like to see where you live, because I don't believe you about that or the fish."

"Quasimodo is not my fish. He's his own fish and he's discriminating about who he hangs out with. You have to swim at night and he won't let you see him until you've stayed long enough he knows he can trust you. Besides, you don't know, I might have a wife there. I might have children."

"You don't. You don't have anyone."

"Tell it to Quasimodo."

"When?"

"A few weeks. When this buries itself."

He kissed her mouth and stood up, thinking how beautiful this woman was in all her parts.

"Please. Don't get killed now," she said.

"No," he said. He pointed off down the spur line. "I'll come along the tracks this way so you'll know it's me. I'll be two hours, maybe more, maybe less, depending on whether I have to wait for Valasquez at the cafe."

She watched him go lower on the spur line until she could no longer distinguish him from shadows.

There was a moon, somewhere. The light was good, the chill air sweet and filled with sounds native to nature in these places.

He found the path they had used at midday, stopping at the spring to drink from his cupped hands. He stayed there for a while, stealing time for a private rite of Bushido—not that he followed the teachings wholly—but rather accepting only those precepts suitable to a fine integration with his own. It was the denouement that he most prized. On a tattered planet too small for Big Wars and too big for Small Wars, he had been victorious in his most formidable conflict. What for others might have been a black proof was for him simply a collision of contemporary samurai—a hunter tracking a hunter until one hunter was brought down. Only the hunters knew. And that was the right of it, as well as the rite. Whether conceived in the human heart or the immortal soul, neither fate had been born in isolation.

He left the spring and went on.

Alongside the road to the bridge fireflies darted busily about under the pines, unusual for land this high. He waited there because his ears had heard something unwelcomed. A minute passed, then two men. In the poor light he could see the faces well enough. They were Indian, carrying shovels. Valasquez and DeJesus were chewing coca as a reward for digging on the mountain. Valasquez carried an empty cage. Holland supposed they had sacrificed another chicken.

He trailed the pair as far as the opening at the bridge, there presenting himself in a way that would not frighten them. They stood over the roaring chute of water and talked a few minutes.

Valasquez asked how the other *señor* was. Holland said fine, aware that the Indian now knew that he was in fact inquiring after a *señora*. DeJesus said the car had been hidden where it would not be found for weeks. Holland advised him that the location didn't matter so much now;

no one would be asking questions. Valasquez confirmed that they had buried the three bodies, prompting Holland to silently total the killings. Eleven; more than all those before, except for war, and none innocent. The killings were not finally a matter of skill, but, like the politics that had inspired them, a matter of numbers.

Valasquez and DeJesus took him the rest of the way through empty streets and corridors of the village. Holland decided that the inhabitants, maybe two hundred all told, were sleeping early due to the wear of the festival. Valasquez led him directly to his place. Like the steps behind, the floor and walls of the cafe were spotless, betraying none of the spoor from the afternoon. Holland's observance pleased the two Indians.

He took a beer to the phone and heard George lift the receiver after three rings.

He mentioned Ebbets Field, deciding to skip the rest of the code, and said, "Having a wonderful time. Wish you were here."

In the morning George dipped the helicopter low over the crest behind the shafthouse, the craft dropping like a slow cat.

Holland had put Moloch's body in the bag and placed it in the center of the apron as a guidance marker, enabling George to set down next to it and keep the Hughes poised while the bag was dumped behind the seats. Max was in the helicopter and clapped Holland on the back as he leaned past to do the loading. His greeting to Rhiana could not be heard over the whine of the engine.

Rhiana got in with Holland's help and pulled the harness over her shoulders and between her legs and around her hips, only then realizing that Holland was still standing outside in the wash from the rotors. She began to shout at him and would have gotten out if not prevented by Max. Holland leaned in the door, taking her outstretched hand firmly. He told her to wait for him, that they would do it all. He smiled and told her that someone had to stay to put the lights out. He gave George the packet of papers, telling him it was a gift, that Rhiana would provide the details. The satchel he handed to Max, asking that they make a pass over the village and float the money down.

He said he didn't want the money and the village was a better place for it than most. He eased his hand from Rhiana's, shutting her in the plastic bubble.

She followed his shrinking figure on the apron below as they lifted and banked out over the canyon. He stood with his hands deep in his Yankees jacket, the shotgun under his arm.

She wanted to know from George what he had meant, why he was staying, why he had not told her.

George explained that it had been planned that way from the beginning, at Holland's insistence, that it would be too dangerous for them if Holland were along and they were stopped for any reason. He thought the chances of that occurring were remote, but he could always explain the presence of the body by saying he was a journalist who had received an anonymous call to retrieve an undefined piece of evidence linked to a story currently getting wide exposure in the press. But with Holland aboard, the conclusion would be elementary, considering the attention now focused on The Doctor.

Sensing that she did not comprehend all of it, he promised an elaboration later. He also said that she should have learned that none of them need be concerned for Holland's safety.

By then they were hovering over the village. She put her head back on the seat and closed her eyes.

Max opened the door and loosed the contents of the satchel. A half-million dollars in American currency rained on Corduran that morning.

The same evening, at dusk, a Hughes helicopter hung over the polo field in Mexico City's Chapultepec Park. Only the pilot occupied the craft on this occasion.

The sides had concluded their match in deference to the fading light and had left the field to wipe the lather from their mounts, some of the players lounging on the grass, contesting the match anew with disputed versions of play and the aid of cool drinks.

They grew silent as a sinister-looking black bag plummeted to the field of play even as the helicopter banked to leave. Horses shied and tugged at their reins, snorting. As a group the witnesses stared for a few brief seconds, glancing uncertainly at one another then back at the bag stuck on the grass. Finally the first of them started toward it, the rest following as people will do.

By seeming coincidence, two of them were journalists.

In the days that followed, the newspapers of scores of countries were flush with revelations pertaining to a man known both as The Doctor and as Clement Moloch. A journalist in New York arrived home to discover that a parcel of papers had been delivered without explanation that afternoon. The delivery was repeated in London, Paris, and Rome. These proved to be the authentic writings of Clement Moloch, and all were agreed that they made for sensational reading. People were moved to compose irate letters to their governments. New movements were organized overnight, and flourished. Waves of allegations were blunted by walls of denials, though a few select individuals did run for temporary cover. But they also surfaced at their old stands soon after the furor lessened, most within a fortnight.

Equal time was given to speculation about the identity of The Assassin. Officially, the various intelligence services assumed the position that if there had really been anyone even faintly resembling "The Doctor," they would certainly have known and done "something" about him. Unofficially, they closed the file on The Doctor, and opened another on The Assassin. The second file, like the French original, remained largely impoverished.

In Corduran The Assassin became a virtual legend, the Indians telling the tale amongst themselves, never tiring of it, particularly on days of festivals. The incident became as much a part of their lore as was the sacrificing of chickens on the mountain.

Le Monde predictably presented the assassin as The Fennec. *Time* magazine carried a series that ultimately attributed the work to Ilyich Ramirez Sanchez—The Jackal (or, at least, one of the versions). The Latin and South American press followed formation, condemning the entire affair as the rantings of left-wing extremists.

Soon the story of The Doctor, well and truly mauled in printing presses and by readers on subways and debates over dinner tables, was laid to rest in favor of the recent phenomenon of terrorist kidnappings in the U.S.

* * *

Holland took the train back to the coast, purchased a boat at Iztapa and followed the lagoon into the canal, then that to El Salvador. Before the month was out he joined Rhiana and Sarah in New York. They were in time to see the Yankees cinch the pennant.

They went on to Venice, then to Little Cayman and his pirate's cove. Rhiana and Sarah would sleep some during the day, so they could swim to the sandspit with Holland at night. Quasimodo slowly grew accustomed to the woman and child, his jealousy accepted then forgotten. On afternoons Holland and Sarah would walk the hot sand for hours, or would sit, sometimes watching land crabs dart into their holes, sand rolling in after. Rhiana liked to walk in the rough guinea grass and bolls of wild cotton, her tailored denims cut off as shorts. They went fishing with Santiago, talked across the breeze of baseball, Quintana Roo, places and things yet to see. Rhiana read Hemingway to Sarah.

Everything after was as predictable as everything before had not been, or, depending on how well we have come to know Holland and Rhiana, was as it should have been.

ABOUT THE AUTHOR

R. LANCE HILL is the author of *The King of White Lady*, a book about the international cocaine trade, and *Nails*. He is a Canadian.

NORAH LOFTS

THE CLAW

Until the reign of terror struck, life in the country town of Hillchester was quiet, friendly and relaxed. But an accidental blow to the head leaves Greg Anderson, family man and father of three possessed by an unaccountable evil.

One by one the women are attacked, raped and viciously brutalized. Then the murders begin ... And as the list of victims grows, the besieged community whispers and watches, gripped in horror by the madman in their midst ...